WILD MUSTARD

Wild Mustard

New Voices from Vietnam

Edited by

CHARLES WAUGH, NGUYỄN LIEN,
and VĂN GIÁ

Curbstone Books
Northwestern University Press
Evanston, Illinois

Curbstone Books
Northwestern University Press
www.nupress.northwestern.edu

This book was published with support
from the National Endowment for
the Arts.

Two stories appeared in slightly different form in the following publications:
"Sage on the Mountain" in *Words without Borders*, and "Forever on the Road" in
The Literary Review.

Printed in the United States of America

10   9   8   7   6   5   4   3   2   1

Library of Congress Cataloging-in-Publication Data

Names: Waugh, Charles, 1970– editor. | Nguyễn, Lien, editor. | Văn, Giá, editor.
Title: Wild mustard : new voices from Vietnam / edited by Charles Waugh, Nguyễn
    Lien, and Văn Giá.
Description: Evanston, Illinois : Northwestern University Press, 2017. | Includes
    bibliographical references.
Identifiers: LCCN 2016044892 | ISBN 9780810134676 (pbk. : alk. paper) | ISBN
    9780810134683 (e-book)
Subjects: LCSH: Short stories, Vietnamese—21st century. | Short stories,
    Vietnamese—Translations into English.
Classification: LCC PL4378.82.E5 W55 2017 | DDC 895.9223408—dc23
LC record available at https://lccn.loc.gov/2016044892

For Nguyễn Liên, who spent his life breaking down barriers between people by translating, teaching, and writing literature. A bright light shone perpetually in his eye, and his voracious appetite for a good joke or a moving story never faltered. He will not be forgotten.

CONTENTS

ACKNOWLEDGMENTS

We would like to thank the National Endowment for the Arts, the Utah State University College of Humanities and Social Sciences and Department of English, the Hanoi University of Culture, and the University of Social Sciences and Humanities—Vietnam National University, Hanoi, for their generous support for this project. Thanks also to Chris Cokinos, Ben Gunsberg, Jennifer Sinor, Michael Sowder, Christina Firpo, Susan Harris, Jessie Aufiery, and Minna Proctor, whose feedback on the translations made them so much better, and for their encouragement and support for this project. We also owe thanks to our wonderful families, who sustained us in so many ways during the project, including giving us the time to make our work possible, and whose forbearance during very loud Skype calls was integral to our success!

Blown by the Wind

An Introduction to Wild Mustard

On April 30, 1975, Peoples' Army of Vietnam tanks rumbled into Saigon, captured the capital, and reunified the country as a single Vietnam, thereby ending a civil war that had been fought since the country had been divided North and South twenty-one years earlier at the Geneva Accords. For many Americans, this event—often referred to as the "Fall of Saigon"— may be the last thing they know about Vietnam. They may have pictures in their minds of helicopters evacuating the U.S. Embassy, or they may remember stories of Vietnamese refugees leaving by boat or of those families settling into various communities around the United States, or they may have seen the run of American movies about the war that came out in the 1980s and early '90s. They may have even read *The Sympathizer,* the amazing 2016 Pulitzer Prize–winning novel by Viet Thanh Nguyen that—among other things—comments incisively on those films and on the South Vietnamese exodus, all while telling the intriguing story of a Vietnamese double agent who resettles in Los Angeles after the war. But ultimately, those stories end up being about Americans and newly immigrated Americans, and they tell us very little about the country of Vietnam and the people who live there now.

And so much has happened in Vietnam since that day in 1975! The Vietnamese had barely finished celebrating their victory when in 1978 they were drawn into a war with the Khmer Rouge in Cambodia and a subsequent war in 1979 with China. And the war with the United States didn't really end so much as transform from a military struggle to an economic one. Until lifted in 1995, the U.S. embargo kept Vietnam isolated from world trade as well as from development aid from the United States and its allies and most international organizations.

Rebuilding the country in the 1980s with minimal foreign aid was a monumental task on its own, but the communist economy made it even harder. The top-heavy decision-making from the Vietnamese government infiltrated practically every aspect of life in the postwar period. Movement within the country was tightly controlled and, in most cases, emigration prohibited. The collectivization of agriculture meant the government decided what crops would be grown and the prices for which they would be sold. The few consumer products available all went through the state store apparatus, limiting choices about what could be purchased and by whom. "No one got rich," goes the saying, "but no one starved"—summing up the best that could be said for the era. Writers such as Dương Thư Hương and Bảo Ninh captured the widespread sense of dissatisfaction with the postwar society in their novels *Beyond Illusions* and *The Sorrow of War*, which the Vietnamese government initially banned. Other writers, such as Nguyễn Huy Thiệp and Ma Văn Kháng, stirred controversy by adding their expressions of disappointment in such classic works as "The General Retires" and *After the Flood*.

Americans who know the literature of this period—as well as literature from the war itself—probably know it thanks to the tireless efforts of groundbreaking translators, such as John Balaban, Wayne Karlin, Linh Dinh, Nina McPherson, Nguyễn Nguyệt Cầm, Nguyễn Quí Đức, Phan Huy Đường, Phan Thanh Hảo, Dana Sachs, Bác Hoài Trần, and Peter Zinoman, among others, and thanks to the courage of publishers such as Sandy Taylor at Curbstone Press, who recognized the desperate need for these works to appear in English.

Part of that need arose from how Americans coped with the war and its aftermath in popular culture in the late 1970s and 1980s. As American studies scholar Edwin Martini has convincingly demonstrated, American popular culture from this period routinely erased the Vietnamese from its representations of the war, contributing to the commonly held notion that America had defeated itself in Vietnam. This belief, along with the lack of representation, the decades of broken diplomatic relations, and of course the tactics of dehumanization that soldiers and nations employ to permit themselves to kill in the first place, all combined in a stark inability for many Americans to see the Vietnamese as human beings.

Wayne Karlin's first anthology of translated Vietnamese and American short fiction, *The Other Side of Heaven* (1995), sought to remedy this problem by presenting stories from both nations in a "work of reconciliation" that would allow for a "sudden mutual *seeing* of the humanness we held in common" (xii–xiii). Similarly, John Balaban and Nguyễn Quí Đức's *Vietnam: A Traveler's Literary Companion* (1996) gave its readers a view of Vietnam outside the context of the war, as a real place outside Americans' machinations and misconceptions. And once those two anthologies had done their best to begin to humanize the Vietnamese to American readers, Wayne Karlin and Hồ Anh Thái published *Love After War* (2003), a volume intended to reorganize American readers' thoughts toward love as the antithesis of war by presenting stories that showed how the Vietnamese themselves had moved beyond the past, and how they looked toward the future with the same anticipations and trepidations as do all peoples of the world.

A few of those collections also included work from writers of the Vietnamese diaspora. In the decades since the end of the war, the first wave of Vietnamese American writers has been joined by a second generation of writers who have spent most or all of their childhood and adult lives outside of Vietnam and who have perfected how to tell their stories in brilliant English prose. Among others, Linh Dinh, Lily Hoang, Andrew Lam, Viet Thanh Nguyen, Andrew Pham, Aimee Phan, and Monique Truong have demonstrated the abundant wealth of talent in the Vietnamese American literary community, with Nguyen's 2016 Pulitzer making it clear that there's nothing these writers can't achieve.

Wild Mustard: New Voices from Vietnam picks up where the previous Curbstone volumes of translation left off, collecting for the first time short stories from a generation of Vietnamese writers who were born after the war or who were young children during its end, and all of whom came of age after Vietnam discarded the communist economy in 1986. Just one of the sixty or so authors included in the previously mentioned collections was born after 1970, which means this new generation's stories have largely remained untold in translation. And yet, so much has happened to shape this generation of writers' lives in ways that are vastly different from the lives of their elders.

Most prominent among these events is the policy shift the Vietnamese government inaugurated in 1986 called *đổi mới* (renovation) that ended collectivization and allowed for a realignment of the nation's economy toward the free market. After *đổi mới*, farmers could decide for themselves what to plant, and the market determined selling prices. The diversification of agricultural products blossomed as savvy farmers turned to catfish and shrimp production, to growing coffee beans and rubber and every type of fruit and vegetable imaginable. In the cities, the state stores quickly gave way to the bursting constellations of newly opened family-run businesses. And in 1995, when the United States finally lifted its decades-old embargo and normalized trade relations with Vietnam, new international businesses and development aid began to pour in at just about the same time that the Internet took off globally as a venue for information and commerce. Suddenly, a country that had been isolated from the world for thirty-five years by war* and sanction was now connected to it in a multitude of ways, few of which previous generations could ever have imagined.

---

* If we include the years the Vietnamese spent fighting the Japanese occupation during World War II and the years spent fighting for independence from the French, this number of years of isolation could be fifty-five.

On the cusp of this transition, as late as 1996, the most ubiquitous medium for community news in Hanoi and elsewhere in the country was the system of loudspeakers mounted at the top of poles scattered across the city. Each morning at six, the price of hogs and rice and other agricultural products along with weather reports and other bits of information would echo down every narrow alleyway. Of course, dozens of daily newspapers also circulated, and three or four state-operated TV channels broadcast dubbed versions of *Little House on the Prairie* in addition to Vietnamese news programs and other shows, but the pole-top loudspeaker's continued use in 1996 can be seen as an emblem of the old way of thinking, a way to get a single, unified message to every citizen that no one could miss, a fundamental part of the daily soundscape of Vietnam.*

And then in a rush international cable TV, the Internet, and mobile phones were everywhere, used by people from all walks of life. The big multinational companies who had raced in when the embargo ended and who had been willing to operate at a loss just to be on the ground when the economy really started to move finally saw their investments pay off because, sure enough, the economy did begin to boom. Cheap labor enabled a manufacturing boom. Vietnam became a trendy place for Westerners to take a vacation and the tourist industry boomed. Money poured in, and hundreds of hotels opened from north to south, up in the mountains and all along the coast. Real estate speculation boomed, turning hundreds of well-connected Vietnamese into multimillionaires. In the cities, motorbikes replaced bicycles as the most common form of transportation; then cars began to shoulder their way onto the nation's narrow streets. In 2009, a Hummer could be seen hulking through Hanoi; by 2013, a Lamborghini prowled Ho Chi Minh City. Boom, boom, boom.

In less than twenty years, in just one significant span of a young person's life, Vietnam had managed to transform itself from one of the poorest and most isolated nations on earth into one with a dynamic, global economy. It went from a state-controlled system embargoed by the United States to a free market economy with the U.S. as its number one partner in trade. From pole-top box to mobile phones and the Internet. From bicycles to Lamborghinis.

This incredible transformation constitutes the primary life experience of the writers whose work is collected in this book. The oldest of our writers—born in 1969—was a kindergartner when the American

---

* In some communities, especially in the Central Highlands, loudspeakers are still used this way every morning.

War* ended, and just seventeen when our youngest writer—born in 1980—was a kindergartner and *đổi mới* began. The stories of their adolescence and coming into adulthood tell the stories of Vietnam's emergence into globalized capitalism and the Information Age, replete with all the best and worst things that have come from these enormous changes. Given that 80 percent of Vietnam's present population is less than forty years old, these stories really do represent their Vietnam, the Vietnam of the new millennium.

And in so many ways, their Vietnam is a Vietnam on the move. In fact, movement has become such an integral part of life in today's Vietnam that in a few of the stories we've collected—such as Phan Triều Hải's "Forever on the Road" and Nguyễn Ngọc Tú's "Lonely Winds"—it's not so much a theme of the story as it is its setting or exposition. Whether this movement means transplanting from a remote village to the city for a job or an education or emigrating abroad to send money back home to support the family or just the ability to travel within the country to sightsee or to take a vacation, Vietnamese today are far freer to move than at any time in the past.

Often these movements have a kind of binary correlation between the past and the present, the homeland and the city. To travel from the city back to one's family home means to travel back to the past. The same is probably true for many people all over the world. But because so much has changed in Vietnam so suddenly, the disruption this movement causes to a person's senses of self and place and culture becomes even more intense. This is why we've chosen to call our collection *Wild Mustard*, after the story of the same name by Dương Bình Nguyên, which explores just how complicated love and relationships have become in an age when people no longer feel rooted, when they instead feel blown from place to place like tiny mustard seeds.

Part of the intensity of this movement-oriented disruption comes from the powerful traditional sense of place that most Vietnamese have. Vietnam is an ancestor-worshipping nation, and ancestors have places to which they are attached. Each Vietnamese has a *nhà quê*—a homeland or native village—that they can point to as the place where their ancestors came from. The farther one moves away from that homeland, the less frequently one can pray at the graves of those ancestors, and the more isolated from that spiritual center one feels. This is different from religion—many Vietnamese are also Buddhists, Christians, Đạo Mẫuists, Cao Đàists, agnostics, and so on. But ancestor worship is more like a sense of self, a way to

---

* While many people in the United States call it the Vietnam War, and many scholars call it the Second Indochina War, our writers and most Vietnamese refer to it as the American War.

remember who you are and how to behave in a way that honors the obligations you owe your family. As Nguyễn Danh Lam's story, "The Land," and Hồ Thị Ngọc Hoài's "Thung Lam" reveal, because this sense of self is so bound with a particular place, life becomes difficult when a person is cut off from that place or when that place itself changes so dramatically that it becomes unrecognizable upon return or perhaps worst of all, when that place has been destroyed by logging or development.

But the stories also rely on another sense of the relationship between self and place. Our title story, "Wild Mustard," as well as Đỗ Bích Thúy's "Sage on the Mountain" and Nguyễn Thế Hùng's "Gifts of Heaven," all convey just how deeply connected the protagonists' homelands are to their environments. They show us how each village in Vietnam has its own microculture in addition to the regional and national cultures they share and, inevitably, how all these microcultures are inextricably bound to their homeland's particular fauna, flora, and topography. This relationship makes sense: Vietnam is one of the most biodiverse nations in the world, with hundreds of microclimates and microecosystems resulting from the way its steep mountains isolate weather patterns and speciation alike. It's no surprise then that its human microcultures are equally unique and diverse.

And perhaps because of the uniqueness of these landscapes, all the stories convey a deep recognition of and appreciation for the natural world. In some cases, a key location—such as the lagoon in Nguyễn Anh Vũ's "Sleeping in the Lotus Flowers" or the beach and sand dunes of Nguyễn Van Toàn's "A Thousand Years Sing the Waves"—intensifies the action and resonates with some important aspect of the protagonist's life. Sometimes it's the contrast that becomes meaningful, as when the two main characters in Kiều Bích Hậu's modern fairy tale, "Waiting for the Ferry," escape the city to spend an idyllic afternoon in the countryside, or when there is no escape from the pollution and poor living conditions of the cities we see portrayed in Đỗ Tiến Thụy's "Wounds of the City" or Nguyễn Đình Tú's "An Unbelievable Story." And in all the stories, the writers' deep appreciation for place and the environment leaves powerful impressions through their rich use of natural similes and metaphors that make us see, hear, feel, taste, and smell their Vietnam in delightful—and sometimes disturbing—ways.

The stories in our collection also show how movement and perceptions of place depend on class differences. While many of today's young Vietnamese have begun to have the disposable income and leisure time to enable them to travel to see their country on vacation, most have moved to obtain an education in the city or a job or both. Undoubtedly, these two kinds of travel are linked. The economy's rising tide has made travel for leisure or education possible. But that doesn't mean everyone who has moved has ended up in this newly emerging middle class. Stories such as "In the White Rain" and "Wounds of the City" let us see just how tenuous life can be for migrant laborers who are lured to the city by the prospect of a good job. Often the jobs are not so lucrative, and the living and working conditions deplorable. People moving from the countryside or the mountains into the cities for work are the ones most likely to end up living in the worst places, closest to the dust and noise of construction sites or in the areas that are the most polluted with garbage and industrial waste.

Naturally, the stories' sense of movement and changing places throws what it means to be Vietnamese into sharp relief. Several of our stories come from writers who belong to one of Vietnam's many ethnic minority cultures. The largest ethnic group in Vietnam is the Kinh, who make up about 85 percent of Vietnamese society and who thousands of years ago came down the Red River Valley and in 1010 CE established a capital in Hanoi (then called Thăng Long). But Vietnam is comprised of fifty-four officially recognized ethnic groups, many of whom settled long ago into the steep mountains bordering Cambodia, Laos, and China. Because of the ruggedness of the terrain, these groups have remained relatively isolated over the centuries and have managed to maintain distinct cultures. So our writers from these areas are not only concerned with how their traditional cultures have begun to change because of globalization, but also with how their culture is changing because of the incorporation into the nation that has resulted from the construction in their communities of schools that teach in Vietnamese and because of the ubiquity of Vietnamese-language television programming and other media. Nie Thanh Mai's "In the White Rain," Đỗ Bích Thúy's "Sage on the Mountain," and Phạm Duy Nghĩa's "Rain of White Plum Blossoms" each approach this dilemma of place and ethnic identity in a distinctly different way.

But the problem of how to fit in is not just a problem for ethnic minorities—it's something almost all our stories address. In the same way Nie Thanh Mai's character H'Linh struggles with being both Êdê and Vietnamese, all Vietnamese now must balance their national identity with being a part of the globalized world. Like so many other people, today's Vietnamese digest an extraordinary amount of international media. MTV Asia, Star TV, South Korean television programs, Chinese and Japanese films, all in addition to movies, television, and websites from the United States and Europe, are as easily accessible in Vietnam as they are anywhere else in the world. The stories in our collection reference world pop stars and famous actors and athletes, demonstrating that there is now no shortage of global examples of what it means to have status—or even just to be a successful, happy, "normal" person in society—and today's young people in Vietnam must sort through them all to figure who they are and who they want to be.

Part of that sorting involves issues of sexuality, and as a result, sex plays a large role in many of our stories. In "Infinite Pain," for example, the global context for understanding sex becomes explicit in "just like in America" comparisons that include bizarre statistics such as how many minutes a typical American supposedly spends having sex. What constitutes a "normal" sex life in light of international values has also come under our writers' scrutiny in other ways as they raise the topics of homosexuality, women's libidos, relationship-revenge blogs, and what seems to be a now insatiable demand from many Vietnamese men for expensive virility-enhancing exotic wildlife products. All this focus on sex in the stories reflects the larger explicit cultural presence and acceptance sex has come to have in contemporary Vietnamese society—there are now adult stores in all the big cities selling condoms and sex toys, and TV shows such as *Sex in the City* and films such as *Bar Girls* and its dancing girls YouTube spinoffs have become wildly popular. But our stories also show the darker side of all this attention to sex. Several depict rape, and others tell the stories of young women from remote areas who are forced into prostitution once they arrive in the city. Just as with mobility, how Vietnamese experience the current liberalization of sexual mores depends on just how much economic power they have.

And finally, given all this tension, opportunity, and complexity, it should come as no surprise that our writers are also experimenting with form and genre, pushing the limits of what it means to write literary fiction in Vietnam. The collection includes a work of speculative fiction by Di Li, whose novel *Red Flower Farm* is considered by some to be Vietnam's first mystery horror novel. We also present a story by Phong Điệp, who has pioneered Vietnam's young adult literary scene. And you will also see a few of our writers, such as Kiều Bích Hậu, Lê Hoài Lương, and Nguyễn Ngọc Tú, take on Vietnam's longstanding tradition of telling fairy tales and ghost stories, but with contemporary twists.

Forty plus years after the end of the American War in Vietnam, it's sometimes hard to believe that the Vietnam of today came from the country that won the war in 1975. The generations of Vietnamese who sacrificed everything to fight for independence from the French—and those who fought for twenty more long years in the war between North and South— could not possibly have anticipated the degree to which capitalism drives so many aspects of life there today. The free market has undoubtedly done many good things to improve the lives of millions of people, but the gains have been uneven—and therein lies the trade-off of *đổi mới*. It has paved the way for individual success under the assumption that the success of the individual means the success of society. Status no longer comes from sacrificing oneself for the nation; instead, it comes from the individual's ability to buy, consume, or flaunt expensive things. And often what's being sacrificed today are many of the aspects of the culture that previous generations would have claimed were what made them Vietnamese in the first place.

Perhaps the more important anniversary for our writers is the one in 2016, marking the thirtieth year after Vietnam's economic renovation. To them, the war is outside their lived experience; it is the struggle that precipitated the poverty of the postwar society. But the changes that *đổi mới* inaugurated are the ones that they themselves have lived through and that have most profoundly shaped their lives. Those changes have given our writers new meanings to their senses of place and tradition, of privacy and property, the sacred and the spiritual, the individual and society, and of intimacy and love, among many other things.

In these past thirty years, our writers have borne witness to countless turbulent changes, and while their work chronicles both the many opportunities as well as the many failures of this new way of life, it's unlikely that any of them would choose to go back to the pre-*đổi mới* era. Nonetheless, it's clear that many of them are still searching for that feeling of having arrived and rooted, that they—like so many people around the world—feel at the mercy of global forces beyond their control, and that they from time to time still feel like tiny wild mustard seeds, blown by the wind.

Charles Waugh
Logan, Utah, 2016

Works Cited

Balaban, John, and Nguyễn Quí Đức, eds. 1996. *Vietnam: A Traveller's Literary Companion*. San Francisco: Whereabouts Press.

Karlin, Wayne, and Hồ Anh Thái, eds. 2003. *Love After War*. Willimantic, CT: Curbstone Press.

Karlin, Wayne, Lê Minh Khuê, and Trường Vũ, eds. 1995. *The Other Side of Heaven*. Willimantic, CT: Curbstone Press.

Martini, Edwin. 2007. *Invisible Enemies: The American War on Vietnam 1975–2000*. Amherst: University of Massachusetts Press.

A Note on the Selection and Translation of the Stories

Wild Mustard: New Voices from Vietnam is the result of a twenty-nine-person collaboration that began with Charles Waugh and Nguyễn Lien talking with Văn Giá over tea after a fiction writing class at the University of Culture in Hanoi. Eventually, we chose the nineteen stories based on the author's age—they had to still be a minor when *đổi mới* was enacted in 1986—and on the quality of the story itself. Each of the stories has been a major prizewinner in the last ten years or so, and each of the writers has begun to garner the acclaim of Vietnam's literary scene. We also looked for a range of themes and settings that seemed to represent the whole country and that touched on a variety of important aspects of Vietnamese society.

Our team suffered a great blow in the middle of our work when Nguyễn Lien passed away after a long struggle with Parkinson's disease. A prolific writer, scholar, and translator, Lien published under the pen name, Huy Lien. As a scholar and translator, he helped bring a better understanding of American, Russian, Korean, and other world literatures to Vietnam. As a teacher, he shaped thousands of minds over the course of nearly fifty years in university classrooms. Vietnam lost a great champion of literature and an insightful mind with his passing. We all miss him dearly. To recover from this loss, our project swelled with contributors. In addition to the nineteen authors and three editors, we have nine translators: Nguyễn Hùng, Lê Thế Quế, Di Li, Lê Thế Quý, Thúy Tranviet, Peter Ross, Vù Thì Tuyết Mài, Charles Waugh, and of course, Nguyễn Lien.

Our method of translation had two defining goals. The first was to retain as much of the original Vietnamese syntax as possible so that the occasional strangeness of the sentence style and rhythm could be preserved. We wanted the translated prose to reflect as much as possible the syntactical way a Vietnamese person might speak or think. The same went for the idiomatic and figurative language. We kept it as close to word for word as possible so that the prose would carry an essential Vietnamese sensibility to our readers. We want our readers to really get a sense of how these stories might unfold to a Vietnamese reader word by word, image by image. Our second goal was to polish the prose in English to be as bright as it could possibly be. We wanted each sentence to be as sharp and beautiful and moving in translation as it was in the original.

Along the way, we've made choices that might be useful to understand. Vietnamese has no fixed first-person pronoun "I" or second-person "you" as English does. Instead, Vietnamese speakers use a much wider range of pronouns that reveal the relationship between the speaker and listener. For example, a man might use *anh* (older brother) as a form of "I" to refer to himself when he speaks to someone younger than himself, but then he might also use *anh* as a form of "you" when addressing any male slightly older than himself. When he speaks to his grandmother, he will probably call himself *cháu* or *con* (child). Each pronoun set helps reinforce the relationship between the two speakers, and sometimes the pronouns change over time, just as relationships do. The same goes for third-person pronouns: Vietnamese is not limited to "he," "she," "it," and "they" but instead employs a range of pronouns that can indicate the age, relationship, or status of the person in relation to the speaker, or—often in our case—the narrator. We have used an array of options to address the issue, sometimes using the relationships indicated, especially when they seem important at that moment in the story, and sometimes replacing them with "you" or "I," "he" or "she," or "his" or "her" to make the sentences flow better for English readers, especially when the relationships are already clear. When some unusual or surprising relationship has been indicated, we have tried to replicate this, as in "Lonely Winds," where we occasionally use "Brother Grandma Finder" as the appellation for the character Dzự. Our overarching goal has been to make sure the reader could understand the relationships while still navigating the sentence gracefully.

A lot of Vietnamese grammar is contextual, so verbs are not always necessary in a sentence, and even when they are present, they often do not indicate tense the way verbs in English do. These features of the language can make for a lot of terse, chronologically ambiguous phrasings or sentences. We have tried to retain as much of the original Vietnamese syntax as possible while at the same time trying to meet our Western readers' grammatical expectations.

We have also left in a good number of *Ois*. *Oi!* just means "Oh!" or "Hey!" But the sound of it is an essential feature of the Vietnamese language's character. It can sound plaintive or endearing, angry or confused, happy or sad. But replacing *oi* with "oh" or "hey" never sounds right. We figured our readers would pick this up without missing a beat. A few other words occasionally left in Vietnamese for sound or flavor have been footnoted when necessary.

And last, two notes about pronunciation. Written Vietnamese has two *d*s: *đ* and *d*. The first, *đ*, is like the *d* in English. The "softer" *d* is pronounced as a *y* in the south and as a *z* in the north. We've used *dz* in English to approximate this sound for names that begin with *d*. Also, many of the names in the stories begin with the digraph *th*. In Vietnamese, *th* is not pronounced as a fricative as in the English words "the" or "thing"; rather, the *h* is aspirated as in the pronunciation of "Thames" or "Thailand." We hope this helps!

WILD MUSTARD

Wild Mustard

Dường Bình Nguyễn

THE OLD WOMAN SAT QUIETLY BEHIND THE PILES OF DRIED MUSTARD, her mouth craving a quid of betel, but otherwise toothless and silent, her darkly socketed eyes leveled gloomily at the road ahead.

Each year, she'd wait for the mustard flowers to fall, the seeds still succulent in the fruit pods, which looked like small, elongated blades. Then she'd cut and dry the mustard stalks. When the stalks became fragrant, she would gather them and bind them into bundles. She stored them in her tiny house made of wood from yellow pine. The whole summer, when she sat in the house, she was surrounded by countless piles of drying yellow mustard. She slept in their pure, mild fragrance. When winter came, she'd take her leave of them, carting them to the district market and selling them to other people. The beautiful little seeds would flake apart, and the blades would break away. Then the mustard seeds would sprout.

Her yellow mustard flowers cascaded from halfway to the sky all the way down to the valley floor, where youth have expressed their love for the flowers in poems so many times they've never known boredom. The mustard flowers became a town symbol—everyone looked forward to them each spring. Her name was Vịn, but I called her Grandma.* She didn't live with anyone, she didn't love my father, and she didn't care much for me. But every time I needed to escape my life, I'd come home and live with Grandma, with the wild mustard's perpetual aroma.

I went home on a day the mist had cleared. The road leading home curved like a quickly sketched line through mimosa weeds in full bloom, the blown flowers flying in the wind and coming to rest on my hair and collar. The town had changed a lot—even the road leading to Grandma's house had been paved. Only Grandma was still the same.

Glaring at my filthy backpack, she sputtered weakly, her voice full of gums and tongue, "Grandma's too tired for this shit—you come all this way

* The narrator calls her *bà nội*, a name that indicates she is his paternal grandmother.

again, and for what? I've got no rice for you. Have you ever brought home that carcass of yours when it smells nice and looks good? Go on, get out of here." As the last words dripped with saliva from her mouth, she pulled her degenerate boy with his grimy, stinking clothes down to a seat on the floor and noisily fanned her conical hat, not so much to make a breeze as to cause a fuss. Her scrawny arms flapped like the wings of a half-starved heron. "God forbid, did they mistreat you? It makes me so tired, every single time you show up asking, 'Can I come home and stay with you?' So goddammit, how many days are you going to hole up here?" "Until you send me away." "Then go now, you little shit, get out of my sight. How come your head's shaved?" "I got a kind of ringworm." "Who made you grow a beard like that?" "A girl I love." "She broke up with you to marry some other guy, right? Just like your daddy. . . ." "Okay, Grandma, leave me alone. Did you sell all the mustard?" "You think I kept some to make medicine for you?" "Grandma, I told you to keep a little for me, how many times did I ask you! What a pain in the ass!" "You stupid whelp, I had to hang it up in the shack or the mice would've chewed it all to hell . . . then you'd really have a pain in the ass! Have you seen that girl lately?" "What girl?" "What girl. The beautiful one you brought here. Back then, I thought you'd marry her." "You were the one who stopped me! You asked why would I want to do that? So much trouble. Every single time, there's always so much trouble, I'm tired of it." Grandma hummed, "That girl was nice, and really pretty, but why . . . ?"

But why . . . why couldn't I keep her? The day she came here with me, it was like Grandma was decades younger. She burbled when she brought water to wash her feet, she boiled mustard flowers for her to bathe in, she scooped cup after cup of warm water to rinse her hair. That night in her bed, Grandma lay between us, not letting me touch my girlfriend's body. To Grandma, she was completely bright and pure. We loved each other, didn't we . . . ?

I boiled stems of wild mustard mixed with fragrant grapefruit leaves and a dried leaf whose name Grandma would not tell. A pot of bright yellow color. Out in the front yard, at the washing place, she still kept a large tub, its bottom valve plugged with a tight roll of plastic. I called to her, "Come out for a bath—a bath on a sunny afternoon like this won't give you a cold. Come on, I'll rub your back and then later you can do the same for me." She sat up decrepitly, her clothes a mess. "I don't know how many years I can stay alive so you can come rub my back. It's nothing but backbone and ribs, so rub softly, Mister Pagoda Guard." After the bath, Grandma changed into fresh clothes, looking rosy clean. "Grandma, don't go away, you have to rub my back." "Let me get some dried coriander—do you still have pimples?" "They're all gone. When I go to the massage parlor, the girls pop all the pimples." "Do they massage you as good as I do? Men like you all spend ridiculous amounts of money at those good-for-nothing places." "So in a little while, you'll rub my back, right? You use a tree oil, right—is it walnut?—that smell is so good." Grandma laughed. "Well, I'm tired, I don't have the strength to keep being your massage girl. . . ."

On a winter afternoon the sun goes down quickly. At night, it's cold and the wind blows down from the mountaintops straight through the wooden planks. But the house was warm and drenched with the fragrance of walnut oil. Grandma lay in my lap, turning her body over and over again. "I'll rock you to sleep, okay, Grandma?" "I want a quid of betel so bad," she moaned. "But Grandma, you don't have any teeth." "Pestle a mortar's worth for me, I'll suck out the juice to quench my thirst." "I'm too tired for such silliness. You'll just drool the betel juice onto my chest again." "God damn you, you little bastard, this mouth full of betel juice is the one that chewed the rice to feed your hole back in the old days." "But now I only love girls with straight, white teeth and mouths as fragrant as steamed sticky rice."

"Tell the truth, how many girls have you loved, how many times have you slept with a girl?" "First you have to promise to leave the whip up on that smoking shelf." "Just tell me, I'm old, I don't promise anything." Grandma found an old betel quid and put it in her mouth, making it smack and pop between her gums. "I've fallen in love with eight girls and slept with them ninety-nine times." "Who did you sleep with the most?" "I forget. They were all beautiful, you know. But sleeping with girls can be a bore too. . . ." She rose and stirred the fire in the stove. "Come lie back down, Grandma. I'll light the lamp and stoke up the stove for you—it's so cold. . . . What are you doing? Hey, I told you not to touch that whip!"

It must be twenty years since I was seven and she got that whip; each year she's had at least one chance to use it, sometimes on me, sometimes on my father. "Strip off those pants and lie down cheeks up." "I told you the truth and still you want to punish me? Next time I'll lie." She whipped me hard, so it really hurt. I managed to keep from crying out in pain and said, "Your hands are too old, it doesn't hurt at all." She whipped me again. "Grandma, why punish me? To love one another and then sleep together, what's wrong with that?" "Then in total, how many times have you gone to the massage parlor?" "There's no way I can remember—after drinks, my friends and I often go for a massage, then get happy endings and feel comfortable." "I'll whip you one more time. How many years have passed and you still act like a wild dog? Do you even remember a single girl's face?" "There've been too many to remember; why keep asking just to whip me? If I can't walk tomorrow it'll be your fault. And if I shit my pants like in the old days you'll have to clean it up." "I should whip to death these bad habits just like your father's. His whole depraved life spent casting his seed like a damn weed, and now that he's getting old he just sits around like a rotten log." "Every time you whip me, you compare me to Dad. That's enough, I won't let you do it any more; it's a waste of time to hit me just so you can compare me to him. . . ." "So where *is* your daddy, huh? All year he hasn't come home even one time for me to punish him."

Where was my father? He lived in some part of the city I could never remember. For the longest time I'd only heard his voice on the phone sounding as cracked as the cascading roar of a midday rain. He said he was weak now, with osteoporosis in his legs, so he couldn't do much except sit at home as his kids left for work and then watch some TV at night. My youngest stepbrother worked as an assistant driver, and the time I met him at Long Biên Bridge, he begged me to come with him to visit our old man, saying he was lying at home unable to go out, his body hurting anywhere it was touched because of the osteoporosis, telling me that his crying in the middle of the night was noisy and horrible. I refused to come, saying that when I could, I would pay the old man a visit, but just then my work at the office was too much and I couldn't take off the time. He said, "What kind of work do you do?" and I said, "I write newspaper articles—investigative reports on the dark side of the massage service." This made him scoff. "You lie to make money? Maybe you *should* stay away from the family." I laughed too, mimicking his bitter voice. "Can you earn a couple million dong* per day?" He said he could earn what he needed, enough at least to buy dear old Dad a can of fortified milk every week. I felt a little bad about myself then and thrust several hundred thousand dong into his hand. "This week I'll buy the milk, okay?" He scoffed again. "What the fuck, my whole life goes by and now's the first time you buy the old man a gift? But thanks anyway. I know he treated you like shit." My old man called me after he got the can of milk, making me jump out of my skin. In my opinion, just one single sentence deserved to be remembered, the one when he said he hadn't taken proper care of his mother, and so now it was up to me to take care of Grandma.

* About one hundred dollars.

But how was I supposed to take care of her? The day I earned a heap of money from the owners of some cut-rate corporations by saving them from imprisonment, I bought an apartment that cost more than five hundred million dong and practically forced her to come to the city, dragging her down here with big yellow bunches of wild mustard flowers still clutched in her hands. But after just three days she'd had enough of the wind on a high city floor and walked out to sit and gossip with the flower vendors in the park, not returning home until way after dark. Then she started going around telling people she had a grandson who was a journalist, but very depraved, and she was bored of staying at his house so she'd come out to make him feel ashamed. I went out to the park and once again forced her back to my home. She moaned, "*Trời ơi*—oh God—at your house, the ice-cream cabinet keeps making terrible noises, like it's possessed by chicken ghosts or goblins." Grandma called the refrigerator "ice-cream cabinet," the air conditioner "cold season machine," the old guy living next door who loved kung fu movies "bugbear," the old lottery-ticket-selling woman who wore too much lipstick "chimpanzee," and the girls who came to my place every afternoon after Grandma had gone to a neighbor's to listen to ghost stories she called "white-bone spirits." She pressed me down on the bed, snatched a paper fan to thrash my ass, and shouted, "You're so stupid! Those white-bone spirits will suck the blood and marrow right out of you!" I told her not to worry, I was too old to pretend to be naïve about such affairs. She said, "A man can be wise from east to west but still die beneath a woman's skirt." "But Grandma," I said, "to die in those parts would be a proper death!" "God damn you, you little bastard, I've said it many times but you just don't listen. I'm going to come meet your bosses and tell them to fire your hide and throw you into the street." "If I'm unemployed, will you feed me?" "Back in the day when you didn't even know how to suck milk or spoon food I could still take care of you." "The past was a long time ago, Grandma. . . ."

The nearer night to morning, the heavier the dew. The palm branches in the roof were so ancient they let the stars in the sky peek through and let the dew wet my cheeks and forehead, stinging my skin with cold like ice cream on the tongue. I told Grandma, "Dad's fine, but I have no idea about Ma; even if you whip me a hundred times, I've given up on her." "Ach, I don't know where your ma went either. Some women are so flaky they can't make up their own minds. Instead they rely on good-for-nothing men like your father." "What about you? Back in the day, was Grandpa a good man? Why do you live alone now?" "He was the most handsome man around. I had loved him since I was just ten years old. Every time he passed the house, I would find a way to get a look at him from as close as possible. I usually clipped flowers into my hair. He would laugh and pat my head. A few years later, it wasn't my head he wanted to pat. As a result, your daddy was born. Then Grandpa left with some people floating rafts of bamboo down the river; people said the waves of the waterfall were so strong his dead body would never be found. As for me, I don't believe that; maybe now he lives along the banks of the Cầu River, but he can't be dead." "Have you ever gone to look for him?" "I have, but I've never found even a trace." "Maybe he married another girl who gave birth to whole villages downstream." Grandma smacked her lips to clear the spit. "Who knows, human life ebbs like the flow of a river, I don't blame him." "If you don't believe he's dead, why do you still burn incense for him?" "I worship gods of rivers and streams; I worship to have peace of mind." Grandma sat beside the stove; in her old age she didn't sleep much, her mouth always thirsting for a fresh betel quid. "Toàn, pestle one more mortar of betel for me, please? My life is a spent betel quid: outside it looks very fresh but inside it's all worn out like rice plants after a big storm." "Have you ever dreamed he would come back?" "I've stayed up late so many years, but I've never dreamed that yet. That's why I believe he's still alive." "A few days ago, someone told me that Grandpa lives in Ba La Tắc Cun, that his family survives on corn bran, eating corn porridge and drinking corn wine, and that his wife gave birth to a pack of children who in turn whelped hordes of grandchildren that are more like pigs, squealing and rooting all the time." "I heard that too, and smacked my tongue laughing, but my legs ache so much, I didn't have the strength to go look for him. It's been decades we've been apart, as long as a lifetime. A reunion might make us feel silly; besides, it's not necessary now. I'd rather let heaven decide my fate. In my life, until now, I haven't lacked anything; I've known it all, had my full share of both good and bad." "So do you want me to try to find him?" "Well, if you have so much free time, try finding a wife to give birth to some children. Any girl willing to marry you would do. Beauty can't be scraped out to eat. If you don't have a job, bring her back here; my land's more than enough." "Silly old woman. You really think a girl would come live in this boring old backwater with you? In all the world, only you could be happy with such a wretched place." "You don't understand." Grandma was really upset, and cried softly while whipping at my legs. "Go away you mongrel, my life has been miserable on this land, but I can't leave it. You've been infected by the city's rotten bait; you're spoiled, living like a wild dog, living the life of a nobody. Without a wife and children, your life is a fallen leaf." I smiled, hugged her, and lifted her up. "Grandma, don't cry, let me hold you in my arms and rock you to sleep, okay?" "Oooh, 'The wind carries mustard back to heaven. Coriander stays behind to suffer a bitter life.'" She weighed nothing; her sobbing dwindled, her tears like autumn dew. "You're rocking me because I used to lull you to sleep this way in the old days. Oh, my puppy, if you don't live kindly, Grandma surely will not be able to close her eyes when she dies. . . ."

Actually, my mother did not go away without coming back to visit, but in those long gone days I hated her. I was an extremely stubborn, impatient boy, living rashly. My mother came home, bringing with her some crappy gifts she'd picked up from somewhere; later, I learned she'd had to beg her husband's children not to sell them to a junk trader just to bring them to me. I used those ugly, musty, sewage-smelling gifts on a scarecrow for the garden. When my mother saw that, she cried aloud, "Toàn, your mother begs forgiveness!" And I laughed; at ten I'd already learned the power of Grandma's scornful laughter. "To use this garbage to make a scarecrow to guard the vegetables is a bit too good for it. Get out of here, and don't ever bring rotten crap like this home again. I don't need you in my life. I'll make a life that will goggle your pathetic old eyes. . . ." Later, I realized I had been too cruel to her, but by then I didn't know where to find her to apologize, or even whether she was dead or alive.

The day I went to university, Grandma gave me my mother's address in the city. Her house squatted along the river bank, her husband worked as a butcher, and all year round she ran a counter selling meat at Quán Triều market, her hand continuously swatting a fan tied to a rag to shoo flies. She told me that a village neighbor once shopped down there and saw my mother waving a pig-sticking blade and dashing over counters to chase a thief who had dared to steal a pig's heart, all while dishing out a slurry of verbal blood pudding. She told me, "Take the bus to Quán Triều—it only costs a few dozen dong (she always converted any kind of money into dozens of dong, whether in the millions or billions), and when you get off, ask for Mrs. Diên, who sells pork. It's been a long time since I checked if she's still there, but she probably is, since it's nigh impossible for her to go anywhere trapped like she is by that pack of brats." I took her advice and figured I'd ask Ma for some money to go to school so Grandma wouldn't have to send so much every month. I searched every corner of Quán Triều market, combed every stinking ditch into the Cầu River, and even checked both banks of the plastic foam choked muddy river, but still I could not find her.

I asked the old woman who sold betel nut at the entrance of the market: "Do you know Mrs. Diên who sells pork?" The old woman looked at me. She said, "I know her, that Mrs. Diên who sold pork to customers and also served blood pudding to her husband and cursed her husband's children like singing a song." "I don't know about that," I said, "but she's my mother." The betel-nut-selling old woman looked shocked. "But you're so handsome, and she was like some kind of weasel, how can you two be mother and son?" I laughed. "Because my father is handsome. But is my mother still here?" The woman motioned for me to sit next to her and, glancing around, told me in a whisper that in the past, my mother's house overlooked the river; her husband wanted to stay there because he said it was easier that way to drop a fishing net at night and to cook chitlins. He always said washing and cooking the pig intestines in Cầu River water made them sweet and crunchy. A plate of his chitlins could wrestle down several bottles of wine and clear the sinuses of a dozen hefty peasants. I don't know about that, but for some reason my mother's chitlins had a huge following. One night, after a storm, my mother's house lay silently at the bottom of the river. And Ma also lay dormant somewhere, leaving no trace, not a single echo to reach back to the market. But like my Grandma with her husband, I also refused to believe my mother was dead. . . .

When I began editing at the newspaper, I made every effort to learn the truth about my mother. She suffered far too many miseries in her life, one of which was having a bad son who flung curses at his mother like pouring acid on the place he was born. During my investigations, I would typically follow my instincts, and each time I found that my instincts were always completely wrong. I followed the Cầu River to its end, stopping at every settlement along its banks. There were so many women, each with a different fate, but all with my mother's same shabby appearance. During these nearly hopeless trips, I trained myself to be patient. I had been avoiding certain truths about my origins, and it's only now that I'm writing these lines that I've found the courage to face them. Maybe my mother was not the person I hoped her to be. She had merged into the grasses and trees somewhere; she had gone someplace with the sea. Ma had been busy, and she had many faults, but she also gave birth to me, a son living wild like a weed, a human son with the instincts of a weed.

There was also the time I phoned my father to ask about Ma. Crying and drunk after the breakup of my first love with a whelp not yet clean of the blood of her birth, a girl with eyes that blinked quickly like an actress in a Korean movie but who had a bad habit of shoplifting. Yet I loved her. I started working like a madman to provide for her but marshaled my strength for our midnight fucking, which was so stormy that each morning after, my knees would buckle and my eyes would turn red, making me look at life as if perpetually drunk. In those days I didn't curse, but goddamn, that woman wasn't worth a shit and I don't understand why I had to feel so miserable and exhausted for her. Dad consoled me: "Women are what men lack; so don't worry, another one will replace her, and you'll see life never has to be boring." "Do you know where my mother is?" He told me after he moved in with my stepmother, he completely lost track of his old life. He would live at that river's mouth to the sea for the rest of his days; his wife didn't let him go anywhere, afraid he'd run off from the life of too many spoiled brats, of boredom and desperation and repeatedly eating boiled spinach and simmered fish. His wife said he was too used to a life of debauchery, that he'd honed his good looks and made the crotch of his pants worshipped by scores of women, but now he had to pay his dues. At that point I almost stopped crying it was so funny. "Is your new wife as beautiful as my mother?" Now it was my father's turn to laugh, a laugh as sour as overcooked rice wine. Then he said, "They're equally good looking." "The old sayings are never wrong," I said. " 'A good wife makes a bad husband.' And 'It's not the green magpie's beauty and long tail that makes it worthless, is it?' " My father said, "You can curse me, but I haven't lived so well that all my good luck is gone." I'd had enough, if he'd gone nuts and insulted me back, at least I would've felt I still meant something to him in this goddamned life. He treated me like a debt he could never pay back, and any time I had a problem, he cried like he expected me to forget what he owed.

Later, drinking beer in a little cafeteria at the top of Phùng Hưng Street, I said to my stepbrother, "What the hell does he think I am? I insulted him and he didn't even bother to argue." My stepbrother laughed bitterly: "Come home with me and you'll see how miserable he is. I come home from work tired as hell, but in the night he wakes me to empty the bedpan for him. The first time, I was pissed enough to spit blood, but later I felt sorry for him. Dad's life is 'A life bitten by a dog,' as 'Sad as the bite of a dog.' " I told my stepbrother, "I know I'm disrespectful, but I'm sick and tired of watching him stagnate in bed, moaning and waiting for death. Tell him I can't stand it." My stepbrother said, "The old man never blames you for anything. You can live as you do now and Dad's still very proud. You're like an unpruned tree but you still live straight." I laughed. "I'm not straight. People are more and more crowded every day. Thạch Sanhs are few, Lý Thôngs legion.* If you want to be noble, the only way is to go live up in the sky." My stepbrother banged his cup of beer down on the table.

---

* Thạch Sanh is the name of a popular folk hero; Lý Thông is the villain in the story.

"Are you telling the truth?" "It's true, my life is shit. I've been fooled a million times and have done the same to others. My life sucks." He pointed at my face and cursed, "Goddamn it, for a long time the old man and I have been secretly proud of you. And now you're just a liar." I laughed. "Don't be angry. In my life, I don't idolize anyone, so I'm never disappointed. Don't demand anything. You live your life, I'll live mine." My stepbrother very deliberately paid for his share of the beer, left behind the milk I'd bought, and went home. He never phoned me again. It's funny, I thought. Why on earth would a pure man like him need to look up to a man like me?

Grandma had not fallen asleep, the weather was so cold; I put a blanket over her, but she shrugged it off. She looked at me. "Did you do something wrong? Or were you cheated on?" "I've never cheated on anyone, and no one can trick me." "What a monster you are." "If not a monster, how can I survive all those horrible goblins in the city? When you lived down there with me, you saw the newspapers every day reporting nothing but murders, rapes, and robberies." She smiled slyly. "But you said the newspapers all lied. . . ." I laughed too. She understood her grandson very well. So what was the story? I wasn't sure whether that girl still hated me, a very mean, good-for-nothing guy, a guy who slept with her countless times, who knew every secret mark on her body as well as every erogenous zone, but who made her out to be some kind of cheap whore. Maybe she'd been swallowed by the fog? Or destroyed by the storms of heaven and earth? I honestly didn't know. "Grandma, I'll tell you this story, but you might beat me to death." She sat up, stroked my beard and hair, and said, "Okay, you tell me."

I looked at Grandma. The fire in the stove had gone out, leaving spots of smoldering charcoal. Outside, the rising din of jungle birds signaled the morning. I used to wish I were a rooster, in the morning crowing so loud it would echo in the forest, and in the late afternoon I'd lead my flock up to a high tree branch to sleep. Each day would be like the next, creation as natural as destruction. If I got my wish, if I'd been a rooster, I would not have been so tormented right at that moment. Grandma looked at me, "What's the story—it's about a woman, isn't it? You'll die because of a woman, boy!" I looked at her. "No, it's about a woman, but not what you think." "So has your girlfriend come back? Are you going to marry her?" I laughed. "She's so beautiful, do you think she'll marry a reporter just to be exhaustingly poor? She'll marry some billionaire." Grandma asked, "Then why did she climb into your bed in the old days?" "Back then, it was love." Grandma exclaimed, "Love? You goddamn cur, where did love get you, making you skulk back here like a dog eating mash on the sly." "Yeah well, she's tangled up with some billionaire, so I have to come here." Grandma said, "Your life is too complicated. "I never understand. . . ."

That's right, Grandma did not understand. But what had I done? What did I do when faced with the difficulty and chaos of earning my daily keep? The girl wearing red high-heeled shoes, the girl with hair to her shoulders, the girl with the beautiful face like on TV. I want to call her Red Shoes because I don't want her to have to read her name once in these words. I know she has lived a life so extraordinary that I haven't completely understood it all until now. On the day she left me—but in fact we were never really on the same road together, so we could never have an actual parting moment—we were sitting at a teahouse on the top of a rise overlooking West Lake. She said, "My life has been worthless, but I know you live well, and that you know how to be a man for woman. You should live a different life. If we keep going on like we do now, soon we'll just be the fat on society's ass. Seeing each other will make us want to throw up." "Okay," I replied, "keep going, but don't try to teach a whore how to lift her skirt." "You're as cranky as a woman selling fish." I cackled, "If selling fish makes money, I'll do it. In life, whatever makes money I'll do, so long as I don't have to go to jail or kill anyone." Red Shoes laughed. "That, I know; I also know you think I'm worthless, just a plaything of the moment; but in the beginning I thought you loved me, so I offered my body for you to handle however you wanted, so you could taste real life for the first time. Now you shake me off like dust from the road, and I don't blame you. Men are all the same. I'll live my life as a lesson to you." Her words were like wind blowing in my hair, but in fact they thrust deep into my heart.

My self-esteem disintegrated when Red Shoes left me sitting there alone to go down and get into the waiting red car of some guy with dyed red hair and then speed away down Cổ Ngư hill. Later, the gossip among the models I know had Red Shoes telling dozens of stories about me. And almost all the models saw me as a playboy reporter, someone who could make love seven times a night from the bathroom to the terrace and who knew plenty of ways to make money from a press pass. At first, I thanked Red Shoes, because as a result of her stories, I had serious status in the eyes of those long-legged girls who'd just become adults. The girls looked at me, not sure if they should love me or hate me. I knew the long legs not because I'd written about them but because I always went out with the assistant directors. They and I lived together like some pairing of symbiotic species, and the long legs were a part of that multicolored symbiotic life. And then one day, I saw Red Shoes sitting and talking with some kids who worked for an advertising company called Viet Supermodels. She said, "Over there sits an amateur model who'd be perfect for the NaNo brief campaign. He's a reporter who just happens to have long legs, a broad chest, a killer six-pack, and an actor's bright beautiful face." The kids from the ad company gasped, almost as if listening to a fairy tale. Back then, finding someone like this was possible only in heaven. The ad company had called relentlessly for tryouts but found only a few people. And they didn't just want beauty. The manager of the project said, "An anonymous model would be perfect! We don't want faces that have already been around the block on television." Red Shoes smiled, while inwardly I seethed. Red Shoes! Why did you hate me so?

That very afternoon, the ad company director phoned me. I knew already but came back anyway. The director looked at me and from that look I knew exactly what he was thinking. I doubled over laughing—I never thought I could fetch such a high price. Had I known, I should have been a model from the beginning, and my life would have been brilliant. The director smiled. "It's not too late, if you want, you can join our agency, on the condition that . . . you must have discipline. . . ." I laughed even louder, just to prevent him from uttering what I knew he'd say next, that I'd have to get into bed with him. I told the director, "I'm not as handsome as Red Shoes said, or I'm only handsome to her. Because she still misses me." The director gave me his business card and said, "I'll pay you two thousand dollars for the campaign; if you think that's okay, call me." I stood up and said, "Money's something everyone needs. It's money, after all. But I'll only model with Red Shoes. . . ."

But things didn't work out as simply as the director expected. Red Shoes fled my pursuit by phone. She left me a message as short as a tycoon's finger: "That Viet Supermodel money—did you have the balls to get it?" She went to Saigon with a plastic and aluminum mogul, a billionaire who I knew had opened a restaurant six months ago that despite having only one customer per day was still lit up like a beacon every night. The place had to be laundering his dirty money. Red Shoes had run away from me. I didn't think she was still afraid of me. Worse, I had no reason to think she still loved me—why on earth would she? Red Shoes had gone. Every once in a while, I'd get an invitation to a Viet Supermodel party. But they were rare, because the long legs all knew the director was a secretive neat freak who lived a life as closed as a jar of fermented wine buried in the ground. But I was thick-skinned enough to attend, even though I knew I would never go so low as to strip naked and play the muscle-bound guy with my picture on a poster just for people to dream about while buying their underpants. The director loved me—this was well known by all the long-legged models. Unfortunately, this news spread even to my office at the newspaper. Even so, I never felt bad about it. In life these days, rumors are as plentiful as grass or garbage. Anyone commonly caught in a scandal just becomes more famous than ever and earns money more easily than before. One long-legged girl, while picking at a buffet with me at the Nikko Hotel, suggested, "We should cause a scandal together, then you can spread rumors in the newspaper and as that loops around we can milk it for all it's worth; without a scandal, you can't become a star." I never had the self-confidence to make myself a character in one of my own newspaper articles but felt the rumors about sex and a relationship with the big-shot director of the advertising agency didn't really harm my spiritual life; in fact, sometimes those rumors made good grounds for upping my luster. As the photo shoot approached, the director said that if I could find Red Shoes, he'd bump my salary up to three grand. I laughed. "I'm not interested anymore. Find someone else; advertising underwear isn't hard, any model can now do something brassy like that; besides, if I take the job, they'll curse me for putting them out of work. But I'll go find Red Shoes anyway. And I'll not take a penny for that."

So of course the scheme to make a spectacle of my body wearing tiny underpants never came to anything. Not because I was afraid. But because Red Shoes had already found her own spectacle. The big shot got caught, stunning no one, except maybe Red Shoes. My editor-in-chief sat waiting for me in his office, the room hot as fire, the struggling air conditioner set below 65 degrees but his fat face swollen with heat. In a panicky rush like his thoughts might fly away, he said, "Hey, bucko, go find that girl right now—who is she, anyway? Where does she come from? What's her relationship with that guy? All you do is fuck around lately; this is your last chance." I was stunned. It had been a long time since I'd last been stuck in my office, sitting in front of the computer behind piles of books and papers, mesmerized by flashing cursors and Yahoo Messenger emoticons. No one wanted to chat with me anymore. Shit. For a long time, I found myself having to think over thoughts like this. Life had taken me away so quickly that my legs had barely tired from one game before they were forced to jump into another. Playing too fast. Playing too hard, from dusk till dawn. Red Shoes, where were you?

I sat in front of the computer, my head whirring like a fan. Well write then! Pay off this debt of life! What the hell, I'd write a book.

At this moment looking back, I just wish Red Shoes had called me.

But she did not call.

I was going crazy, but I didn't know it.

She said we were the same, both of us roots without soil to cling to, both living lives as fleeting as flying sand. But there was a time, exhausted by booze and making love, that she and I sat next to each other on the terrace gazing at the sky full of stars, and she told me about the rock she crawled out from under and the land she came from. She spoke to me as if speaking to herself, saying she'd never go back because she no longer had faith in it. I went like a sleepwalker to Red Shoes' village. Her mother had left a long time ago; there was only her stepfather sitting sprawled on the porch. He said, "Yeah, she came home. She brought some money and then took off. That whore, a few days ago I saw her on TV, wearing a shirt open at the chest, her ass hanging out; what kind of animal is she? Just like her mother." I asked the old man, his face black as water chestnuts, "Did you hear the stories about her?" "She's just like her mother, greedy for money. In the old days, when I still traded wood, her mother stayed with me for that. But now I'm broke, and she left me all alone to go to the city to wallow in filth. Yesterday, reading the paper, I saw her face, no honor at all. Such a shame." I scoffed. "What are you to her? You tried to rape her when she was barely fifteen." The old man whizzed a cup past my ear. "Get out of here, you rude little shit, where'd you get such crap?" I ran away.

Sensational story! Beautiful article! Such an exclusive!

Dozens of congratulatory SMS messages swarmed my cellphone the morning the first story in my series about Red Shoes ran. I looked at the article, at the words I'd strung together. People say when fingers don't hold the pen, the words don't come from the heart, and like so the pages of my manuscript turned cold. Digital words don't know how to tremble. I'd often said the person who thought up that saying was an idiot. But now I've found that I myself am the idiot.

Eventually, Red Shoes's scandal sank into silence. Hooking up with a big shot was no crime; people could curse her for a hundred days, but she wasn't actually guilty of anything. Red Shoes reappeared in the city, alone. She made the effort to find me. "Hey big guy, I was with that billionaire for a while but now it's over. Will you let me stay with you for a few days?" It was like I'd been struck dumb. She carried bags of her clothes into an empty room of my house. After begging me to drink with her, she cried, telling me, "I'm the bad girl so I should be the one to suffer, why won't people leave my mother alone? I don't even know where to find her. . . ." Red Shoes gradually stripped off my clothes. My body burned hot as a fever. I lay there, with my empty body stretched out flat on the mattress, and she collapsed on top of me. She gasped, "I think you still love me. We've both lived a dog's life, we both no longer have parents, and we both love each other. But I'm in such pain." Sobbing now, she said, "They dug up every last nest of my secrets. Who are they to judge my life?" I lay there, her tears trickling over my broad chest. I lay there, my body tingling with energy, but I couldn't do anything, I couldn't possess her body as I'd done on all those nights we spent together. I lay there, still. I cried.

While Red Shoes slept, her soft white body spread on the mattress like a challenge, I ran away. I returned to Grandma. "In fact, I came back here to tell you this story. Are you going to keep whipping me?" Grandma wouldn't look at me; instead she gazed out to the mountain slopes laden with morning dew, her voice choked with water like mimosa weeds after a winter night. "Oh Toàn, how I wish I could be strong again . . . I want to beat you to death, you rotten whelp. . . ." She cried full voice, sounding like wind flying through the fences, dry and rasping. She cried like that a long time. I stood before her, weeping, but never daring to embrace her in my arms. I cried like I'd never yet been myself.

I took for granted that Red Shoes would stay. But by the next morning she was gone. When I returned to the city, I found she hadn't left anything in the room except a pair of my underwear that she'd taken at our previous parting. She'd said they made me look like a heavenly statue. She said she was taking them with her so whenever she missed me she could take them out and imagine me in them again. At the time I thought the whole thing was silly. But now, after so many whirls of time, the fact that she'd kept them and only now returned them to me meant I'd lost her forever. I returned to the newspaper and asked the chief to switch my beat to something different, like culture and art, so I could spend all day reading books and watching movies. The transition wasn't easy, but it made me less likely to have to meet or connect with other people, and at the time I loathed the complicated entanglements of the human race. The chief didn't understand, thinking I was crazy or that I had some sort of megalomania of the young-and-famous-too-soon. He said to be a journalist meant covering domestic and social affairs maturely. In a Phi Tiến Sơn film, the lead character was a journalist covering society who was busted down to writing on art and culture because of his . . . breach of discipline. I had promise but seemed already infected with celebrity disease.

I explained to the chief that by working diligently in the vast and dusty on-site library, I would read and wipe clean the books, and my own record as well. Though new, the books had not been opened in a long time.

The first lines of this story I wrote on my blog. And so it grew out of my frivolous thoughts over many days. Many people have written to ask me about my grandma: How is she? How does she live now? Has she come back to the city to see the ice-cream cabinet? I've been silent because I never know what to say. Grandma loves me, loves the treasure of her life too much. So she will never forgive me; she will not concede to me and my streets.

Once, while scrolling through the pages of a blog, I recognized something familiar in an ambiguous passage. It turned out more than half the personal blogs in Vietnam were all quoting this same blog, which was blazing red and unfinished. The entries ceased abruptly at the end of July 2006, with its owner writing that she would forgive the faults of the man she loved, even if he had rubbed salt into her wounds, if only her man knew how to use his kisses to erase her sorrows. But that man didn't do a god-damn thing, his muscular and naked body was like a waterlogged corpse, a heavy stone that would not move even when her tears became a stream, a river.

That man did not dare to make love to her after so many painful days. She knew then she had nothing left. So she went away.

I often wish that those were not pages from Red Shoes's diary.

I don't go looking for Red Shoes any longer. Because everything I've ever looked for during these days and months living on this earth has become distant. They may have appeared to be near, but gradually they have fallen out of reach. On the day I left Grandma's land of wild mustard, I thought I had the whole world; I would accomplish the impossible and give Grandma the grand life I'd seen in movies and on TV. But I've hurled my life this way and that, and in the end I still have only the past from which I have tried so desperately to cut myself apart. Empty-handed, I've learned I am a wild mustard seed, grown unbidden in the sand, intent on flying with the sand. And it's with the sands of passion that I've been washed away, merged into streams and rivers.

This year I am twenty-seven years old, and I know it's too late—oh so late!—but I must go back, for a new beginning.

Translated by Nguyễn Hùng and Charles Waugh

A Thousand Years Sing the Waves

Nguyễn Van Toàn

THE OCEAN HEAVED UNDER THE DARK BLANKET OF NIGHT. A WIND BLEW the little plants growing along the beach. Battery-powered lights swept slickly over the faces of the men working on the floating wooden ship. One, two, three, four. New shadows arrived on the beach. *Oh, I want to stay,* groaned the shadows, their voices hushed like from the silenced muzzle of a gun. The old local men's hands were held tightly by their wives. *Don't go my love,* sobbed the women. *We can't back out,* said the men. *Money has been handed over already.* The husbands' expressions crumpled with pain. *Come back my love.* The women slumped down to the wet sand to watch the shadows of their husbands swim out to the boat.

The sound of the engine gurgled effusively in the waves. The boat nosed toward the open ocean and began the journey to search for the promised land. The dazed women looked at the shadow of the boat as if it were a coffin slipping into the sea.

The next day, and the day after that, the whole fishing village maintained a Buddhist fast. Incense smoke whirled up into the heavy, breathless atmosphere. They waited, buzzing with prayer. They prayed for their men's journey to go smoothly, for only a little bad luck and for a lot of good. *Why these past few days has the surface of the sea been so dark? Why have the silver edges of the clouds looked so gruesome?*

The omens became clear one morning as watchman Châu's long shadow stretched down the middle of the village road. Every family had a body on the Thuận An beach to claim. Mothers and fathers starved for good news now cried to each other to eat sand. Châu's voice rang out. The alarm fell down to the open thatched houses and to the whole fishing village, stampeding out like a flooded anthill. *Father! Husband! Child!* Tears fell endlessly from the knots of people wailing on the sand—the sand soft and fresh and natural like the skin of teenaged girls. Dark tumultuous waves rolled beneath a distant corner of the Thuận An sky, rocking forty horror-stricken and wide-eyed corpses. Forty dead bodies now rotting into fish food. Forty pairs of cold stiff hands tied together with the sunken boat's lines. In an unplanned suicide, these ill-fated men had entwined themselves with one another hoping to prevent their descent to the bottom of the sea.

* * *

I could never escape the haunted feeling of those men's return to our breezy village. Cut off from the world by smooth sand dunes that stretched without end, our tiny fishing village consisted of dozens of gray rooftops spread like a flock of birds prostrating themselves between a poplar forest and the curling green waves, singing jagged fragments of time. The ocean thudded relentlessly, the beating of an insidious heart.

My memories of my childhood all relate to images of a normal, lolling little neighbor girl alone on the beach. She liked making sand houses. The houses had hedges and flower gardens made from green poplar branches and red and white corals. Her eyes perpetually looking up at me. "Let's play pirates!" "Again? Okay." So much fun. We had robbers and police and kidnapped hostages. Really fun. A soft tender child. Then one day I saw her trussed under a tree, her eyes wide with fear. This guy Dzương had nearly strangled her half-naked body, obsessed with this one so little she still sucked her mother's breast. The little girl burst out in unintelligible wailing that shattered the hurt, strangled places inside me. I plunged in like an animal. My punches knocked Dzương onto his back. He sat up spewing curses. We steamed into each other, tangling and hatefully giving each other the beating of the century. Ready to kill each other if some other kids hadn't arrived in time. "Go home," I shouted at Lam. She'd stayed, watching me. Seeing her underpants were wet, I pursed my lips. She blushed. Because of him. She told me when I fought with him she worried that I'd get killed and that just a moment ago Dzương had said something nice to her. He had asked her to take him as her husband. I went berserk again, feeling hatred, feeling the sleaziness of his disgusting delinquent voice. I growled, then turned and walked away. My bewildered little friend ran after me. "Wait for me," she called. I chided her: "He asked, but you didn't say no. Horrible." She began to cry. After a silence, she blurted, "I'll never take a husband." Horrible. Then she streaked away. Her hair red with sun, her dangling arms swinging. "I'll never take a husband." Her voice clinking like a crystal glass breaking on the sand.

We, the children of a fishing village. A poor village, poor approaching wretched. The old boats kept crumbling like they hadn't enough strength to cope with the wickedness of life, with the vicious muddled coastal fishing. That craving for the ocean, that dream of heavy nets of fish kept swooning in the hearts of the boys. My grandfather's life was a series of long, beggarly, dark days. My father's life never had anything different, and maybe my life would be the same. By the age of three, children in my village already knew how to swim, at five, they could sit in any boat, and by seven, they knew how to row. We memorized the faces of the fish before we memorized the letters of the alphabet. To get from our village to the school, endless scattered patches of sand, cactuses, and wild stands of firs had to be crossed. Several acres in the middle held a gloomy cemetery with protruding mounds. Patches of sand piled up in dunes all around the side of the fishing village bordering the ocean. All around the rest was the busy village market and good long fresh fields and gardens all the way to Tam Giang lagoon. Two worlds, two lives. Going to school each day, we stepped from one world into another, a fact that could have given me some kind of complex. I was a bored kid at school. Sometimes I called or whistled for Lam to come with me past the row of luxuriant green bamboo, down into the field to embrace the refreshing wind. Sitting at the edge of the grass one day, we gazed absentmindedly at the choked yellow fields beyond the dried-up ditch and stiff bulrushes. Swarms of golden dragonflies danced, their wings shining, gliding back and forth over the cracked field. "Are you hungry?" I asked. She nodded awkwardly. I waded down into a spongy patch of sugarcane stalks and passed through to a field of potatoes. Lying pressed to the ground, I dug into the earth with my two bare hands and scraped up two purple potatoes. I broke off the roots and brushed away the dirt and took several ravenous bites. Then I dug out a few more potatoes to carry back in my shirt. Just as I came up the bank, a shout made me jump. "Stealing potatoes, huh? Stand still—don't make me shoot." I turned around, frightened. Châu stood at the top of the slope, an AR-15 rifle in his hands. I slipped like a mouse into the middle of the sugarcane. A deafening explosion and the sound of the sugarcane spraying behind. Fear made me numb. I ran blindly through the sharp sugarcane leaves, getting slashed all over my body. When Châu's curses reached me, I just lay down in the red earth trying to breathe. Faintly, Lam's voice came through the rustling leaves: "Phong! Phong oi!" She came down from the bank calling and I crept toward her. She hugged me tight, then slumped down crying. I burst out laughing. "Silly girl, no need to cry." She wiped her tears and puffed her cheeks. "I imagined you were dead already." "What mischievous death could get me? Here, eat." I put one of the surviving potatoes into her hand. Seeing her two skinny legs covered in grass, her small mouth shyly munching the delicious raw potato, I felt a love beyond measure. I knew she was hungry. Like the whole fishing village was hungry. The poor had turned into the hungry after so many years pursuing collectivization. We had to go through that period just to understand what collectivization meant. Knowing our village people couldn't sell fish at the market but would still have to pass by all the merchandise was horrendously difficult. To be able to buy something required a painstaking process. Emaciated rice fields under the hands of collective care and cultivation became barren in an astonishingly strange way. Hunger spread, trapping people in an invisible wire net, and in their deprivation and despair, people turned their gaze toward the ocean. They placed on the road to the horizon all their flickering, insubstantial hopes for a new life. My village beach with its advantageous terrain became an assembly point for the oceangoing departures to all places abroad. Overnight, our otherwise well-mannered fishing village became a shelter for the traitors and criminals who aligned themselves with Châu, the commune leader who also ran the police. A bloodthirsty public demanding diligence in official business gave him the perfect opportunity to make arrests. Like a fox in charge of a chicken coop, Châu received the authority to swear in bullies as his deputies. People said he took special pleasure in beating people with a rubber sandal. To fall into Châu's hands for stealing or trespassing—or really any offense—was to have him take off his sandal or pull out his big jungle knife and immediately shove it into your face, for sure to be beaten every time. If there was ever a whistleblower letter sent to District Chairman Thang or to some other notable person, no one would know how, but all would be settled silently. Châu just became crueler and crueler, denouncing on the spot anyone he suspected of betraying the nation by trying to flee. But hunger forced a person to take risks, to catch and sell fish betting against the odds. To cross the sea. In that deadly attempt to flee, both my father and Mr. Đại, Lam's father, were lost.

* * *

For a long time I just did not think of loving or hating her. I still saw her as ordinary and a little absurd. And I thought it was absurd when I heard others call her pure or charitable, an immaculate angel.

My older friend Kiếm always told me: "The nature of women is the same as cats—deceit and false-heartedness lurk within like dormant seeds. Love is never the lofty ideal it's made out to be, because their goal is simply to get into bed." I admired Kiếm for many things, but in this matter his opinions made me sick. Because in my life, love was a blessed thing. Because I loved her, silently, head over heels. A pristine love like white paper.

After many years apart, I met Lam again one day on a late ferry. She sat leaning to one side, daydreaming while gazing out at the viscous river water in the afternoon light. For ten minutes the ferry crossed the river; for ten minutes I sat as if drunk, looking at her from behind the cockpit. Wearing a yellow shirt with embroidered chrysanthemums and green pants in a tight mossy pattern, she floated above the group of other passengers like a fresh and proud flower budding above its leaves and stems. The ferry drew up to the dock, and she received her bicycle from my hand. "Hey, thanks." Her voice was the same as her: clear and sweet. Then she smiled, her teeth flickering prettily. Just that and I lost my appetite, I lost sleep. Others knew her only as the daughter of Mrs. Tư, the head of the afternoon market. She lived and studied in Hue now, and usually came home to visit her mother by taking the Perfume River ferry, not mine. As soon as I saw her, I felt desperately hopeless, the kind of desperation and rejection the dwarves must have felt when loving Snow White. But I couldn't control my feelings. I loved her more than my own body, and making her know that alone would be enough to make me happy. I'd fallen for her like this without even having talked to her! Truly, back then I was still a fool, full of silly ideas. I did not yet understand that true love always comes with shared thoughts and complete commitment. Or that sacrifice without condition was a delusional charade. Kiểm said there was something wrong with my way of thinking during all this. I forgot to tie up the ferry, forgot to oil the engine, and confused a lot of other stuff, like the many, varied river navigation signs I'd failed to figure out in the past four years. I was seriously indebted to Kiểm. He gave me a set of primary experiences with life. If it weren't for these, I'd still be like the pack of fishing village friends who day in and day out sat yoked to their round boats casting nets, blindly dragging another generation through life. I'd always lived true to myself and to others, but then things began to change. Most nights, I waded across the patches of sand and returned to the village by dawn just to turn around and go out again to the dock to run the early ferry. On moonlit nights, I didn't return home but instead went up to sleep in the boat with this little devil named Ngợi. Ngợi was old and short and as hard as the heartwood of a teak tree, all year working his fingers to the bone. He spent all his life on the water, always on the river or in the cove, in shallow, narrow passages and on the lagoon. A person of extremely few words, always making up some new story to tell in his murmuring voice—his great stories told of the ways of the ocean and the habits and legends of different kinds of fish. One type of perch lived far out in the open sea and only occasionally appeared in the lagoon. Ngợi said that's when the fish missed people. Waiting for a

clear moonlit night, the fish would jump into the bottom of a boat and lie
still for people to stroke them and let them back down into the water to
go out to sea. Some sacred magic let the fish know how to choose people
who would never be ruthless. To have fish leap up into your boat was a
great fortune because the fish could grant wishes. All these stories I heard
were preposterous, but I still wanted to believe them, I still hoped that
some moonlit night the fish would jump into my boat. I waited, cherishing
this hope. And I probably would have kept waiting forever if not for a bout
of drinking with Kiếm one night. Kiếm knew everything about wine and
usually liked to drink alone, only sometimes inviting me to join him. So I
was kind of surprised on that dark afternoon to hear him tell me to go buy
wine. I jogged up to Mrs. Tư's bar. Lam had returned home recently, so I'd
had more chances to see her. Despite being the awkward guy who couldn't
speak in front of pretty, decent girls like her. Maybe she knew this, since
she voluntarily and naturally took the initiative for me. I drank only a little
while there, otherwise I'd have fallen on my face in front of her. I carried
her sweet sentences the whole way home.

Kiếm and I anchored the ferry beneath the shadow of the rice plants.
The tide began to go out, the river knocking loudly on the sides of the boat.
A green color spread over the surface of the water beneath the weak moonlight, the wind blew with a frosty chill. In the distance, golden lights like
kernels of corn bobbed slowly on the fishing boats. Kiếm lounged in the
bow drinking quietly. His disheveled hair hung to one side, covering part
of his face and chin. He was handsome in a hardened way, the turmoil of
life having given him a bit of savage mystery; in fact, most of his life was a
mystery. No one knew how he'd drifted to Thuận An. Even more mysterious were the dozens of years whose stories of his wife and child he never
told. Some people guessed he'd wanted to live a life committed to another.
Others supposed he hated love, so he felt hatred toward women. Some
rumored he'd had a breakdown. He had heard all these stories but calmly
refused to say anything about them. Only I knew he was still a lady's man.
Because I always smelled strange perfume in the ferry on mornings blurred
by fog. Because I kept finding long hairs twisted on his pillow and blankets.
Strands of hair not the same color or size. At first I meant to throw them
away. But then, because of my crazy yearnings, I began to keep them in a
cardboard box, so when I was free I could spool them out again to contem-
plate their meaning. Each strand, each type. Glossy, velvet, curly, black,
blonde. The owners of these strands—who were they, what were they like?
I moonily imagined the shapes of the faces that went with each strand. At
the same time, I began to feel there was a fuzzy hidden memory inside me,

something like a feeling of resentment toward Kiểm. A disgusted feeling I couldn't fully comprehend, like when I saw Dzương pull that depraved trick with little Lam all those years before. My suspicion increased after finding a curl of thick hair. For sure Kiểm couldn't know about this.

The wine had softened Kiểm's lips, giving his voice a twang. The smooth twang trembled with each accumulated feeling of excitement, passion, loneliness, and grief. Each tone sparkled on the water, dissolved in the moonlight, and sank into my blood, making me feel faint. *Better to be like a raindrop drying on a stone statue. For a hundred years people return along a wide river.** For many years I've heard singers and guitarists sing this song. But none of them have made me feel as haunted as this extraordinary twang of Kiểm's that night.

At the end of the song, it was just two guys lying on the boat deck. He asked, "Phong, have you ever been in love?" I hesitated. "You just never know," he said. "Love can be all right, but never compassion. Because compassion almost always requires some unnecessary sacrifice." I was surprised. "Why do you say this?" "Because sacrifice is taken advantage of—it always gets repaid with lies and pain." After a silence, he continued. "You probably don't know, there was a person who left to join the marines for the South during the war. As the boat evacuated after a storm capsized it in the middle of the ocean, he gave the last life preserver to his wife, and to save himself, he hung on to a piece of driftwood for three days and nights before washing ashore. His wife was rescued by a passing ship. She was taken to America, and after a little while, she cold-bloodedly sent word to divorce him, abandoning him naked and poor in Vietnam. He was devastated, and in all the time that passed since, he's never loved again." Kiểm's voice fell silent. Already a little tipsy, I began to argue. "But all women and girls aren't the same." He sat up and looked at me with surprise. "Exactly right, but how can we make a distinction, how can we understand their hearts? Depravity always puts on the mask of innocence. And it always traps people, poisons them with false appearances." Without reason, I got the feeling he was referring to Lam, to the girl I loved. I felt myself being abused and dishonored. I swelled. "You don't know for sure. I feel there's one person not like this." He turned around and looked at me strangely. "Who? Tell and we'll see." I spoke dryly, "She's around here." He frowned, thinking, then blurted, "Ah, you must mean Mrs. Tư's daughter." I was silent. He nodded gently, a savage light flashing on his face. "Wait and see," he said cryptically.

---

* Lines from the poem "Thà Như Giọt Mưa" by Nguyễn Tất Nhiên, made popular in song in the twentieth century by Phạm Duy.

The next few days, we didn't speak of this again. Kiếm became close-mouthed, which made me vaguely anxious, feeling like he was plotting something horrible. Each night, I went to bed restlessly. What's he doing now, with whom, I kept asking myself, feeling tortured and regretful because of what he'd said the other night. My mother worried for me because she thought I was sick. For years, I'd shared every sad or happy thing with her, but I couldn't share this. A long week later, Kiếm said to me, "Tonight there will be something really interesting at Cane Break beach, you should go see." There was something bitter and viperous in his voice that gave me chills. I could tell something really atrocious was about to happen. I agonized like a tied up dog about to be slaughtered for meat. All afternoon, I cursed my powerlessness. At eight o'clock that night I went to the designated place. Cane Brake beach lay in the middle of an endless length of thickly growing reeds, so few people went there. The full moon was rising over the beach, the surface of the water glowing white. I saw the old familiar ferry partially hidden behind a luxuriant patch of cane. I took off my clothes and slipped down into the velvety water and swam like an otter. Near the ferry, I clung to the reeds to have a look. The ferry not flat on the still water but bobbing. A sound of stirring or struggling from the hold. Then the sound of breathing, the sound of a girl's soft moaning. I floated closer and peeked inside. I was dizzy, my hands and feet felt limp. In the dark hazy hold, a man and woman lay entwined, stroking and squeezing each other. Four sweaty naked calves curved together on the white floor beneath the moon. Nearby, Lam's yellow shirt and green pants lay rolled up and tossed aside. I gulped hoarsely in my throat, wanting to roar, to tear open the earth and sky as wide and deep as the pit of resentment in my heart. But some glimmer of clear thinking in the back of my mind held me back. Not able to look any longer, I turned and swam back to the beach with trembling hands.

Cursing my wet body and soaked underwear, I came ashore like an exorcised demon. Across the beach, through the market, I bolted like a maniac on the sand. Sinking my teeth into my own shaking muscles, I hated that I'd finally come to hate everyone. I needed to feel this fiery pain broiling into resentment. I wanted thunder and lightning to streak down and turn me into ashes. I wanted the earth to open and swallow me down into a pitch-black grave. I saw myself standing in front of the ocean. Beneath the moon, the surface of the water was beautiful like in a fairy tale, with soft waves rolling onto the beach like bolts of silk. My body seethed, hot. I took off my underwear and waded down into the water. The ocean embraced me like a lover. I knelt to submerge to my neck, letting each wave roll like a caress over my body. I satisfied the thirst burning inside me. I made love to the ocean void of all devotion, pleasure and pain. Then I shook myself and listened to the crashing of the waves.

I floundered up the beach and sat down on the sand. A feeling of shameful humiliation grew inside me. Clenching my lips, I let my tears run in bitter, salty drops. I lay down to dry myself beneath the refreshing moonlight and remembered I was only eighteen.

Over the next three days I holed up at home. The shock of that night put me in a desperate mood. Lam came to my house and with my mother cooked rice porridge for me and looked for herbal supplements to cure my depression. Since the episode in the ferryboat, I hadn't seen Lam. Now her tan skin began to have a beautiful, salty hint of the ocean about it. My mother said, "You're only human. Make mistakes, try hard, pray, get and give all the same. Don't curse your mother's lifework. You've got something good here, it looks like. . . ." My mother left her sentence half-unsaid on purpose. I knew my mother loved Lam, but I could not be moved. What happened at the ferry was like a death inside me, making me apathetic toward everything. Early the next morning, I went to the beach. I took the lock of curly hair and set it on fire. Each strand, each trembling strand burned from my hand and flew into the wind. But this only made me miss her more. I went to the dock to find Kiếm. He listened indifferently as I asked him to take a break, the whole time looking at me like his work running the ferry couldn't be interrupted. I searched his face for some expression that would reveal something from that night, but he kept calm and just looked tired. He was such a miserable wretch. I shouted in his face, ready to get an angry punch in return. He remained still and silent a long time. Then he said coolly, "Yes, but I'm not a hypocrite. And you should remember how every person who has played tricks and lied to you is also wretched." "Go to hell." I calmly turned my back to him and to the four years I'd spent working the ferry on the river. And that was the last time I saw him because, shortly after that, he sold the ferry and went away without saying anything to anyone. But Lam, I met her a few more times. She was still young and beautiful but now there was also something somewhat bleak in the light of her eyes.

I went up to Hue and joined a work crew. After six months of brutal physical labor, I returned to my village. The gloomy cemetery had become even gloomier as bodies were dug up for reburial.* The money sent back from

---

* In some parts of Vietnam, the dead are buried twice, the second time roughly three years later when all the flesh can be assumed to have been stripped from the bones. The coffin is dug up, the bones cleaned and meticulously accounted for, then reinterred in a burial urn.

Western Heaven* was able to be used without criminal offense to construct
new tombs. In some kind of crazy rat race, ignorance provoked people who
were already beaten to keep building because no one wanted to be bested
by anyone else. In the middle of this broad, sandy lot, the cemetery rose up
like some bizarre city of the dead. Too many shapes, materials, and garish
colors. I didn't want to be a part of a heretical project like this, but I needed
a job while I looked after my mother. Besides, I wanted to feel again the
untroubled feeling of being in a deserted place surrounded by silent souls.
By five most afternoons, I'd be on my way back home. But one moonlit
evening, I stayed late to finish some work and left for home about nine. I
was taking a shortcut across a sandy valley of recently planted cottonwoods
when I heard an unseen voice stammering behind the young trees. Thinking
it must be some kook, I hurried along. Then I froze. Under the silver moonlight two thugs had a hold of a girl in the sand, one guy straddling her and
the other pulling apart her legs. My eyes bulged and saw red. Roaring with
a voice that tore the sky, I flew into them with punishing kicks, each equally
terrible. One guy splayed out across the sand, shouting in surprise and pain.
He sat up and looked around. It was Ban, the son of District Chairman
Thang. I was astonished. Then, over my left shoulder, I heard a bitter voice.
I clenched my teeth and turned in time to see Dzương swinging his wooden
nunchaku around. I leaned my body to dodge the way Kiểm had taught me,
then chopped his wrist. The nunchaku fell to the ground as a screech came
from the girl. "Watch out, Phong!" The flashlight in Ban's hand lit up a knife
blade in the other. Suddenly, he screamed and dropped the knife and held
his face. Sand, along with rocks and shells, flew into their faces, making
both guys turn toward her. Handfuls of sand continued to launch from the
girl, along with screams of "Die! Die! Die!" Then the two guys fled, rubbing
at their faces, leaving her just sitting there, sobbing. I gently tugged her torn
clothes back onto her shoulders and comforted her. "It's okay, Lam, shh,
are you hurt?" She shook her head and toppled into my chest. "Oh Phong,
I'm a wreck." I sat numb and speechless, not having the heart to push away
her tight embrace. Lam's tears burned hot on my chest, the sweaty smell
of an impassioned girl, strangely enticing. The moonlight slanted down to
her round face, revealing her curved lips, open and pouting. Lam shuddered as if she were freezing and then seized my hand and held it against
her warm breast. "Phong, I want . . ." She spoke urgently, short of breath.
Her young woman's breasts felt taut and smooth like a pair of throbbing

* A play on the Buddhist concept of Sukhavati, the narrator refers to Vietnamese émigrés living in
the West who send money home.

doves breathing beneath my hands. A tingle ran through my body, making me rigid. She leaned her body into mine and kissed me, her kisses like rain and wind on my face. We collapsed down to the sand. "Phong, Phong," Lam whispered, her eyes half-closed, her hands all over my back. In my head at that moment flashed the scene in the ferry from the other night. I shook myself. A bitter feeling of sorrow welled up, bringing me to tears and making me numb to every other sensation. "What's wrong?" she asked when I held up my hands and sat up. "I can't . . ." I stuttered, clutching at the collar of her shirt. "I understand," she said glassily. Then, standing, she looked straight into my face. "You're such a coward." She staggered away unsteadily, her windblown hair flowing in the moonlight. I stood calmly watching as her shadow shrank and disappeared behind the undulating sand dunes. Alone again in the middle of the vast white sand spilling over with moonlight, I felt sad, slow, and stupid. I stood there alone with a feeling like loneliness but not called by a proper name, not clearly shaped like a one-syllable word,* more like being born from a past life. I lit a cigarette and silently looked out at the ocean, the night, the distance.

After that, Lam took a husband with an expensive house in the city. Sometimes he had epileptic fits. People gossiped that a mouse had fallen into his family's rice jar. As for my mother, her cheeks were frequently wet with tears, telling anyone and everyone about her self-tormenting baby. I wasn't happy or sad; I just had this intense feeling of fleeting loss. The cemetery work came to an end. I went up to Hue to join another crew of itinerant workers and fell in love with a girl named Thúy, who sold smoothies at the market. Thúy was pretty and very quiet, but after she got to know a person she seemed really genuine. She had large dark eyes that bedazzled everyone who looked into them. My mother urged me, "Marry her!" And though I was head over heels for Thúy, I still worried I'd discover something about her I couldn't get over. But eventually we did marry and had a long and happy time together. Shortly after the wedding, my mother passed away. Then I understood the magnitude of my mother's urging me to take a wife. I cried, holding the gold my mother had quietly saved, hoarding it for me. With my mother's grave finished, my new wife and I went south, cherishing the dream to make it rich; in Saigon I already had many friends who had started businesses years before.

We rented an apartment on the edge of the city. Every day, I went to work construction, and Thúy shouldered a tea stand to peddle refreshments

---

* Most Vietnamese words are formed by two one-syllable words written together. For example, *hoà bình* means peace. But there are also some three-syllable and some one-syllable words.

at the schools. We knew that by suffering through one hard year, we could scrape together a decent sum. With the money, Thúy wanted to go to school to learn to cut and shampoo hair. I agreed because I did not want her to have to work so hard. I didn't want to make the mistake of killing a person, because my compassion was affected by instinct. We rented a spot near the railroad to open a shop. Through word of mouth and Thúy's cunning, the shop was always full of customers. By then I was managing for Thành, a young, up-and-coming contractor. Many nights I ended up sleeping at the office. One night like that, suddenly and desperately missing Thúy, I ran the eight miles to return home. Arriving late at night at the top of the alley, I saw Thành in the porch light creeping from my house like a thief. A moment later, Thúy opened the door for me, her clothes gaping to reveal her flesh, sweat beading down the side of her face. After a confused glance, she circled her hands around my neck coquettishly. "Why are you coming home so late like this? Are you hungry? I'll make you something to eat, okay?" I shook my head, already on my way straight into the bedroom. The pillows and blankets were rumpled, messy, still warm from the heat of two bodies. The smell of Xmen cologne faint on the pillow, the brand Thành used. I asked, "Did anyone come looking for me this afternoon?" "No, no one came. I was at home all by myself, sad and missing you." Her slick, honeyed voice gave me goose bumps. Whore. I held my curses in my throat as I stood in the hallway. My mind felt like an overblown balloon about to pop. "Are you sick?" Thúy put her hand on my forehead, her eyes wide open, innocent, without blame. With a violent slash of my hand, I shoved her away. I spoke haltingly. "Don't play any more. Tomorrow morning, first you admit the truth and second you vanish from this house. I don't want to become a murderer. You understand?"

All that night I wandered the streets like a sleepwalking monster. I ached, going crazy and ready to jump on any bastard who might inadvertently run into me. At dawn, I returned home. Thúy had left. On the table was a small piece of paper. *A thousand times I beg you to forgive me. I know I have to go. Goodbye.* I crumpled the piece of paper and raised my face up to heaven, cackling like a lunatic. I crossed over to the neighbor's to borrow a wooden hammer and hauled our bed out into the courtyard. This was our heart of gold wooden wedding bed that we had carefully carried all the way from Hue. Breaking, cracking. The wooden fragments flew everywhere. I vented hatred with each hammer blow. I split the rest of our love bed by myself in the deserted kitchen, slowly feeding each chunk into the fire in the stove. The tongues of flame squirmed and licked the chunks of wood in a beautiful way, the fire flowing into my bosom, turning steel to water. One week, two weeks, then three weeks. The firewood gone, the fire dying; in the middle of my heart, freezing ash surrounded a bright blue steel blade. A frigid blade insensitive to love. I carried this blade in my heart without flinching, making my life as a bachelor fierce and expedient. I gradually improved my standing in the construction business. With money, I began a series of conquests. I went through many girls, calmly, without an iota of emotion. And after each affair, I bitterly realized again and again that I'd become a bastard. In those moments, I often thought of Kiếm and found that I respected him again. Then, in my dreams, I always saw myself returning to a sandy row of cottonwoods, with the fishing village wind blowing gently. To Lam, to her clear laughter, to her hair flowing in the moonlight, and her voice tinkling like crystal falling on the sand.

I returned to Hue to find her. Summer rumbled and hummed along Thánh Gióng road. The three-story house had plenty of room for just Lam and her mother; by then they'd lived there for three years after the period of mourning for her husband. Lam felt anxious seeing me cry quietly. The tears paralyzed me with sadness. I couldn't speak a word, and Lam was the same way. It looked as if everything was too late in life already. Lam's son had been at school, and when he returned, he greeted his mother and me very politely. I hugged the little guy to my chest and kissed his chubby cheeks, and then was on my way out to the station to return to Saigon.

* * *

I returned to Tam Giang lagoon at the end of March, the rice plants near the ferry glowing in bloom. However many months and years had passed, the old dock was still the same, but Kiếm, my friend and teacher, was still completely silent from all directions. That imp Ngợi was still alive, still lucid and strange and shy, inviting me one night to come down to catch shrimp and drink wine. It seemed like the whole fishing village had moved into the lagoon dock. I strolled up to the afternoon market. In the middle of a vacant lot, crude tents bustled with people buying and selling. In a tilting dilapidated tent at the corner of the market, a swinish stinking crazy person sat absorbed in swatting flies. His rubber sandal raised high, the crazy person remained passionately on watch for each fly in a very entertaining way.

People said that Châu had begun to go mad the day his wife died, and then went truly crazy the day he learned District Chairman Thang was going to be well taken care of for a long time. The chairman had retired really rich thanks to money sent back from the parts of his family who'd fled. I went past Thang's residence. In its place was an expensive karaoke bar thrown up in the middle of a vacant field, and it was full of fresh-faced red-lipped girls giggling, inviting, flirting. Ban and Dzương stood nearby, wearing suits and sporting mustaches.

I went out to the cemetery and found myself in the middle of a wind-storm of incense. The next day, my village would have forty families honoring death anniversaries. I painfully remembered a forest of white scarfs, the mourning during all those awful days that year. I placed incense at the grave of my mother and father, and at Lam's parents' grave. I had tears in my eyes, my head hung low before the cold gray tombstones. Then I heard soft footsteps. Looking up, I was surprised to see a woman in a bright dress the color of warm sand standing there. The same chubby face and curving lips, her red-rimmed eyes looking at me with both happiness and reproach. Lam. She collapsed into my widespread arms and choked through her tears, "I knew you'd come back for this."

"I only married for the money," she told me later. "Because my mother had been diagnosed with cancer. Then she passed away soon after, and my husband died of a heart attack during a seizure the next year. After that I found out my three-story house was still in my husband's parents' name. Before they left for America, they arranged to transfer ownership, stipulat-ing that I couldn't go anywhere before my son reaches fifteen. If I stay put until then, the house will belong to me. And if not, we'll lose it all. I stay not for the house but for my child. He must be able to study decently in order not to have a hard life like the kids from the fishing village. Any time I've thought of coming to you, I've also believed you would return. I've saved myself completely all these years. What a loss. Do you believe me . . . ?" Lam and I sat on the sand, looking out at the late afternoon sea. Seagulls banked their wings, flying above the dark blue surface of the water. The ocean was still young, the way a thousand years is still young. The waves babble and sing for all time. I felt like I'd been blown into the wilderness but had now returned to sit surrounded by my homeland sand dunes. I felt there might be one green seed just beginning to sprout in the barren field of my heart. Behind us, our windblown footprints had blurred away. I turned to Lam. One teardrop out of a thousand was slowly falling from her cheek. *I'm sorry, Lam, why are you still crying? Don't cry Lam, don't cry . . . .*

Translated by Charles Waugh

In the White Rain

Niê Thanh Mai

1.

The red dirt road stretched to the horizon, smoking with dust. H'Linh dragged her aching feet, foolishly shod in high heels, over the rugged, pockmarked path. She'd already gone forever and not yet arrived, and her feet were throbbing with a dull and lasting pain. H'Linh took off her shoes and carried them in her hands, her feet still hurting but each step easier to take. Familiar and strange. Somehow close and yet still far away. Ahead the mountain path, slender as a red thread, meandered through a valley of white flowers.

Not watching where she was going, she stepped into something hot and wet. Squishy. Cow shit. Disgusted, she hopped to the side of the road and dragged her feet through the grass until her red lacquered toenails turned green. A pungent smell wafted up to her nose and H'Linh sneezed repeatedly. After so many years absent from her village, the sight of a cow alone was enough to make her uneasy. The cows with their short necks and golden hides. Lumbering. Slowly chewing the green grass. They looked as if they were staring at her each time she passed. She felt nauseous. The smells of cow sweat and cow shit were no longer familiar to her. The valley darkened with dusk. A hundred thousand mosquitoes swarmed her, darting into her eyes and nose. So annoying! A few flew straight down her throat. Oh, home! So many of her memories were like this. She turned off the road, taking a shortcut to the village across a field thick with sharp-bladed grass.

2.

Droǎl Creek stretched out before her. A rock shaped like a big-bellied jar lay in the middle, called Ceh ÊKei by the villagers. Ceh ÊKei meant male big-bellied jar. Ancient as the forest, never changing, Ceh ÊKei remained impassive and unbroken, never worn by the water running past, never afraid of sun or rain. Had it been placed in the garden of H'Linh's landlord, would it have looked so natural, so primeval?

The Êdê people used the big jars to ferment rice and wild forest leaves into wine. Every family had its own jars, and even the poor had at least one. They regarded each jar as a kind of person. When a jar was old enough, they felt it needed a partner. So they looked for a mate. Rich households might own up to eighteen jars. A tuk jar could be exchanged for several buffalo or cows, and an eight-handled tuk jar could be exchanged for an elephant. A jar became fond of its owners over many generations, and so it would come to have a soul and be regarded as sacred. Even so, the jar still had to stand miserably beneath sun and rain alike.

Róc rách went the water. On and on continually. White pebbles of all shapes could be seen in the crystal clear stream. H'Linh scooped water to her face. Fresh and cold. Her weariness melted away. *Rì rầm rì rầm rì rầm . . .*

"Ceh Mniê has come back."

"The female jar has returned."

"So happy, oh village!"

It sounded like the voice of Ceh ÊKei. H'Linh remembered back . . . and felt sadness . . . and disappointment. . . . The sound of the wind howled in the mouth of the rock.

As the elders told the story, there was once a terrible flood that destroyed the village of the Kdăm people on the other side of the valley. The flood had rushed down the mountain, tearing through the village and wrecking everything in its path. It pulled down the pillars of the houses of the poor. Old people were drawn down into the water; young children had screamed up at the sky. Villagers floated tree trunks to the victims to save them, but everything from the houses was swept away by the water and disappeared. A pair of jars was also swept away in the stream.

No matter how the waves rose and fell, no matter how fast the water flew by, the pair of jars floated together. Tree trunks, branches, and logs coursing down the surface of the river could not separate them. Further downstream, they plunged over waterfalls and were at last sucked down into a whirlpool. The male jar popped to the surface and bobbed in a circle seeming to panic at losing the female jar. The current was very fast. Searching, searching but never seeing the female jar again, the male jar called out to her with his hurt voice. The sound of sorrow howled from the male jar's mouth and spread over the surface of the water, then dove beneath the current. It sounded heart wrenching.

Then the flood subsided. The male jar came to rest in the middle of Droăl Creek. In the deserted forest, the trees looked haggard and desolate from the catastrophe that had just passed. The male jar began to hear the echoes of a familiar voice singing softly. The voice of the female jar. She had drifted into the house of a rich tribal leader not far from Droăl Creek. Either the female jar hadn't heard his call or deliberately did not want to hear anymore. The male jar was hurt. He heard her whisper her innermost feelings to a strange male jar in the tribal leader's house. Oh! She had already committed her soul into the realm of the rich and bright. . . .

He waited, calling her name for a day. He waited, calling, for five nights. He waited, calling her for a whole month. One day, the male jar could not cry any longer. Ceh ÊKei had transformed into a rock in his endless hurt. Only in nights of heavy rain or when the moon sparkled golden on the forest or on days when thunderstorms rumbled in could the Yanghao villagers hear the hoarse voice of the male jar call to his darling.

Many hoarse nights. Wavering. Fading. H'Linh had heard the love story of the male and female big-bellied jars many times, and it now rose before her eyes.

Hands together, scooping water to her face, H'Linh could not splash away her sadness. The clear water could not cool the love story in which betrayal came from the fairer sex.

3.

A shadow passed over the surface of the water. Like the shadow of a bird flying by. Like the round shadow of Ceh ÊKei. H'Linh trembled. She looked up nervously. Oh God! It was Y Thi, her older brother-in-law. As if come from the sky, he appeared out of nowhere beside the male jar. He held a long forked spear in his hand for catching fish.

H'Linh was astonished. Her brother-in-law too. His eyes had a shaking fire in them. The stretched out collar of his T-shirt revealed his broad white chest. The bright sun shone on it brilliantly. She hurriedly straightened her own low-necked T-shirt to cover her breasts and their many dark purple bruises.

He opened his hand and the spear fell to the rock beneath his foot. It clattered and bounced from the rock into the water. He was family. Close. His chest was broad. His forearm muscles bulged. His thighs looked like coils of rope. His skin was copper. His brown loincloth heaved and bulged. He looked so strong. So powerful. The wind carried his smell of salty sweat and wild grass.

H'Linh looked strange. Printed on her yellow T-shirt were the words FOR GET ME NOT in red letters. She wore torn fringed jeans. High-heeled shoes. Her carefully coifed, long hanging hair had been dyed a golden yellow like the wildflowers on the mountain. It smelled sweet and fresh like the mountain forest.

So happy! But still a little awkward. Their greetings, questions, and answers had no beginnings or ends, no harmony between them. But she could tell he fished in this stream every day.

4.

H'Linh and her brother-in-law returned home together.

She stood for a moment at the base of the rough-hewn log ladder to the stilt house. Her father sat cross-legged on the porch smoking tobacco. Seeing H'Linh, he rose, trembling, like he half wanted to step nearer and half wanted to step into the house. H'Linh dropped her bag to the red dust when she saw her father's body. Months and years of endless hard work had turned him to gristle and leather. Time had taken his black hair, taken his strong muscles, taken the bulging sinews from beneath his skin. Her father looked like a tree whose leaves had already fallen.

Her father cried. Tears in the wrinkles of an old man. Tears from the corners of his eyes pouring over his dark cheeks. That his daughter had returned home. H'Linh blinked and her eyes too filled with tears.

Her brother-in-law went upstairs first. Then he lifted her from the last rung up into the house. His hands were big, rough, and warm. Hers small and soft. She looked up to see his eyes also brimming with tears.

The villagers also recognized H'Linh. With difficulty. It was hard for them to accept that she was still a daughter of the village. Maybe they recognized her because of her eyes. She had taken off her long, curly false eyelashes. Now they were again the familiar big dove eyes that had attracted so many of the village boys. But now, oh God! Where did the strange eyes with thick black lashes go? Now H'Linh's eyes were dazzling and round. The children crouched behind their parents. They stared at her as if she were someone strange from far away.

The villagers shared the news, like the sound of a gong echoing from house to house. The villagers came to visit, partly to welcome her but mainly just to see her to satisfy their curiosity. They crowded in, sitting shoulder to shoulder, making the house hot and noisy. H'Linh sat in the middle of the crowd. The children remained outside, clustered on the porch, scrambling to divide the candies and chocolates; big ones and little ones all clamoring to be included. She felt embarrassed. Did the adult villagers want candy and chocolate too?

Some curly-haired girls sat in the corner of the house laughing together. And a few teenaged boys with skinny arms and chests huddled next to them. When H'Linh's eyes met theirs, they blushed self-consciously and quickly looked away. Only a few of the girls wore traditional Êdê clothes. The rest wore shirts and trousers like the Kinh, long over the ankles. The trousers had been patched together from several different colors of cloth. She felt a sad, unsteady desolation sweep over her heart.

"Did you come back because you were homesick or are you up to something else?"

Her father's voice sounded rough in his throat. His scrawny shadow stretched up the wall. Old too. Stunted. She could not remember how old he was. She stared in amazement, then gave a reluctant smile.

"Don't talk like that, Dad. I miss our house, miss our family. How many years has it been?"

Yes, it had been many years. When first meeting her again, no one could recognize H'Linh. She was very different from when she'd left. She missed the time when there were people in the village who recognized her face, people who shook her hand, people who kindly patted her on the back. Where did her healthy tanned complexion go? This pale lily white skin was not the skin of a village girl. The kind of rosy cheeks a person got from pink powder did not belong to a girl who had to work in the fields and carry buckets of water every day. That kind of thick red lips was not the same as the natural color of the ylang-ylang vine. Everyone found her strange. Everyone seemed shy and confused when they saw her now. Only her brother-in-law looked at her with a close, sympathetic, and silent expression.

But the villagers were not silent. They asked each other: "Has H'Linh come back to marry her brother-in-law, Y Thi?" "Yeah! Y Thi went down the mountain to the city to find her a few times, but she kept disappearing." "Poor Y Thi, every afternoon he goes to the male big-belly jar at the creek to catch fish and wait for her to return. Oh!" "The guy's caught all the fish in Droăl Creek and now H'Linh is back." The villagers also said: "How much longer does the poor guy have to stay an in-law anyway? H'Lan died a long time ago already."

H'Lan was H'Linh's older sister. She had a bent back just like their mother. But all Êdê women went everywhere with their backs bent low.

H'Linh's village had sloped hills, sloped mountains, sloped roads, and even sloped fields. The slopes made the Êdê girls walk hunched everywhere they went and made their feet big too. Her sister's feet had been huge. Her mother's feet had been huge. And H'Linh's feet were huge too. Big feet and hunched backs. Êdê women wore short skirts to make it easier for them to walk into the forest and to work hunched over the sloped fields. Êdê girls like H'Linh carried everything in a wicker basket strapped to their backs. Water. Bamboo shoots. Corn. Wheat. Brocade. . . . They carried whole meals and heavy jugs of water on their backs even when they were just little girls. They carried their baskets into the time of silver hair and even into the grave. Baskets and slopes made Êdê women hunched and their feet big. Êdê women had such a hard life!

5.

H'Linh's Êdê people did not know how to make gongs or bells; they had to buy them from the Kinh. But the Êdê knew how to play them, and how to arrange a set of them to play a harmonious tune. Not all Êdê men had been selected by the gods for the talent of bringing the gongs into tune. In all of the Yanghao area, only H'Linh's father could speak with feeling with the gongs, and now that her father was old, he'd begun to pass this gift to his son-in-law.

A windy afternoon. Yellow leaves fluttering to the ground beneath the trees. Her brother-in-law sat on the porch tuning the gongs. *Chut chut . . . chat. Chut chut . . . chat.* The wooden hammer's cadence was so joyful. A clutch of village boys who often came to his place had assembled to watch and to get a chance to practice. A young Kinh woman who had come to the village seven years ago to teach school was also there.* She had curly hair and wore traditional Êdê clothes and spoke Êdê as if she was one of the girls from the village. Her chest swelled high, her large breasts as shapely as two hills of grass at the beginning of the season. She sat on the porch leaning back on her hands and staring wide eyed up at Y Thi. A passionate look on her face. The hardest to bear was when the teacher poured water for him, then brought a towel for him to wipe the sweat from his brow. . . .

The clutch of boys cried: "Hey H'Linh! Can you remember any folk songs? Sing, H'Linh, sing!"

---

* The Vietnamese government sent native-speaking Vietnamese to remote areas of the country to give ethnic minority villagers an education and to ensure that they would learn to speak Vietnamese.

Then they laughed and, not waiting to hear her response, began to sing a song of their own.

> You hang your wet dress on a branch of tung,
> I hang my wet shorts on a branch of rieng,
> Tomorrow you take the long road home and remember my face,
> Tomorrow far apart our names will be forgotten,
> Like all our wishes to be together,
> To drink water together from one gourd,
> To smoke together just one cigarette.

Y Thi's steady hand rapped the hammer. His fist rested on the knob of the gong. His shoulders rocked. His eyes sank into the sound of the spirit. The Kinh teacher swayed her body to the rhythm. She swayed but her eyes remained fixed intently on Y Thi, not straying even for a single minute.

H'Linh paced back and forth. She intentionally kicked her foot into a heap of nearby gongs. The gongs went this way and that, falling apart noisily. The song "Buôn Tul Kmăn" stopped right in the middle. Her brother-in-law stared at her, his face confused.

6.

After dinner, Y Thi took his rifle to go hunting. In the house on stilts, the cooking fire still burned. Soot blackened the walls and pillars. The house was older than her father. The cook fire had been burning since before he was born.

"You don't love your mother or your sister, do you?"

Her father hesitated, then continued.

"You've got to love your sister's children though."

"Don't say that, Dad. I love my whole family. Don't bring them up just to make me feel bad. I haven't forgotten anything."

H'Linh had not yet forgotten anything, only nearly forgotten. The flood that year had been terrible. Her mother and sister had gone to the fields and were returning home when they were swept away. Her father and brother-in-law spent three days on the stream searching for the bodies. In the village, every three or four years, a flood would take several unlucky people.

Her father was silent. His face pensive. He stood and dusted the seat of his pants, then lit a torch and went outside. Halfway down the steps, he turned around and said, "I'm going to the terraced fields. All along the forest there, early in the morning, the monkeys have been coming down and trampling our corn. Tonight, I'll give Y Thi a break. He's been working like a buffalo for our family for a long time."

"Take me too, Dad."

"No! Stay and sleep with H'The. In all these years now you haven't held your niece a single time. Her mother's dead, and you're her aunt."

H'Linh didn't respond. The shadow of the old man gradually vanished into the dark. She knew her father was angry. The fact that she'd been gone from the village for how many years and had not written him or visited was also making him angry. In truth, she really loved her father; she wanted to live at home and to carry water from the stream to wash his face; she wanted to weave cotton to make clothes for him to wear. But H'Linh dreaded coming back and having to smell the stench of dirt, the stench of cow shit.

Late at night, very quiet.

The forest trees ceased rustling. The deer did not bellow beside the deserted stream. Birds roosting in the trees slept. And H'Linh felt restless. Her emotions roiled inside her. She sat up and scraped the bamboo window open to one side. A gentle breeze blew onto her neck and caressed her face. So refreshing. It had been a long time since she'd felt such a refreshing wind. She bent her head to look outside. The door of the stilt house was wide open. Moonlight shone on the porch. H'Linh startled when Y Thi appeared at the top of the stairs. The floor of the stilt house porch creaked. Her brother-in-law sat down by the cook fire and stirred the coals into a crackling flame. His head, hair, and shoulders were wet with the night fog. His strongly built body looked like an ironwood statue. Broad chest. Curly hair, falling down to his bare shoulders. Poor Y Thi!

Since the day H'Linh's sister disappeared, he had been like this.

H'Linh rubbed her eyes and got up.

"The house must seem strange, making it hard to sleep, huh?"

Strange house. Hard to sleep. It was *her* house, and her brother-in-law asked her this. H'Linh felt very sad.

"H'The keeps squirming," she said, taking a coat from a peg and draping it over his shoulders. He seized her hand.

"I can't wear this coat, dear Sister."

She understood. Without intending to do so, she'd given him her own coat. She tried to withdraw her hand, but his warm hand remained holding hers. His eyes glittered in the fire light. She felt her chest heave, constricting her breath, her knees trembled like they wanted to collapse.

From the bed came the sound of H'The turning over and murmuring in her sleep. H'Linh startled and freed her hand from Y Thi's grip. She stepped to the bed and hugged the little girl into her lap. The child murmured in her sleep again and hugged her aunt tightly.

Chat . . . chat . . . chat . . . . The sound of the hammer on the gong echoed from below the stilt house. Repeatedly. But not in the double rhythm as in the afternoon. Oh god! Y Thi was tuning his gongs in the middle of the night. It was so confusing. *Chat . . . chat . . . chat . . . .* The tapping of the gong was like a tapping in H'Linh's ear.

She hugged her niece tightly as if trying to escape the sound of the hammer tapping the gong. The hot dry smell of the little girl's hair filled H'Linh's nose. The girl was so thin, her neck so long. Her two hands were rough and chapped, her two hands too small to catch the rope halter of a cow. Miserable! One big stilt house, one wide-open door, and three generations caring for each other. . . . The little girl nuzzled her face into H'Linh's chest. Tickling. Sad. Then easier to bear. Warm. Familiar. A feeling of family closeness came into H'Linh's heart. Like being of the same blood. Like that of a mother and child. . . . She felt a warmth spreading over her. Holding her niece in her lap was not like the feeling she had when taking care of her boss's daughter in the city. One was real love, the other just a responsibility. Her Êdê patron had a house and garden in the heart of the city. His Kinh wife had gone abroad ten years ago and never returned. He sold antiques, intending to become rich quickly to wash away the insult of his wife leaving him in poverty. That was what people said anyway, and H'Linh hadn't heard anything different. But sometimes she wondered if he'd brought her home to spite his wife. He'd met her in a karaoke bar. He had feelings for her. H'Linh was unusual. All the men liked her. She could make them laugh, but she was also sad. After several nights singing together, she came to his house. She didn't have to work hard. She only had to care for the garden and trees and to teach his child to speak Êdê. . . .

7.

Early the next day, H'Linh was still in bed, half-asleep. A noise came from the yard below. Why had Y Thi tuned the gongs all night long? Did someone want to borrow the gongs already this morning? It sounded like the gongs were different each time. Oh god, why was her head so silver white?

She startled awake when she opened her eyes and immediately saw the slow steady gaze of her niece with her chin propped on her hand, looking back at her. She could have been staring at her for hours while H'Linh slept. The child popped up and raced down the stairs when H'Linh sat up.

Her back ached because it had been a long time since she'd slept on a bamboo floor. The bamboo floor of the stilt house hung suspended in the air and was usually cool. The wind felt like it was coming up from beneath the house. She'd grown used to having a thick mattress, the waffled kind that massaged your back.

Her brother-in-law came up into the house.

"The kid's not used to you yet."

He took a chunk of salt pork from where it hung on the wall and placed it in the kitchen. His voice hesitant, and not daring to turn to look at H'Linh, he said, "Are you all right now? This morning I made some sticky rice. I don't know if you still remember the taste of our village's sticky rice, do you?"

She startled. Overnight, his hair had become streaked with silver. She spoke like a person with a twisted face: "Of course I remember, I could never forget that flavor." Then H'Linh blushed, and smiled. A forced smile. Since she'd first stepped foot in the house, all her smiles were forced. She did feel strange in her own house.

Her father told the story of her sister and mother's disappearance. He calmly spoke about the flood that swept two of their loved ones away. He seemed accustomed to the pain, so his voice remained calm. H'Linh felt silly. She did not understand why she never felt grief. Exactly like there was a gaping hole in her heart. Her brother-in-law and his daughter had lived with her father for nearly four years. Her father said that from the day her mother and sister disappeared, he could do nothing at all. Playing the bamboo xylophone, for which his hands were held in high esteem, had gradually become painful and could not be borne anymore. He could only wander around the house doing housework. She asked him if he was sick. He shook his head. Then he looked at her pointedly. A look both sympathetic and angry. She never could bear it when he looked at her that way. He said slowly: "I've been punished by Yang* . . . because I cannot . . . teach my daughter." She wanted to apologize to her father. But seeing his blood-red eyes, she felt afraid.

8.

Y Thi led H'Linh to the stream where her mother and sister had been swept away.

---

* Yang is the name of God for the Êdê.

She found a big banana leaf fluttering back and forth and slashed it once with the machete to cut it, and the leaf fell down to the ground softly. Her brother-in-law gave her a look of satisfaction for the good stroke of the knife. He handed her several sticks of incense. The thick white smoke wafted around her body, hovering over her brother-in-law's silver-streaked hair. The smoke did not smell of perfume. The wind swirled it into her eyes, stinging them. Y Thi knelt on the ground, his crying sometimes short, sometimes long. All heartrending. His long moans sounded like singing. To see a man cry is like a crime. H'Linh felt the heavy burden of her heart as she sympathized with the young man with the silver hair who had stayed so close to her family for more than ten planting seasons.

She saw Y Woan standing on the other side of the stream. At one time the young man had her wound around his wrist. He smiled coyly, happy to have met his girlfriend once again. When he turned his back, his image vanished amid the head-high grass. H'Linh gasped, feeling strange. Y Woan had vanished, not walked away. Her hands went cold.

"Brother-in-law, has Y Woan from the end of our village taken a wife yet?"

"He's dead."

"Dead!"

H'Linh gaped at Y Thi. He spoke but didn't raise his head. In a sulky voice, he said, "He was very angry with you. You left without promising to come back. People from the village joked that you were scorning him."

She listened to him, feeling terrible.

"He waited three years for you. You didn't come back, so he married a girl from his mother's side of the family."

H'Linh hung her head, staring at the ground, wringing her hands.

Y Thi's voice was sharp. "He didn't love his wife. All day, he refused to go to the terraces or into the forest; all he did was drink. And once drunk, he'd sing to himself. He still loved you. He still hated you too."

She reeled, her head spinning. Faster and faster, images from the old days surged and receded in her mind. Y Woan had sung very beautifully. He had often sung the song that went: "When I die our stream will still go on, and though I die beneath the river, beneath the stream, I'll always remember you standing here, oh my dear."

H'Linh always got angry with Y Woan for singing a song with such a bad omen. But he laughed and said that even when he died, he wouldn't reach the end of his love for H'Linh. He loved her dearly. Nonetheless, H'Linh left the village knowing she would not return. One rainy day, years ago, Y Thi and Y Woan went in search of her. In their back baskets they carried gongs down the mountain, going to a shop that sold brocade and other highland handicrafts, looking for a woman from their village who worked in the city. She took them to the karaoke bar where H'Linh worked. The woman from the village was older than H'Linh by ten years. She was really pitiable, had lost all her charm, and envied H'Linh. She arranged for Y Thi and Y Woan to be seated in the same room with H'Linh. They sat to see what she was up to, to watch everything she did. That day, H'Linh was really drunk, her face red like a fighting cock. An Êdê girl with a face as red as a fighting cock meant she was up to no good. H'Linh clutched the shoulder of a white-haired man, who led her by the hand out of the bar and into a big black sedan. Y Thi and Y Woan ran out and pulled her back. But the two strong Êdê men could not fight the four karaoke bouncers. Y Thi and Y Woan were thrown into the street like two banana tree trunks. H'Linh could see through the car window that her brother-in-law's neck had received a bloody wound. Before passing out, she saw the images of her brother-in-law and Y Woan blur and lose shape in the middle of the street beneath the heavy white rain. . . .

H'Linh told herself it was time to stop remembering this old story. It was so bitter. It just kept reminding her of all her sadness, making her cry.

Y Thi returned home first. He didn't say anything more about how Y Woan died. And H'Linh couldn't seem to open her mouth to ask. Maybe he was still angry with her. And he was right to be angry. She had been surprised to see Y Woan's face, and at the same time had felt both happy and sad when he appeared. And worried. And numb. When she was happy and earning money in the city, how many people in the village had missed her, how many had waited for her? Why had she never burned with such impatience, burned with such longing for anyone there?

9.

H'Linh went alone to the cemetery.

She was never afraid to go anywhere alone. When she left her village and went down to the city alone, it was the same. But now, stepping into the cemetery, she felt shock and horror. As a child, she never came here. The villagers never allowed children to come to this place. Except for the days villagers had something to do there, the cemetery was very cold and gloomy. The cemetery was only crowded when people came to worship their ancestors or when a family had a funeral.

Y Woan's name had been scrawled on a rectangular piece of wood. Vibrant purple flowers adorned his grave. The leaves of these plants closed when they were touched. Like the leaves were shy. Or sulky. H'Linh tossed a small coin into the jar on the ground in front of the low funeral hut. The coin clinked inside the jar. She thought, You're sulking so I've made offerings, Y Woan. Everybody before you also had to pass at some point into the grave. H'Linh will also one day enter the grave. But for what else must I apologize to you in this grave?

Y Woan's tomb had many monkey symbols and many faces of gloomy monkeys carved all around it. She strolled past the other ramshackle tombs. A horror arose in her as she saw the wooden statues guarding them. The deeply carved lines in the statues' faces filled her with sorrow. Lines carved in the uplifted head of a wooden bird. What kind of person would make statues with such horrible expressions? A family of these grotesques had been born, and why did the outside world find them all so desirable?

H'Linh lit incense for her mother, sister, and Y Woan before returning home. The sticks of incense fizzled out. She relit them several times, but they wouldn't stay lit. A strong wind blew. Soon it would rain.

10.

H'Linh wanted to leave the house.

Outside, thunder rumbled, foreboding rain. Y Thi saw her wearing a cotton jacket but didn't ask where she was going. For several days they had only exchanged glances without speaking. This time, she heard him whispering with his daughter below the house. She felt a tender love for him.

H'Linh spoke with her father. "I'm leaving today, Dad. Next time I'm free, I'll come back."

Her father told her: "You should stay here at home. If you don't want to marry Y Thi, I'll won't try to force you any more."

"It's not like that, Dad." A hundred thousand voices cried inside her heart. "I still love Y Thi very much. But I have to go."

Her father did not answer, nor did he rise. H'Linh stepped down the stairs. There, her brother-in-law followed after her, murmuring: "Take a raincoat with you. It will rain today."

She looked at Y Thi, her eyes knowing how to say thank you. She stepped briskly away. Her brother-in-law followed behind a little while to see her off. H'The also ran to catch up to H'Linh to walk a ways with her. They stopped at Droăl Creek, near the place where the jar-shaped rock stood, patient and quiet. H'Linh took Y Thi's hand and placed in it a bundle of new bills. He would not take them. She implored him: "Take them to make me happy. Our family needs money. Dad is still angry with me, so don't tell him about it." He shook his head. "For so many years we haven't had you at home, and we could still live, dear H'Linh." Her face turned red, and she hid it in the chest of the child. The girl had tears in her eyes too as she clung tightly to H'Linh's skirt. H'Linh freed her skirt from H'The's grasp and looked away. She knew that if she looked into her brother-in-law's or her niece's eyes, she would not be able to go.

The day was already stiflingly hot. Having gone just a short way, H'Linh already felt that her legs were very heavy. She remembered the light in the sad, patient eyes of her brother-in-law a moment ago. He had wanted to say something, and she didn't understand why he'd kept silent.

She had just made it to the village cemetery when it started to pour. It rained so hard she couldn't see the trees in the forest. Her bare feet turned cold and clammy. Maybe she'd stepped in cow shit. She hated the smell of cow shit, hated that squishy feeling. But at this moment, she couldn't stop to clean her feet. Despite the rain, she uprooted one of the wooden statues with a sad monkey face and slid it into a jute bag. The statue was feather light. She grasped the bag, her fists flashing red from her painted fingernails.

H'Linh traced her way back to the road. She only needed to hold out her hand and a truck stopped and took her down from the mountains.

11.

H'Linh returned to her Êdê patron's house in the middle of the city.

She felt relieved when the truck stopped in front of the gate. Seeing the wooden monkey-faced statue, the patron was deeply moved. The immense garden with its many plants and trees became even more picturesque when she placed the wooden statue in its center. The patron bent his head to closely examine each carved line, each crevice. A broad smile. Maybe he was thinking of the luxurious banquet he would throw for his wealthy friends. They would be amazed when they saw the delicate craftsmanship of the artisans of Yanghao village, which was a far cry from the fake statues sold in souvenir shops at a price that would cut your throat. She liked her patron's smile. And the sweet looks from the little girl studying the Êdê language. H'Linh had furtively glanced into her smiling face as the girl galloped excitedly up the stairs to the second floor. H'Linh received the praise from her patron with a sigh of relief.

Coming down from the mountains this time, she couldn't sleep. Every night, knocks sounded at her door. She would switch on the light and open the door, but no one would be there. She would shiver with fear, return to bed, and bury her face in the blankets and pillows, trying to get back to sleep, but as soon as she was dreaming again, she'd again hear the knocks. Monotonous and persistent. Many times the patron had told her, "I am a serious man. I only want you if you offer yourself willingly to me."

"But you wouldn't be my first."

The patron said: "Don't speak of these things with me. I only need you to love me, that's enough."

Yes! So it would be love. Hot. Poignant. Passionate. But—

"Why, sir? Are you toying with me?"

"I'm so sorry—it just does this sometimes."

The more impotent he was, the more he pawed at her, tormenting her. The more he clawed at her breasts and thighs during the night, the more he'd apologize in the morning. He told her: "You gave yourself to me freely, and you're also free to leave if you don't like it."

"Yes!"

But it was such a shame! So miserable. H'Linh was still a young woman. A vibrant young Êdê woman, bursting with life, with fertility.

12.

H'Linh became haggard, wandering stunned into the kitchen every morning like a lost person. These days it seemed like there were no more knocks at her door during the night. If she had grown used to those monotonous persistent sounds, she also didn't know it. But still, she could not sleep. Each night, she felt a heavy burden in her heart and a lot of pain in her thighs. Night after night, the dark wrinkled face of her father wavered before her eyes and disappeared. Her father worried, her father sulked. Tears wet his wrinkled cheeks. Then images of her patron came and went. Moonfaced. Potbellied. Heavy. Clumsy. With teeth like fangs. Bites on her breasts and soft thighs. . . . H'Linh was afraid.

She longed to return to her brother-in-law. For a long time, she had missed being with a normal man and had missed real intimacy. One night a long time ago, she had followed Y Thi when he went to catch fish in the stream. At night, the fish liked the places in the water in the shadow of the moon. He taught her how to work the long fork. Hold the right hand like this. Hold the left like this. His hands were very warm. Her heart fluttered in her chest. She hurled the fork down at a nearby fish and slipped from the rock down into the stream. He dove in after her. His arms circled round her breasts, the breasts of a young woman, firm, round, and heaving.

H'Linh's sister saw her come dripping back into the house. Her wet skirt and blouse clung to her flesh. H'Lan scolded: "Fell into the stream, did you? You better leave Y Thi alone down there." H'Linh remained silent. The next morning, her brother-in-law tried to evade his wife's suspicious looks.

Nights in the city sweltered. So far away, so very strange. H'Linh wept and wept. The sound of her cries came from her heart and soul as the bitter tears streamed down her face. She trembled all night. She drank glass after glass of wine, of foreign liquor. She remembered the warm smell of her village's strong sweet wine. Their rice wine warmed the chest and had a nice mellow flavor. H'Linh felt her mouth sour. The liquor in the Italian crystal glass had become bitter, caustic. She cried as the burning liquid slid down her throat.

H'Linh heard her father crying.

H'Linh heard her brother-in-law's hammer tuning the gongs.

H'Linh heard the Kinh teacher singing a folk song.

H'Linh saw Y Woan's wide-open eyes, sad and sulking.

H'Linh saw the image of a man flying in the air, floating in the heavy white rain. It was Y Thi, lifting the sad monkey-faced statue from the patron's garden onto his shoulders. She ran, struggling to catch it, hugging the statue to her. Tears from the sad monkey face mixed with the rain and her own tears and trickled down her cheeks. The monkey statue's tears and H'Linh's tears poured like the rain in the night. Heavy white and bitter cold. Then lightning! Thunder split the room. The smell of cow shit mingled with the smell of rain.

Her brother-in-law shouldered the sad wooden monkey-faced statue and disappeared into the obliterating white rain.

Translated by Charles Waugh and Di Li

The Well

Di Li

HE STARED AT THE NEW CLERK, AN EXPRESSION OF PAIN PULLING AT HIS broad cheeks. So far, all she'd done was ask him a series of irritating questions about his drive to the resort, the new road from the city, his luggage, and on and on with the same stiff and stupid expression on her stiff and stupid face. Finally, she arrived at the question that would end her inane chatter: "Your name, please."

"Andy Trần."

The hands that had been fumbling over the keyboard stopped immediately. Perspiration began to bead on the milky white skin of her forehead despite the coolness of the lobby. At once, he was no longer upset. Instead, he wanted to see the nape of her neck. He wanted to see the place beneath her jet-black hair where the chiffon of her uniform had begun to stick with sweat to her flesh. He wanted . . .

"I'm so sorry, this is my first day . . . I didn't know . . . I thought you were . . . an ordinary guest." In her embarrassment she knocked over a glass of water on the counter. She began to panic.

"When attending to your guests, there's no such thing as *ordinary*."

"Yes. I'm sorry. I'm new."

"Never make excuses." He stared intently at her face as it flickered with terror. "You are a beautiful girl," he said, "but that's no reason for me to stand here waiting forever. Come on, give me the key to my room."

The poor girl continued to fumble with the computer. She had become so flustered she could not remember what she was supposed to do. She flushed, searching his face for the answer. "Room number 13?"

Genuine anger now welled up from his chest. "How stupid are you? The hotel has no Room 13. Call Mỹ Hà out here."

A young woman in a red uniform appeared from a doorway behind the counter. With her smooth white skin and doe-brown eyes, she was just as beautiful as the first girl. Seeing Andy standing there, she gasped.

"Mr. Trần, the schedule doesn't have you here today, sir."

"What kind of goddamned schedule makes me play golf on Sunday?" He kicked his bag. "Explain the rules for this beautiful, stupid girl here. She tried to give me Room 13."

A puff of indignant air escaped Mỹ Hà's lips. "Andy Trần's room is on the fourth floor," she puffed. "4014. And that room only. It's his private room." Then, turning to Andy, she said, "I am very sorry, sir, the regular girl's sick. Mai Lan's just filling in—she needs another week's practice."

"Okay, enough already. Just give me the key."

Mai Lan seemed about to cry. "But . . . I've already assigned that room."

"Room 4014?"

"We had a lot of advanced bookings today, plus a lot of walk-ins. There's no room left."

"I am very sorry, Mr. Trần," said Mỹ Hà. "Mai Lan didn't know any better, and since your schedule didn't have you here, I failed to tell her not to assign your room. You . . . could . . . use the office to change clothes, couldn't you?"

It was just past two on a sunny, scorching day, so all the hotel's guests had already returned to their rooms for a rest before going to the golf course when it got cooler. In the empty lobby, the huge flat-screen in the corner barked out news of Tiger Wood's return to the tour, Phil Mickelson's huge winnings, and Nikki Garrett's latest photo shoot. Mai Lan and Mỹ Hà gazed anxiously at Andy, taking in the fineness of his silk linen suit, their plans to find new jobs after their certain dismissal from the resort clearly visible behind their eyes. Andy rubbed the mole on his left cheek, a gesture whose meaning even the new girl could gather.

"You want me, the second largest shareholder of this club, after travelling forty miles today, to enter the pigsty of your office, and then go out in this sun?"

The two beautiful faces crumpled, Mai Lan's porcelain white skin flushing at first, then going pale and finally purple. Andy found it interesting to observe these changes. He didn't care much one way or the other about the beauty of these girls or about where to change or when to golf, but he liked to see changes like these come over them. Andy shrugged, gave them a half smile and glanced above their heads as if that were the place where his mercy might be found.

"Don't let this happen again. I won't forgive you a second time."

He swung his heavy golf bag over to one of the lobby's plush lounge chairs, removed his golf shoes from the bag and put them on. The two girls whispered to one another and peeked at him from around the computer screen.

After a few minutes, three men came down the stairs carrying their clubs. Andy rose and shook their hands and spoke to them in Cantonese. At dinner in Saigon the night before, these new partners of his had cheerfully, if not a little too drunkenly, wagered an enormous sum on the final hole.

On the fourth, with a distance of 350 yards, Andy Trần needed just two strokes to reach the green. After nine, the Hong Kong men had fallen behind by ten strokes, and by the eighteenth tee, they didn't try to hide their gloomy faces. Andy shrugged. People who couldn't restrain their emotions whether in victory or defeat were easy to control in negotiations. He squinted against the sunshine to read the fairway and prepare his drive. One of the caddy girls couldn't restrain a cough. The way she kept at it made it seem as if she'd been paid to interrupt him, so he lowered the club and glared at her, expecting her to look afraid. But the girl kept coughing, tantalizingly so. Her face remained calm, as if she had no idea that she'd done something wrong. He gave her the club and jutted his chin toward the cart.

"Give me the three wood."

She ran to the cart, found the club, cleaned its head, and coughed.

He returned to the tee, settled into his stance, inadvertently opened the clubface and swung. Without even looking, he knew the ball would drop into the sand trap three quarters of the way to the green.

One of the Hong Kong guys jumped from the cart, excitedly shouting, "It's a duck hook!" Sensing the possibility, each of them drove straight down the fairway, each just a little further than the last.

Sweating now, Andy climbed into the cart and took off, abandoning the ignorant, silly caddy girl. He drew his sand wedge and stepped down into the trap. He knew he was close to blowing it. He needed some inspiration. He thought about the terror on the new girl's face and felt the iron in his hand go light as air. Earlier, on the eighth, he made a spectacular putt from the edge of the green. If he missed, the Hong Kongers had a shot to win the hole, but then an inspiring thought bloomed inside his bold and glossy dome. The face of the girl standing at the lobby desk went fuzzy and dim. *She* was afraid, her eyes looked at him beseechingly, her body buckled to the floor. He mouthed the word "Soon" and tapped the ball lightly toward the hole. The ball rolled out and back as if turning by remote control, then dropped into the cup. The Hong Kong partners looked at him as if they'd seen a magic trick. When it really mattered, he thought to himself, he would never fail.

In the sand trap Andy Trần carefully adjusted the clubface and stroked through the ball. A handful of the dry sand splashed up. But to his surprise the ball kept getting smaller and smaller in the sky. It wasn't floating down straight to the green; instead, it yanked to the left as if an invisible hand had flicked it out of the air.

Andy sped the cart off the path to follow the ball. His luxurious cotton shirt had completely soaked through with sweat. It was hard to understand. It was impossible to shank a ball in that awful, wrong direction even for a beginner. Stress began to pull at the cords of his neck and throb uncomfortably at his temples. He thought of *her* again. Whenever failure loomed, he knew he could think of *her* and turn failure into victory.

Before a court of law, three witnesses had confirmed that he had been at a gentleman's birthday cocktail party. And because *she* had no witness to testify on her behalf, his witnesses confirmed that Andy Trần was a prosperous businessman and eligible bachelor with hundreds of women trailing after him. There was no logic to the story that he had tried to rape an ordinary girl with nothing special about her, well below his position.

She stood at the plaintiff's table, the hatred in her eyes nearly masking her terror. He felt aroused, which made him read the speech he'd prepared with just the right heightened state of awareness, and the judge in the end showed his frustration with such a "brazenly slanderous girl." It was unlucky for her because she had hesitated to make a case against him—the evidence on her body had already healed.

He passed his finger along the scar on his neck that she had made. She hadn't been able to raise her frightened and hopeless eyes to him. He wedged his knees between her thin legs and shoved them apart. One of her nails dug deep into his neck, the other tore at his T-shirt made untidy by the struggle.

Her swollen mouth distorted in pain, the glare in her eye—ah! Such a look of intense anger and fear always aroused him. Most women he met had a look in their eyes like they'd drop their skirts on command. But Andy Trần had always felt that a soft, compliant woman's body might as well have been a pillow.

The ball had certainly fallen into the trees. He plunged the cart down the slope and into the little grove, crunching the dry leaves underneath. He left the cart and began to kick through the leaf litter, first one way, then another. It had to be there somewhere. Sweat continued to pool between his shoulders. He regretted leaving the caddy girl. If he hadn't left her, he could have just sat in the shade of the cart, waiting for her to find the ball. It seemed invisible beneath the thick leaves. The stress continued to throb in his ears. It was something that he'd lived with as a child but had gone away as he'd found some success in life. Only now it had come back like a chronic disease, the childhood taunt ringing again in his ears, "Bastard Andy, bastard Andy. . . ."

Back then, he was frightened and silent because he knew the place of a mixed blood child without a father. The worst were the other half-breed kids whose mothers had found big strong husbands to protect them and who relished their power to abuse him. One afternoon, he caught an abandoned cat on the road from school. He tied her tail to a tree, then wound a rubber band around her thin neck and tied it to another tree. The poor, frightened cat had cried out miserably, its meow constricted when it struggled against the tightening rubber band. Every so often, he would loosen the rubber band to let the cat recover her strength, but then he'd snap it taut again. After he bored of this torture, he picked up a large stone from a crumbled villa wall. He raised it high above the cat and let it drop. The cat jumped to one side, its eyes glassy with fear. After a dozen rounds of this new game, the traumatized cat finally collapsed and the stone dropped straight onto its back. She didn't make a sound. For the first time, his fear subsided. A calm settled over his body like a drug that he would need to try again and again. When he turned toward home, he found a crowd of children had gathered, watching him from the corner with disgust and fright. A black boy, twice as big as Andy, shouted at him, "You sick bastard!"

Riding the high of the torture, he threw himself at the kids, each of them falling just like the cat. From that moment on, he knew victory didn't always go to the stronger or wiser, but to the one more willing to take a risk. He had suffered the horrors dealt to him and now he would pass them on to others. Andy Trần had become a sick bastard, and now all the kids in his neighborhood would know it. That wild cat, his first victim, had made him unstoppable.

But as with all addictions, the dose would have to increase. The day several years later, when a frightened neighborhood girl turned her face from him as he passed, mumbling "Sick bastard" under her breath, was the day people found her nearly naked in pool of blood outside a garage.

He escaped to Saigon, gambled all his money in the new stock market, and won big. Money led to money, and with each successive victory, stranger, more addictive fetishes took over, convincing him he could never fail again. Most of his victims never said a word because now he could buy their silence; for the others, the shock left them too numb to do anything.

Only *she* had the courage to face to him in a court of law.

But Andy Trần still had his victory. And now it seemed there was nowhere he could not do as he wished and then retreat to the safe place his newfound wealth had made for him, protected on all sides as if in a well.

Kicking up leaves, rooting down to the soft soil beneath, Andy searched the entire area where the ball had disappeared. Still he could not find it. He tugged his chin, thinking. He knew this golf course so well that even with his eyes closed, he could sense the distance to each hole. Losing the ball was exceptionally ridiculous. All at once the sky blackened with clouds, and a wind swirled with leaves and dust. He scanned the course, astonished. Just a moment before, players had been on the greens and tees, uniformed caddy girls sitting carelessly in the carts, and now everyone had disappeared. It was so strange. Even if they knew it was going to rain, they couldn't have gotten back to their rooms so fast. Then a voice inside him told him decisively that he must find the ball at any cost, even if he was all alone on the course. He could not be vanquished. And just then, away from the trees, past some bushes, he saw something small and white pinned beneath a concrete slab.

Happily, he considered his next shot. It might take an average golfer two strokes to reach the green from here; he felt certain he could do it in one. But the ball had somehow wedged itself tight beneath the slab, and the heavy slab could not be moved easily. He knew what this was. When construction on the resort began, the local workers had refused to work in this area. They said an ancient well had kept this highland barren for thousands of years. According to their superstition, a terrible spirit inhabited the well, some intangible force they couldn't name. Contact with it could ruin their lives. When the president of the management board examined the construction site, he agreed to narrow the area a little. But to the workers he said, "The course is fixed. There's no reason to meddle with our perfectly engineered plan just because of superstition."

Andy Trần himself had arranged for the concrete slab to be hauled in to seal it off. Encouraged, the workers finished the course. Nothing had happened then or after and soon the whole idiotic ordeal was behind them.

He tapped at the ball with his iron, but it didn't move. He knelt down to try to pry the ball loose, but still it wouldn't budge. The golf course behind him was quiet and the sky became dark as if it were no longer a summer afternoon. He sat down and tried to push the slab aside with his feet. With a groan, it slid half an inch and then completely crumbled apart. A funnel of cold air tore down from the sky into the well, pulling Andy Trần with it. He fell, spinning around and around in the dark, empty space. At last he splashed into the viscous, icy water. He cried out but even his voice was trapped in the hole. The sky above faded to black. He saw lightning overhead but could not feel the thunder. He felt like he'd begun to disintegrate. Maybe he was dead.

Something moved in the water beneath his feet. Then a very strange thing emerged, dark and thick like black jelly, rising up to his waist, then his chest, and then facing him. He could see through it, not with his eyes so much as with a sense newly born into his consciousness and rooted in the rank spring of terror. The very strange thing was a face—not human, not animal, not ghost—that suddenly split into hundreds of other faces. They split and flowed and then merged again, finally forming terrified eyes. *Her* eyes. A moment later, he realized the eyes were wide open, the pupils swelling and going clear as a mirror. He could see his own face, tremendously distorted, and his own eyes filled with horror.

Then, something fell into the well.

His golf ball.

Andy Trần fainted dead away.

Something brushing softly against his face woke him. He was lying on the couch in the hotel office, the shades drawn, the room dark. The new girl, Mai Lan, peered down at him. "He's waking up," she said.

"What happened?"

"You hit the ball into a tree and it bounced back and knocked you out," said Mỹ Hà.

"No, I fell into the well."

Mai Lan and Mỹ Hà looked at one another in surprise.

"Your partners found you lying on the ground."

As Andy Trần gazed into the girl's eyes—the last time he ever looked a woman in the eye—her pupils opened wide, black as the bottom of the well, reflecting his own terror as unmistakably as a mirror.

Translated by Nguyễn Lien, Di Li, and Charles Waugh

Lonely Winds

Nguyễn Ngọc Tú

Why can't people see me when I'm still alive?
—said by a ghost

THE MIDDAY RAIN BLOWS A LONELY WIND OVER THE GRASS IN FRONT OF the long-haul truck. Tamarind leaves flutter onto the glass. The wipers cannot cope with so many of the small, tender leaves. The driver swings his body out behind the open door to clear the windshield, his curses slinging in time with the blades. The oil-smeared towel he uses to wipe his hands conjures before my eyes an image of the Grass Market in the throes of the declining day.

Two blocks of houses alongside the road end abruptly in abandoned fields. In an afternoon market, everything withers; the sunshine after a rain slants withering light over withered vegetables and the slabs of meat also wither beneath the sated buzz of the flies. A woman seated beside her stall yawns indifferently through dry lips. In the long sigh of the Grass Market, I cannot hear the mist rising up.

Another young man from the truck has unloaded the last pots of salted colza leaves to the market. He opens the door, his sour stench assaulting my nose, and touches my hand. We're at the Grass Market, little Miss, please wake up, get off the truck.

I quietly thrust my hand into my pocket and take out a little more money. His pulse throbs heavily at his neck. Not for the money, but in surprise. Where do you really want to go, he asks. I look at him a moment, then close my eyes. I don't know where I'm going or where they will go after this. I like sitting here, on the torn seat cushion, my thigh touching the steel frame, the dense chaos of overwhelming smells all around. I feel at ease because I don't feel nauseous.

Yesterday, from Xuyên Mỹ to the city in a small, crowded bus, I vomited when the driver's assistant asked the passengers to get off at a deserted communal market, saying, "You'll all be fine. We're just going to run and mend the tire, then we'll come back to pick you up." Noodles spilled from my mouth as my stomach turned inside out. In the group of disheveled passengers who'd bought cheap tickets along the way, there was an old woman who pooh-poohed him and rubbed balm into my temples, into my sadness, saying, "The little girl's carsick, so pitiful," and the smell of the betel from her two pockets was so warm. I felt my throat unknot again.

* * *

Not remembering the color of the sunlight or the direction the sun fell, in the afternoon they left in the truck from a crossroad restaurant toward the Grass Market. Not yet knowing whether the day would have any good signs or bad—a spider in the face, a bird in the cabin, a broken cup in the restaurant—and then the moment when the girl appeared in front of the truck, her old blouse wrinkled, her hair loose on her pale slender neck.

She stood there in the way, the driver heatedly blasting the horn. She waved a green bill. The money raised its glittering voice. It said this girl was its master and she wanted to come along in this crushed old truck carrying pots of salted colza leaves from the city to the Grass Market.

That day, the lonely wind took a step into the new season. When the driver's assistant, Dzự, opened the door to let the girl in, the wind drew a cold line across his black face. He muttered, "Cold as a mother—." He leaned close to ask her whom she knew at the Grass Market, but the girl had fallen asleep already. Maybe she wasn't asleep but had closed her eyes to avoid answering, her small backpack the color of mouse fur held tightly in her lap. Her face, her hands, and in fact everything about her suggested silence.

* * *

There are several ordinary questions people usually ask, like Where's your house? and Why do you tramp the dust of life like this? Don't you have any relatives? What's wrong with you, so pale like this? Where do you want to go? Who's waiting for you there? What's your name?

The chubby question mark hovers over the point of a knife, and a person only feels the knife's sharpness when it begins to enter the flesh.

* * *

The driver called her Ái. The nickname, which meant "ouch," originated from a small accident; just as he asked for her name, he absentmindedly slammed the door, catching her hand in it, and she screamed, "Ouch!" The tip of her finger flattened and just minutes later, it was swollen. She didn't cry or faint from pain. He felt bad for her, so he offered to rub it with some balm, but she shook her head and sucked her sore finger until it wrinkled with saliva and went numb.

She remained silent. Yet she traveled with them for two days, and this trip seemed to be a long one. She needed a name to be called at meals, to get on or off the truck. But after a few days, the driver recognized something wrong with her nickname, with it sounding like a cry of pain, like something stunned, and it reminded him of his careless mistake, even when the wound had almost healed.

That afternoon, after eating, he called: "Mỹ Ái, get on!"

"Beautiful Ouch"—the first gift to make her smile.

* * *

I have many names; in the cornfields of Mai Lâm, they call me Peanut; on the roads I pass through, children call me Mute, and adults ask, "Honey, can I give you a lift?" The other night, at a roadside bus stop, my name was Lam. The one who so nervously called me Lam was a sprawling drunk young man. Even his voice tottered, listless. From the patter of his stammering lips came nostalgia. Bicycles. Journeys. Dizziness Pass. Curling his legs over one another while sleeping in the fog. I thought he was babbling; he didn't talk about himself, as he calmly wiped the tough strings of tears from his eyes. Rice wine had pickled his back; it could no longer support him as life bent him further and further toward the ground.

"That time at the pass, there were six of them. I didn't run away, I only searched for someone to help."

It was almost like he couldn't keep his head on any longer; it nearly lolled off his neck. His whole body had been soaked with rain, wine, and sorrow, everything wet to the bone. The diluted blood and that tired heart had to push back against such dreadful currents. I shouldered my bag, wary of the drifting, slippery flow of blood.

I sidled away, my back foot tripping over the front and scuffing my shoe. I felt from one heel a stabbing pain that rose slowly up my leg. As if I really was the one named Lam.

Mỹ Ái seems like a name that's come out of the blue. I like it, because for me it has no past, no sorrow.

* * *

The girl had remained in the cab of the truck since the day she vomited in the restaurant, when the driver's assistant, Dzụ, reached out with an arm crisscrossed by scabietic scars and grabbed lasciviously for the waitress, telling her that he'd dreamt about her the night before, then tossed and turned all night, sweat all night, "missing you terribly. . . ." Mỹ Ái dropped her chopsticks and hunched over, then ran to the back of the restaurant before fumbling her way into the truck, and then did not get down again. It seemed she'd chosen that small space to be her home.

Thunderstruck, Dzụ said, "Boss, that girl is not right. . . ."

The driver crammed a load of vegetables into his mouth, gobbling through his words: "She can't bear to hear you lie."

"That's why she vomits?"

"Go ask her."

"Boss, you're joking; she's mute."

"Whatever."

By idly making up stories, guessing and theorizing, each day they shared more thoughts about her, said a few more things. That surprised the driver; he and Dzụ had a common interest after all.

He had bought this Landu truck five years ago, at the price of seventy-three million dong*—twenty-one years' worth of working as a porter in an ice factory, as an assistant driver, as a co-driver, holding the wheel, clinging to the roads. The truck's former owner vouched for the assistant driver with the long hair covering his eyes, his skin black and sun-dried from a laziness toward bathing, older than his real age. Dzụ. He didn't need Dzụ, but the truck did; Dzụ knew by heart where the jingles came from and how long that smell of burning would make them stop for repairs. If the truck jerked and stalled, and Dzụ looked alarmed, saying by God the mosquitoes would tear them apart, the driver knew they would be stuck all night.

Five years together like this, and still he thought of Dzụ as he would a lone bowl of cold rice. The driver did not need a family so he never made an effort to start one. When cleaning up at a truckstop, they did not care to notice each other. He had his own life, his own dreams and his own women each night.

But the girl brought into his truck so many curiosities, so many mysteries. Seeing her so pale after vomiting and not being able to repress his feelings, he let slip, "She looks like a ghost. . . ."

* * *

I always have a feeling that it's my blood that I throw up. After each bout of nausea, I'm exhausted, worn out, unable to hear the swish swish of my

* About $3,500.

arteries, my heart heaving dryly. I feel I am at the edge of death, just half a footstep away, that I will fall into some dark black water, then sink, forever. On the day I met my father again, on the television program *Farewell to Wandering*, my father took me to Dr. Lanh's house. The doctor hastily performed all the important tests while examining me. He asked what came up when I vomited, and my father smiled painfully, telling about the sour smell of regurgitated sweet potato in front of so many guests. The doctor laughed; maybe eating too much sweet potato gave me indigestion. Or, maybe it was because of my restlessness, my constant movement; seven to eight years of wandering was no small matter. Then the doctor patted my head and said that when he himself was emotional, his nose was itchy and he sneezed a lot.

That day, it seemed he was emotional too; when my father announced he'd just signed an appropriation for the hospital, the doctor's face glowed. Affectionately, he slid a prescription into my hand, saying, "Take the trouble to get a transfusion, you look so pale. You said she used to live where? In Mai Lâm, right? My heavens, I lived there when I joined the Youth Volunteer Corps; that sacred forest's water is really toxic. Poor child. . . ."

The prescription relaxed and cheered my father. He didn't know that the slip of paper was worthless, its words written quickly, without hope.

*   *   *

The lonely winds made him care more about a place to spend the night. It became impossible to sleep anywhere, let alone in a market stall or in the bed of the truck. No one could rest in the persistent tricks of the wind; it was like being torn apart by an invisible hand. And since the winds themselves came in separate, individual gusts, they tormented everyone they touched. Chills came and went, like a fit. Covering up with a blanket became a small struggle; they couldn't know when the wind would come, and without the wind, their whole bodies would drench with sweat. The winds never tired of this game. When the travelers finally wore out and fell asleep, the wind would wake them by gliding slowly from head to toe, like a soul, like a ghost, just passing through.

To escape the wind, the driver put the word out that he'd transport anything anywhere, giving the cheapest price to his network of market women at all the familiar places. In this way, the lonely wind season could pass peacefully through his life. "At least you won't have to pay for a place to stay," giggled Dzụ, surmising the plan. He schemed with the driver about such things. Dzụ was young, passing bewildered through this bewildering life.

But even lying in a warm and cozy room, he still tossed and turned with the wind that night, wondering, "Why won't that mute little one come inside the house?" The next morning, meeting her again, he couldn't tell whether the girl had become paler because of the wind. Maybe her two legs weren't able to stretch out straight because the wind had come into the cab and frozen her crooked.

* * *

The maize field in Mai Lâm welcomed the lonely winds with its rows of leaning plants. Sometimes a gust of lonely wind swaggered across the field and made a funny scene, with some places still straight, others slanting and tangled. In the morning, the wind pummeled the flowering maize down to the ground, leaving a clear line of sight to the house of Mr. Tám Nhơn Đạo.* I saw him washing the hair of his disabled wife. She lay on a bench. He held her heavy head with one hand, poured the water and shampoo with the other, and then both those big, wide hands sank completely into the white foam.

The morning wind made the hair washing go faster. Mr. Tám carried his wife into the house; they disappeared behind the dark door. I turned toward the myrtle tree. Purple constellations from all over the tree had been blown to the ground by the wind. Separation from the tree had caused the myriad flocks of stars to dim and tatter.

The dog named Crane ran dutifully, excitedly, from Mr. Tám's house, the fur at the corner of his mouth still smudged with a little bit of burnt fat. He ran and barked in surprise, even though he had already barked all night; in the early morning light, the wind-twisted scene of the field looked strange. The roof of the hut where I lived fluttered up and down like the hair of a person who just woke up.

In the bundle of familiar sounds of ants touching their legs on their way out of the nest, of the thousand rustling leaves, of dew dribbling down, and cuckoos clanging in the reeds, there was also the sound of the trees secreting resin to heal the wounds where the flower buds had fallen.

* * *

Dzự woke early. As soon as he sat up and felt the pain in his back, he ran to the Landu to see if the girl was still . . . alive. Despite seeing that she was fine, just sleeping, he woke her, as if to confirm she could still open her eyes. He smiled slightly, whispering, "Damn lucky."

---

* *Nhơn Đạo* means "humanitarian."

Seeing her still alive, Dzụ felt alive too, with rays of hope filling his heart. Life kept going despite the severe lonely wind season; somewhere, his grandmother was also waking up, opening her eyes to vaguely greet the new day. In his enthusiasm, Dzụ swung on the driver's shoulder, freely and closely, like a younger brother plays with the older. But the driver scolded him, not wanting to be touched.

Dzụ hated roads. Whenever the truck stopped, he'd run to push back the hat of some beggar, hoping to find an old familiar face, and he would curse the road that carried his grandmother away, seven years ago. The driver would sit silently in the truck, looking at Dzụ's hopeless shoulders and thinking that choosing to love other humans also meant losing joy. It also meant death, desolation, infidelity, destruction. . . .

The driver loved roads deeply. They were always alive, fertile, refreshing. A road had no death. A road always knew how to wait.

* * *

I like looking at the truck driver's face after morning coffee. His lips hold a cigarette vacantly. He sits behind the wheel, silent for a moment before beginning the journey. Smoke and beads of coffee mingle in his bristly beard, making his face glisten. After that, his face holds only a condensed thoughtfulness; his body, a rhythm of sorrow.

A sad person.

Each time we wind through a turn or look out over the far distance before us, I realize his heart beats the same as mine, the blood running indifferently, frigidly, with never a problem, the heart always on the right beat. There is nothing after the next turn or out in front of us waiting.

The other man sitting beside me is different, his breath is always bustling. He is eager to take note of each moment, each change of scenery alongside the road the old Landu travels.

* * *

The girl had no money left. In the afternoon, when he bought her a rice box, the driver thought he'd drop her off at the Mỹ Đức market, where the truck would stop to deliver bundles of sedge that would be used to tie crabs. It was dark when they reached the market; they wouldn't get paid until the next morning. Silently, he tossed her shoes out of the truck, then the bag, and then at last the girl, her tiny rounded shoulders enclosed in his rugged, hardened hands. Dzụ felt it was a bit heartless, saying, "Poor little one."

The girl seemed to know this end was coming, so she drifted over to lie on the market veranda. She curled up in the lonely wind, an expression of silent resolve still on her face, but the market loomed so large behind her that she looked small and lonesome. The driver tried not to look in that direction, despite Dzụ continually smacking his tongue and hissing. The goods unloaded, close to midnight, Dzụ said, "Let's sleep right here, when we get paid in the morning we'll go, we don't need to find a place to sleep, Boss." He didn't want to leave her alone—maybe the big man would reconsider and bring her along.

Curling up in one of the stalls, Dzụ fell asleep with a faint hope. The driver sat there, smoking desperately. He'd just begun to doze, still hearing the lonely wind rustling lightly on their faces, when the girl screamed, sounding like a fallen cup breaking on the floor: "Fire!"

He and Dzụ ran through the dark, smoky doorway. Dzụ did not forget to haul the girl along with them. Pulling out from the narrow road alongside the market, a fire blinked in the rearview mirror. The night closed in on them. He saw dreams, heard the girl's scream, smelled the fire. His cigarette ash had caused the disaster—he hid that thought in his mind.

The next morning, the TV news said the Mỹ Đức market had burned to the ground, only soot-blackened concrete frames remained, a billion dong reduced to ash, the authorities were looking for the cause. The driver lowered his face nearly into his noodle bowl, apparently absorbed in eating. Dzụ felt glad to have escaped death. Holding his chopsticks upright he wondered aloud: "Wow! I really thought she was mute. Good God, now how can she speak?"

The only one who could answer was sitting outside in the truck. The driver wondered whether the fire was fate or if it was she who wanted it to happen. Now, if he abandoned her, maybe she'd tell someone what she knew about the Mỹ Đức market fire. She was not mute.

* * *

Once when I was six, I stole my father's razor to shave the fur of our dog, Lu Lu; unpredictably, my mother and father quarreled because of that; my father pointed at me, asking my mother, each word as tight as blood leaking between gaps in the teeth, "Who did you lay with to give birth to this thing?" My mother didn't answer but quietly went to her room and locked the door from inside. Three hours later, my father found her swinging from a beam. Her rebuking tongue survived in death because she did not accept its uselessness, having spoken but never been listened to.

I stood staring at her and wet my pants with fright. Old Mrs. Chín stood nearby, covering my eyes, but her withered hands could not close tight, and before whisking me out of the room to change my clothes, I saw again my mother's contorted face. When I returned wearing my new lime green dress, Mrs. Chín burst into tears, crying out painfully, "Oh God, why is life as short as cooking noodles?"

Over the two whole funeral days for the desperate woman who had just discovered she had stomach cancer—according to my poor, bereaved father—I sat crouched against the wall near my mother's coffin, silently feeding votive paper* into the flames from my hands, fire perpetuating fire, never fading. My face and my hands grew extremely hot; they felt like they were going to bleed. At the end of the second day, Mrs. Chín confronted my father, asking fearfully: "It's been days, why won't she speak?"

My father turned to look at me, somewhat relieved. Silence was necessary for secrets.

* * *

The first question Dzụ asked was simply, "Where's your home that you've chosen a life of dust, little one?" But she did not answer. She still looked like she didn't want to speak. It seemed her cry of alarm at Mỹ Đức was only a dream.

The driver regarded her continued silence as a relief. He never asked anyone a question like Dzụ's because after they answered people always wanted to ask, "And you?" He never replied, even with the women he held in his arms. It was a very salty answer, one that burned the lips like sea water.

* * *

From Thổ Sầu, avoiding traffic, Mr. Sad (the name I've given him) drives the Landu along shortcuts at the edge of the city. I realize I just passed my house with its high gate bursting with bougainvillea. It had been tidy before I returned. And then it was spattered with vomit.

Many people brought gifts to congratulate my father and me; they said the reunion broadcast live on TV made them cry like they wanted to die. They didn't know the chairman's life had so many tragedies, that his first wife had died, that his daughter had been missing for nearly ten years. A person must have great willpower and rare courage to overcome such personal pain to care for public affairs. I heard all these things with some bewilderment, then threw up, wanting to run to the bathroom but

---

* Many Vietnamese burn paper versions of things that deceased loved ones enjoyed in life so that they may enjoy them in death too. Money, gold, cars, houses, etc., have all been made from paper for this purpose.

not remembering where it was. The food spilled all over the carpet. As the day's guests multiplied, the more I vomited. Finally, Ms. Băng said I could go lie down in my room.

Actually, the guests did not feel the need to meet me; they only wanted Ms. Băng to remember that they came and to remember the imported toy dog and the platinum ring and the expensive handbag that had been brought for me. If she remembered, then she would mention them again, when my father returned. Her job was to make my father remember them.

She also had another important job to do every morning: buy food for the crocodiles she kept in a cage. She rode her motorbike with its two big baskets on the back. People at the market came to expect this sight, and everyone praised the chairman's new wife for being so good at enduring hardship; other leaders' wives could only be found at the tennis court. She just smiled, telling people that to stay home and do nothing but live off his salary would be unbearable.

Everyone knew the story of Ms. Băng raising crocodiles to renovate the villa. Lots of other people also raised crocodiles, but none of them ever built a villa.

* * *

Suffering a high fever, Dzự remained in Lạc Mai to rest, so on the trip to Đập Đá, the Landu had one empty seat. But the driver felt no emptiness. He was accustomed to change and uncertainty; the next morning, maybe Dzự would have already gone home forever after finding his grandmother either alive or a sack of ruined bones. The girl sitting here was the same— she climbed into the truck one day on a whim; because of another, at some point she would silently hop out. There was only him and the roads. He never wanted to leave this life and so refused all chances to live like a normal person, having to shave his beard, cut his hair, dress properly, wake up in the morning and drink coffee, eat phở,* and go to work, to love a person and marry a wife.

It started to rain as the truck passed a rubber-tree forest whose leaves had begun to change color. Looking through the stippled glass, the girl blurted, "How deep are these tears already?"

Her voice quivered shyly. The driver felt funny; maybe it had been a long time since language had deserted this girl, and when it returned in such a whirlwind, she'd have to sort through a chaotic swirl of words, choosing each one separately to form a sentence.

---

* Vietnamese noodle soup.

"Let me *dig* that for you."

At dinner that night, after he unloaded the truck, she had scrambled to serve him rice. He nearly choked because of the word "dig." The wind gusted outside, the same shredding wind that was so painful and cold. He drove slowly to find a guest house; the small town had already begun to close doors and switch off the lights.

* * *

Lying in the cornfields to gaze at the floating moon, I used to wonder, if I ever spoke again, what my first sentence be.

"Don't lick my foot, it tickles!"

That's what I'd say to Crane. He often woke me with his uncontrollable excitement from some shadow cast by the moon, from falling leaves, or the smell of a strange female dog at a distance. . . . His cold wet tongue would wander from my heel to my calf, then to my knee. From there a shudder ran to the top of my head, a cycle of waves burning up my body.

I hated that sensation, so I intended to speak first to the dog. But when the time came I said something else: "Go."

It was the morning I left the cornfield behind, as I walked along the road lined with flickering reeds and floating butterflies. At the intersection, I reached an empty tea shop. Crane came along behind; in truth, he didn't understand the word "go" since I'd never said that to him before, but he knew the pain from my bloodshot eyes, from how I pointed, from my averted face, my frowning eyebrows, my heavy step. . . .

* * *

Three days in the infirmary were like three years to Dzụ. Beneath the blanket, he imagined the truck in the morning passing a small temple, inside of which his grandmother lay asleep, a broken conical hat covering her face, her head resting on a torn sack. Seven years of drifting had torn the old body to pieces as well. The conviction that he'd missed his chance to find her unsettled him. Tomorrow, if he followed the same road to the same temple, Grandma would no longer be there. The roads would sweep her along with them.

He held his grandmother's photo; it had been twisted, crushed. Hundreds of hands had held it, only to return it with a shake of the head. The day Dzụ left home, he had shaved his head clean so it shined like a vow: "I will not come home until I find Grandma." His mother broke into tears, saying, "The world is boundless—how will you find her, my son?"

He couldn't believe the world was any bigger than the city. A hot steel sliver had lodged in his heart, burning there since the afternoon he left his friends at the pool hall to run home and take care of his grandmother.

"Grandma's such a pain," he had said. "The sooner she dies the better."

Dzụ felt certain it was because of this impertinent remark that his grandmother went away. He had to find her and fall on his knees to beg forgiveness. He could never remember what he would say to her when he met her again. Everything was so exhausting; he searched for her only because he wanted to find her, that was all.

Lying around in bed or in the hammock, not driving, not loading, not cleaning, no longer getting any pleasure from teasing the host's maid, Dzụ felt exhausted. Yes, he would find Grandma some day, but then what? "Then what" had become a transparent, everlasting space.

The afternoon the Landu returned, Dzụ ran outside, so happy, feeling they had been apart too long. One part of it was the girl; after coming back, she had begun to babble some crazy talk—"are you *free*?" or "the button *broke off* there." Dzụ felt funny and forgot his cold. When cleaning around the holes in the truck floor, she lamented, "This spot's been *torn* . . . ."

* * *

I can't remember what I said to make Mr. Sad smile that day. From his mouth, the smile flared, and his face became brilliant like a coal ready to burst into flame, feeding the warm glow of the coals nearby.

When the words came from my lips, I was thinking of the woodpecker's nest on the roof of the hut at the end of the field. I never knew where their stories came from but they chattered the whole day. I imagined the husband bird saying: "I just found a dead elephant in the forest."

His wife would reply, "Heavens, why did the elephant die?" So the assumption was made and the story became endless, and at the end of the elephant part of the story there were ants crawling, maybe to the elephant, then the spring running over the elephant's body, then the tree branches swaying above. The following day came the story of a falling flower. All the stories were serene and happily without end, regardless of rain or sun, regardless of the lonely gusts of wind. I often wonder, whether in this life any bird seeks its death because of the singing of another bird? Has there ever been a dog who smashed its head into a rock because of another dog's barking? Does any cow drown itself in the river because another cow says moo?

The voices of animals are not used to hurt each other, I think. Up to now I still think this way. So when I speak in the way of birds, it makes those two laugh. There was a time I practiced speaking human, just some little bitty words, but they made me sweat, exhausted: "Why are you so sad?"

And the one receiving the question frowned and spat. It seemed he didn't like human speech.

* * *

When he shaved, the driver looked at himself. In the mirror it was his father's face, his mother's deep eyes, and his older brother's thick, unruly eyebrows. All of them had sunk already, into the deep blue sea or into America.

He still had the roads. He went to work as a driver's assistant when he was thirteen. With several sets of clothes, he went from place to place, traveling like a leech in a banana garden in the rainy season. Only needing some small purchase, the leech stretches itself to another place, and from that new place, it continuosly reaches for another. The difference is the leech needs blood to live, the driver just needed to keep moving.

Dzụ met him the first time and called him the Boss because "I know right away when I see a man from the street." With an innate stubbornness, homelessness, and landlessness, using the truck as his home, making the road his friend, from time to time devouring women, not giving a damn about what he earned . . . he was more of a wanderer than anyone from the street.

Even now, traveling back and forth between the markets, he never let himself feel sad. The roads changed every day: a lady shopowner had her hair cut short, the raintree leaves turned colors, one more cigarette booth opened on the pavement, the rubbish bins were changed to new ones, a restaurant sign was repainted, some street lights burnt out, a banner over a tennis court gate lost a letter and made a dirty pun.

Roads never disappeared after someone overslept in the attic, like the whole family did when he was eight.

* * *

Sometimes I forget that I . . . have . . . sadness. Like the time I lived in Mai Lâm. My job was to keep the cows from the next village from coming into Mr. Tám Nhơn Đạo's field. Mind the cows, weed the field, spread manure. In season, I gathered sugarcane, harvested maize, transplanted cassava. When I was hungry, I came into Mr. Tám's house looking for rice to eat, and sometimes I'd find him chopping firewood or writing poetry, and sometimes I saw his wife in her wheelchair, watching movies from Hong Kong. Then, if I felt sleepy, I'd dream of talking to Crane, of listening to him complain that his girlfriend dog must change her heart, not love him anymore, and try to move on. Conversations like these with my pets made my dreams so interesting and pleasant.

Now I sleep whenever and wake whenever, no day, no night, no memory clear or deep enough for me to sit and look into. The big winds go and the lonely gusts come, each season of winds with its own voice, so the sound around me always feels refined and serene.

Time has passed, and I no longer recoil from human voices. But the day Mr. Tám came out to the hut, I was oblivious. Without warning, I felt myself pressed down into the spotty, worm-eaten boards, a hand sliding under my blouse. I struggled. I screamed, but a hand stinking of rice wine, meat, and piss trapped my voice inside. I could not be sure the burning voice inside my throat was human, and even if I tried with all my strength from the small hut out in the field, only the woman in the wheelchair could have heard. Maybe she also wasn't sure it was my scream; maybe it sounded more like the howl of a dog, the cry of a restless night bird, a cat yowling in the grass.

I silently planned Mr. Tám Nhơn Đạo's funeral. Every detail I knew about him disappeared, faded away: the sticky rice he gave me in the corner of Mai Lâm market, the strip of cloth he tore from his shirt to bandage my hand when I'd been cut by a knife, the portion of salty food he left for me in the cupboard, the cheery verses of Lục Vân Tiên* coming from the house in the early morning, the way he sat patiently washing his wife's hair on sunny days.

A strange man had fumbled on top of me, like Crane always stuck out his tongue to lick me and to complain about his life. Strange, I couldn't feel anything all over my body. It was like all feeling had died. Hearing human voices too, smelling human smells.

That was the first time I realized some things have names that differ from their real essence, like Crane was actually a dog, Tiger was a fat and lazy cat, and the maize field that season was a maze of death, just grass and ragged wind. . . .

* * *

There was no way to know Dzự's grandmother had come to rest beside the road that the Landu truck had traveled at least ten times. A road that ran between the coast and a limestone mountain, with many pagodas on the mountain, and clouds of incense smoke in the pagodas. He usually went

---

* An epic poem of the mid-nineteenth century by Nguyễn Đình Chiểu.

quiet traveling this road, but before this day, he'd always thought it was "just because it looks so beautiful, so sad. . . ."

Until this one afternoon, Dzự kept thinking the same; because the road had so few people, its desertedness made him feel anxious. When they stopped at a roadside cafe to drink tasteless instant coffee, Dzự's grandmother compelled a woman carrying a sea cucumber to approach them; he felt something strange and bent to look at the creature waving in the air like dark moss. Dzự's grandmother compelled the woman to say vaguely: "Your face looks like an old woman who used to wander this neighborhood."

Dzự stared at her, his eyes bulging, as he took the photo from his pocket, and asked, hesitating, "Sister, was it this woman?" His grandmother had already told her yes, so the sea cucumber woman nodded immediately, "Yes, that's her."

The woman took them to the resting place of Dzự's grandmother. A shirt of grass mixed with red moss roses covered a mound along the roadside. The flowers had been grown by her. Then more people from the village came, nodding and saying yes, that was her.

Dzự collapsed on the grave, crushed flowers dotting his hair, and howled. The driver sat silently pulling weeds. The girl ran to the truck and came back with an old, gray handkerchief that she slid into Dzự's hand, saying, "This thing for *drying* . . . ."

* * *

There is a human sound that is still beautiful, the sound of crying. Once, I entered Mr. Tám Nhơn Đạo's house to look for rice, and I heard Mrs. Tám crying. He had gone to a death anniversary memorial.

The sound of her crying was the glossy, shining black sound of sorrow; it had not mixed with the color of pain, the color of anger, or the colors of self-pity or gloom. It was very deep. Deep like a dark sea in which she dove up and down with just one hand. Quietly, I carried a rice bowl to sit outside by the broken stump where Mr. Tám had stacked the chopped firewood and drank in the sound of her streaming tears.

Then another day, quietly looking for some rice, I heard the cry again, muddied and crushed, but then she said through ground teeth: "Whore! Why are you still prowling around here?"

I tapped on Crane's head. Go. And he followed me to the shop at the three-way intersection. Some people knew I was the mute girl who looked after the fields for Mr. Tám. They expressed surprise that I intended to go somewhere without any money. One woman with a very tender voice squeezed my hand for a long time, saying over and over, "Oh God, so pitiful, lost from father lost from mother, come home with me, won't have to work much, I can even pay you a little."

I felt choked; I could read something not true in her face. I could smell the smell of her sweat, feel her slippery breath and quickly beating heart, see the muscle fibers twitching on her sharp face, and my stomach writhed, my throat curved, and I vomited. The first vomit happened there, at the small shop at the three-way intersection, surrounded by dust and flies. That first time I had no idea it would keep happening, in places with people, lots of people, places where people often tell lies.

Crane knelt at my feet, tentatively lapping the vomit of dried rice and dried fish. His long, soft tongue touched my parched heart. I felt cooler with each stroke. Several buses stopped and invited me on board, their doors opening to reveal the people teeming inside. My stubborn nausea kept me still, desperate.

I returned to the hut with Crane. I lit a fire to roast sweet potatoes to sate my hunger and lay that night listening to water threading through channels underground, to a lizard's tail slithering down the wall, to a mouse gnawing lamentably on a root to sharpen its teeth, to the sound of a dry leaf skittering over another dry leaf. . . . I went too far, hearing every deep sound of the dark night, and now I can even sense the blood coursing through a person. I don't know what to do with this strange ability of mine.

Three days later, a man came saying he was from a television program called *Farewell to Wandering* and "Your father asked me to find you. . . ."

* * *

Going home. Dzụ left the Landu the next morning as clouds billowed on the horizon; it seemed it would rain all day. No long goodbyes, he just opened the truck door and swung down, glided into a waiting bus, and then it became just another trip. So light. So normal. The driver hardly waved his hand. The girl gazed at Dzụ, her face still indifferent and a little bewildered. When the bus pulled away, she closed her eyes; it seemed she'd exhausted herself keeping her eyes open so long.

The rain soon enveloped the truck in a dazzling white veil. He smoked slowly, pondering how the dictionary of his life was so simple that it didn't include such words or phrases as *going home, send a letter, buy a gift, kitchen,* or *birthday.*

From the first page to the last, it held only a few expressions: *time to go, hit the road,* and *drift.*

* * *

The car stopped in front of a high, locked gate, and my father said, "Come in, this is our home." I couldn't believe it. The walls, the roof, the porch, the bricks . . . everything had changed. The cardboard candle box that I kept from my mother's funeral was no longer in the corner between the two wardrobes. The red candle wax always reminded me of clotted blood; burned by fire, it would bleed in currents. When I was small, I once imagined that if I could warm my mother's body, the blood would run through her again.

Unable to find the candle box, I truly believed the house was not my home. That place belonged to Father and Ms. Băng's two kids because they knew how to keep the carpet clean, which way to turn the faucet so the water was warm, which button to press so the TV would show shirtless men beating each other in a roped-in cage.

Luckily, I liked the crocodile pens. I sat listening to the bones of the small fish crunching between the sharp jaws and wondered at the running tears. The crocodiles didn't cry for their food, but still their tears ran. It was strange—I didn't vomit because of them, maybe because crocodiles don't have much blood or feeling in their hearts, no sweat, no saliva. That mess didn't torture me. Not like the time at the studio when they invited Mr. Tám Nhơn Đạo to come in, and he told the story of how he found me sitting at the market hungry and torn, how he raised me up, how he cherished and protected me: "My wife and I are childless, so we coddled her like our own child." That's what he said. And an extremely bitter spout of vomit gushed from my mouth. The whole studio fussed.

Apparently, if I hear some bird whose chirping lies about the coming of spring or some dog who sees the moon and barks the lie that a thief is near, then I'll have no problem.

* * *

"Just send the girl away," said the woman in a voice choked with emotion as they turned over in bed. The driver reached for his shirt and asked, "Jealous?" She said no, it was because she was so ghostly, so weird. But the driver realized he'd had enough. He sat and smoked a cigarette, casually regarding her and the room that had protected him from the lonely winds that night. Intricately tangled spiderwebs dangled along the cord to the lamp; faces stared out at him from newspapers pasted to the wall. When he came into this room, he never thought of the thousands of miles that had passed in the two years he'd known her. The people on the wall were the same, with this beard or that hair, that one particular stare, that smile, that look of worry.

But now he would not see them again, the same as her. She had broken their agreement, she had loved. Jealousies were what happened in a family, but he had no role in such a family.

He went out to the truck. The girl blinked her eyes, bewildered by his return in the dark. She climbed down from the truck and entered the house to wash her face in the sink. The woman sat there, combing her hair, and called out: "Eating and sleeping like a sponge off a long-haul truck driver, what kind of girl is worse than a filthy rag?"

The girl silently splashed water on her face, then left. The Landu would never park its chassis on that ragged broken brick pavement again. The woman knew it too and threw the comb at the wall pasted with human faces.

*   *   *

Stray comments will sometimes make me remember things I've lost. Looking at swimsuit models posing loosely in faded calendars, I think calmly, I used to have fresh skin like them. Not any more.

I can only remember the loss. No regret, no intention to get whatever it was back. Between myself and my body there exists only a few connections: when I'm hungry, or in pain, or when I vomit. A lifeless body going anywhere with anyone does not matter.

And that's why Mr. Sad lets me stay in his truck, because when I close my eyes, I don't exist anymore. I disappear into the sounds of water spilling out of the fish tanks in the back, the canvas top of the truck flapping in the wind, a broken steel weld trembling on the truck body. . . . But I feel happy because he doesn't see me, which means I can go with Mr. Sad for the rest of this life, this sky, this land. And from time to time I let out one of my animal voices, and he bursts out laughing.

One dawn the truck arrives in Lạc Mai, and Brother Grandma Finder is standing there waving his hand like crazy. He says he's been waiting there for several days. Sitting in his usual place, he claps my shoulder in a very natural way and says, "I've gotta teach this girl to speak like a proper human being. . . ."

Brother Grandma Finder always sees me. Speaking like a human . . . there are times I also think this way. Like when I remember the voice of the old lady who had the two warm pockets that smelled like betel. Or when I remember Brother Grandma Finder's saying to me each morning, "Wake up, don't die, okay?" Or the time I kept my eyes closed a while longer than usual, and he worried, "Oh! Are you really dead?" Or when I remember the unfamiliar man selling newspapers who looked in through the window and wondered, really caring, "How can she lie like that and let her legs go numb?"

Of all the things I lost, it's only my voice I still think of sometimes. At noon, listening to the sounds of women selling sweet soup, singing out "Hey! Ho!" or calling out to one another from afar, I crave speaking-like-a-human. When Brother Grandma Finder collapsed in tears over his grandmother' grave, I would have consoled him, saying, "You go ahead and cry, I'll sit right here, I'll wait." I also want to talk with Mr. Sad; I like it when he laughs, when the blood running inside him is like a real living human being's.

But if speaking-like-a-human means I have to tell lies, to cause pain, to torment someone. . . . Who knows, I will probably speak and vomit at the same time. I will speak and cry.

One late afternoon as I sit in the truck, I can hear the woman in the house tell Mr. Sad: "Tâm, have some more, the perch are so fat right now. This morning, I scoured the markets to find these scarlet wisteria flowers to make sour soup. I just knew you'd come this afternoon."

She tells more stories, ordinary ones that happened since the last time they met: a broken ladder, a neighbor's house that had been robbed, a runny nose that lasted for days. . . . The sound of chopsticks in a bowl. The sound of a spoon on china. Two dogs tirelessly wrestling over bones. A warm family always has these sounds, these ordinary aimless stories told human-style.

I curl up as a lonely wind passes through, freezing me to my bones. And just a minute later, Mr. Sad comes out to the truck. That night he does not sleep with her, just because dinner was too cozy, too much like a family.

He doesn't like human-style, that's for sure. I have no worries; I will speak bird-style forever, or cow-style. . . .

* * *

Dzư boasted, "I'm cleaning up my life," the day he climbed back into the truck with his hair cut high and tight, showing the girl his weird white nape against its dirty black background. He became diligent about bathing, more proper in how he dressed. About returning to his nomadic life, he said only, "Sitting around at home with no idea what to do to earn money, I decided I'd better follow the Boss a while longer." He didn't say anything about the first night at home, tossing and turning in bed as a limpid and endless tomorrow stretched out before him, about suddenly seeing the girl loom toward him from out of the dark.

Dzự missed her, in a strange way—the pale green skin, the fluky vomiting, the quirky things she said, sleeping half the day, dreaming the other. . . . Missing her made the night so long.

The next morning, Dzự came to Thổ Sầu and asked all the long haul drivers about the Landu; they said they'd seen it parked at the Xuyên Mỹ crossroad the day before, but now they had no idea. A familiar driver clapped his shoulder, saying, "I want to ask your boss to go to the border to pick up some Chinese electronics. If you see him, tell him I want to talk business." Dzự nodded, knowing that going back and forth he would never find him. He decided to wait at Lạc Mai.

Long day after long day, he began to worry maybe they would never come back, maybe in some wild wanton moment, the Boss drove the Landu into the woods forever, taking the girl with him. What had happened during those days Dzự spent at home? He imagined some typical situations between an experienced man of the streets and a missing girl, and those wild imaginings plaited themselves together, becoming a thick noose that slowly tightened around his throat.

* * *

There are many emotional situations I don't hear—or can hear but don't understand. And I don't want to understand everything because I don't know if then I would vomit less or more. One day, the truck stopped at a market crossroad, and I got down from the cab to clean the windows while Brother Grandma Finder and Mr. Sad loaded boxes. A noon market has a lot of flies, but few people. Scattered here and there were some groups of shirtless men playing cards, and women who had left their stalls to gather and pluck eyebrows and trim hair. A skinny, dull-looking young man sauntered up to one of the women and whispered: "You think leaving me's as easy as leaving a dog?"

She collapsed to the ground with a terrifying loud sharp sound. Blood spurted past the knife stuck in her chest.

I choked with regret. I'd listened to that man's heartbeat, to his breath as he'd passed by. I heard his insides boiling, blood rushing into his heart like waves, his heart nearly bursting. I could feel all that but didn't know the name of it was *murder*.

There are so many things about humans I don't know. Like when Brother Grandma Finder came back, the breath inside him was very different, like a puzzle, like twisting, and his heart somehow dragged, and at the same time seemed anxious. I wanted to ask what that meant, but still speaking bird-style, it came out: "*Suffering* some *strange*."

* * *

Dzụ grumbled: "When are you going to talk properly, for God's sake? You have to say it like this: 'It rains really hard early in the morning.'"

What she'd said when he woke her was: "When *a tiny bit near to morning* rainy *skies* a lot." He complained a long time. He felt happy reproaching her; it was the feeling of caring for someone, which had disappeared when his grandmother left and had now returned full force.

Plus, he had a lot of time for it. The Landu was being dismantled in a garage; the driver wanted it repaired before going to the border with all its twisting, mountainous roads. The girl had to leave the truck cab and live like a human, sleeping in a room closed off in all four directions.

Dzụ took to hanging around the girl, lying spread out on the floor, propping his legs up against the wall, grinning because he felt things had begun to seem like a family; yes, they lacked only a kitchen and the cry of a baby. . . . He hoped the mechanics would work on the truck as long as possible.

But not everyone shared that comfortable feeling. The surrounding walls made it hard for the driver to sleep. Every night, he lay in a hammock swinging by the window of the guest house, silently listening to Dzụ's resounding snore. The idea of going back to the mountains made his heart clench. He remembered roads like threads drawn along the edge of an abyss, zig-zagging the precipitous limestone slopes. He remembered hands flying like a dance. Car horns hiccuping at each stony curve, echoing until their sad refrain died at the top of the mountain and then fell in heavy clusters to the bottom of the void.

When he drove a bus along that route, he liked to sound the horn, just to hear its voice of loneliness. It was not his voice, and he did not speak to anyone. Just the hanging echo of a voice in the middle of the sky. Here, a soft sound could be answered; a flung rock rolled down, its rolling sound tapping and clacking for what seemed like forever. Many times, when he stood at the edge, he'd shout, "Quyên!" and the stone mountain would cast back its fearsome, dizzying echo: "ên . . . ên . . . ên. . . ."

At the hospital, he had called Quyên a hundred times, but the woman remained silent, her heart still and the raised round abdomen beneath her blouse just as void of life. He hadn't slept for two days before that, but then he only needed to turn his back. Everyone always left. Only roads remained.

This nostalgia had no purpose; it just kept gnawing at his sleep. When he'd nearly dozed off, he'd hear the sound of wheels tearing through puddles on the road as they whipped along, and some buzzing sound kept coming from far away. He realized he'd been out of the Landu for more than a week.

He lit another cigarette from the last one. At the end of the hall was the girl's room. She was vomiting. The guestroom's thin plywood walls trapped her so close to other people. He imagined her pale and immovable face. He pushed open the door to step inside.

* * *

The sounds of closing doors are never the same. Because they aren't simply the sounds of wood meeting wood or the creaking of rusty metal. Each door closing is a ghost.

I remember the house gate, the day I closed it and left. It had no click, just a soft sliding sound. And I heard Ms. Băng whispering in her children's room. "That girl will die soon. You don't need to be sad."

It seemed the children worried about the expensive jewelry I wore and the few moments after dinner when my father passed by and quietly caressed my head. My father's hands were soft; the first time he let my hand slip to greet some acquaintance at a crowded fair, my journey started.

And then I myself tore my hand from my father's a second time with the closing of that gate.

In the hut in the windy field at Mai Lâm there was no door, just a curtain made from a cement sack, stiff and rustling all night, impossible to tell if its sound came from Crane, the wind, or a person. It was all the same.

When Mr. Sad steps inside the cramped and narrow guest room, I realize instantly that the sound of the door depends on the hand that closes it. It sounds deliberate and gentle, like when he shuts the truck door.

He comes close to me and lays his hand on my neck, making that place burning hot, then sits on the floor near the bed and smokes. The rhythm of his deep, dark breathing shrouds the chaotic noise coming from the couple in the next room. Everything cools down, slowly turning pleasant, and I gaze at the face that glows red with the cigarette at his lips until, in a daze, I fold myself in three, like in the Landu, and sleep. When my eyes close, there is still a flicker of fire.

The next morning, I wake up very late. Brother Grandma Finder didn't come to rouse me.

* * *

The road was just thirty footsteps wide. In front it looked just as short. Mist swirled round, darkly. From time to time the sound of a motorbike glided by, ghostly, just that sound and then a dark space tearing through the mist, plunging, and after that just a dull feeling around the waist as the mist swirled to erase the body.

The driver walked in front to lead the way, the flashlight in his hand flaring. The pass from here to the Puvan summit still had many incredibly demanding, sinuous turns. He had driven through many of the difficult parts by himself and had now given the wheel over to Dzụ. He remembered this stretch of road, each rock, each turn. For ten years his hands had danced over this route; even if the mist obscured it, he could still sense the abyss near his feet. He waved the light. Dzụ drifted sluggishly behind.

Dzụ's hands felt numb because of the cold and because of the muscles tensed to follow the light ahead. He felt exhausted. He had no idea when they'd be out of the mist, past this jumbled road. The other side of the mountain had sun, had a fire to warm the body, had some restaurant with some familiar food. But beyond this misty pass, who was waiting for him?

No one at all. For Dzụ, even the other side of the mountain was misty, fogged by hopelessness, without even the shadow of another human being. For seven years he had traveled these roads thoroughly absorbed by his belief that his grandmother waited for him somewhere. After finding that his grandmother had died, he saw only the girl waving her hand from the distance. But when he woke one morning to see the Boss stretching his shoulders easily as he left her room, Dzụ felt his heart pull apart. And when the nights with the squeaking sound of her door closing continued, he felt the choking loss swallow him whole.

She would never be in his tomorrow, even as she lay still beside him at this moment, dozing. Over her body lay draped the shirt of the man brandishing the light ten steps ahead. Dzụ suddenly thought, if he drove the truck into him, if he made it seem like an accident, out of his control, waylaid by the mist, by the hand-freezing cold, if he just slid forward a little faster, he would lie down forever with roads, just as he'd said he wanted one afternoon as they passed a funeral and Dzụ had asked, When you die, where do you want to be buried? Without hesitation, the Boss had pointed, the side of the road.

Dzụ pursed his lips; if he surged forward, maybe on the other side of the mountain someone would wait for him.

*　*　*

I hear some fast chunk of sound nearby, and I remember it's like when the young man twisted the knife into the woman's heart in the middle of the market. My stomach tumbles, and a profusion overflows upside-down into my throat. A swirl of mist clears, and Mr. Sad signals toward the open road.

He doesn't know the truck is coming right at him. In the bitter vomit everywhere, I feel my hands pull Brother Grandma Finder's hands, heaving the truck to flow to my side, the side without him, without light. Trees and shrubs fall flat before us, limning a very deep and jarring road. And I feel I am floating, bobbing and dreaming in a space that grows darker and darker, and then the dark becomes endless.

In the deep dark, I hear Brother Grandma Finder say—he too now is already an unhappy ghost—"Oh this girl . . . I only meant it as a joke. . . ."

How can a person make a joke out of *murder*? I, also a ghost, am confused by this aspect of the human I had just known. A slow hopelessness envelops me: for now and forever Mr. Sad will never hear me speak in the way of mice, birds, butterflies, ants, of a thread of water from a spring or the leaves on a branch of a tree. . . . Smiles will never return to his lips. This thought squeezes the blood from my body as if wrung from a shirt.

* * *

The mist closed slowly, self-stitching the gap the truck left along the wet and slippery road. He reeled beside the grass, his face dripping. He did not fall asleep, did not turn his back, did not even blink his eyes, nothing he could do could stop that journey. The third time he was denied, was left behind with only the roads, no one ever asked, "Why are you sad?" nor did anyone know how to embrace his shoulders to share his sudden joy.

He groped toward the edge of the abyss, wanting to love people, numb with loss, and let out a solitary cry, exhausted by the lonely wind, by the mist, the rocks, the trees. . . .

Translated by Vũ Thì Tuyết Mài and Charles Waugh

Sleeping in the Lotus Flowers

Nguyễn Anh Vũ

*I don't believe in miracles. I only believe in
things that are true. I also know what you
intend to write. But hey! I don't believe it!*

*Yes! I'm no writer. I only record the things I know, as I've
seen them, somewhere. And those are the things from
deep down that I want to reveal. Old or new, believe
it or not, it's up to you. But this time, let me speak!*

1. Toại

Full name: Nguyễn Văn Toại.

Born: 19—

Home village: Hamlet 10, Dâu Village, Dậu Dành Commune, —— District,
—— Province

War invalid with classification of 1/4. Toại has just one-and-a-half remaining limbs. Meaning on Toại's body there's just the whole left arm and half the right leg—the right arm was lost completely, and the left leg has been removed up to the hip. Toại's parents died, and his younger sister left home to marry a husband in a new development zone. Toại had been living in Army Nursing Camp 27/7* for nearly ten years when Thoan came to find him.

2. Thoan

Full name: Chu Thị Thoan.

Born: 19—

---

* A common name for wounded veteran rehabilitation centers; July 27 is War Invalids and Martyrs' Day.

Home village: Hamlet 3, Cầu Quả Village, Dậu Dành Commune, —— District, —— Province

Reddish brown skin. Cheekbones a bit high. At the top of her nose a dim reddish mole. Thoan went deaf when she was very small from the concussive pressure of an exploding bomb. Thoan led production unit number 6 at the Hồng Kỳ rubber plantation. Then, in 19—, learning that Toại was still alive, Thoan petitioned to return home.

3. A request

The paper cost five dimes and two pennies and was printed in light purple Hong Ha ink. Its handwriting was not beautiful but carefully followed the slightly puckered margin. It said:

Socialist Republic of Vietnam
Independence—Freedom—Happiness

Dear Board of Directors of Army Nursing Camp 27/7:

I am Chu Thi Thoan and currently live alone in Hamlet 3, Dậu Dành Commune. According to the need and my abilities, I hereby submit this petition to the Camp Board of Directors to ask permission to welcome back and care for Mr. Nguyen Van Toại in his home village.
    Looking forward to receiving consideration and agreement from the Board,

Thoan

4. The reunion

In the morning, Toại had a regular physical exam and heard that his health was sound, his weight just forty-six pounds. In the afternoon, Toại read the board's response, not saying a word, just shaking his head. Still alone, Toại reached to rub the place where his left leg used to be, his tears pouring down. At the beginning of his stay there, when he found it difficult to sleep at night, Toại's hand roamed all over his body, feeling for what remained and crying. Cupping his crotch, Toại wept noisily. Many of his camp mates who had lost legs and arms always kept their trouser legs and sleeves neat and smooth as if they still had everything, as if not missing anything at all. But Toại always knotted up the now extraneous and dangling pant legs and sleeve.

Thoan burnt incense at Cầu Quả Temple, bowed toward Hạ and then went to the camp to find Toại. Before leaving, Thoan wrote that if Toại didn't want to come home, she would get work at the camp to be near him.

Thoan had been at the camp a few days when Toại agreed to return with her.

5. The return

The Commune Youth Union got together for several days to reroof the house. The Commune People's Committee had approved an allocation of several hundred roofing tiles, but Toại wouldn't take them, asking instead for the old-style thatch roofing. Thoan bicycled down to Duyen Hung; it took her a whole month to buy enough reeds. In the land of reeds and jute, everyone knows a thatch roof makes the house cool, but nobody actually makes their roof like that any more. The People's Committee Secretary said: "How awful! This guy's like some kind of lord. In the old days, only a big-shot landowner could have a thatch roof three feet thick." The Veterans' Union said they would take up a collection to help buy floor tiles. Toại didn't accept those either, saying a pounded-earth floor would be fine. Thoan remembered when she was a child and often came to Toại's house to eat jambolan fruits and would push the deep purple seeds into the smooth pounded-earth floor in the shapes of flowers. . . . Oh, oh, oh, they had laughed so joyfully together all those years before Toại joined the army. No one could know what the future held.

Thoan set up the altar, placing upon it a small pot with sand to hold burning incense for Toại's deceased parents, and then moved in to live with Toại. She also set out small cakes, candy, and tea, all at one time.

Thoan cleaned up the kitchen, installed a brand new cast-iron cooking tripod, made food offerings to the ancestors, and cooked the couple's first meals. Then Thoan fenced in the garden, went to the commune fields, and finished the paperwork to get Toại's special compensations. Several days later, Thoan put together a loom on the veranda for weaving mats and spread sedge out in the yard to dry, turning it dazzlingly white. Not having woven a mat in a long time, Thoan bungled the start, the sedge threads lining up too loose and irregular, so that the mat ended up deformed. The double-sized mat twisted, and when spread out on the bed, it looked crooked like a pancake fried in a hurry. Thoan and Toại rocked with laughter. Toại said, "The longer we lie on it the flatter it will become." Thoan nodded, her hands pushing and stretching at the edges.

Like so, the mat received their two bodies lying side by side for the first time. Thoan began to remove her shirt until stayed by Toại's hand. In the dark, Toại said something, but Thoan could not hear. The two lay holding hands like that the whole night.

Tears fell silently.

6. A bath

Gradually, Toại came to understand the sign language of Thoan's hands. Thoan wanted to register their marriage officially for "proper reputation and favorable speech." Toại agreed. Thoan carried Toại out to the racked back seat of the bicycle and rode to the Commune People's Committee office.

On the way home, Thoan took a shortcut through the rice field. The dirt road shook the bicycle noisily. Several times, Toại almost fell off. Toại squeezed his thigh against the saddle, his left hand wrapped tightly around Thoan's waist. The field bright in the afternoon sun, the sun burning down like a tray of blazing red charcoal. The rice plants ripening, fragrant. For the first time in how many years he could not remember, Toại again had the chance to luxuriate in this view of his village's fields on a spectacular day. So beautiful! The smell of Thoan mingled with the fragrant rice. Toại breathed deep. He wanted to shout, "I have a wife! This lady, Thoan, is my wife!" And so he did. Toại felt as if his voice traveled far away floating on the waves made by the wind on the rice plants, running past the tombs of his parents, past Cầu Quả shrine, past Hạ Lagoon, running over the river-bank, spreading out endlessly toward the horizon. In the distance, a flock of laughing doves startled, flapping their wings and flying into the air. Thoan couldn't hear a thing, only felt that Toại held her tightly, then turned back smiling and took one hand from the handlebars to place it over Toại's hand.

That evening, Thoan pumped water into a large washbasin, added half a kettle of boiled water, then carried Toại on her back out to the well. She removed his faded green shirt. The right sleeve and two trouser legs had each been knotted tightly for many days, making it very difficult for Thoan to untie them. Thoan tried to press the wrinkles flat.

"Today, a new wife can bathe her husband."

Moonlight.

Endlessly drifting clouds.

Water.

Thoan's hands.

"Today, a new husband can be bathed by his wife!"

Thoan's hands.

Endlessly.

Water.

Moonlight.

The hands rubbed his back, scrubbing as gently and meticulously as if taking inventory: massaging, scrutinizing, and recording every detail like an impoverished peasant counts her pennies.

Toại grasped the lip of the well, obediently allowing Thoan to bathe him. Thoan could sense the change in Toại's skin, which in the presence of warm water was expanding beneath her touch. Her hand slid down to his belly, circled his navel, and slid down further still. Toại startled and released his hand from the well to stay hers. Thoan pressed her lips to his face and gently tugged her husband's only hand up to place it on her breast.

And moonlight.

And kisses. Finally, at this age, Thoan and Toại kissed one another. Thoan made a stuttering sound in her throat. Toại wrapped his arm around Thoan, squeezing her body to his over and again. And Thoan held Toại up, holding him tightly while her hand stirred up and down. A long time. Then, all at once, Toại collapsed, lowering his face to Thoan's chest, sobbing, "I'm sorry, Thoan . . . it's no use . . . nothing will work, love . . . forgive me. . . ."

Thoan just shook her head and smiled. She dried Toại's body with a towel and then lifted him onto her back and into the house. The moon hung in the sky. Moonlight streamed through the door and into the bed, a light so blue. The mat woven at the beginning remained twisted even though slept on for days.

7. The market

Toại received a wheelchair from the Red Cross and the Fatherland Front. A brand new wheelchair. Thoan hefted Toại into it. With his one hand, Toại rolled the wheel forward, around and around in the yard like a revolving lantern. Big shots from the organizations, offices, and unions cheered. But with just one hand, despite his efforts, the wheelchair would only spin in circles. Narrower each time, the whirling circles dizzied the well-wishers. Toại gave the chair back, telling them to give it to someone who still had both hands.

Thoan visited Đót Hamlet to ask a carpenter to make a wooden wheelchair for Toại. Low like a small chair, with four wooden wheels each one hand wide. The backrest held some lengths of rubber bicycle tubes that helped hold Toại's body secure.

In the morning, Thoan lifted Toại into the wooden wheelchair and then left for the fields. Toại fastened the rubber tubes across his belly and pushed a half-meter-long bamboo stick against the ground to make the wheelchair roll around the house. Getting down to the yard presented a challenge that with practice became more and more familiar. Toại poled against the ground to the left, then to the right like paddling a canoe. At first, it was very tiring, but at least the wheelchair went straight . . . left . . . right . . . left . . . right . . . left . . . right . . . and it had covered the distance from one end of the yard to the other. Toại flooded with happiness; while pushing the wheelchair he sang: *Baby made of cotton. Cheeks of pounded tin. Two iron hands, two leaden feet. Wife buys wooden wheelchair, fastens baby to the seat. When the* . . . laughter, interrupting.

Once it became familiar, Toại handled the wooden wheelchair with ease. He cruised out to the garden to pick eggplants, sow sesame, pull weeds, and kill pests; he rowed into the hamlet to visit with neighbors. When an old woman asked him, "Happy being married?" Toại beamed and answered, "Happy!" Young people would ask, "Mr. Toại, at night, how do you share secrets with silent Ms. Thoan?" and Toại would reply, "Just like your parents," and then grin broadly and row for home.

The ninth, nineteenth, and twenty-ninth days of the lunar month were market days at Đồng Luân. When finished weaving twenty mats, Thoan would bind them to the bicycle, then connect Toại's wooden wheelchair like a trailer to the tail end of the bike. On trips to the market, his wife's back bent into powering the bicycle toting the mats and tugging the husband all at the same time etched itself into Toại's memory. The wooden wheelchair clacked and clopped on the road. Everyone in the area got used to seeing the couple parade to the market this way.

Thoan chose a corner in the shade for Toại to sit selling mats; then she'd leave, which Toại felt was a bit strange. Sometimes, when Thoan disappeared like this, Toại wondered whether she was doing something or meeting someone secretly.

One afternoon, after the market had broken up, Toại waited a long time without seeing Thoan. All the mats had sold. Finally, Thoan came back, her hair plastered with sweat to her round red cheeks. Her eyes glittering. Asked where she went, she didn't answer; instead, she just pointed at the bundles of jute she'd lashed behind the saddle and gestured confusingly for them to go.

On the way home, the couple met Sật, the jute seller, who grinned at them from his bike. This guy Sật was the party secretary's little brother and a fellow villager, with yellow teeth from smoking too much Lao tobacco, and curly hair and a bushy beard that spilled from around his mouth down to his neck; when he spoke, the two thick wings of his nostrils dilated, making his already big nose look even bigger. Sật had six kids and had been widowed for a while. He offered to help push them along, then awkwardly wedged his fingers onto the saddle where Thoan sat and away they went. Sật stood into the pedals, cranking hard. The two bicycles flew along the dyke road. Toại and the wooden wheelchair galumphed behind, fishtailing wildly. It looked to Toại like Sật's hand had edged even closer to Thoan's rump. He shouted for them to stop the bikes several times, and Thoan tried to push Sật's hand away, but Sật held firm and continued to pedal, whooping with laughter. At Cầu Cô Hill, they bounced over a buffalo-shaped mound and both Toại and the wooden wheelchair toppled over, dragging behind a ways before pulling Thoan down too. The wooden wheelchair shattered into pieces.

When they finally got home, Toại fed the chunks of broken wheelchair into the kitchen fire.

For the next dozen days, Toại didn't say a word. Whenever Thoan signaled to say something, he turned away, angry. Thoan didn't know how to get through to him, but then one day she wrote I WANT TO HAVE A BABY! on the back of a page torn from the calendar and tucked it into his side of the bed. Burning with anger, Toại wrote back: GO FIND SẬT! Thoan read the note and burst out laughing. Later that day, he saw her change the cotton cloth from the bottom of her panties and wash it at the well, tears in her eyes.

Over the next few days, many such cloths appeared, hanging to dry on a pole in the backyard.

8. Sật

Without explanation, Thoan occasionally absented herself from home. She'd head off toward the district or to the province center, sometimes staying away the whole day. Toại remained at home, feeling like he was sitting on a hot stove. Repeatedly, he looked toward the door.

One day, Sật came to visit, carrying with him a wine bottle and a small bundle. He called noisily from the gate: "Hey, Toại, you prick, you home?"

"Go away you son of a bitch!" mumbled Toại. "Your mother's dog balls, is that why you're here?" He beat the palm fan on the mat, waiting for Sật to come in.

"You should be calling me older brother," said Sật. "I'm three years older. But okay, let's forget about that, we're both fellow villagers, and we

used to tend buffalo together, so let's choose something more equal, okay?"
Sật drank the tea from a cup on the tray and threw the half-drunk tea from
Toại's cup out into the yard, then poured both cups full of rice wine. "I
made this wine myself—cheers!"

Toại had not drunk wine in a long time. With the first cup, he knew
exactly the effect of the wine on the different parts of his body. By the third,
his stumps had begun to itch.

"Sật," he said. "What happened the other day's no big deal, just a little
pain is all. You didn't have to come here bringing me wine. But listen. If
you're with Thoan . . . ach . . . if Thoan comes looking for you . . ."

"Hey man, don't talk shit! You don't know what the hell you're talking
about!"

"Well, all I do is hang around the house, so I don't know shit. But, by the
way . . ."

"Stop saying *but*. I'm not after your wife. This village has a lot of girls.
And . . . and . . . and *seducing* somebody else's wife is fucking useless."

"Just please listen." Toại drank a big gulp of wine. "Thoan wants to have
a child. But I . . . as you've seen . . . I had to surrender. My gun and ammuni-
tion are lost." Toại let forth a burst of loud, uncomfortable laughter. "Does
it sound pathetic? But Sật, I'm serious. Maybe Thoan hasn't come looking
yet, but if . . . then you, please be good to her! She really wants a kid. The
situation's already been hard, so if it keeps going on, for sure. . . . Better it's
you, at least then I'll know where it came from. . . . You understand?"

Sật seemed shocked. Toại pushed a newly filled cup of wine into his
hand. To health again! After draining his cup, Sật laughed, his sides shaking, toppling himself over to the ground.

"You're killing me! Bloody hell! I never would've guessed anyone would
ever ask me to do that kind of work!"

"But . . . because . . . you look . . . you're a stud! You've got six kids, birds
and butterflies both, with more birds than butterflies. If you and your wife
hadn't quit she might've given birth to a whole squad. . . . Why the hell are
you laughing?"

"You've got it all wrong, man. Seriously wrong! Yeah, I'm a stud all right.
Back in the day, any girl who got to know me once would never forget me.
I had the first kid with my wife and then went into the army for three years
before making it back home. Like you said, I'd been set on making a whole
squad of kids. But son of a bitch! On the battlefield—Boom! A piece of
shrapnel cut off the thing most precious to me! An arm or a leg wouldn't
have been so bad. Son of a bitch! Man, at the time, I just wanted to die. I
missed women, but I had nothing to give them. I felt terrible for my wife

too. When I joined the army, I was still intact, but when I came home, I was a dead end. Fuck, if I could even dare look into my wife's eyes. I thought maybe I should become a monk. No way! You know me—I'm more likely to become a drunk! Ha! Well, I could still come home and bury my face in the wife's carpet for pleasure. Why not!"

"No way!"

"It's true, why would I joke about that? Only the first one's mine. The other kids came from my wife's *fishing trips*. Her tits and ass made good lures, you know. . . . I didn't resent any of that, the more children my family had, the more cheerful it became. At night, my wife still pounced on me like a tigress. And I didn't disappoint her. My beard and mustache got bushy like this for a reason. And these things too. . . ." Sật stuck out his long tongue and wagged a fat middle finger. He grinned. "Understand? You can do the same thing! But you still don't believe I lost my *gun*, do you? Take a look!"

Sật stood and dropped his pants down to his knees. Sật's thighs looked like a pair of ironwood pillars, and in the place where that monumental tool should have been, nothing. Toại cast a quick glance and turned away.

"Sật! Pull up your pants. I believe you!"

"So now you believe me? The whole package is gone, right!" Sật pulled up his pants and buckled his belt, tears streaming down his face. "And you. Give it some thought. If you still have a gun and bullets, then get some treatment! There's still hope. I brought you some Chinese herbal medicine that Thoan asked me to help purchase the other day. Soak it in rice wine for a while and then give it a try."

* * *

Late that night, Thoan came home, carrying so many things, including a new wooden wheelchair. Her face looked as fresh as a bouquet of flowers. Toại asked where she'd gone; she just shook her head and gave Toại a package of Western medicine that looked as if it must've come from far away in Hanoi. Toại kept asking how she got it. Eventually, Thoan couldn't keep the secret and showed Toại a talisman she'd been given by the master monks of Cả Pagoda. The talisman came wrapped with a prayer and instructions on how to perform a kind of ritual, but Thoan snatched it back before Toại could read them.

9. Hạ Lagoon

A full moon in May, bright and sharp.

Fresh, young sedges crowded the banks and lotus flowers spread like a carpet over the surface of Hạ Lagoon. The lagoon fed a tiny creek named Diếc that eventually joined the Dâu River. In the middle of the lagoon, there used to be a small island called Hạ. As a child, Toại would swim out to the island to trap starlings. At one end stood a pagoda that people in the village called Cầu Temple. In a year no one wanted to remember, the island was bombed and all but disappeared. Later, villagers rebuilt the temple along the shore, near Quả Bridge, so it became Cầu Quả Temple. In recent years, maybe because the lagoon receded or because termites had excavated the earth there, Hạ Island had begun to rise again from surface, exploding this time with bushy reeds. In the center of the island grew a large fig tree. On a full moon night, Toại rowed a boat on Hạ Lagoon.

Before getting into the boat, Toại and Thoan burned incense at Cầu Quả Temple. When the three sticks of incense burned out, Thoan prayed, and then came with Toại out on the lagoon. Toại sat in the prow, rowing. Several years of rowing the wooden wheelchair had made Toại's arm big and strong. His body had developed unevenly because the side with the remaining arm had exercised so much more than the other. Shirtless, the muscles of his only arm and of his shoulders and back shone glossily in the moonlight, rippling with every stroke.

In turn, moonlight streaked each side of the boat with white. Left . . . right . . . left . . . right. . . .

Thoan carried Toại on her back onto the island. She plugged the three spent incense sticks into the base of the fig tree and lit a whole new bundle. After praying, the couple bowed to the four directions. When the incense burned out, Thoan lit offerings of money and gold made from votive paper. Toại searched the ground beneath the tree and found a ripening fig, which he broke in half to share with Thoan.

Lotus petals covered the floor of the boat. Toại rowed slowly as Thoan scattered petals on the water and prayed.

Toại circled Hạ Island three times before Thoan finished. Utterly exhausted, Toại pulled out a bottle of rice wine and drank. Thoan also took a few sips. The husband and wife curled into each other on the floor of the boat and subsided into sleep.

* * *

The boat drifted slowly toward Diếc Creek. The floating lotus petals followed behind, closing a long streak of light shimmering on the dark surface of the lagoon. And Toại dreamed. In the dream, he saw Thoan kiss him all over his body. She kissed his amputated limbs. Wherever she kissed sprouted a shoot, crystal-clear and growing very fast. At some point Toại saw that his arms and legs had grown back entirely. He held Thoan tightly and ran, then lifted her into his arms and flew into the air. Flying, with the voices of children singing:

> Little baby, hold you tight,
> Your two cheeks so rosy bright,
> Little baby, for shelter we'll start,
> Your Mama's bought you a wooden cart,
> Little baby snuggled into seat,
> On Victory Day, we'll roam the streets.

The children's singing voices echoed again and again.

And Thoan. Thoan lay her body on top of Toại's, feeling that something was growing, a shoot emerging, germinating. Sprouting inside Thoan's body.

And their little boat passed through Diếc Creek.

* * *

I wouldn't call myself a writer. I only write what I know, what I've found somewhere, what I want to express from deep in my heart. Old or new, believe it or not, it's up to you! As for me, I believe in miracles. I myself am the proof of a miracle.

I was born in 198—, in Hamlet No. 10, Dâu Village, Dậu Dành Commune, —— District, —— Province. . . .

Translated by Nguyễn Hùng and Charles Waugh

Heart of the Land

Đinh Ngọc Hùng

"WE HAVE TO GO BACK TO THE VILLAGE."

My father spoke to the whole family. Except for my mother, everyone was puzzled. What village? Since we'd been born, apart from this place, we'd never once heard our parents mention anywhere else. Ma sat in silence.

"It'll be the end of us, but we have to go. We'll have to sell everything." My father spoke as if to convince himself.

The day Pa left his village, he left empty-handed, alone. The day he returned, trailing behind him were my mother, the three of us, and forty-one head of cattle. At the time, my brother Sơn was eight years old, my sister Mài, seven, and I was six.

"There's the village!" My father pointed to a murky black grove of trees shimmering in a distant field.

When closer, we could see an ancient banyan tree. The return of five people and forty-one head of cattle became a Gò village spectacle. People poured out to watch. Several people rushed up, crying with satisfaction when they recognized my father.

The first night back at the village, my family and our forty-one head of cattle camped on the biggest mound at the top of the village. My mother and Mài brought down the firewood, set up the kitchen, and fanned the rice. After such a long journey, the herd of cows lay about in disarray. Being late fall, the dew came down quickly spreading a web of white over the field. I couldn't help but notice the recently moved graves,* discolored boards and old clothes strewn about. Sơn wrapped his arms around me. Without explanation, the two of us began to shiver.

My village was poor. You couldn't have counted a handful of well-to-do families in the whole place. The scenery was nothing special. The sole

* While in some parts of Vietnam, the dead are reburied after about three years, this story also involves moving whole cemeteries to repurpose the land for development

thing villagers ever pointed out to strangers was the temple of the lady with its eight stone steles recording the names of those who had passed their mandarin exams. Then one day, the eight stone steles disappeared. Later, we found out Mr. and Mrs. Độ had taken them home and crushed them to burn lime. Whatever. The village's last remaining old Confucian scholar died eight years ago—was there even anyone left in that village who could read that script?* The stately row of steles at the temple gate looked impressive with their sophisticated carvings, but it was like staring at a wall. So whether or not they existed didn't really matter to us.

After the eight stone steles had been destroyed, the ancient banyan from the days of the village founding—the banyan my father had pointed to as the first sign of the village when the whole family came back from upstream—withered up and died. Like every year, in winter the tree shed its leaves, and at the beginning of spring it should have burst forth with blue-green buds. But even by the end of summer not a single branch had budded. In the end it had to be cut down; otherwise, the branches would rot and in a windstorm fall and wreck the temple's tiled roof.

Not long after that, a team of archaeologists came to the village. The researchers wanted to study the eight old inscriptions—if they were genuine, the government would give the village a cultural relics certificate. Now then, where were they? The eight inscriptions had become mortar lime. The archaeologists were astounded. They said the earth beneath our village still held countless mysteries. The old people in the village gaped with recognition. That explained the funeral boats several brick-making families had dug up from the marsh.

Mrs. Độ went crazy. Who knows whether it was payback for taking the eight steles or because the villagers were cursing her? It was most difficult on her little ones—with their mother going hospital to hospital, it was like they'd been abandoned. She saw a shaman who said: "The gods have dealt their punishment. For the rest of this life you'll work to repay the debt." Seers were brought in, amulets pasted around the house, and spirit worship bells and gongs clamored all over the village. Then she visited all the temples and shrines; continuously seeking anything they held sacred, hoping to be told the madness would soon be over. Who transplants rice by hunching over a few seedlings, then in the dark pulling them all out?

---

* The narrator refers to *chữ Nôm*, the Vietnamese logographic writing system similar to written Chinese. It was replaced with *quốc ngữ*—the writing system based on Roman script—by decree of the emperor Khải Định in 1918.

The old people in the village lamented that since the eight stone steles had disappeared and the banyan had died, the good earth—the fertile mind of the village—was gone, and no one would ever get into a university again. And there you had it, now there was no one to go out and make a good reputation for us. The villagers just hung about the village. My father said a kid's success depended on the care of his ancestors' graves. In the past when trouble arose, a scholar could be invited to come bury a talisman in the ground, but now . . .

When we returned to the village, the first thing my father did was sell eight head of cattle to buy back the old house, even though it had fallen to pieces and wasn't worth the money. My mother complained, but my father roared, "If I had to sell everything we owned, I'd still buy it."

As usual when my father had one of his outbursts, my brother, sister, and I were pushed out into the garden to avoid getting whacked by anything that might come crashing down on our heads.

The second thing he did was to call someone to butcher two cows so he could invite over all the families of the village. There were the Phùng Vǎns, the Trần Quốcs, the Nguyễn Đứcs; I asked about our family, the Đinhs. He hawked up a ball of saliva. "In this village's eyes, your father's just a piece of shit."

The rancor in his voice gave me the chills.

It would be another ten years before I dared to blame him for my mother's death. The first time he didn't yell at me. He said that if with one's own eyes a person witnessed the murder of a loved one, the only thing he could think of would be revenge. I was indignant. Because of the dead, my father had abandoned the living. Why do people only recognize the pain other people cause them and not the pain they cause other people? I couldn't understand why one after another of the village women came into my father's hands. Did he have some magic power? When my mother died, I realized that life is only the present moment. The future may come, but it isn't certain. The past will never return. Each time I stand before my mother's grave, this fact is reconfirmed.

Even though we're brothers, I am the complete opposite of Sơn. He is tall and skinny, his dark face sullen and spiteful. But I inherited a fair complexion and my mother's red lips. Everyone always says Sơn is the pigheaded one. I'm doubtful. I don't know how many times Mài and I have seen him give his back to the whip when he wasn't to blame. Those times we pitied him, awash with tears, dragging him out to the riverbank to console him with foolish words. But later, I was the person who dared to spite Pa, not Sơn.

I still remember the moment I saw Sơn dragging himself along, begging on the bus. By then, he had to use his hands as feet, each one inside three plastic flip flops stitched firmly together. I grabbed his hat and tore it to pieces, tore up even the little money the passengers had given him, and threw it out the window.

"Come home!" I said, stressing each syllable. "Come home now!"

"Finally lost it, eh Lộc?" he said, staring at me without feeling.

That look sent a chill through me like the one on that long ago October afternoon before the white dew erased the recently moved graves. When I calmed down again he said: "That was my fate. When a person is born, he has to have his own fate. If you live long enough, you'll learn. Don't tell me it's not true."

My brother was the first in the village to buy a motorbike. The sound of that bike astounded Gò village no less than my family's return from the mountains with forty-one head of cattle. But that motorbike also caused him a horrible accident. He ran into a milepost; luckily, the gods only took his legs. The cause of that accident was, well . . . he had lost at gambling, he was bankrupt, he was drunk. And he'd found out the baby in his wife's belly wasn't his. He tormented himself trying to forgive her. But unable to forgive her, he ran into the milepost. With his two legs sawed off, there was no need for torment—my sister-in-law took off. Only then did he learn how faithless people can be. When you haven't yet weathered the storm of life, when you haven't yet met your downfall, faithlessness has yet to show its face.

"Can you really live like this?" I asked.

"Sure," he snorted. "Fuck dying."

"To be without the hands of a woman, is that your fate?"

"Fate? Some jobs whores do best, regardless of fate. Stuff a little money down their shirts, and you're set."

I don't know why I attributed the fetus in my sister-in-law's belly to my father. I loathed what I was thinking, but in no way could I banish the thought from my head. I can still see the moment the little fellow came into the world between my father and my brother, the so-called dad. In the eyes of the villagers, my mother died of some sickness. But my mother's illness originated in those women. Each woman who came into my father's hands pushed Ma a little closer to death. A mother resigns herself to such things. Tears can be shed, but pain is swallowed inside. A destiny too small, a pain too big, they ravaged my mother until she had nothing left.

She watched as my father sought revenge on the village. One day, he dragged home a flabby chunk of blood-red meat, cooked it up, and laid it out on a platter on the floor in the middle of the house, got some liquor, sat down, and began to eat and drink. Seeing Sơn and me, he called us in.

"Meat here, eat up."

Sơn ate. I ate too. It was good. Crisp. When we'd finished eating my father said, "It's human flesh . . . afterbirth."

Covering our mouths, Sơn and I tumbled out into the yard spitting and spluttering. We stuck our fingers down our throats to throw up but could only dribble out a few scattered drops.

My father grumbled, "You're still not as low as your father."

From then on, when a woman gave birth in the village, my father would go and ask for the placenta. There were some who were suspicious, but my father assured them it was to make medicine to cure some illness, and they all gave in to him.

"Eat up." After he'd fried it up again, he always called me and Sơn.

"Why, and what for?"

"So I can feel like the people in this village are being eaten like meat."

Was it the liquor talking, or my father? The words of a person, or the words of a devil? Sơn ate cautiously. Not knowing was one thing, but knowing, I could never do it again.

"Lộc, you're not eating?"

A cup of wine was thrust in my face. I panicked, choking on the stench.

"Let me eat for him, Pa."

Sơn clasped his arms around me. I brushed him aside, catapulting out of the house. Why would people have to eat human flesh? Among those dripping red placentas, who would ever know if there were any of my father's blood? I shuddered and felt nauseous. My mother held me as I wept that night. Several years after that, my mother passed away.

Mài brought her children home for a visit. My nephews, Hậu and Thuỷ, glanced timidly at their grandfather and at me.

"Come here," I said, "Uncle will give you a present."

The two boys didn't move an inch. Why was the look in their eyes the same as Mài's in days gone by?

"Thập still treating you well?" I asked her.

Mài's response was neither a nod nor a shake. I felt something moving in the pit of my stomach.

"He's down South now. Maybe by Tet he'll be back."

"Are the rumors about those women true?"

She shook her head as if talking to herself. "No. He's not the ungrateful type."

I squeezed her shoulders. It had been a long time since I'd felt the touch of a loved one. I said to her, "Tell Thập, even if Pa drove him out, he still has to come back."

Mài nodded dutifully. My whole life, I will never forget that afternoon behind the meeting house. Three young men, one dear sister. They were workers digging up a section of road that cut across the front of our village. I went insane, grabbed the nearest brick, and pounded them repeatedly. Red blood flew everywhere. Until I regained my composure, there was only me and her. I was stunned. It was the first time I had looked at her clearly with the eyes of a man. Hey Sis, no wonder everyone says you're so beautiful. Her cowering beneath my gaze made me come to my senses. I told her to hide in the cornfield to give me time to go back and get some clothes for her. That night, and many other nights too after the hatred subsided, I obsessed over the image of my sister that afternoon. My father collapsed when he heard the story. Never before had I seen his face so fearful. Never had he been in such pain. Was it like the pain he caused? Every time a family in the village had a fight or dragged one another to court, I suspected my father was behind it. And I asked myself, of the thousand young faces now growing up in the village, who shared my family's blood? It was a question whose answer I did not want. How much pain had this village caused him that he resented it so deeply? By the time my father found the row of shacks belonging to the road crew, the three troublemakers had run off back to their hometown. Later, I heard they'd been transferred somewhere else. It was the first time my father was powerless because there was no evidence. That night, the row of worker's shacks went up in flames. I didn't do it. My father didn't do it. I believe him. From then on, I swore I would beat to a pulp any guy prowling around my sister. Poor Thập, now my brother-in-law, learned this lesson the hard way, having been given several dunks in the river in the middle of a freezing cold winter. Even now, I still don't understand why, when Thập repeatedly asked to marry Mài, my father refused to agree.

Father turned to grave moving. When he came into the house, he reeked of liquor. The miasma that emanated from him made the room cold and cheerless. I'd been to a few coffin moving ceremonies. After each one, images of coffin lids and skulls with gaping eye sockets came back to haunt me, especially when we placed the headstone for my mother. Many years later, in dreams, I sometimes still feel shocked. Is that really the destination of a person's life? Why did Father choose to be a gravedigger? Before the accident, Sơn was a gravedigger too. If I had listened to my father, maybe now I'd also be one. The profession came to my father when a project was started to build a road near the village. A shaman had predicted that the land in the village was extremely prosperous and about to come into great wealth. The weather was mild, the terrain advantageous in every way, the only question was which way the hearts of the people would lean. Everything was just as it was foretold. At the beginning of the next year, cadres surveyed the land, marked out this place, outlined that, and announced to the villagers that the land within the scope of the plan would be appropriately compensated for. In the village's whole history, had this land ever been good for anything? Harvests always came in stunted—you could only sell them at a loss or give them away. The several dozen acres of land the road would cross were cracked in the dry season and boggy in the wet. The trouble was the road would run through several big mounds in which many people's ancestors had been buried. It took forever to make the arrangements, but in the end everyone agreed to move the cemetery to accommodate the new plan.

While the Gò villagers waited for the day to move the graves, early one morning my father bundled up some things and went down to the river to rent a big boat to travel upstream to Bắc Ninh. Where our father was going and what he would do, Sơn, Mài, and I did not know. All we knew was that he told us to go down to the landing the next afternoon to meet the boat. The next day, my father pulled into the landing with a boat full of reburial urns. We spent the rest of the afternoon hauling urns back to the house, filling the entryway and garden. In fact, my father had been up to the pottery village at Phù Lãng. He'd calculated on leading the work of relocating the village cemetery. By the end of that day alone, more than half the urns had been sold. Seeing the pile that remained, Sơn said, "If we don't watch out, we're gonna get stuck with these."

My father cursed and said, "Before bringing them back I spent several days surveying the field. Even if some families already went and bought urns outside the village, there are still all those graves that have lost their names lying deeper down."

Then he said, "Just you wait, soon Gò village is going to have something to see."

When the number of urns in our garden was down to a dozen, old one-eyed Chác brought home a cartload too. Who knows how he knew where to get them. One-eyed Chác's wife, with a babe in arms, sobbed from the top of the village, "I told you, you haven't got half the brains they've got. Don't even think about it. He said he's the only one in the whole country to come up with the idea, but now come and see. How many lifetimes have people been eating and crapping?"

One-eyed Chác sat down with a thud at the village gate, sweat running off him like a shower. From that day on, the sound of bickering never let up from one-eyed Chác's house.

"During his lifetime, old Trí was extraordinary; dead, he's still extraordinary," my father announced one day as if he'd made some huge discovery. "Today as I reburied him, holding his bones in my hands felt so satisfying. Even when an old conniving bastard dies, all that's left of him is a bunch of water-soaked bones."

I could see the contentment in him clearly.

"You need a new job."

He shook his head.

"Why not?"

He did not reply.

Only near the end of the meal did he say, "I don't do it for the money."

Then he opened the cupboard, dragged out a butter tin, and poured it out in front of me. I was dazzled. It was the gold from when he sold the herd of cattle.

"I want to see what people have left when they die."

"When you die, you're left with your bones, what else?"

He shook his head. I shuddered. He said: "You know. Every time I pick up a skull I ask: 'Do you remember me, sir? Do you remember when you were alive, what you did?' Obviously I'm not talking out loud. But those skulls understand it all. Some are terrified to face the truth. Some grin as if wanting to pretend it never happened. Some hang their heads and look repentant."

"You're drunk again."

"It'll be a while before I'm drunk. Only when there's no more booze am I drunk. The times when the booze gets into me, I'm awake in one stroke."

Then he moved the conversation around to me. "You left because of Lý, didn't you? You good-for-nothing. Leaving because of one woman is bullshit."

Maybe my father really was drunk. Drunk but still capable of rekindling the pain in me. Lý was one of our neighbors. She had no father. When her mother remarried, she stayed and lived with her grandmother. When her grandmother died, her mother wanted Lý to come live with her, but she couldn't do it. She lived alone in her grandmother's house. Lý was beautiful, but she also had epilepsy. She was older than me, older than Mài. Lý let her hair grow long and kept it twisted up in a bun on top of her head. She only let it out when she bathed or washed it. Between our two houses was a jackfruit tree, and below the tree was the bathhouse. Every evening, I would climb to the top of the tree to spy on her. Life with my severe father was soothed by the sound of the clanking buckets, of the splashing water echoing from inside. And every night, I sat quietly up in the tree until the electric light in her house switched off. Then one day, I reeled as I saw the silhouette of a man come out of her room. My father. Never before had I hated her or hated my father so much. Her palace within me came crashing down to dust. I had thought the sound of clanking buckets and splashing water could soothe the imperfections of my life, but I was mistaken. She and my father, they were one. I left the village and found work as a day laborer. Life and pain took me from one place to the next: Hoà Bình dam project, Yaly dam, Sơn La dam. And by now I'd also started a family.

I don't understand how she could've ever possibly loved my father, but Lý did eventually leave and get married. She found a husband somewhere far away. So far, most people don't even seem to remember she'd ever lived in the village at all.

Past the mouth of the river, now a beach, was the place my father had lived for a few days after leaving the village by boat. I've never asked him why he left the village by the river but returned through the forest. This beach was where my father first became a man with the boat captain's wife. Maybe the captain discovered my father flirting with his wife, so he had my father thrown ashore. Maybe there was some other reason my father took off and met my mother. My mother was one hundred percent Thai,* according to my and my siblings' birth certificates. Pa said, "We can't let the little ones lose their roots. If the chance comes, we should take them back. Even if they run away they'll never escape where they came from."

Soon my village had many multistory homes sprouting up between the bamboo groves and tiled rooftops. The village was beginning to stir. The new sat on, pushed aside, and swept along the old all at once. It was truly different. Not too long ago, the village was just the village, tranquil, unassuming, lying sheltered by the sweet-flowing Kinh Thầy River. Now the village was like a teenage boy, making trouble, capering about, prone at times to taking risks. My father, whose mind worked similarly, also received a dizzying blow from these changing fortunes. How many schemes had he dreamed up to bend this village toward his own ideas? And now he himself

---

* The Thai are one of the many ethnic minority peoples living in the Vietnamese highlands. They are distantly and linguistically related to the Thai people in Thailand.

was being bent by it. The old man had aged swiftly, had thinned. People murmured. Old Nhan the gravedigger has contracted Yin disease. Only his children, Sơn, Mài, and I, knew what ailed him—an incurable, demeaning, long-lasting disease, ravaging him and all the people around him. I knew he'd never stop.

"Rotten to the core, ruined, just a shell." He clutched his head in his hands.

In all my life I will never understand his hatred for our village, the place he'd given up everything to return to.

Not too long ago, Sơn called me to his house to have a drink. Having seen him with his homemade motorbike hawking drinks at the bus station, I'd felt at peace.

"Pa says it's all for a reason."

I glowered, but Sơn maintained his easy manner.

"Like today, for example: the farmers have had to give up lots of things. The factories are shrinking the fields. Pollution is making the river smell all round the village's water sources, running all the way down to the delta. The places we used to hunt for crabs and catch mussels are gone, and now even birds flying through there fall in flight; nothing can live there anymore."

The more he drank, the more he talked.

"Village structure has really broken down too, bro'. These days, families don't even stick together anymore. Out of a hundred families in the village, maybe sixty or seventy have someone away doing export labor or have moved out permanently for work. Our homes are spacious here, but five in ten families are dysfunctional, with just a mom or dad. These days, everybody thinks divorce is just a joke. It's the era of the practical, the material."

A motorbike clanked to a stop out in the yard. A buxom woman with piercing eyes stepped in carrying several small plastic bags. So this was the woman Sơn was living with? I got no feeling for her because of the haughty look on her face. I felt something breaking apart inside me. But I consoled myself. With my brother Sơn as he was, her sincerity and courage must've been proven when she moved in with him.

"Lộc, right?" she said. "Sơn called and said you were coming, so I bought some snacks so you two could have a long chat." One by one, she laid out the different dishes, then sat and had a few drinks with us before sneaking off to do some end-of-year debt collecting.

"I'm worried about Pa."

Sơn quietly drank his rice wine. After a while he said, "Everybody has one life. Whether an evil life or a good life, both are still a life. The Buddha sat in meditation to find a way to save lost souls. Living a human lifetime is also a meditation for finding your way. If you can live your life without worry or regret, you can be satisfied."

When had Sơn become so philosophical?

Life helps us work out a lot of things. But there are some things whole lifetimes can never solve.

Translated by Peter Ross and Charles Waugh

Wounds of the City

Đỗ Tiến Thụy

THE TRAIN STATION IN THE MIDDLE OF THE NIGHT. A SLEEPY SAIGON voice on the loudspeaker. Exhausted faces, stale air. An electronic display hung from the station roof running red glowing lines: "Welcome . . . *Kính chào quí khách* . . . Welcome . . ." Happily, I make out Dziu's bright eyes in the midst of the scattering crowd. I want to rush to her, to embrace her. But the question she asks stops me at once: "Why are you here?"

The hot iron tracks sizzle with rain. I too feel like a glowing hot bar of iron doused in cold water. If the return train were leaving immediately, I would go right now. But Dziu already has my pack in hand and has started walking toward the gate. I force myself to follow. Our cyclo circles through streets lit by flickering electric lamps, then drops us into a slum.

The sky is not yet light. Dziu tells me to sit and wait outside the door to let her roommates sleep a while longer. The many things I intended to say suddenly disappear. I lean my back against the damp moss of the wall and close my eyes. I left the army more than two months ago, but my mind keeps bugling reveille each morning at five. I open my eyes with a start as Dziu knocks on the door. A dozen gaunt faces with ruffled hair and disheveled clothes peer out. I stand as detached as heaven above the somewhat familiar, somewhat strange crowd of girls and their excited voices. "Brother Vũng!" "Don't you remember me?"

I nod rashly. "I remember, I remember. . . ."

But I don't recognize any of them. The day I joined the army, they were all still sickly, skinny little girls. But now . . . "We heard you were coming!" "We've been expecting you night and day." "How are your parents at home?" "Did Chút pass the high school entrance exam?" "We asked our families to send our local fish sauce—did you bring it?"

One of the girls dives to my backpack and lets loose a scream: "Why is it so light?"

Seeing their fallen faces, I regret very much that I hadn't imagined their longing for the simple foods of home and threw away the sack containing their sauce to lighten my load before boarding the train.

I avoid the girls' eyes by peering into the room. It's shabby, with clothes strewn everywhere. Two years of military service has taught me a passion for order. I despise sloppiness. But I can't just keep standing outside forever, so I force myself into the room, strangled by lines of drying clothes. The girls resume the barrage of inane questions for a few more minutes and then busy themselves preparing for work. Before I know it, the house is quiet. Dziu sits in thought for a moment and then looks up and asks cautiously, "How will you live?"

I feel the sting to my pride. "Naturally, I'll find some job to do. I'm no parasite, don't worry about—"

"I meant," Dziu breaks in, "what long-term job. . . ." She stands to escape the awkwardness of the moment. She boils a bowl of noodles for me and then sits watching me eat. When I set down the chopsticks, she whispers, "You . . . you should repack your bag and follow me to Uncle Cuông's place. It's not proper for you to stay here."

I set my jaw and sigh. Having met again without a fond word spoken, I have no choice but to pick up my bag and leave.

Uncle Cuông lives in the slum surrounding the export-processing zone. His gnawing questions unsettle me. His five children are poor learners and had to repeat their classes several times, and his wife, exhausted by worry and caring for the family, is now in the hospital. I force myself to lie to him according to my aunt's advice. Hearing the good news I make up about our family, he shines with happiness just for a moment.

"Rest for a few days to get well," he says. "I'll find a job for you."

Listening to him, I feel hesitant. He already has to watch out for the hundred-plus children of his fellow villagers who left the paddies to follow him here with hopes of changing their lives. I don't want to be another burden on his thin shoulders.

Each day, I scour the papers for some opportunity. Full of stories about robberies, rape, and murder, they make me throb with fear. I see hidden dangers everywhere. At night I can never fully fall asleep.

When Dziu visits, she doesn't ask whether I've found a job, but concern always shows on her face. One night, Uncle Cuông comes home shouting for joy from the door, "Somebody needs a security guard! The ad says, 'Requirement: male, age not over thirty, good health. Priority given to demobilized soldiers.'" I snatch the notice from him and read the whole thing at once. Dziu leans her head close to read with me and lets out a sigh of relief.

"So!" exclaims Uncle Cuông. "The two of you will work near each other, then you can get married, rent a private house, and no longer have to have one in the east and one in the west like now!"*

I immediately prepare a resume. The garment factory will require me to spend my own money to study at a private security company. But that's nothing to worry about. After so many years in the military, drilling over all kinds of obstacles, I'm not afraid to do anything.

I had been a commando, so at the security school, I am invited to be a tutor for shooting and martial arts. The hardest subject for me is the detective work. Apparently, in civilized society many people spend their money to hire detectives to follow their husbands or wives around. I have to learn how to place hidden microphones, to take surreptitious photographs, and to follow subjects in order to locate their "dragonfly nests."

I have no experience with love, so this form of exercise pains me in many cases. But for my future, I try very hard to learn and to pass.

On graduation day, my mind feels like a trapped bird beating its wings, wishing to fly away to Dzịu. But I have to wait, making my legs ache, and wait again some more until a flashy car pulls into the courtyard accompanied by uniformed guards riding big-engined motorbikes. At first, I think it must be some politician's convoy. Then I learn it belongs to Linh Trường, the famous singer. Dressed in a fancy shirt and wearing black sunglasses, Linh Trường looks from one end of the row of "soldiers" to another. Surprisingly, he stops and stands looking bewildered in front of me. I alone am asked to meet with him in private. "Will you come work for me?" he asks. "Your task will be to stay by my side and to close and open the car door for me." His offer of a five-million-dong monthly salary brings the blood rippling to my face. I nod.

When Dzịu and I speak about it later, she gives me a panic-stricken look and says, "Why don't you come work at my company—the wages are low but at least we can be near one another?"

I try to appear wise and say, "Let me go work for him to earn money for a wedding; that's when we'll really be together forever."

When I have the first month's salary, I decide to rent a private room for Dzịu. I don't want her breathing the foul air coming from the old place's black water drainage ditch filled with floating garbage. I don't want Dzịu to have to see drug addicts every night dropping their pants to shoot up as if no one was around. I don't want Dzịu to have to close her eyes and

---

* A reference to workers who in the past had to leave their families to go to other Communist countries for work.

cover her ears when passing through the garbage dump to ignore the boys and girls having sex. Even so, the move arouses the criticism of my fellow villagers. But I put it out of my ears. I have to stay beside the singer day and night—there's no way I've rented the private room for me and Dziu to use together. Still, with the new place I worry that Dziu has to pass an old deserted airport on her way to work. When I mention my concern, Dziu just smiles, pulls a big pair of sharp-pointed sewing scissors from her purse, and says, "I dare anyone to try to mess with me!"

I get used to traveling with Linh Trưởng from one show to another. In the evenings, I buy flowers from street stalls to give to Linh Trưởng's fans, then at night, when these same people climb up to the stage to give him the flowers, I slide in between and pull them back down. When Linh Trưởng has an outburst of passion and jumps down from the stage to greet the audience, I sweat it out acting as his shield. Though he's already very famous, Linh Trưởng is never satisfied. He organizes live shows, hangs banners overshadowing the sky, and sends fireworks exploding into the streets. One night, the whole stadium is overpacked with fans dancing and screaming. To our dismay, Linh Trưởng has sung just one song when heaven plays a nasty trick and unexpectedly pours down a torrential rain. Like a rooster soaked in rainwater, Linh Trưởng struts around the stage angrily for a few minutes and then furiously rushes offstage and into the car. Stunned, our team of bodyguards races to our motorbikes to look for him. As his personal bodyguard, I always ride in the car, and so I have no motorbike. I have to run out to the street to hire a motorbike taxi to chase after him. At home, Linh Trưởng darts inside and slams the door. I stand transfixed under the haughty statue of himself that Linh Trưởng has installed in the foyer. With a hungry belly and soaked clothes, my teeth chatter uncontrollably. But I don't dare go any further. Late that night, Linh Trưởng calls for me. It's the first time he's asked me to enter his bedroom. The room is magnificent, like a real palace, complete with a throne flanked by a majestic pair of elephant tusks. Frightened, I stand with my arms crossed, waiting for an order.

Linh Trưởng is crying, with tears streaming down and snot running from his nose. He feels terrible about the concert that night and the ten thousand people in the audience. When he tires of crying, he sends me to get some booze. His cellar contains hundreds of bottles of Western and Chinese varieties, all stacked together on many shelves. Rice wine impregnated with a bear paw or a tiger penis or velvet antlers or exotic flowers and plants preserved in all sorts of jars.

"Drink!" Linh Trưởng cries. "Drink with me! A singer's life is thankless, you know."

I reluctantly take the glass he offers, thinking hard about what he said. He called his life thankless. What, then, can my life be called? Unfortunate? I was born in a rice paddy. But the rice paddy could not sustain me. Some days I had meals, others I did not. Some days I went to school, others I did not. The university gate was too high and too big, but the sweet potato and rice seeds were too small. Many of my ambitions have already been buried at the bottom of my backpack, and now I'm living the life of an errand boy. So I'm the one who has the right to drink and get drunk. At first I'm cautious, but soon I'm right there with the singer, holding my own. When drunk, people like to talk a lot and to smash things. The singer throws a half-full bottle of Napoleon brandy at the large lacquer painting on the wall, and I pound my fists on the flower-patterned carpet. The singer cries again. And when he tires of crying, he sings. His gummy, flat voice makes me laugh.

"What are you laughing at?" he snaps.

I don't respond but instead raise my voice in the only song I can really sing, "Love Song." Listening to me, Linh Trường gapes in amazement. "Your voice," he says, "it's so good! You're a natural tenor. But that song you sang . . . it's . . . pagoda music. A famous singer from Hanoi could come down here and maybe get two hundred thousand dong for a show like that." He snickers. "One of my shows pulls in at least twenty million. Damn! The same thing some musicians call sentimental, people slobber all over themselves to hear. Critics flame me for singing 'cheap music.' Motherfuckers—as if I give a fuck. I sing cheap music to be able to buy expensive things. You get me? Do I lack anything?" The singer sweeps his hands in a circle meant to suggest the whole world. "The only thing I don't have . . . is love."

I gape at Linh Trường.

I've often felt jealous, seeing him onstage with thousands of girls rushing to him like colorful butterflies plunging into a flame. But seeing the smoky eyes of Linh Trường in the desolate room, I can tell he really is a lonely guy. We drink. Drink and drink and drink. In a body exhausted by booze, my mind floats without direction. I give up and let Linh Trường sweep me into a crazy game against all reason and whose passion could never be satisfied. When I wake in the middle of a slimy mess, the first thing I feel is a burning sensation in my crotch. I sit up, holding my raw, red manhood, and sob. I quickly put on my clothes and run from the house.

"Why are you like this, darling?" Dziu asks, her voice strangled with fear. Tears well in her eyes. "What did you do? What happened?"

Her incessant questions utterly shame me. I lie crying quietly as Dziu gently and bashfully hovers nearby. Suddenly, Dziu stops and her voice turns hard: "I understand now!" She turns away. "Why not ask me?"

My throat chokes on her question. Yes, she could have given herself to me. But we were born in the rice paddies. The rice paddy opened the door for our love, but it also erected an insurmountable wall of propriety between us. In all the days we'd been in love, our most intimate moment passed the night before I left for the army, when we sat close to each other on the river dike. The full moon sparkled on the gold-plated waves, dancing with the river's rippling current. We spoke in wandering sentences without beginning or end. Our hands unintentionally pulled up all the grass surrounding us. I had to take a deep breath to find the courage to wrap my arm around her shoulders. During my years in the army, every night I dreamed about her soft body trembling in my arms, and like a skittish bird, I trembled too. My silly virgin lips had until now retained the sweet taste of the brief kiss we shared on the dike that full-moon night.

But now this bad thing has already happened, . . . and I know Dziu resents me for it. I don't know how to explain; I just bow my head and hope she can forgive me. Finally, Dziu softens. "You have to come work with me at the factory. My monthly salary is six hundred thousand, enough for us to live frugally. All your salary, saved this past year, will be enough for our wedding."

I breathe a sigh for escaping my offense, happy to try on a security guard's uniform.

Every day, I stand in front of the gate, checking visitors' papers and keeping an eye on the workers going home after their shift to see if anyone looks suspicious. Each morning, I give Dziu a ride to work. At lunch we eat at the same table. Only at night do I have to leave her to go sleep at Uncle Cuông's. When the afternoon shift ends, I can always pick Dziu out of the exhausted crowd right away because of her bright, beautiful eyes.

Six months pass this way, and then I begin to worry that the light in Dziu's eyes is going dark. The doctor diagnoses macular degeneration. I nurse her with some cheap fish oil and clumsy words of comfort. I tell her to rest, but Dziu shakes her head. Her lips press tightly together, and her eyes light up faintly. Somehow I know something serious is about to happen, so I question her closely. Dziu stammers to say something but does not speak. Later, I ask Uncle Cuông and some of the other workers, but they only hint that I will know soon.

And that day finally comes. The workers have just started their shift when the factory siren sounds. It's not the shift siren but the alarm. My walkie-talkie barks continuously. The Korean manager, Hun Suk, shouts, "The workers are on strike! All security guards must assemble to keep order." I run toward the crowd, shocked to see Uncle Cuông and Dziu standing at the front of the strikers. Her face hardens. In her clenched hands she holds a protest sign. Her eyes light up among the boiling sea of protesters. I stand shoulder to shoulder with the security team to create a protective barrier behind which Hun Suk can negotiate. "Increase wages! Increase wages! Increase wages!" demand the protesters. "No! No! and No!" Hun Suk screams back. The workers shout a series of slogans like rolling thunder, their fists raised toward the sky. Confronting the will of hundreds of people, I feel scared, my feet unsteady. But the manager Hun Suk's attitude does not change.

"Go back to work if you don't want to be fired!" he shouts. "If you want your wages increased, please just increase the number of shifts you work!"

The manager cuts his hand through the air to give orders to the security team and turns back toward his office. The crowd rushes up but can't get past us. Unintentionally, my billy club whacks into Uncle Cuông's face. I quickly look away but not before I see his watering eyes.

That night, when I return home, I see Uncle Cuông lying with his hand crossed over his forehead. Skulking in like a bad dog, I skip changing my clothes and climb straight into bed. The silence becomes a lack of air. Unable to bear it any longer, I speak first: "Uncle . . . I am sorry! I had to perform my duties. . . ."

Uncle Cuông just lies there silently.

I try again. "Is there no other way than to strike, Uncle?"

Uncle Cuông then says vaguely, "What a pity! Those youngsters are at the age of flying high, but they have to face down sewing machines all day. When they get home, they just fall asleep. Their minds have become dull, knowing nothing of a life outside. At this rate, none of the girls will be able to find a husband!"

After three days of the strike, the factory becomes a wasteland. Manager Hun Suk's face has started to look worried; his way of speaking wavers. Everyone thinks that sooner or later he will make concessions. But heaven is on the side of the strong. News of a big tropical storm sweeping through the northern delta during the flowering season of the rice plants falls like a thunderbolt. Surging seawater floods the crops. The women workers hug each other and cry. Exhausted, they ask each other: "What do we do now? We must return to work. We have to work to send money home to help them!"

Dzịu insists on signing up for more shifts despite my best attempts to dissuade her. "My sisters are all working extra hours too," she says. "How can I stay home?" Every time I watch these women begin to weave home on their bicycles, I feel ashamed. I sign up for more shifts too so that Dzịu and I can come and go together and still find joy in that.

But one night, I have to stay on duty through the early morning and cannot take Dziu home when the shift ends. I stand guard through the early morning feeling hot in my heart as if it were on fire. I have a premonition that something horrible has happened and leave my post to rush home. I stand as if dead in front of a raucous crowd. Dziu sits motionless on the bed, her tattered uniform streaked with blood. She stares back at me with the withered, no-soul eyes of someone looking at a stranger. Several police officers have arrived and are taking statements from witnesses. I rush to Dziu, hold her by the shoulders, and ask repeatedly, "What happened? What happened to you?" Seeing me, people in the crowd ask each other, "Who is this man?" I scream back at them, "I am her husband! Her husband!" The crowd looks at me with disgust. "Her husband? What kind of husband lets his wife go home alone in the dark through such a neighborhood? Such a husband should be thrown to the dogs!" Through the cacophony, the painful facts begin to take shape. Six students—the sons of tycoons from other provinces renting houses in the "aristocratic quarter"— had gathered together to drink. Thoroughly wasted, they egged each other on to race their motorbikes at the abandoned airstrip. When they saw Dziu cycling home alone, they surrounded her, popping wheelies like wild rearing horses. Within seconds, Dziu became a rabbit surrounded by wolves. The garment scissors in her hands were nothing, like a prop used to scare children.

I squeeze my hands into fists, clench my teeth, and roar. I race out, running toward the airport. But the police and the neighborhood watch has already rushed to the homes of these "heavenly sons," handcuffed them, and taken them away.

The police bring us to the station. They ask Dziu to describe the incident. She holds the pen, sitting silently for hours. They ask Dziu to have a medical examination. She faints in my arms like a withered leaf. Hugging her cold body, I have the unnerving sensation that I'm holding a dead body on its way to the morgue. Later the next morning, we are finally sent home. We haven't yet regained our composure when a woman with a thickly powdered face comes to find us. She introduces herself as the mother of one of the six goat boys. Not beating around the bush, she lays a sharp, square pile of money on the table.

"What's done is done; our family would like to offer you ten million dong to compensate you for . . . your health!"

I don't yet know what to say, but Dziu grabs the pile of money and throws it into the woman's face, shouting, "Get out of here! My whole girlhood . . . do you have any idea?"

Taken aback, the woman picks up the pile of money and timidly steps backward to the door. But she quickly regains her composure, looking sideways at me and then curling her lips. "Girlhood," she sneers. Then she spins away, brushing off her rump like she's putting the dust behind her. She speeds off in her shiny car, spewing a plume of exhaust that burns our eyes.

The next day, Dzịu and I are again asked to come to the police station. The police captain who receives us says cordially: "You should think twice about this. To make a lot of noise won't do you any good; it'll just waste your time."

I shoot back, "No good? We can see justice done! Just do what the law says and take action! We're not going to settle or withdraw."

I take Dzịu's hand, and we storm out across the police station courtyard. A lieutenant with a very young face snatches my arm and whispers, "Take this to the end, you've got us on your side, don't be afraid of anything!"

I nod in place of saying thanks. Just then, I catch a glimpse of the woman from yesterday standing in front of the cell door, looking back at us and the young police officer, saying, "Son, set your mind at rest; they can't do anything to hurt you."

The question burns in my mind: Who does she mean by "they"?

For a week, I lie holding and consoling Dzịu while she cries. Since the day we first fell in love, she has never cried in front of me before.

"I have nothing for you now. . . ."

Her teary words, biting and cold, as if shocked with electricity, freeze my heart. But I have to be strong. I kiss her eyes and say, "Don't say that! With me, you are still pure as heaven."

Dzịu shakes her head.

I say, "Don't think too much about this. I've also been used badly. . . ."

Dzịu looks into my eyes. "You are a man. You may be corrupted but that just makes me sad; I would never blame you for that. But with me . . . like this, how can you still love me?"

I don't know how to answer her. All words at the moment have no meaning. I hold her tightly in my arms. I have to love her! Have to love her! Only by loving her in this moment can I hope she will recover from the shock. Thus, reason urges me while my heart remains confused. The scratches and bite marks as if from vicious animals are still fresh on her body. She lies still, her eyes searching my face. My tears fall to her face, joining the stream of her own. I caress her cheek, my touch like a breeze gliding over a field crushed by a storm. At first, she acquiesces without emotion, but the waves of our love resonate deeply in her emotions, gently and gradually overwhelming her. She sinks both hands into my tangled hair, her fingers tingling with electricity, transferring to me a kind of numbing happiness. Falling asleep in each other's arms, I submerge into a strange dream. From the middle of a black stream full of floating debris and white fish bones, freshly blossoming purple water lilies emerge, emitting an utterly pure fragrance.

A few days later, out of the blue Dziu says, "We have to go back to work. Staying at home like this means we'll starve to death."

"Oh!" I say. "Shouldn't we wait for the court to settle the case?"

"I won't go to court. I . . . I . . . am afraid."

"What are you afraid of? What do you have to lose?"

Dziu doesn't answer other than to shake her head. Looking at her glittering eyes, I finally understand. Dziu doesn't want to go to court. So far, we have kept what happened to her a secret. Uncle Cuông and her coworkers from our village don't know. Going to court, the whole story would come out. We are country people. That's all there is to it—to forget it. We will just have to regard the whole thing as a nightmare. We have to live, to raise ourselves up. . . .

I return to playing my role in security, each day watching streams of workers in their grayish-blue uniforms slowly jostle into the factory. My Dziu grows paler and skinnier with every passing day. I try to encourage her to keep up her strength by joking with her. "Eat more!" I say. "You're as thin as a stick of dry wood, how can you have a baby?" Dziu smiles back.

One day, she says, "We've saved enough. This Tet let's go visit our village. I'll buy presents for our parents, and the rest of our savings can be spent for the wedding." Is it necessary to have a wedding when we so completely belong to each other? But we are the children of peasants. We have to obey the rules handed down to us by our ancestors. We agree to celebrate our wedding twice. Before going back to have a nice warm wedding in our village so our relatives will consider us husband and wife, we will have a wedding here to give our hard-working fellow villagers the chance to enjoy a happy day. We ask Uncle Cuông to be the master of ceremonies because he can represent both our village and our coworkers. We have the invitations printed, book a restaurant for the reception, and make an appointment to go to the people's committee office in our ward to register. We count down each day, wishing for the arrival of the moment we can put the rings on our fingers.

But the wedding has to be postponed. I'm on duty one day standing guard when Manager Hun Suk calls me in. Security monitors of all sizes line one wall of his office. Facing the opposite wall, a skinny worker stands with his head bowed like he's being punished. With a start, I realize that the worker is Uncle Cuông. Before I can speak, Hun Suk jerks his chin toward Uncle Cuông and says, "This lowlife is a thief! Rough him up for me."

I freeze, unable to believe my ears. I've seen two girls forced to run a hundred laps around the dining hall, just for coming into the kitchen for a drink of water during their shift. I've also heard a story about two girls who'd been strip-searched on the suspicion of hiding fabric under their clothes. The degrading way this foreign manager has punished "these illiterate hicks" makes me ashamed, but I have no chance to defend them. There's no way Uncle Cuông is a thief. Country people may be nosy, but because we are, we know each other like the hair on our scalps. I know Uncle Cuông—even if he were starving—would never steal.

Seeing my doubt, Manager Hun Suk smacks his lips and thrusts his chin at the monitor in front of him, which shows an unclear shadow of a male worker doing something equally unclear. The angle of the shot makes it difficult to see anything.

"He plotted with other workers to steal two rolls of fabric from me."

The fact that Hun Suk's explanation sounds more like an accusation chills me.

"Beat him!"

His urgency startles me. Hesitantly, I approach Uncle Cuông. "Uncle!"

Uncle Cuông turns his austere but sturdy face toward me.

"Is it true—you stole something?"

He shakes his head.

"Beat him! If you don't hit him, you're fired!"

Hun Suk's Korean-accented Vietnamese sounds like a loud growl.

Uncle Cuông looks at me sympathetically. "Just hit me! Never mind. I can take it."

I lean in to Uncle Cuông's ear and whisper, "I don't believe you're a thief. Why should you be punished?"

Uncle Cuông whispers back, "Just hit me! Hun Suk wants to send a warning. If I don't plead guilty, he said he'd fire everyone in the workshop."

"Beat him!"

Now I understand the situation. Uncle Cuông will take the beating not to get a morsel to eat for himself but to protect the hundreds of girls from my village whom he loves like his own children. And I . . . I will have to beat him to do the same.

I blink quickly, trying to signal an apology, then raise the rubber club. The blow raises a cloud of fabric dust from Uncle Cuông's clothes and makes a loud plopping sound. I intentionally grazed the seat of his pants but can still feel my own buttocks twist with pain.

"Hit him! Hit him! Hit him!"

After each of Hun Suk's cries, I swing my hand. The rubber club becomes heavier and heavier until I cannot lift it again.

"Son of a bitch!"

Hun Suk jumps at me, snatches the club, and strikes. The sound of the solid thumps bounce off Uncle Cuông's skin and flesh, echo, and swirl in my ears, causing me sharp pain. I stand with wide-open frog eyes, watching my boss beat my fellow villager and not knowing what to do. At first, Uncle Cuông clamps his mouth shut, but then, unable to bear the pain, he can no longer hold his tongue and a string of curses bursts forth. Like a big strong buffalo stung by hornets butting a tree for revenge, Hun Suk rolls up his sleeves, rips off his tie, and clenches his teeth, striking repeatedly. The more he beats Uncle Cuông, the more it becomes like an addiction he enjoys. When Uncle Cuông can no longer stand, he collapses onto the floor like a body without a soul. Hun Suk goes mad. He roars curses and throws the club away. He kicks and punches and then kicks and punches some more. Before his eyes now, he no longer sees a worker but a sea of stubborn protesters inciting each other to complain. He wants to trample them underfoot, to crush all opposition. He jumps on Uncle Cuông's body, bringing all his enormous weight down on him. Uncle Cuông's painful groans drone in my ears. The sight of the splattered mess of half-digested rice, shit, piss, and blood sends a blinding white light through my eyes. Blood rushes into my chest. Peasant's blood, pumping mightily and about to explode, demanding to be released. I react. I am a twenty-four-year-old boy. Rice paddies have given me strength. A soldier's life has taught me how to attack. With my left hand I yank Hun Suk's head by his hair directly into my solid and pointed elbow, thrusting right into his red upturned face. I hear a scream and the sound of a body falling down like a butchered animal.

I rush to lift Uncle Cuông up into my arms and run into the street to call a taxi.

For a while, everything is blur. Only when I see Dziu and the other girls of my village rushing noisily toward me can I realize that I am standing with my head down in front of the emergency room. My body feels limp with weariness and completely hollow. I rejoice when the doctor pokes his head out to tell me to put Uncle Cuông on the stretcher and bring him into the examination room. I slip my hands behind his neck and knees, attempting to lift him, but I cannot. The doctor snatches my hand to look at my arm, his eyes big with surprise. "What happened?" I bend my arm to see and shudder when I find two of Hun Suk's teeth embedded deep into my elbow.

I return to my rented home exhausted and curl into a feverish, shivering sleep. When I wake, Dzịu cleans my wounds, looking at me in a doleful and worried way. "Go into hiding," she says, "I beg you!"

No, I have nothing to hide. I am waiting for irons to be put on my hands so I can stand in a court of law and say the urgent things that need to be said.

"You must go into hiding right away! They'll hire someone to kill you!"

That makes me think. I am not afraid of facing the law. But I am the son of peasants; I will lose to the law of the jungle in the dark.

Dzịu packs all my things into my backpack for me. "Go back to our home village," she says. "The city is not our place."

"Will you come with me?"

"No, I have to stay. I'll stay and work to support you and the rest of my family. You have to do it again . . . do it all over from the beginning. We're still young, you know. . . ."

Dzịu pushes me to the train station. The train lets off a melancholy burst of a whistle. I stare through the train-car window. City lights twinkle red, yellow, purple, and green. Advertising banners hang everywhere like spiderwebs, some flying the picture of Linh Trường. Grimy bars emit dim lights and flat voices singing. Everything rolls backward behind me as the iron wheels clack over the rails.

I am out of danger. But behind me, she and the others from my village still struggle in the streets. I desperately want to know what happened with Uncle Cuông and Hun Suk. I search through the pile of newspapers left behind by other passengers. Several papers feature articles angrily condemning the common use of violence against laborers, along with photos of Uncle Cuông's bruised face and an apology from Manager Hun Suk, who promised not to fire Uncle Cuông. All the articles I read focus mainly on the role of the trade unions and the press. Not a single word mentions me. What I've done was just some foolish game, and no one seemed to care. Still, I know Hun Suk will not allow me to return.

Absentmindedly, I take up one last old paper. It is a literary journal with an ancient black typeface. I am young and indifferent to worldly affairs, so I've always ignored newspapers like this. But in this moment I need to feel connected to something else. My eyes drift over the lines loaded so heavily with the ways of people and the world, and then stumble on lines of poetry by a Buddhist monk named Lương Tử Đức:

A paddy wind bathes the exile's face
I return home to heal the wanderer's wound.

Were these lines written for us? No. We are the children of peasants, we can
not be wanderers. But we can be exiles. Exiled in our own homeland, then
struck with fatal wounds. Aching wounds that still smolder in my heart.

Translated by Nguyễn Hùng and Charles Waugh

Sage on the Mountain

Đỗ Bích Thúy

MA AND MY NEPHEW, SINH, MET ME AT THE FORK WHERE THE TRAIL turned up the slope that led to the house on stilts. It perched precariously above everything else, old, obsolete, tiny. Anytime I remember something about my mother, I also see that house with its nine stairs where my wobbly legs first toddled into the life full of storms I'd just returned to.

My eyes suddenly blurred. I was confused. "Ma! You're healthy? Good God, I was so worried!"

"If you knew I was in good shape, you wouldn't have come back, would you, Dzin?"

"Look . . . I beg you, Ma. Don't make up stories like that. I came, didn't I? Don't you love me?"

My mother turned away, silent. She sighed gently, but it pained me as if a wind were twisting through my chest. Sinh hugged my neck, pressing his runny nose against my cheek.

"Auntie, Grandma's gone senile."

"Don't be rude!"

"It's true! Dad said so."

My parents had two children, me and my younger brother, Dzân. My father sacrificed himself for the country when I was just ten years old, and Ma stayed in my grandmother's house to help take care of her and her flock of little ones. Then, seemingly all at once, Grandma died, Pa's younger brothers and sisters all got married, I left, and Dzân got married and moved out of the house. It was like Ma was all by herself again. Fortunately, Dzân married a girl from our village, and since Sinh's birth, Ma's at least had this small comfort.

Ma went ahead, her hand in Sinh's as they slowly climbed the slope. I couldn't believe it—could my mother really be so stooped already? It was the mark of time, starkly changing my mother's body without deliberation, without warning. Her legs also seemed out of her control, and the path seemed longer, steeper, more uneven. In the old days, on this very same

path, I would sit Dzân on a palm leaf and hurtle down, screaming and dragging him behind. Once, we both fell down it, tumbling again and again, our
faces digging into the sandy soil, both of us trying not to cry out. Grandma
knew, but she didn't let Ma punish us. Dzân told me later: "Even then I
felt sorry for Ma. She couldn't even raise her kids the way she wanted." He
meant it as a criticism of Grandma. My grandmother had a reputation in Tả
Choóng as a terrible in-law. But she stayed with Ma all the way up till the
day she died, saying she couldn't bear living with any of her own sons or
daughters.

At the house, my sister-in-law was just coming home from our terraced
paddy. Dropping her bundles of harvested sticky rice plants at the bottom
of the stairs, she exclaimed: "Dzin, you're back! I almost didn't recognize
you. Each time you're even more beautiful—oh, you're really going to
make our village boys suffer!" She smiled, her dimples deep in her cheeks.
My sister-in-law was four years younger than me. The day she married my
brother, the boys of our village got so drunk many of them couldn't get
back to their own houses. People in Tả Choóng said that because Dzân
could read and write, he was better than the other suitors, and her father
agreed to give her hand for just thirty, even though a beautiful girl like
my sister-in-law could easily have fetched a hundred. One hundred silver
coins, one hundred pounds of chicken, one hundred pounds of pork, one
hundred pints of corn whiskey; if not from a wealthy family, a boy might
work until his death without fully repaying the bridal debt. My first day of
having a sister-in-law put me in high spirits; I could finally have some peace
of mind when I was away from home. And it was as if she had been born to
be an in-law in my family. She even ate just like my mother. In her, Ma had
another daughter—the one she actually wanted, not the one I was. I could
never hear what my mother needed. I rebelled. I went away. There were so
many times I felt exhausted from living and working in a foreign land and
I wished I could bury my face in my mother's bosom and cry. But still I
stayed far away from my mother, far away and for a long time.

The whole load of rice plants was about four big bundles, but my sister-
in-law just swung it onto her shoulder and trotted up the stairs, leaving
behind nine wet footprints, firm and steady. Taking one of the bundles of
rice plants, she deftly flipped it back and open, spreading it out like a flower
on the drying floor at the gabled end of the house. Several dozen bundles
had already been laid out.

"Looks like you've harvested a lot of sticky rice this year," I said.

"Yes, a lot, a bumper crop," she said slyly. "Plenty to cook for your wedding party. But will you ever come home to get married, Sister Dzin?"

"These days no one wants to marry a twenty-six-year-old, you dear girl. I'm an old maid already."

She smiled sweetly and said, "A tall tree is for strong climbers, Sister Dzin."

I put away my suitcase, took the bamboo shoulder pole, and followed my sister-in-law to the terraces to bring home the rest of the harvested rice. She walked very fast despite the thorn bushes snagging her calves. "This year everybody abandoned their terraces to go down the mountain to farm the lowland paddies. Even sticky rice seedlings can be transplanted down there, and lots of new types of rice can be threshed, so we don't have to pound any more. But Sinh's grandma said we still had to plant a few grains of the old sticky rice to eat at home, to make full-moon cakes, and to save for your homecoming."

Piles of harvested plants lay scattered along the terrace. Soon, when the rice stubble dried out completely, a fire would be lit to burn the stalks to the ground and then a new crop would be started. The afternoon sun fell on the golden yellow mounds of rice plants and on the gleaming velvet forests of oak and chestnut in the distance. A breeze crept over the mountains sweeping with it the smell of kitchen smoke from the silvery houses of the village of the Phù Lá.*

A boy with a dirty face was driving a crowded herd of goats down from the mountaintop. When he passed me, he suddenly stopped, his eyes wide with curiosity. I gave him a friendly smile and said, "You there, what's your name?"

He stared at me blankly.

"Your house is near the spring isn't it?"

I asked because when I waded across the stream at the entrance to the village, I saw a house with several rows of sheds nearby that looked like a goat farm. But the boy didn't speak. He just made some quiet unintelligible sounds. Then he thrust a handful of dark purple grass toward me, stuck out his tongue, and turned away, cracking his whip above the goats. My sister-in-law whispered: "That's Câm, the mute boy. Maybe you don't remember. In the old days when you were still at home, he usually brought fish to sell to Ma. Now he lives at different houses a few days at a time. He's nearly twenty, but it's like he doesn't grow up. What did he give you? Sage? He must've gone really far up the mountain if he's coming home this late." Now

---

* The Phù Lá are one of the many ethnic minority peoples of Vietnam. They live mainly in the northern provinces of Hà Giang, Lai Châu, and Lào Cai, which border China.

I recognized the familiar scent wafting up. This spicy, sweet, ever bitter scent had stayed with me, keeping me rooted to my whole peaceful childhood. It was so simple, but since I'd returned home, I had been unable to figure out what was missing and making me feel so unstable and empty. Câm's bunch of sage began to wilt with the heat.

After the sun went down, my brother Dzân came home carrying an oilcan on the back of his motorbike. He looked much older with his skin dark from work. And people say commune officials are idle. . . . On the dinner tray we had soup made with bamboo shoots and frog meat, a chicken roasted with lemon, and sage fried with a vinegary fermented rice extract called mẻ. Looking at the disk of cooked sage, I felt hungry but didn't dare take any with my chopsticks. I was afraid to eat it.

My sister-in-law was surprised—"Why did you say you liked sage?"

"I do," I said, "but . . ."

"But it's been so long," said my mother in an angry, hurt voice, "so long without eating anything bitter like this, you've forgotten how."

I was silent. Dzân repressed a sigh. On the wooden tray, the disk of fried sage wavered from my sight as I felt a roar from the back of my mind, echoing the sounds of a flood-rushing waterfall, the forest trees' bark cracking in the dry season, the little goats bleating at their mothers, the winter winds gusting on the roof of the house. That year . . .

The heavens had made the land dry up, and I followed Ma carrying bamboo tubes over two mountains, half a day's journey from Ta Choong, just to get to a small puddle of water full of moss. It was bitter cold. White frost sparkled in the air. The trees were full of dying leaves, the pumpkin creepers in the garden all dried up before giving fruit, and the radish seeds Ma had sown a month before never sprouted. Without pumpkin or radish, our village didn't have any vegetables for winter. One day, two days, then a month, every meal just grated cassava with salt. Dzân sobbed convulsively, making Grandma and then Ma cry. That evening, Ma went to the garden and gathered a handful of sage. Grandma said, "Don't risk it, mother of Dzin." My mother wavered a moment, then said, "The goats can eat it, we can too." Without proper meals for so long, everyone had cold sores. But sage had always been baked over a hot stone and used only for aromatherapy. No one ever ate it.

Ma boiled the sage, then fried it with mẻ. Mẻ was sour, and salt was savory, but the cooked sage remained bitter. I made the effort to swallow a few sprigs, but Dzân spit it out immediately and cried again. Eventually, however, we began to regain our strength, and as we gradually got used to it, the pains in our insides went away. Grandma took some of the cooked sage to our neighbors. Then the whole village followed our example. The more the villagers picked, the more the sage grew, despite the winter winds ravaging the earth. On the terraces, in the garden, even under the floor where the dried-out water barrel sat warping, sage could be found everywhere, compensation for the severity of the earth and sky.

Sinh had already curled into sleep, exposing his chubby round belly to the fire. My mother took up an unfinished piece of net to weave, and my sister-in-law made a pot of rice bran porridge while threshing the sticky rice at the same time. Dzân sat smoking his pipe. As the pot of bran porridge began to bubble on the stove, Ma raised her voice: "Dzân! Tell your sister what you wanted to say. You expected her to come home more often!"

My sister-in-law said deliberately, "As a commune official, you have to talk to outsiders all the time, how hard can it be to talk to your own sister?"

Dzân squirmed and spluttered, "Dzin's staying a while so I can say it tomorrow. I'll let her rest first."

"I'm not staying for very long," I said. "One or two days and then I'll have to go. I've still got a lot of work down there."

Dzân was like that. With outsiders he had no patience, but he had endless respect for his sister. Since childhood I had always had power over him. Not that I wanted it. My father was the head of our family, and he had only one son.

Dzân gave Ma a hard look, but she showed no response. It turned out he was having difficulties with her, over the new and the old. The commune's cadres had been urging all the villagers to adopt new social and cultural conventions that required changing some ways of living and eating. More than one tradition had been deemed unhealthy or obsolete. But Dzân, one of the community exemplars, came up against Ma as if he'd stumbled over his own doorstep. It was awkward and problematic for sure. He didn't know if my being at home for a few days would help or not.

Ma announced it was time for bed, then opened the trunk and took out my clothes from when I hadn't yet left home. "Still know how to wear them?"

"Yeah, but with my hair short like this, I don't think I can wind the turban."

My mother sighed. "You're so grown up now, I could never keep you home. Not even the forests or the high mountains could stop your feet from walking away. Later, when I die, will you come back to Tả Choóng? What kind of person will you marry, Dzin? Why don't you bring someone here so I can see his hands and face? Are you scared he won't respect you or your home? I might never know how big or small a cup of wine my son-in-law will offer."

I burst into convulsive sobs. For a long time, I hadn't cried like that. I hadn't known what to say to Ma when I left to follow my own path, when I struggled to escape the dim and the immense and the solitary, when I was afraid to fall into the expectations of being a mother or a sister-in-law. How could I explain anything in a way that would please my mother's heart? I held Ma's tiny cold body tightly. Where was her warmth, her vitality? Where were the full breasts of the mother? Where was the hair that smelled of rice, of pungent sage, of the savory aroma of burning grass?

It was a quiet night. Water murmured softly in the bamboo pipe. I had no idea how many times since I left that Dzân had been forced to replace that pipe. All at once the geckos began to chirp anxiously. I teared up, remembering Pa. When my father was still alive, he caught some geckos to raise at home. If you release a few young geckos on the roof during a rainy day, they'll stay there and never leave. The family of geckos grew to nearly a dozen, became totally used to humans, and with staring eyes would crawl back and forth over the threshold. Days when an odd number of geckos chirped would be sunny, evens would be rainy. Pa followed that forecast to arrange all our family affairs. When the border conflict broke out, our family evacuated together, leaving only my father behind to lead the commune militia. We didn't return home until the ceasefire. My father had sacrificed himself. Our old house had been ravaged, going gray with mold, the family of geckos long gone. Grandma began to cry, saying they must've followed my father. But this night, the geckos were calling again. I didn't know if any of them were the descendants of our old gecko family. I counted again and again but couldn't tell if the chirps were even or odd. My mother complained that in recent years the weather had swung erratically between sun and rain, our crops sometimes thriving, sometimes lost.

"Dzin," whispered my mother, "are you still awake?"

"Yes," I said. "What's the matter?"

"Tomorrow, I want you to talk to Dzân. Tell him if he doesn't like living at home, he can move into the commune office."

"Oh no! Why would you say that, Ma? Dzân would never dare do that."

In a strangled voice Ma said, "For more than sixty years I have been like a stream flowing downhill. Soon I'll reach the big river, soon I'll follow your father, and now he asks me to turn back, to flow upstream. He . . . your brother Dzân . . ."

"But I don't see what's so complicated, Ma."

"Ugh! Nothing! You're just like him, Dzin. How many years have people lived in stilt houses with the buffaloes, horses, and geese kept under the floor, and now suddenly your brother demands the buffalo be brought out to the garden, even though she's just had her calf and been sick night and day, unable to recover despite having plenty of salt. Geese used to stay put, and now, for no reason, they've been driven out from under the floor and I have to go find them every morning, one goose here, another over there, all over the village. Both of you learned to sit and walk on the floor before you got all grown up like that, and now he brings home a table and chairs. He said we'd have frequent guests, so our manners would have to be top-notch. But who decides what manners are good? All the guests wear nice clothes but keep their shoes on in the house. When they sit down to have a drink of water, they turn their backs on our ancestral altar. If they see children in the village, they pat their cheeks and run their hands all over the children's heads. But when I open my mouth, he tells me to tear down our wooden house and build a new tile-roofed house. When I was sick, I asked him to slaughter a goat and get a shaman to chase the ghost away, but he just shook his head and gave me a handful of red and green pills. Now that he's so smart, he wants us to follow the lowlanders in all we do. I don't need it. I don't want to have a child like that. I'll die right here." Ma's fragile chest heaved as she cried without tears. At her age she had already shed every drop of human suffering.

After a long while, Ma began to stir, slipping out of my arms and pulling back the blanket, waking me. "It's so late, Ma. Where are you going?"

"Go back to sleep. I'm going to check on the calf. I told Sinh's mother to pile dried rice husks to bank the fire, but I bet she forgot."

Earlier that afternoon, Mr. Tào from Ngàm Đăng Vài had come and asked to buy the newborn buffalo when it grew up a little. White buffaloes can't be used for plowing because it's taboo. But it was a pity to sell the calf, and a pity for the mother too. So even though Mr. Tào said he wouldn't take it home for a long time, Ma still hadn't agreed to take the money.

I couldn't sleep. The later the night grew, the colder it was. The weather here was like that; no matter how sunny the day, no matter if it dry-roasted the roof thatch a handspan deep, the night was still cold. The blankets were never put away. The blanket I pulled to my chin was heavy. It smelled of memories.

During her engagement, when my mother was sixteen, she spent a whole month weaving this blanket and a scarf and some dresses. She told me their first night together was very cold, but she absolutely refused to share the same blanket with Pa, forcing him to go out to the kitchen fire and sit smoking his pipe until morning. My mother came to her husband's house empty-handed, owning almost nothing because her father died very young and Ma had to live with an aunt and uncle. So she was like the cat crouching in fear near the kitchen of her husband's family. From morning to night she never looked up. At meals she never dared to eat her fill, and so at eighteen, she was even smaller and skinnier than when she'd married. My older sister was born and lived less than a month before dying of pneumonia. Another ten years later I was born. . . .

In the mountains winter always comes early. When the first leaves of the peach and plum fall, the spring begins to go dry, and the water flow falls beneath the layer of white pebbles. Winds from the canyons rush down, bringing the chilly air of the stones and rice leaves. The sage begins to dry, its roots clinging to the soil, hardening and turning dark brown in the frost. Many days, weeks, even months sometimes go by without sunlight, and in the middle phase of the moon, night is merely dim. This is the time of the least work during the whole year. Girls stay at home spinning linen; their cheeks warm by the fire and become a bright and cheerful red. Out on the terraces, only barley can be planted. Grains of barley are not as delicious as corn or rice, but the barley flowers are beautiful. The colder the weather, the brighter pink and green they are. The whole mountain range, with the terraces of one family connected continuously to another, flares in the colors of the barley flowers, outshining the sky. A family's whole terrace planted with barley yields only half a basket of grain, but all families plant it. There's nothing to it. Harvest the corn, the weather turns cold, then sow the barley seed. Grass can't grow, and the barley sprouts up very green; no one leaves soil unplanted.

Then the time comes when the horses clop at the gable, the pear trees bloom flowers white as snow, and spring has just arrived. Fathers wear sheathed knives and go out from their houses to search the village to see who has the biggest pig to share for celebrating Tet. Spring has come already but it will still be cold until March or April. Children driving cattle down the valley are not yet ready to leave their straw firestarters at home; all have chapped faces. Only the soil begins to break up and soften. Cows and goats can eat fresh grass, and water begins to flow in the bamboo troughs again. After Tet, sometimes the festival of one village overlaps the festival of another, and so the celebration can last up to a month. The markets teem with boys and girls dressed beautifully, wearing bands of silver, shopping less but watching each other more. A long time ago, my father saw my mother with her hair wound in a turban at a market like that.

Coming back in, Ma didn't return to bed but instead sat by the fireplace, poked the coals to rekindle the fire, and brought out the net she'd been working on. The flickering firelight shone on Ma, on her silver hair and wrinkled face, like something both real and unreal. A fear from nowhere rushed into me. The image of an open coffin with Sinh and his friends jumping in and out to play appeared clearly in my mind. My mother had prepared for the longest journey, to the hereafter, some five or six years ago. Three goats exchanged for a huge chestnut log that Dzân dragged home with the buffalo.

I went out to sit with Ma. A moment later, the rooster crowed and my sister-in-law also got up, standing on tiptoe to reach the flat winnowing basket of salt drying on the smoking shelf above the fire. The upcoming July full moon would be a big feasting day. Even in the poorest family, children would have new clothes. In each house there would be mincemeat pastries, banana cake, and steamed red or purple sticky rice. When I was little, I used to make Dzân follow me and my friends all the way to Khuoi Nam to meet with other children to play games of sticks and spin the top. When we got hungry, we could run into any house and be given enough cakes to eat our fill. July was normally a rainy month, but on the day of the full moon it stopped. Men went drinking at their friends' houses and sometimes got so drunk they didn't come home for several days.

My sister-in-law said, "This July full moon, you'll have to come home for sure! The last two July full moons, we made so many cakes it took weeks to eat them all up. Ma was worried that if you came back home and brought friends, we wouldn't have enough, so we just kept using more flour and more bananas. . . ." I looked at Ma. I wanted to ask if she just always wore an angry look but secretly really did love her daughter, but she seemed not to notice anything.

When it was not yet light enough to see someone's face, Dzân got up to leave, saying he had a meeting at the district office. Dzân looked at me as if he wanted to say something, then hesitated and left with his briefcase, the sputter of his Minsk engine fading away. My brother's sad eyes from when we were kids scrambling for each baked cassava kept tormenting me. It was rumored that people wanted Dzân to work in the district office, but he didn't want to go. Dzân was, unlike me, tied to his birthplace and could never leave, even though he'd had many opportunities to rise up. I felt both sorry and grateful for Dzân; he shouldered part of my responsibility for Ma, and surely my father's spirit was also happy.

Sinh got up and, without washing his face, pulled me down the stairs. "We have to go find the geese or Grandma will scold Pa."

"Where should we look?"

"I know where. Let's hurry!"

Sinh ran, pulling me to the stream where the waterwheel was pounding up and down. The flock was indeed sleeping there, all with one foot up and their heads under a wing. Unwillingly roused, they made a huge racket. In my village, every household raises geese to protect the house. With just two geese it was all right to open the gate and go out to work the whole day.

When we returned home herding the geese, my mother was waiting at the foot of the stairs. "Why aren't you wearing a coat, out so early in the morning, Sinh?"

Shrewdly, he ignored her. "I went with Auntie Dzin to fetch the geese. They are very obedient, Grandmother. They just need a little place outside near the water trough, that's all. Oh, Grandma," he said, "Grandma, don't scold my Pa, don't be angry with him anymore, my poor Pa. Grandma! Grandma, please agree. Just give me a nod." The boy nodded several times to prompt her. My mother looked at him, a twinkle in her eye that seemed close to a smile. Sinh was just like my brother, from his dark skin and small eyes to his wavy locks of hair. The spitting image of Dzân twenty years ago. It seemed like Sinh was trying to do what his father had struggled with for a long time but did not know how to manage. And my mother trusted him. Perhaps because she could still pick him up and hold him, even as her own children had spread their wings to fly so high and far away.

At the foot of the stairs lay a huge blue stone, large enough for four or five people to stand on. My father had dragged it from the edge of the stream after a big flood. It was on this stone that I stood with my father for the last time, listening to his instructions with tears pouring down my face until I finally let go of his shirttail. I can't remember how many times since then I've stood in that same spot, facing up to the soaring Tây Côn Lĩnh mountain range wreathed with white fog, feeling a warmth, a certain vitality that I can step confidently into the world and into my life.

The sun rose. Red like a halo of fire. Signaling a very sunny day. With sun like that, in just three days the sticky rice would be dry, ready to be placed on the smoking shelf. Every year after the harvest, the shelf running from one end of the house to the other was always packed full of rice and corn. Ears of corn tied into knots dangled below, rice piled above. In good years, when all the rice from the previous year had yet to be eaten, the new rice would be put on top. My mother used to say in the old times that at my father's parents' house there were bundles of rice older than the youngest uncle.

A bell tinkled outside along with the sound of heavy steps. It turned out to be the mute boy, Câm, herding goats up the mountain. He stopped at the gate of my house, waiting for my sister-in-law to drive out our goats. I said, "I'll go with him."

"What for?" asked my sister-in-law. "He can tend the animals by himself. Besides, it's really far, Dzin."

"It doesn't matter how far," I said. "I'll get there. I want to go find some sage."

"Then tell him to get it for you. There's no need to go and get tired."

"No, I want to do it myself."

Ma grumbled, "In the old days, sage sprawled everywhere, even to the ground under the house, and even begging you, I couldn't get you to eat it. How come you're so hungry for it now?"

Câm's face lit up. His eyes twinkled, his face suddenly both happy and sad. Maybe always being alone, he often felt this way. We walked up toward the rising sun. Still behind the mountains, its rays looked like the blade of an enormous paper fan, reflecting upward. The goat path grew steeper and steeper; mosquito larvae wriggled on the scattered yellow leaves soaked in dew. The higher the path led, the gloomier the forest became. In forests like this, kids busy playing wouldn't know when night fell. Overhead, the canopy of leaves was thickly knit and filled with the whirring of bees. It was hard for me to keep up with Câm. The goats needed no urging to run ahead, scouring the dense, thorny bushes.

And then I was standing on top of one of the most majestic mountains of the Tây Côn Lĩnh range. The wind gusted as if it wanted to sweep me flying high into the air. And there, bursting out before me, intense green, deep purple, silvery white, drifting like waves, the whole mountainside was alive with fresh young sage that had just awoken from the blanket of fog. I rushed into it without thinking, lowering my face down to it, half-dreaming, half-awake, as if transported back to the years of so long ago. Those years sometimes seemed to give way to the fast pace and constant struggle of modern life. I met my father there. He was still strong and whole. I wrapped myself in his warm embrace.

I had returned to the place I was born, the place where the sun rises late and sets early.

I'd come home to the high mountains.

Translated by Nguyễn Hùng and Charles Waugh

Waiting for the Ferry

Kiều Bích Hậu

CHIẾN'S CELL PHONE RANG, VIBRATING NOISILY ON THE TABLE. CHIẾN pushed aside the computer mouse and checked the name of the caller flashing on the screen. Liêu! Again already! Chiến wanted both to pick up the phone and also to just ignore it. Calling at this time of day meant Liêu had succumbed to another one of her bouts of wanderlust, but he was so ridiculously busy today!

The phone kept flashing and skittered crazily on the table. Chiến clucked his tongue and picked it up.

"Chiến's escort service, what can I do to you, Madame?"

"Hey! I should slap your mouth, you naughty man. Where are you now?"

"Where am I always at this time?" said Chiến, scratching tentatively at the top of his head.

"Can't you ever stop doing paperwork, you poor stiff? In fifteen minutes come down to the gate; this Madame will be there to pick you up."

"Oh all right." Chiến hung up and glanced around the room.

The secretary's plump freckled face was bent toward her computer screen as her fingers pattered over the keyboard like rain. The girl from marketing, wearing another of those short skirts, put one hand on her hip as she spoke loudly into her cell phone, a curl of her dyed blonde hair falling onto her shoulder. Every few minutes, she let loose a burst of laughter like a foghorn. The two technicians, so alike they were practically twins, had their eyes glued to their computer screens. And the shaggy, gray-haired department head sat at his desk scowling over a notebook, his thick glasses hanging from the bridge of his nose.

Chiến took a sudden deep breath. Every day was the same. Nothing special whatsoever. He clicked the mouse to shut down the computer. He picked up his hat and said to the department head, "Mr. Minh, I'm going out for awhile."

The department head, still bent over his desk, cast a suspicious glance toward Chiến.

"Sure, sure, go away."

Chiến closed the door. He still had the designs for two advertisements to complete this week. For sure, Mr. Minh would be on him tomorrow morning. Never mind! Go already! As he left the gate, he saw Liêu drive up on her Attila motorbike. She smiled at him, her eyes bright. She wore light-blue jeans, tight on her long legs that she was so proud of. She usually pinched his ears when she caught him staring at them. Her short pink T-shirt showed the top of her jeans, and she looked as fresh and delicious as a cold slice of apple.

"Hell's bells, I must look a mess for you to look so confused. Get on the bike already."

Chiến obediently sat behind her on the motorbike. Liêu never let him drive when they left the city. She told him she wanted to drive for him, and also this way he wouldn't block her view, so she could enjoy the scenery along the banks of the river.

Liêu drove fast. Her dyed blonde hair, loosely curled like egg noodles, blew back with the wind, splashing into his face. He could smell the strong familiar scent of her perfume. Such pleasure! Chiến dared to nuzzle her shoulder, wanting instead to nibble it just a bit.

Liêu shrugged him off.

"Sweetheart, get that cobra nose off my shoulder. Unless, of course, you want me to crash us into a truck."

Chiến forced himself to sit up, his hands clutching at the sissy bar behind him.

"Hey, by the way," he said excitedly, "I found a fat hen for you. One of my buddies is getting married. He's fixing up his house and wants to redecorate the whole thing, wants you to do the interior design. He's rich as hell; easy for you to cut his throat. He says he just needs something beautiful and luxurious. Monumental, he said."

"Fantastic! If it works out, I'll give you a big commission."

"You don't have to do that, but I do want something else."

"What's that, sweetheart?"

"You . . . should find work at a company. Always staying home like you do, it's crazy."

"It's not crazy at all. Anyway, any half-decent company would fire me in less than three days. What kind of boss would put up with me?"

"Be patient—you'll find the right boss."

"No way! Unless it's a dream, or a fairy tale."

"You just need confidence and to look for a job—the right boss will appear, one who'll put up with your craziness. You only need a little grace, and the fairy tale will happen for real."

"You said it would be easy. And you just said I was crazy. You really must want to be slapped today; don't think I didn't notice."

Liêu lifted her chin, sending another maelstrom of hair into his face. He caught several strands in his mouth and tasted them. A little bitter. They tingled on his tongue and made it feel numb. Liêu now drove the motorbike slowly along the winding path. The wheels rolled over patches of dry white soil cutting through the thick grass.

Chiến didn't want to quarrel with Liêu. He straightened his back, rested his chin lightly on her shoulder, and with wide, appreciative eyes took in the yellow and green cornfields along the riverbank. It was late afternoon with big white clouds flying slowly across the sky, but the burning July sun still shone. The cornstalks looked like sword strokes against the sky, the tassles blossoming like fireworks. The fields of corn soaked in the golden sun, rolling like silk before his eyes. Liêu was also silent. She looked far away as if wanting to record every detail of the beautiful scene. The path cutting through the corn looked like the line on the back of an enormous green beetle, the motorbike just a tiny mite crawling along the green beetle's shell. Liêu stretched herself, breathing deeply to smell the cornflowers' sweet perfume. "Please green beetle," she murmured, "I'm standing on your back, let's fly."

Chiến wrapped his arms around Liêu, his chin still resting on her shoulder, and whispered, "I have to hold you tight. Seems like you might fly away."

Liêu let him do it. She just let her body go slack. Wind from the river blew over the cornfield, its voice murmuring. The cornstalks leaned with the wind. Liêu craned her face to the sky and shouted, "Hey, I'm here!"

Chiến also sat up and shouted, "Hey river!"

They burst into happy laughter, the sound mixing with the murmur of the leaves.

"Why not say more?" Chiến's chin pressed more firmly into Liêu's shoulder. "Let me say it for you. I wish we would dissolve and become the wind and fly away. Fly away. We are the wind on the river. Blowing forever and ever. Loving the banks of the river."

"We're here," said Liêu. "Look at the best driver on the riverbank."

The motorbike rolled down the bank to Mrs. Hà's little snack stand next to a bamboo pier on the edge of the Red River. Liêu and Chiến left the motorbike near one of the stand's four old bamboo poles. The palm thatch roof swayed with the poles, which had not been fully set into the cracked earth. Several sun-bleached wooden benches surrounded a small table made from an old door, its paint faded and peeling. The table sagged with the weight of its load: a large jar of strawberries steeping in juice, a basket full of teapots, soda bottles, cups, glasses, and spoons. Several bottles of sticky-rice wine stood beside a plate of green guava. And behind all this stood Mrs. Hà, her face already old but her lips still smiling and lively, her eyes heavy-lidded as if she'd been drinking.

"Hello Miss and Mister, you're early today."

"Early how?" asked Chiến as he sat down on the bench and laid his hat next to him.

"I only know earlier than usual," Mrs. Hà murmured. She opened the jar of strawberries and ladled juice into a glass.

Liêu sat beside Chiến and stretched her legs. A man sitting across the table glanced at them as she stretched, then looked back toward the river.

"Here you go," said Mrs. Hà. She set two cold glasses of juice in front of them.

Chiến immediately raised the glass to his lips and took a big swallow. "Whew, nothing tastes better than this." The flavor was sweet and strong but also soft, nearly fermented but not yet wine. He chewed a strawberry slowly, let the sweet taste spread slowly over his tongue.

"It's too sweet for me, Mrs. Hà. Will you bring me some ice, please?" asked Liêu.

Mrs. Hà dropped some ice into Liêu's glass. The spoon clicked against the glass as she stirred.

Chiến asked, "How long till the ferry?"

"Just a bit longer," said Mrs. Hà. "It left here a long while back."

"Hey Liêu," said Chiến, turning toward her and sounding a bit cross. "Every week, you rope me into going across the river to Bát Tràng with you. What do you want to keep going there for? Don't you think it's getting a bit old?"

"But I couldn't bear *not* going. Every time I go to Bát Tràng and buy a bowl, I want to come back and buy a vase."

Chiến laughed. "Would you rather I just buy everything in Bát Tràng for you? It might make you less crazy."

"Are you bored? I, for one, am never bored. I see each of my little plots of land beneath every step. Changing shape into bowls, vases, cups, and plates, anything that can be flung into some corner of the house or placed on a table and brought to the lips or set on the altar to look down imposingly on the people bowed in prayer."

"You and your imagination," Chiến yawned, "it's so exhausting. . . ."

"Whatever, Captain Corporate. I love getting out to relax each week, and all you do is whine and complain. Keep it up and next week you won't hear from me. I'll find another friend to come along."

"No one will want to go with you, your highness."

"Every time, you two quarrel like this," broke in Mrs. Hà, "but then you keep coming back!" Pointing toward the river, she said, "Here comes the ferry."

Chiến got up and pushed the motorbike onto the flat-bottom boat. Liêu paid Mrs. Hà and mounted the bamboo slats of the little pier as several passengers joined them: a woman with a bicycle stacked with baskets, four clean people with motorbikes, a dirty woman with a baby in her arms.

Chiến parked the motorbike in the middle of the ferry and stood beside Liêu, his arms folded across his chest. The putt putt putt of the engine echoed over the river as the ferry slowly crossed. Neither spoke to the other, each silently admiring the slow rippling waves. Chiến's thoughts returned to the past. It had been eight years already that he'd known Liêu. The first time he saw her was at a charity exhibition of children's paintings. She had stared at him deliberately, and he couldn't turn away. She urged him to buy one of the paintings to help raise money for the children. He gave in easily. They introduced themselves. Very directly, she said she liked him. He just laughed. In fact, she was not beautiful. Her cheekbones were too high and her face somewhat bony. Only her long, thin legs set her apart. He told her to wear skirts, but she never did; she never gave him the chance to see her legs. The more he got to know her, the more he saw her stubborn and erratic sides. In school she studied graphic design and could have gotten a great job, just like him. But she only liked to freelance, designing interiors here and there, never amounting to anything significant. Sometimes she dabbled with painting, but then her paints just made a mess of the house, also to no end. And she was always right beside him, sharing her feelings or sometimes just quarreling. In fact, did she love him as a lover should? He didn't know. She always met with him, but he could never do anything, could never even kiss her a single time. Part of him wanted to find another girl, to have a normal, loving relationship, to satisfy his needs. But when he held another girl in his arms, nearly forgetting everything else in the world, Liêu's laugh—or one of her funny phrases—would echo in his mind, making his bones go loose. It was so crazy—did he even love her? He didn't yet dare be sure.

This time was just like all the others. They drove the motorbike around the winding roads of Bát Tràng village, where he had to hold his breath because of the sooty smell of the charcoal-fired kilns. They'd charge into every shop and look at every last thing, but then she would buy just one small item. He was so bored with this passion of hers. He couldn't understand why she felt so elated by this or that particular porcelain bowl. She said she would eat rice with it. So crazy.

On the way back, the ferry drifted over the surface of the river, already dark. Above the riverbanks, the city sparkled with lights. He felt as if he'd been in some strange and distant world, not the one with which he was familiar. He was returning with nothing, and as with all the other times, an unattributable sadness descended upon him. He said without thinking: "The river looks so peaceful, but the waves lurking beneath could surface at any time; they could swallow the ferry, they could make us disappear."

"Actually," she whispered, "only I would disappear. You would continue to exist because you serve a purpose for so many other people."

"*To know yourself is to know others,*" Chiến teased.*

"Yes, I realize just living my life and following my desires sometimes makes others feel miserable. They worry about me, while I feel happy."

"Your happiness scares me. You spent all that money on thousands of flowers to decorate the company's gate on my birthday, then listened to chanting tapes all week locked in your room, making your mom have to call me for help. Maybe you should see a therapist. If you keep this up, you'll make me crazy too."

"Oh, how wonderful of you to say!" Liêu exclaimed. "To have a man crazy because of me makes me so happy! A crazy person can do anything he likes but remains free of other people's pains, never has to worry because of what they do. He can get sent to the nuthouse and go completely bonkers and be taken care of."

So their conversations on the river always went. Then, also as always, Chiến felt exhausted. He wished he'd stayed at home and could now be sinking into a hot bath, only later to go to bed and sleep oblivious to both heaven and earth. But still, he had to make an effort. The ferry had crossed the river. He drove the motorbike up onto the riverbank. Mrs. Hà had closed her stand, and now it was dark. They switched places; he would drive Liêu home. After the long afternoon, they both felt so very tired. Next time, he swore he would not go like this, despite the yellow fields of sweet ripe corn, the wonderful cold strawberry juice, or the cool wind on the river. He would not go again, not go anywhere, not go crazy. Liêu's long legs may have been arousing, but he never got to do anything with them. He needed his work to go smoothly, he needed days of peace. He needed his life to have order and to go according to plan.

When they said goodbye at his company gate, he felt so tired and bored he couldn't even manage to smile. Liêu pulled his shirt, her lips pursed sullenly.

---

* Vietnamese proverb—*Biết mình biết người là tốt rồi.*

"Tell me something, sweetheart, before I go."

"What should I say? Sleep sweetly and have a beautiful dream, right?" Chiến said the words to her, but his eyes looked away.

"No, you have to say something else." Liêu did not let go of his shirt. "If you're bored, sweetheart and don't want to cross the river with me again, I don't want to live any more."

"To live or die is not important."

"Then what *is* important, sweetheart?" asked Liêu, beginning to smile.

"Love . . ." Chiến said, caressing her cheeks between his two hands. "But you only . . . *like* me, right?"

Liêu removed his hands from her face.

"Whether I say yes or no is also not important. The important thing is how you feel."

Saying that, Liêu sped away on her motorbike. Chiến shook his head, watching her go. Then he let himself into the company parking lot and started his motorbike toward home. On the road, his mind continuously returned to Liêu. Where would she lead him? Things would go on like this forever. He was a man, he needed to control the game. He would change—or at least try to. He should have done so a long time ago.

Chiến's mobile phone buzzed over the table, startling him. It was Wednesday afternoon. Liêu. All week he had tortured himself over this decision. Surely Liêu would be sad and disappointed. It must be so. But he needed to live for himself. He needed to know clearly, when away from Liêu, whether he could bear that distance, whether he needed her to come as she did.

He glanced at the cell screen, and then he pressed *Ignore*. He had ignored her. He sat up straight, closed his eyes, inhaled deeply, and listened to his body. He felt a silent space inside, a very silent space. So pleasant.

The end of the year was very busy. Chiến wanted to stay focused on his work. He intended to send Liêu a message—"I just need some quiet time"—but thinking this and then thinking that, he did not. Keeping silent was also a message.

Liêu didn't call him again. Silent, no news, however small, like a cold war. Chiến bought several books on meditation, trying to find some peace. But on a Wednesday afternoon, he decided to make some noise. He called some friends to go out for a drink, came home very drunk, went to bed without having a bath, and slept like the dead.

Thursday morning, after such a boisterous Wednesday, he oozed into the office like a slug. Following his routine, the first thing he did was read through the newspaper. His eyes died on a second page brief. A ferry had sunk: one child had drowned, a woman was missing.

For several minutes, Chiến didn't know what to do. Then his senses returned, and he snatched his phone and pounded out Liêu's number, his fingers trembling over the familiar numbers he had dialed a thousand times. Her cell was turned off. Fear twisted the moment inside him. He sat there, waiting, for what? Someone would call him, would give him the news. News he didn't want to hear. He still needed peace and quiet, didn't he? To live or die was not important. The important thing was whether he loved her or not. If he loved her now, was it even possible any more? He did love her, he wanted to rest his chin on her shoulder, hug her around the waist, and listen to the tides in her heart. Was it even possible, something as simple as this?

Empty-handed, he left the office, not saying anything to anyone. It was not important. He walked slowly, trying not to think of anything. He feared the appearance of any thought in his mind might cause it to explode, over-freighted with memory, conscience, conjecture, and pain. Near noon, he came to the field of corn by the river. He raced up the path through the rows, the stalks blown by the wind cutting each other with their leaves. Liêu!

Mrs. Hà's restaurant wasn't open yet, the hour still a bit too early. A ferry lay on the water moored to the landing. Several sampans ran along the river. A knot of people had gathered at the heap of earth where the boat-man usually laid out wooden planks for the passengers and motorbikes to board. Chiến approached them. The search party was dredging for Liêu's body. The ferry had sunk, and Liêu had saved one child, and then she continued to dive after an infant and two women who could not swim. After that, no one saw her surface again. She saved the two women and retrieved the body of the infant. But Liêu was lost. Chiến listened to each detail as they lodged in his heart, but he wanted to grasp only one: Liêu was lost. What was going on? How could a person, close to him here, having such a large effect on him, be gone so suddenly, and without having told him anything? He sat on his heels in the grass and wrapped his arms around his knees, watching the river, ignoring the hot sun on his head. Mrs. Hà came and set up her café, but he remained where he was, savoring the lovely view of the riverbanks, almost like nothing had changed. Why was it like this? Why? Why was everything so silent? He had needed quiet, but the silence of the river at this moment was something he could no longer bear. He could no longer deceive himself. Painful misery came with the realization of how much he loved and needed her. He felt sorry for himself, not even one time having dared to hold her close, not even one happy moment to hold onto for the rest of his life. If he'd done so, his stomach would not be burning like it was now. He had saved money for a trip to Russia, a place she'd wished to see once in her life with him. He envisioned all the special Russian figurines, so meticulously made, that they would bring back. He wanted to tell her about them so she could hear. That was it—he would do it for her now, for himself, no more waiting.

He took a seat on the faded wooden bench in Mrs. Hà's riverside stand. Not needing to be asked, she brought him a glass of cold strawberry juice. She fluttered around the stand, telling him about the strawberries she'd picked from the patch near the river, big and ripe, prepared following her mother's secret recipe, the most delicious in the city. Strawberries had just one season for picking, fermenting, and pressing in the whole year, she told him. Sometimes they had a poor crop, and the whole patch would have just a few fruit, barely enough for several jars, but even so she always had enough for the whole year, as if the jars were charmed, selling continuously to customers and never running out.

The ferry slid toward the riverbank. Chiến stood and pulled out his wallet to pay. Mrs. Hà waved his hand away.

"Go get on the ferry. You don't need to pay. She paid already."

"She paid already? She who?" He looked startled.

"The girlfriend you're always with. Last night, she came back on the ferry by herself, drank two glasses of strawberry juice, and paid for three. Said today you'd come to take the ferry. Like usual, she paid for you already."

Chiến hurried onto the ferry. Liêu was always like that. She never let him pay for the strawberry juice for the two of them, and she never let him drive the motorbike when they went to the landing to wait for the ferry.

Chiến tapped his forehead, smiling with astonishment as the ferry landed. She had paid for the strawberry juice. He imagined her standing on the far side of the river, waiting for him. When he landed, she would take his hand, and they would run up the riverbank together. They would enter Bát Tràng and look into every shop. He used to promise he would buy everything in Bát Tràng for her.

The next day, and every afternoon for many days after that, Chiến went to the bank of the river, sitting next to a glass of strawberry juice at the stand, waiting for the ferry, thinking, Hey ferry, did Liêu cross today, did she cross the river with you? Why does Liêu pay for me every day but won't let me see her? I love you, Liêu. Do you want me to shout it to the surface of the river? These past few days, I finally understand how much I love you. You are my whole world. You'll come back to fill this world to the

brim with your voice: "Sweetheart, board the ferry. Cross to Bát Tràng."
Yes, I will go to Bát Tràng with you, one thousand times, one million times.
Until the end of my life. I'm so bored with the silence of not having you.

Mrs. Hà kept smiling sleepily, kept ladling strawberry juice for him, kept
bringing it in a glass. But she never took his money. She told him, "Last
night, after you left, she came to the ferry and crossed the river. It was
really late, I was just about to close. She sat drinking strawberry juice and
asked me how you looked, whether you were well. I said to her, 'If you miss
him so much, why won't you meet him here; he's always sitting here waiting for the ferry, every afternoon waiting for you, so loving, so miserable.'
Her eyes fill with tears, and she says she can't meet you, she wants to but
she can't."

Chiến jumped up. "How did she look? What time did she cross the river?"

"No one knows what time. What I know I told you already. She looks so
thin, her skin a little green, almost translucent."

"Tomorrow I'll wait for her, for however long."

The next day, Chiến did not cross the river in the afternoon. He sat at
Mrs. Hà's restaurant from dawn until dusk. Lights sparkled on both sides
of the river. Mrs. Hà said, "It's the last ferry, get aboard, then remember
to come right back. Tell the boatman you'll pay for the round trip so he'll
bring you both right back."

"Today," Chiến sputtered, "why didn't she cross?"

"Board quickly, don't ask." Mrs. Hà's eyes sparkled strangely. "How miserable you are, looking but not seeing each other, waiting but not meeting.
She just boarded the ferry."

Chiến felt cold, his skin prickled and shivered. He hurried onto the ferry.
This last one was nearly deserted. Only him and a middle-aged woman, in
ragged clothes, with a small dog. The woman glanced at him a moment,
then sat, slumped down holding her dog, her eyes following the lights
at the landing they had just left. The ferry engine puttered incoherently.
The ferry seemed to hang motionless in the middle of the dark river. How
cold the water was. The dog barked three times. Chiến saw Liêu's solitary
shadow on another ferry sliding past behind him.

"Liêu!" He raced to the ferry rail and called her urgently. "Liêu!"

Liêu did not reply. It seemed like she smiled and waved her hand. She
wore a thin white shirt, dim against the dark surface of the river.

"Wait!" shouted Chiến.

The ferry carrying Liêu swept past. A cold wind swirled behind. The
middle-aged woman huddled into her seat. The dog growled. Chiến ran to
the pilothouse and shook the boatman's shoulder.

"Turn the ferry around, follow that ferry over there. I just saw her."

"You're crazy. I don't see any ferry. This is the last ferry. Go sit down and keep quiet."

Chiến turned around and around, but he could no longer see the ferry with Liêu anywhere. He rubbed his eyes. It was as if the ferry had dissolved into the air. Clearly, he had seen Liêu. She was slender and pale. She had smiled and waved her hand. His heart felt like a hand had grasped it and held it down. He screamed, his lonely voice reverberating over the surface of the cold, deserted river, "Liêu!"

Translated by Di Li and Charles Waugh

Infinite Pain

Nguyễn Vĩnh Nguyên

As of this moment, my mind is empty, and I cannot even write an opening line. And immediately, I write about such an emptiness that it is like a lizard eating its own tail. It eats the nothing too and makes hunger no longer mean anything.

Is it even possible to start a story this way? The first disadvantage is that readers are waiting for me to write about familiar things—a story that makes them burst into gentle tears like the Chicken Soup books so popular these days or something about sublime magnificence. But instead, I've started to write at a bad time like this. Pathetic. Like the man who goes around naked right from the start of the day. He strolls along the bank of his vast pond kicking at weeds until exhausted. Maybe he wears himself out kicking around, so when he plunges into the pond, he sinks. Sinks not because he's not a good swimmer but because he makes too much of an effort for something not at all related to swimming.

But I cannot sink just yet because only now does everything seem to be starting. It's miserable to be a man sitting at a computer keyboard imagining that the guy reflected in front of him has a face full of words. He will say into the void, I have phantom limb disease! I feel pain coming from a part of my body that does not exist. At every waking moment, I feel pain coming from outside my body. It's hard to believe. How can a person extend nerves outside the body and receive signals from that pain?

I call it a symptom of the pain of reaching out.

This story is truly like a fable. Even now, I can feel and see that pain myself. But around here, people don't have permission to depict such agony from outside the body like this. Because writers must depict only joys or the kind of pain capable of making a reader burst into tears. You cannot characterize contrasting views with vague illnesses or speak out in ambiguous language. Because these ambiguities are sometimes considered to be too close to concrete reality. But if I write about a joy coming from outside the body, it means I'm writing about a feeling of meaninglessness, a total lack of real experience.

Did I lose some certain unessential part of my body? No. I am a completely whole man like any other. And I have never lost any part from which pain can arise.

So in emptiness, I've found the source of my pain. My friend says all this is just the pain of loneliness. It's unfortunate that he voiced such an opinion while sitting in the middle of a group of people who had no idea what being alone is really like or what aspects of it must be examined. Amid the group's confusion, and illustrating the difficulty of conveying isolation, some musicians asked their band's young singer to stand and sing some golden oldie songs with idiotic lyrics like:

My life is lonely so I still feel lonely with anyone I love,
My life is lonely so my love for anyone always leaves me alone.

It's a tragedy because any concept that can be illustrated with monotonic lyrics and a rhythm that only seems to prolong the unimpressive life of a totally simplistic nation seems not to know how to escape its own banality.

*It's like that, it's like that!**

All this despite the fact that these people are artists. Because after that conversation, he (who struggles to truly comprehend loneliness) will go out to the bars with them and continue to discuss the typical features of isolation in creative psychology and philosophy. These are the syncretic theories of solitude in which can be found the Buddha's enlightenment, the tragic who seek the gates of paradise with God's resurrection, the gullible of the world who protest violence and protect the peace of Albert Einstein, the *Übermenschen* who transform from lambs to lions according to Nietzsche, and sometimes just the guy who goes out for dogmeat and takes the chance to explain the importance of individuality in the pursuit of freedom according to John Stuart Mill.

As a result, no one feels alone at all. Demonstrated by the extremely delicious dogmeat, which goes so well with the taste of banana wine, and by all the people talking and all the people listening. Everyone wants to prove how hard it is to escape from their inner pain. This is the way it always is. But my pain lies outside me. Always taunting me to search for it and to paint its face. I am a skeptic and sometimes wonder to myself if all this is just some game of self-deception or the paranoia of an idiot.

---

* The lines are a parody of a silly, contemporary song. —Author

I am a sick man. I try to convince people of this fact as eloquently as I can. For example, I willingly sit beneath a razor to shave off my hair. The only things left on my bare scalp are scratches. The bloodied clumps of hair fall down, bit by bit. They cause no pain. Most days, they seem like they're just old useless antennae protruding without meaning anyway. They make me think that the real pain can be located through its vibrations buzzing into my brain. But that's a big mistake. I doubt the razor's sharp blue edge and continue to use my teeth to strip bamboo fibers to cut my fingers. I clutch a strand of the sharp bamboo and use the other hand to pull hard, gushing blood from the cut in my flesh. But the outside pains do not come from there. These cuts do not answer the questions: Where does the real pain come from? What does it look like?

Bald. My head is a fist. Very white. Confidently strutting down the middle of the street, I step out with my fistlike head and with that pain hanging in the air, outside my body, my hands full of bloody sores. But the pains from my hands that feed into my bones are meaningless compared to the aching pain outside me. I step forward and wave my arms around like an idiot accustomed to hallucinations. I groan when the invisible knife cuts. I struggle to embrace the pain, but even when it fits inside me, I still cannot stand it. That feeling of pus swelling. Barely touch it and it will burst like an ulcer. My nerves cannot last when constantly sending the brain such unendurable pain.

I stand like a statue and invite the pain to surround my body. I reach out with my hand, my tongue, my legs, and even my cock, and still cannot catch the tantalizing pain that devastates me so.

Some might call it a mental condition. But it might also be a dysfunction of the body.

* * *

The fist goes to the end of the street. Immediately, it feels a pain nearby. It stops at the sidewalk and pulls out its cock to piss on a utility pole. Piss splashes everywhere, glistening in the sunlight. The pain is now somewhere really close. Its body senses the proper frequency and latches on. But now's not the best time to receive pain signals from outside. He knows that.

The wife is something completely impossible to him. Each day, he spends half an hour making love. The same as Americans. But even when pressing her down into the mattress and stuffing his cock inside her, in his head he feels an indescribable pain. The pain doesn't come from any direction. It's impossible to know its cause or reason. He lies in bed and cries. At these times, his wife makes worse a pain that's difficult to share.

You hurt me.

Yeah, I'm sorry. I hurt too.

Where do you hurt?

Outside my body.

She pulls him close and tells him that what he said makes her happy. She likes to share pain with him and simple human contact. He cannot completely feel what it's like to be a woman; he hasn't had the opportunity to feel that way. He thinks that if he has another life, he will vow to be a woman in order to better understand his wife's pain and at the same time to escape the pain of being a man.

* * *

At any moment, emptiness can arrest me and chew me like its favorite jellyfish salad. And I, in those moments, again will seek this pain outside me. Maybe it will be beneath my fingertips as I press the keys to write this story. Maybe it will be at the top of my cock after a cold fuck with a prostitute or while making love to my wife. This business is so boring I simply cannot find any excitement in it at all. Once, I had to use my fingers to stuff the wrinkled bag called my penis into that dank region just as a farmer puts fertilizer into the ground and waits for the next crop to sprout from the earth. Right in the middle of that time, pain reached up from inside me, from the direction of my pasty-skinned member. I was sore from the friction against the wet parts of someone else's body. I curled my body to try to absorb the pain of that feeling of sustained impotence.

For now, it—that pain—can lurk beneath the chair I sit on here with my not-so-imposing ass. Then again, it might also be on top of my bare and lumpy head—a weak fist always shakes in the air in vain. Sometimes I feel the pain right in front of my eyes. But not in the eyes. My eyes are still bright. Not in the forehead. But somewhere. My forehead protrudes forward and never senses any extra parts of mine.

The Buddha says life is suffering. Sages always speak concisely. That makes it hard to understand how the stories illustrate an opinion. Everyone wants to understand in their own way. That experience of making language mean something is how dull-witted descendants can become a little wiser. Anyone who's certain God exists will die without having questioned his own life.

That whole subject lies outside my abilities. Nor can I speak concisely about this cloying pain that hangs about me. It seems like it's a circular, revolving mass, like a dance. It reaches me by some invisible thread. I know it's always with me every second, every moment, always toying with some new bizarre agony. Sometimes it's also rather awkward. I have to lie on the ground and wait for the pain to pass. Aching and suffering. One hand continually claws at the emptiness where the pain resides. The sharp blade perpetually cuts another exquisitely cold slice to separate chunks of flesh from my body. I cannot stop it. I sniff the air, my hand reaches out, and I am floating in the sun-filled sky like a crazy man, my lips puckering in search of wounds to lick; even the hairs growing from the mole under my jaw that I have long tried to forget tingle with the effort to find some invisible point of contact. From there, pain bowls me over, driving me insane. A pain not lingering but festering, about to burst. A feeling of abandonment and outward abundance. A sense of being beaten, tortured, and torn from one nowhere to the next. A spot I can feel like the space where one hot and one cold streak collide in the middle of a roaring thunderbolt that splits the sky. I scream chaotic sounds. Scream and hope the screaming can thwart the pain in some intangible place.

Phantom pain?*

It's not a phantom pain. I am whole. Not yet has any part of my body been amputated.

The pain is just an illusion. The nerves must have some kind of damage.

No. I'm completely functional. I'm always alone when I fall into a fit of pain like this. What must I do to stop it?

You are a special case, says the doctor. A patient unaware of a constant pain. I will record and monitor your symptoms. Maybe it's a new disease that medicine has not yet discovered.

Are you going to research it like some pompous critic who lacks experience and can only see the pages of this story through Coke bottle glasses?

No. I don't know what else to do. And you have to accept that. Because you can't identify where the pain comes from either, or even where it is. And if it's like that, how am I to pinpoint what nerves are in pain? We have no medical notion of invisibility, sir. . . .

So I have to wait while the pain carries me away until you establish a pattern of old pains based on the coordinates X, Y, and Z marked in monstrous red ink on my flesh?

I am a scientist. You're only a patient in this study with my permission, sir. If this conversation isn't over, we're all going to be very unhappy since we can't even come to a basic agreement about what the problem is. Now keep your invisible pains to yourself and get out of my office.

* Phantom pain is pain experienced after an amputation as if its source were the missing limb.—Author

Motherfucker. Useless thing!

Like so, it's perfectly reasonable to suspect my flesh or my nerves are the problem. To explain it is truly a difficult matter. I have to try to peel off these layers of sensitive skin and replace them with layers that can cover the nerves to keep them from interacting with the outside world and in this way seal the outside pains from coming in.

But this, no one can do.

On the way home from the hospital, the pain becomes excruciating. I feel it can swallow me and all my fear and disappointment. I hug myself, reeling and choking. On every tiny surface of my skin I can feel the spreading of the pain. At home my loved ones stand nearby but can do nothing to help. All my fists—even the one that is my shining white head—break out in a sweat. They are receiving a reeling pain. I see myself foaming at the mouth and my legs go hollow on an empty balcony. A jump in the afternoon. The setting red sun ulcerates a corner of the city sky. And below, streams of people congregate. I will plunge into that pain like a release or submerge myself into it to find its location and appearance, its relation to my body. I'm flying through a space containing many pain signals. The signals go through my body like a parabolic wave, freeze, ripple, then slide down. And I throw myself into it like a broken radio tower in free fall. Wind from the river blows softly across the sunny sky. The city chokes on the clouds of dust raised by the wind and on fumes from engines, factories, and people. When the winds rush up the face of the building, they lift me on a soft caressing breeze, lift me flying horizontally on the air. But the fist, my shaved head, weighs me down. I ride many currents of air before sinking into the stream of panicked people below. A sound of collision. White waves come up. In my eyes, waves so intensely white. Waves roll into the shape of a lonely monster erupting into broken bubbles and a confusing moment without boundaries. The river of people swallows me into the heart of an excruciating pain with its panic. The river abrades my flesh with a pain that remains floating outside me. I've spent so many afternoons floating in that pain trying to scream it out just like James Blunt in that video singing *you're beautiful* while peacefully removing his clothes in preparation to plunge from a jetty down into the deep black sea. Darkness closes in. And the chorus keeps humming *you're beautiful* until the end of this video hallucination.

Now, I am lying in bed. Freedom. And pain. My whole body has been wrapped in white bandages. And outside that, a nylon bag, clipped closed with the same clips I use to hold together my unpublished manuscripts about these pains reaching out. I feel claustrophobic and stifled, and the air around me feels condensed. They are killing the excessive pain. The pains melt into an unbounded loneliness. I am like a bird with torn and tattered wings, alighting outside a window. Trembling, waving for the last time, then leaving without ever expressing its pain.

Sometimes, in the extreme emptiness of my self, after eight hours working at the office and half an hour of routine sex, I like to search for the pains that have been abandoned outside me. I like to be lonely and empty. But then I have no pain. I have no emptiness. They abandoned me indifferently after my jumping escape, after the white bandages and the nylon had been clipped closed in such a careful way. Someone reached in and locked fast my invisible pain.

Maybe I've had emptiness surgery to become a different kind of person. Right now. When finishing this short story. My emptiness has been different from the very moment I pressed CTRL+S to save a new file.

It all ends here.

Translated by Lê Thế Quý and Charles Waugh

An Unbelievable Story

Nguyễn Đình Tú

AT SEVENTEEN I LEFT MY ANCESTRAL HOME TO COME TO THE CITY AND work for a high-end wooden furniture store. My job was to sit ready and waiting, so that when customers finished buying I could deliver the furniture and move it into their house for them.

For this job I needed only three days of training, that's all. Most difficult for me was learning how to ride a motorbike and having to memorize all the streets. The city by nature had a lot of streets and alleys and shortcuts, and I was still just some hayseed who'd never even sat on a motorbike before. But then I gradually got used to everything. After just a little while, I'd earned an "expert" certification. I boarded in a small alley not far from the store. Evenings I was usually free. Very free.

The alley I lived in was full of poor laborers. This guy named Hùng also lived in the boarding house with me. Hùng had studied at the College of Social Sciences and Humanities in the Sino-Vietnamese Studies department and after graduating couldn't bear going back home, so he stayed to work for a foreign insurance company. He had a motorbike and a mobile phone, went out all day, and never showed his face at home. To me, he was a mirror for study, but I didn't understand why he constantly complained; the word that always came out of his mouth was "wretched." In life, he always regarded whatever came up as wretched. He told me many times: "The same way a stupid hayseed like you turned out to be good, the more you study and know, the better you'll see how wretched everything is."

At the end of the alley lived a few guys studying at the Labor Union school. Every time these guys stepped out the door, they were dressed in nice clothes, but when night came, after they'd already been out and come back, I'd always hear them talking in front of my house about ways to borrow money from someone to "save themselves from hunger" on the days when their "families had not yet sent their allowance." On the other side of the alley was a strip of partitioned boarding houses with fiber-cement roofs, containing all kinds of people. Almost all of them were small town folks like me gathered here to rent themselves out to make a living. It seemed as if everyone was living with one another, but during the day each person went to work alone, leaving the alley deserted, and when night arrived everyone went to sleep early, the alley remained completely quiet, and the boarding folks barely got to know one other. Even Brother Hùng and I were like that. Two people living together in one house but not eating together, not working together, not sleeping together, not using each others' things, only sharing the rent and the electric and water bills. After two months I got to know—or to speak more precisely—became familiar with a guy named Bền, who lived in the strip of partitioned housing on the other side of the alley. Bền came from Phú Thọ, was already thirty-eight but never married, and had come to the city seven or eight years ago to work as a cyclo* driver. Bền was big and tall, towering like a bear, with a very kind personality. He lived by himself. Some considered that a waste because groups of poor laborers usually lived together to save money.

I went inside his house once. That was the time Bền had come home from drinking somewhere and couldn't seem to shove his cyclo inside. I helped him and then saw the extent of his life of poverty. The cyclo took up half the place, and crammed into the other half was an old bed, a tiny dresser just as ancient, and a wooden shelf hanging lopsided on the wall holding some rough clothes, the sleeves and pant legs still rolled up. That was it—in the whole place not a single thing of any value. When he rolled into bed and fell asleep, snoring like a storm, I silently closed the door, thinking to myself that even if the door was left open all night, no burglar would ever bother with this place.

After that, Bền became close with me. I have no idea what he managed to sock away after nearly ten years living in the city, but I could see he was generous in his spending. One night after I'd just gotten home from work, I was showering when Bền ran over still in his underwear. At his place at the end of the street, the water only ran in drips during peak hours, not enough to do anything with, so frequently he'd come over to my place to clean up. He was standing there watching me pour water over my body when out of the blue he reached over and grabbed my most sensitive parts. He laughed and asked: "Has this thing of yours gotten any use yet?"

I was shocked, my face red, completely embarrassed.

He spoke again: "Tonight I'm going to treat you, okay?"

"Treat me to what?"

Bền said, "A woman, of course."

---

* A pedicab with a two-passenger bench seat in front.

That evening, we left the house a little early, with just me dressing a bit nicer than usual. Bền took me to the flower garden past the five-way intersection, up into the park and then down to the lake. I followed him, curious, expectantly nervous, worried. Honestly, I'd never imagined doing something like that even though I was already a young man. Because Bền had ignited this need for discovery, I now felt a great thirst for satisfaction, whereas before I'd always been quite shy, but at the same time I was cracking my knuckles to calm my heavy breathing and to give me an air of confidence while walking beside him. But we walked forever, until our legs got tired, and we still hadn't found a place for us to experience this "capability" of ours. After another lap around the lake, Bền turned to me and said, "I'm not sure why, but we're out of luck—there's no one to see. Maybe there was some bust, so they all took off. These days the cops are really after them."

We resigned ourselves to walking home. That one experience was enough for me to get an impression about daring to be a playboy and about Bền's generosity. His generosity also made its mark at the Horny Goat Weed Bar. A few nights later, he took me to this bar at the end of the street—which sold this liquor with a really "arousing" name—to hang out and mingle with all sorts of people, including a group of his drinking buddies who called themselves the Chicken Head Suckers.

The bar was a little crowded. Bền said, "City people really like this liquor right now. When the bar first opened, it was even more crowded, but now there's lots of bars like this, so this one's not so crowded, just a third of what it was like before."

The horny goat weed liquor was sold in small La Vie* bottles—it had a brownish color and could be purchased with all sorts of appetizers: dried seafood, green and pickled fruit like green guavas, bananas, cucumbers, plums, apricots or vegetable salads or finger foods like salted peanuts and chips. Basically, this was the kind of sidewalk bar where the working class, artists, and poor intellectuals could all hang out together. After following Bền to the bar a few times, I was still confused about two things: one, what was the difference between the horny goat weed liquor and other liquors? And two, why would his drinking buddies—all of them poor, hard-working laborers and migrants coming from all over to make a living like himself— call themselves the Chicken Head Suckers?

On the first issue, Bền explained roughly that the horny goat weed liquor was primarily a normal rice wine, which the bar owner then infused

* A popular brand of bottled water in Vietnam.

with a type of grass called "horny goat weed." How to do the infusion, for how long, and with how much of the grass were all secrets of the house. "But what's drinking this liquor good for?" I asked. "Well, if you believe the stories, more stamina, more strength, more vitality—the name is 'horny,' right?" Bến's face held a look like that explained it all.

To answer my second question, Bến said simply, "They were just joking around."

"Joking how?"

"Well, my buddies were all sitting and drinking together, and a guy who had nothing better to do made up the story of the Chicken Head Suckers, and after that the story became a thing with us. That's all."

"But what *is* the Chicken Head Sucker story?"

"It's a story about a bunch of guys who'd been drinking a long time, and when all the snacks were gone, all they had left was the head of a chicken. These guys tied the chicken head to a string and whirled it around, continuing to drink and twirl, each taking turns sucking on the chicken head. At the end of the night, the drunks realized only the string was left because the chicken head had disappeared into their drunken mouths. It's a crazy story and a downright lie. The guy who told the story, we grabbed him by the neck and threw him out to the street. But his story stuck in our heads; there was no way to erase it. From that moment on, any time our guys showed up, right away the word would spread: the Chicken Head Suckers are here—let's see them drink!"

The gang of Bến's drinking buddies wasn't very big, just about six or seven, nearly all middle-aged and unmarried. They worked all sorts of jobs: porter, market guard, motorbike-taxi, cyclo driver, store security, construction worker. They'd get together at the bar once or twice every week. Every time they met like this, they'd all start with surly looks on their faces. But after seven or eight La Vie bottles of the brownish liquid, they'd turn and start to speak with each other. The stories they told were usually bland and meaningless, but for some reason they seemed to hold their interests and arouse their passions. For example, one time I heard them talking about crab lice. One guy said: "You get crabs because you're dirty." Another said: "Living clean you can still get crabs." Another guy chimed in: "If you think you have them, you do. If you don't think you have them, you don't." Then they started a debate. The first guy said: "If you shower every day, and scrub antibacterial soap all over your body, then the crabs have no place to live." The second guy said: "Crabs migrate down to your ass hair and then hide in there, where they're safe from any kind of soap." The third guy said: "If you think crabs are only in your clothes, then change your clothes and you'll get rid of them, but if you think crabs latch on to you, then the itching will never end."

Their silly debates always left me feeling so bored and so tired. But Bền told me: "Not understanding anything about crabs means you still don't understand anything about life." Yes, I still didn't understand life, but I also didn't plan to explore the lives of these little crabs that lived like parasites and got crushed between fingernails. At the end of the night as usual, Bền tried to pay in front of his buddies' hesitant eyes. And then they all shook hands, their tottering shadows lingering on the sidewalk, and disappeared into the dark corners and alleys of the city.

One time coming home from the bar, Bền stopped beneath a tree a few steps from our alley to relieve himself. Suddenly a "humanlike thing" from up in the tree jumped down onto his neck. Startled, he grabbed for the humanlike thing on his back and was shocked to find a mass of fur like a dog's draping over his shoulder. At the same time, a long, chain fell from the tree and looped round his neck. Bền yanked the chain and threw the humanlike thing to the ground. *Keek . . . keek!* A monkey. Maybe it got away with his chain and hit the town, not wanting to go home? Bền wound up a leg to kick the monkey sending it back home to its master, but then, unsure what to think, he decided on a whim to bring it home with him.

On that particular evening I hadn't gone with him because I had to stay home to write to my father. That morning, I'd gotten a letter from him that said:

> I received the money you sent. I saved half of it to buy medicine for Mom, and will use the other half to feed the family from now until the harvest. The pigs at home eat a lot, but even so we have to raise them so we'll have meat at the end of the year. I know you're working hard, and because of the family you had to leave school to work for the money to send home to us. Try to take care of yourself, son; this weekend one of our villagers will go up to the city and I'll send you some fresh corn; boil it and eat some with all your meals to keep up your strength.

When Bền knocked on the door to show me the monkey, I'd just finished writing back to Dad.

Bền examined the monkey carefully then said to me: "This little guy's light gray fur looks clean—really easy on the eyes—and I bet he'd look great with a little red or blue shirt. Maybe I'll keep him—what do you think?"

I said: "Yeah, he's great, you should keep him, and if you can't keep him, you can always sell him for a bundle."

After that, the monkey began to eat and sleep with Bền. It had obviously received quite bit of training, so it knew how to please its master. Bền liked him a lot. He brought the monkey along everywhere he went, even to the bar. Whatever he ate, it ate—if he drank wine, it also had a taste. If he got drunk, it would be tipsy. The strange thing was that its tolerance for booze seemed to get higher each day. Every time Bền brought him to the bar, it would wander off to other tables. If a customer invited it to drink, it drank. At first it looked like it was causing trouble for the owner of the bar, but in fact a monkey who knew how to drink made people curious, and the bar got more crowded each day. The owner begged Bền to sell him the monkey, wanting something to keep his customers coming back because the competition between bars in the city was getting fiercer every day. But Bền wouldn't sell. He did, however, agree to rent it out. The bar owner agreed, and without question, the monkey helped to increase sales. The arrangement brought Bền quite a bit of extra income. He rented the monkey to the bar in the evening, and during the day he kept him at home to rest. But many esteemed customers came during the day, so they didn't have the chance to see the monkey drink. They blamed the bar owner and seemed ready to pay a lot more money to drink with the descendant of Tôn Ngộ Không.* The owner really wanted to please his customers but he couldn't persuade Bền to rent the monkey during the day as well as at night. He tried going up to the highlands to buy a few monkeys, but none of them could drink, regardless of how he tried to train them. After a few days, each of them keeled over dead.

I was truly happy for Bền, because it seemed like it had become easier for him to breathe in life. He had new clothes and had even bought a few things for his meager home. I teased him: "You should get married now; what are you waiting for?"

He said: "I still have a lot of debts—seven mouths back in the village all still rely on me. And besides, I've never known what to say to women. They always think I'm an idiot or some kind of lout."

But then he did get a girlfriend. She was a woman about his age who sat selling drinks at the botanical garden. I said: "She looks like one of those old broads from a brothel, Bền, not someone from a good family."

He sighed. "Well, her whole life she's had to work like that—she's gotten old squatting on the sidewalks, and if she dies she won't have anyone to

---

* The Vietnamese name for the Monkey King, from the Chinese legend of Sun Wukong, made famous recently in several literary adaptations and martial arts movies.

bury her, so feeling that wasn't right, I made my intentions known to her, and she agreed right away. I'm almost forty, and with a life like mine, near the end. At least we'll be together, maybe out of a sense of humanity, but if we can have a kid together too, then heaven's looking out for me—you think I can hope for anything else?"

Right in the middle of Bến's plans to get married, I received a letter from my father asking me to return home. My father's letter said:

> Because our family is poor, and your mom and dad so pitiful, at 17 you had to roll into adult life to earn a living. I think a lot about that. I finally got permission from the commune to develop Dog Mouth Swamp near the graveyard bordering Thượng Village, so our family has a chance to make some money. Come home and develop this swamp with me. For sure our family will end this hardship, and your younger siblings will have better luck and be better off. When you get this letter, make arrangements to come home right away. Your siblings and I are waiting.

So I bid farewell to the high-end furniture store, shook hands with Bến as he prepared to start his own family, shook hands with Hùng, who continued to "mop the streets" all day to sell insurance contracts, said good-bye to the city and to my little alley, and went back home to work as a farmer.

It wasn't until three years later that I had the chance to return to the alley where I'd spent my entire seventeenth year. Naturally, my father's project at Dog Mouth Swamp failed miserably. I brought my strapping twenty-year-old self back to the city to shoulder the burden of earning money to send to Mom and Dad to pay debts and to raise my younger siblings. I hurried to find the people I used to know. It had been just three years, but no one was familiar except for Hùng, who still lived alone like the day I left.

"So you're back up here to share rent, huh?" Hùng greeted me with a straightforward question as usual. "Wretched! Leaving your home a second time is just wretched, dear boy."

"Yeah. Is Bến still around?"

"Nope."

"Did he take his wife back home?"

"What wife? Don't you know that story?"

"Not yet, what happened?"

"It's a long story but . . . so wretched!"

Honestly, I didn't know if Bến had good luck or bad since with Hùng everything was "wretched." Graduating from university was wretched, living in the city was wretched, leaving home—wretched. Going to work by a motorbike, having a conversation by mobile phone—wretched. A lover coming to the house and crying her eyes out—wretched. Even winning a lottery was wretched, so how was I supposed to know how to take this wretched story of Bền's?

That night Hùng told me Bền's story. It went like this: After refusing for so long to let the Horny Goat Weed Bar owner have the happiness of renting the monkey during the day, suddenly Bền changed his mind. It seemed like he needed money, a lot of money, and of course the bar owner always wanted to please his customers. So they came to a verbal agreement: Bền would bring the monkey to "work overtime" at the bar on Saturday and Sunday afternoons in addition to the evenings as usual. The first "overtime" afternoon that Bền brought the monkey, it was drizzling rain, and patrons had packed into the bar. Bền chose a corner of the place to sit and eat alone. Like every other day, the monkey jumped from one table to another, dumping liquor into his mouth, then tossing the glass back to the customers. It also ate cucumbers, peanuts, and chips, and when it was drunk, it tottered lopsidedly, looking very funny. The later it got, the harder it rained. Water poured down, shutting down the city streets and alleys. Customers drifted away. The owner eyed the rainy sky and decided to close early.

Bền carried the monkey back to his house. The rain poured down, soaking them both. At home, Bền felt queasy and fell into bed. The monkey climbed onto his chest, looking for warmth, and Bền wrapped his arms around him. They both fell sound asleep. It was dark when he woke up. He had a cold feeling in his chest and sat up. Just barely hanging on to him, the monkey fell down to Bền's lap. Bền sat the monkey up, but it was already dead. Dead but as if he was asleep, the hair on his chest still warm. Without hesitation, Bền breathed into its mouth, trying to give him some of his energy, hoping he would live again. But his efforts proved useless. The monkey turned cold, his limbs began to stiffen. Bền covered his face, terrible cries rising from his throat.

The people in the alley had never seen Bền cry before, but that evening they heard him crying loudly. It's difficult to imagine the cries of a man nearly forty years old who had weathered the sun and rain like Bền. His wailing was so pathetic, so heart-rending! Bền just sat there holding the monkey and crying. Outside, the sky still rained. Light rain, faint rain, not the vehement pouring of that afternoon.

It didn't take long for the news of the monkey's death to reach Bền's Chicken Head Suckers. They decided to come share Bền's grief. Each guy brought two La Vie liquor bottles bulging in their pants pockets. They circled around Bền, and just like that they started to drink. As usual, at first their faces remained blank. Only after half the La Vie bottles had been drunk did they begin to speak. One guy said: "Can't save the monkey now, let's figure out a way to send him off equal to all the things he did for his master."

Another guy said, "Cremation is cleanest." Yet another said, "Bury him." Another followed with, "Let the birds take him to heaven." As these opinions circled about, Bền just sat there in silence, his eyes dim, his left arm wrapped around the monkey. "Food burial! Only a food burial makes sense because the monkey's blood and flesh will mingle with ours, so it'll never be gone, it will remain in his master's cells. If we're happy, then it will be happy. If we're troubled, it will have to bear those burdens too. Isn't that the best way to honor the master-servant relationship?" Truly, it was an unusual idea, but it brightened Bền's eyes. After a moment of stunned silence, all the Chicken Head Suckers clapped their hands in agreement.

So while Bền lit incense and arranged an altar, his buddies boiled water to cook the monkey meat. That night they drank until daylight. Every once in while, they sent someone to fetch more liquor. The head of the monkey was placed on a plate, right in the middle of the tray. Each participant kowtowed toward the monkey head and then turned it to face the next. They pointed the monkey's face at each person when it was their turn to drink. The following morning, Bền woke to find no one else around. He had no idea when his drinking buddies had gone home. The monkey head was still there, in the middle of the house, facing Bền. Wherever Bền went, the monkey head swiveled to follow. Bền got so scared he dropped to his knees and prostrated himself to the monkey. When he looked up, the monkey also nodded up and down, returning his bows.

Bền let out a single scream and passed out cold. People took him to the hospital. Then his father came up from his village to take care of him. When Bền finally woke, he couldn't talk, and each and every thing had to be signaled, his mouth murmuring, _Keek . . . keek!_ When he got better he came down with an intense itching. The doctors removed his clothes and were shocked to discover his entire body had sprouted grayish-white fur. His father asked to take him back home to be cared for there. They went home and within a month, Bền passed away. The day he died, even the bar owner went to honor his spirit.

"No!" I shouted, unable to believe Hùng's story. "No way it was like that—how could you imagine something so cruel? Why would Bền deserve such animosity from you?"

"Wretched! I told you right from the start the story wasn't nice! I only told you what I know; if you don't want to hear more, that's fine. I'm not the type who likes to *gossip*."

Hùng looked resentful and went back to bed, leaving me to sit at the coffee table by myself. All that night, I couldn't sleep. The next morning, as soon as the alarm went off, I went over to the place where the students lived at the end of the alley to ask them about Bến's story. But they were gone. They'd graduated and left already. I ran over to Bến's house. It had a new owner. The new person showed me the monkey head hanging on the wall, saying: "When I got here, it was already hanging there—who it belongs to I have no idea, and I don't know anyone named Bến." I ran to the head of the alley, to the Horny Goat Weed Bar of the old days. A lady stepped out and mistook me for one of the regulars, raising her voice: "You're out for liquor pretty early, aren't you, young man? Crazy for the grave, huh? How many pints?"

"No, I want to see the guy who owns this place."

"What guy?"

"The owner of this Horny Goat Weed Bar."

"Nonsense. That guy disappeared a long time ago."

"Disappeared where?"

"Nobody knows. Now we sell *sán nùng** liquor here, young man. That's what city people drink these days. Why would you use that horny goat weed liquor anyway? You're so young and already you need that stuff? Besides, what does that horny goat weed liquor even do? It's all a scam! I've been selling liquor since I was ten. Whatever liquor you want, I can sell it to you, no need to waste your time looking for that useless old bar owner—besides, you'd probably end up with rubbing alcohol!"

I left the bar and ran to the city's botanical garden. All those old ladies were still squatting there at the gate, but none of them looked like Bến's old broad. "Who? Oh, that old hag, you should go up to the rehab center and ask them. But why are you looking for that old thing so early? At this hour, they're all still asleep, no soul's up this early. If you can wait, then wait."

Well, that was it. I didn't know who else to ask for Bến's story. If the story were true as Hùng told it, then it really would be hard to believe. But in this life, there's no lack of unbelievable stories. And with Bến, would I just have to believe an unbelievable story like that? For the first time, I uttered the word from Hùng's mouth: Wretched!

* A popular type of rice wine flavored with special forest leaves made by the Dao ethnic minority people along Vietnam's northern border.

That evening, I sat down to write a letter to my father. I wrote:

> Dear Dad: Life in the city is a lot easier for me now. I will try to work hard and send money home for you, Mom and the kids. Don't worry about me being young and green, Dad. I'll be able to do things here that you'd never believe. You'll see. Don't worry!

Naturally, I'll never stop trying to find the truth of Bên's story, a story as hard to believe as it gets!

Translated by Thúy Tranviet and Charles Waugh

Thung Lam

Hồ Thị Ngọc Hoài

IT'S NO COMPLAINT TO SAY PEOPLE CALL LIFE COMPLICATED. THE LONger I live, the more inexperienced I feel, the more naive. What could twenty-five years have taught me about being a woman, about this world? Three years thrown into preparing for a college entrance exam. Four years of study in the capital. The rest was just what everyone else had experienced. A teensy bit of learning and a weensy bit of life hardly mean a thing.

Work was very different from what I imagined. Gloomy. Stultifying. Any higher purpose completely hidden. Meanness grew like weeds on wild, stagnant land. People often complicated everything unnecessarily just to strangle anything out of the ordinary or free-spirited. Then they oversimplified the things they actually needed to pay attention to. The superficial got adorned with affectation and falsehood or left naked, stupidly exposed.

I recognized there were some things I had to let slide. Many nights, I lay awake thinking hazily. My look of confusion (people often say this about me) must have come from the forest, thanks to the serenity and purity of the mountains around Thung Lam,* or because no one could ever teach me to be wise or even clever. The fast-talkers I've met have always thought I'm a bumpkin.

From the beginning, I wanted to go far away from home. I'd urge myself, passionately, ardently: *I've got to get out of here!* Every Saturday, I'd diligently bicycle the twenty miles between work and home to talk with my parents, to argue. When the time ripened, when I had the strength for a final attempt to escape, I had to work myself up to telling them. My parents looked like I'd poured oil onto a fire.

"Every day," I said, "I see people full of contempt, fear, and ridicule hiding behind flattery, spitting in each others' faces with disgust, only to pretend nothing is wrong."

---

* Thung Lam means Lam Valley, and is pronounced "Toong Lam."

"What a misery, child. No one wants that, certainly they can't be happy being like that. But don't be rash." My father was gentle. But I couldn't go back—not to the city, and not back home. I didn't want to be surrounded by waxen, uncaring faces.

"Manipulative, greedy women with only a shred of power win over the others in the most conniving ways. It all makes me so bored. Dad, let me go!"

"Bored! Is that all? Doing what you want to do? If it's so great, go away for good!"

My father had become angry. My mother took pity on me, crying, "What a terrible shame. What misery! It's driving her crazy."

My father drank more rice wine, the troubles of life whittling him down to an insensible shadow. I felt ruined and miserable, but I couldn't go back. With no other choice, I left silently, with unspoken apologies and promises to make amends burning in my heart.

On the bus, and then on the train, I made some simple plans. A friend in a town by the sea. A tiny bit of money. A university degree. Twenty-five years making a person, with one age-old thing perfectly clear: money comes from strength and will.

On my long and quiet journey, I kept myself in high spirits by daydreaming, occasionally raising some fear or wandering back to the past.

"Nguyện, sweety, it's settled! Damn, so many months of looking for a job for you has made your father a lot wiser."

"I can tell, Daddy."

From the distant mountains my father traveled near and far, living high and low to learn the ways of the world. After each excursion, he told Mum and me the stories. Once the work was all done, it could be summed up in a simple sentence like that. He admitted it was unendingly difficult, trading sweat labor for hard-earned money, blood for silver truly so. Once my brother and I started going to school my parents had to sell their bones and marrow to provide for my honor and position, pawning every bull and cow, one after another. Next the breeding stock would go too.

In the most remote backwaters of the district, I had a couple of school friends who had to eat manioc and went everywhere on foot like my parents and managed to pull it all off. But when I got the faintest whiff of the world, I had to find some excuse to act crazy and make people stare.

Right from the beginning, at the office job my father found for me in town, I was never a beauty like from America or Australia, but people still felt the need to make comments.

"From the hills and yet so arrogant."

"What arrogance? She's naïve, practically an idiot."

"Does she have some kind of brain damage? Maybe she's possessed?"

"A pile of years already but never in love. Something's got to be wrong with her."

I'd check, review myself, then shrivel.

Only much later, one of the older girls said to me: "You can't avoid these cud chewers. You've got to join in their nitpicking and know how to follow the herd. Speak up. The more you yammer with them, the more they'll respect you as a wise and experienced person. Don't you know that?"

After a year of work, I realized I'd learned a few things. But were they worth two head of cattle? Ugh. Must the lessons that make someone a person be so dear?

* * *

After the train ride, a woman nearly forty years old, with a very fine and beautiful face not at all resembling a madam's, took me to the newly built hotel by the sea. They chose me, but I also got to choose the face that guarded my gold. They needed me to be businesslike, simple. And I didn't hesitate when I got a foot in the door like that.

One afternoon, on a balcony overlooking the sea, the man renting room number six on the third floor made my acquaintance and asked for my story. Listening to me, nodding repeatedly, his faithful square-shaped face radiated waves of light. The details of his face suggested erudition, and certain standards, clearly not an ordinary person.

"Really?" he asked me. "Graduated with a degree in literature? Why work here?"

"I"—I had to choose the proper form of address*—"I want to live in direct contact with the 'ever green tree of life.'"†

"Excellent! Can you get by?"

"I can save a little bit."

"How long will you work here?"

"Until I need a change and have enough to do it."

"Freedom's wonderful, but you have to pay for it."

"That's right!"

---

* The narrator uses the personal pronoun for "child"—what a grandchild or niece would call herself when speaking to a grandparent or uncle.

† A line from a famous poem of the same name by the twentieth-century poet Xuân Diệu.

"Many arrogant people regard themselves as this or that, but they cannot escape from what they don't want. Pride lives on in slaves and masochists."

That didn't seem like something he said for me to hear. He seemed to have sunk into something else there. After our chat, the guest looked at me kindly, with affection, and the next day when he bid me farewell, he said we'd meet again.

A month later, I did again meet the guest who loved the ocean so much that whenever he felt stressed, strained or depressed, he'd hop on a coast-bound bus. I was as happy to see him as to grow to know his voice, and unexpectedly, this meeting brought a change in my life.

"I don't want to settle into work at home for a lot of reasons. It's so tiresome that everyone just keeps imitating everyone else, turning life into a rut, then thinking that it's the only way, an ideal, and attacking anything new. People with power are blind and deaf, crushing real values to death. . . ."

I guess I'm fond of speaking like an old lady. I spoke like I was afraid of not being able to speak. Whatever I knew, whatever I thought, gushed out like water from an opened dam. After that, the guest helped me like a fairy godfather helping the poor in a children's story. I was anxious, unmoored, and in a big hurry to follow him into a new life based on my love of literature.

* * *

Another departure, and I forced myself to hide all my feelings, as if I'd wrapped up a present to myself and set it aside until my birthday, so that when the day finally came I could open it and burst into rapture. Then I'd know the exact day joy would return to my life, to my whole body, even to the roots of my hair. But nothing went as planned. Instead, I took the train home because of news that my mother had become seriously ill. The whole long journey I cried impatiently, imagining evil things. From the station I ran, stumbling, deeply inhaling the smell of my homeland. Along the road, I met many of my fellow villagers, and seeing their faces and hearing their unusually soft-spoken words, all my scattered, unhappy prayers solidified in the shadows of the still afternoon light. In the lane to my home, the smell of incense turned my legs to lead and I lost consciousness. Pain robbed my soul.

At the funeral, I staggered to my mother's grave.

I tried to mollify my inner feelings but ended up torturing myself anyway: "Mum didn't blame her daughter, did she?"

Then pensively, again and again: "Mum wasn't sick because of me, was she?"

Everyone there soothed my pain. It wasn't until we'd returned home and only my father and I remained that I realized that my return had revived him, that the melancholy, isolation, and loneliness had gradually begun to thaw from his face. The harsh wrinkles of old age melted behind his affectionate eyes.

I sat with him on the porch as the afternoon sunlight faded from the lane.

"Do you miss Thung Lam?"

"I miss it a lot!"

"I've kept the hut for you."

"Really, Daddy?"

Thung Lam and the old days came back to my mind.

When we were teenagers, my brother and I took turns walking our oxen deep into the valley. For a second and then a third year, I struggled to prepare for the college entrance examination. With rice balls for lunch and dinner, I took the oxen far up the valley, staying until late in the evening so I wouldn't have to hear my mother's wheedling not to leave. I felt indebted to Thung Lam. My friends all scattered, then got married everywhere else, and still I rode the oxen into the valley. In the first days, I followed my brother and I was afraid, but as I came to know the valley, I fell in love with it. The most pleasant thing for me was to lie in the hut, swinging in the hammock, reading books, listening to the birds sing, especially the wild doves. The songs and smells of Thung Lam soaked into the marrow of my bones. In the late afternoon, the oxen's bellies were as fat as if they were pregnant, and both the oxen and I walked slowly, laden with bamboo shoots, banana flowers, or dry wood. I never believed the stories of this valley having ghosts. There were never ghosts, but occasionally we saw animals from the forest. The first time I saw a snake, I rushed to the hut, but afterward I became braver. Never could I forget my father's warning: "Don't go alone into the valley—you might run into wild animals."

Missing my home, missing Thung Lam, I thirsted to return to those days filled with joy, but . . .

My father changed the subject.

"You've seen many years already but aren't worrying about a husband and children?"

A husband and children? Here was a man who'd just lost his wife, silently giving me the things to create a life unlike everyone else's but never asking for anything in return. I felt spoiled, coddled like a strange flower.

And then there was the guest from room six of the third floor in the hotel by the sea. And also Song, the boy who conquered me with his strong will, pouncing on my hesitation as if seeing right through the complexity inside me. Song, a city boy who looked like a gentleman but whose inner qualities were more instinctual than sophisticated.

The story of my feelings crossed back and forth like a mountain trail. My thirst for giving myself up burned, but I didn't dare to hurt anyone. Not strong enough, not having the right to hurt either of these two people, I resigned myself to abstain, to languish in silence, to let the heat burn inside while outside the ice failed to melt. When people cannot feel untroubled, cannot be decisive, they are miserable.

I missed Thung Lam, missed those carefree, innocent days following the oxen and carrying books to read. It was another time in my life, when my head strained, aching because my heart had stopped at a crossroads. Should I stay safe at home, resigned to a life like my mother and father's in Thung Lam, without troubling my head with tests and challenges, or should I continue to hope while plunging myself into the corners of the world? But that first story would have been too simple, too locked into letting things run their course than this story.

My father waited. And I never wanted him to know anything about how conflicted I felt. It came to nothing, what can I say. He seemed to suppress a sigh in the evening light. I stood up to begin making dinner, talking for the sake of talking.

"Don't worry Daddy, in cities people like to get married very late, some even like to live alone."

The next morning, my rapture on the old road to Thung Lam made me love every pothole, every eroded bank, every jagged rock showing through the macadam, even every angle of the long, sloping road. I shivered and shed a tear when I saw the hut from a distance. I know that when it had begun to fall apart, my father had tried to repair it. The hut was small and simple, but it contained the infinite.

One August afternoon years ago, as I lay swinging in the forest hammock, my father walked up holding a letter of admission, making me jump up and down and hug him with joy. I felt the whole valley swing with me in ecstasy. That moment, that image of my father and of Thung Lam, flutters in my memory always.

I strolled along the path searching for feelings to connect yesterday with today. At the hut, I was stunned to see that the whole valley had changed dramatically. And then a familiar voice, as generous as an old friend, made me feel calm and light. Was that Song? How could that gentlemanly city boy be . . . ? I stood motionless, but my coursing blood flushed my cheeks and throat. I couldn't believe my eyes. How could it be so? The hut perched in a remote, desolate and forested mountainous area—not one from a fairy tale—so how could he so magically appear? But to be fair, it was not such a strange thing for such a strong man, someone who longed to conquer whatever he'd committed himself to. Coming there, did he know he had charged my heart and blood with the miraculous dream that in the city I had craved and at the same time felt compelled to flee?

He made me tremble, he burnt me to the ground.

Then he began a daring, adventurous game, calling me to the edge of the lake without knowing its depths, pulling me into the water. I let myself be entranced, let him overcome me with his sensual caresses. He carried me in his arms.

The hut—and all of Thung Lam—took on the glow of our passion as I was led through the realm of ecstasy into womanhood. The obstinacy, the firmness I presumed to be permanent in me soon became liquid, a light smoky cloud drifting away. I felt both close and strange at once, both me and not myself.

Stepping from the realm of passion, I left behind my feelings of weariness. I felt justified being myself. He had returned natural feeling to me, had dispersed the turbulent air that had arisen from regret, dissolved my perfectionism with a passionate gaze and a silent sharing. He too was happier, stronger, and more confident.

Then he brought some young forest banana leaves back to the hut to make a skirt for me. I just wished the wind and sun of Thung Lam were really strong. It's only love that's tricky like this, reducing people to such crazy situations.

I gazed out wishing the sunshine and the wind would quickly dry our trappings of urban civilization hung on the bushes nearby. My face reddened as I glanced down at my primitive figure, wishing he could weave the banana leaf skirt more quickly. I looked at him, naked, well built, designing clothes. And I loved him even more passionately when I realized that he had dissolved the trappings of urban civilization with the primitivism of Thung Lam. He had set off one more vibration inside me, one new emotion. Did he know? If there had been something dubious about the sophisticated, civilized façade he wore, in that moment it had completely disappeared.

Thung Lam allowed me to know the most extraordinary feelings a girl can have—feelings I couldn't have imagined would be like that, especially not in Thung Lam.

We returned from Thung Lam into exultation. Then came a time when I truly felt the accumulation of all my innermost feelings. The sorrow of the loss of my mother surged up inside me, as did my love for my lonely father in his deserted house. Seeing me brush away my tears, my father said: "I am burning incense for your mother, for our ancestors. Set your mind at ease and go, don't worry about me. When you get married, I will come."

We returned to the city. Song and I and the man of the sea were different now. Those days weren't like the old days. I wasn't unhappy, putting on a nun's robes to run away from love. Song happily introduced me to all his friends and relatives. Yet the gentle caressing moments on the balcony of room number six on the third floor of the hotel by the sea, the boundless sentiments, and the tender affection and the warm, sad, faraway eyes of that man made me feel as if I was somehow being punished every day. When in Thung Lam, Song had made me forget there was another man, a man who loved me deeply. But even though I respected and admired Song, I didn't know if it was love. As always in the stream of life, I worked steadily, and silently. In rapid succession I became Song's wife, gave birth to two children, and turned into the caregiver for a whole family. . . . Meanwhile, the man of the sea remained alone and continued to have warm and pure feelings for me that seemed unreal in this life full of earthly things. However much I prayed for him, he remained silent and alone, unwittingly punishing me all the more. I'd been possessed already by Song's strength when he arrived in Thung Lam, but never again did the great depths of the man of the sea rise up to me.

* * *

The poorly made road to my homeland was immersed in mist and rain-clouds. The solitary, unassuming shadow of my father made me miss him constantly, tormentingly, but I resigned to accept my guilt as part of my jumbled and wide open future. My father was satisfied with his life, but like Mum, he passed away unexpectedly, without giving me even a moment to see him alive a final time. Why would both my mother and my father leave so suddenly, like a punishment to me?

All the same, for several years I had been preoccupied by the birth of my second child, while Father aged and weakened, no longer able to travel, and he and I couldn't see one another. Three years passed. That span of time coupled with my father's sudden death nearly made me lose my mind.

Song? My older brother? My sister-in-law? My niece and nephew? My children? None of them came to Thung Lam with me after the grief-stricken funeral. Only I believed Thung Lam could dilute such concentrated sorrow. Only I traveled the lonely forest path whose moods I knew so well.

But this time the valley's skirts didn't flare as proudly and splendidly as if twirled in a dance; they were roughly torn here and there, revealing painfully stripped flesh and bones. Its strength and vigor could no longer conquer the people. Its miracle and mystery did not force man to yield. The sounds of the animals had disappeared—there was only somewhere the sound of a lone bird calling for its flock.

The hut? I should have known. Daddy must have been too ill to look after it. My tears streamed down. The thatched roof and bamboo screens, they seemed to have decomposed, as would the flesh of my father in the ground. Only the frame remained, like my father's bones, which would also gradually crumble. My thoughts and imagination drowned in tears. I sat on the rock beside the hut without moving.

Heart Lake had become shallow and muddy. The handful of wildflowers nearby thirsted for its life-giving power.

The valley's voice choked with emotion. I fell apart.

My brother returned to his city. I also returned to our remote city. I pitied myself for living in a deserted, desolate house, depending on my relatives and neighbors to care for our family home. I no longer had Thung Lam to return to for peace and quiet. Little by little, it had been lost, even the things that could hardly be perceived by sight.

In the endless days of the city, when I shared some story about my homeland or my family, my husband just said:

"You look for perfection in everything. That's so tiring."

"Some things we can't change! We have to accept the facts of life."

"If it weren't this way, life would just be a fantasy, there's no one to blame!"

"Everyone just does the same thing! Save your energy for other things! No one lives in the Thung Lam house, it should be sold!"

"Men use wood—the forest must be cut!"

The path to the spiritual world must be very lonely. That's why the secrets of the soul insist on appearing in one form or another. For my daughter, I made up a fairy tale based on myself and on the story of how my parents and grandparents lived in the mountains in Thung Lam.

> Once upon a time, there was a prince who eloped with a poor village girl to settle in a distant mountainous region. Every morning and afternoon, the silken strips of smoke, along with the smell of sweet potatoes and manioc, flew very far, summoning other couples to join them to build the village and open new roads. The new roads were filled with snakes, sharp rocks, and thorns. One road in particular grew wider and longer, leading back to the castle of the

king father. Then one day, hearing news that the country was in trouble and that the king father had died, the prince left his wife and son, seeking to serve the world and save the country. The prince was unyielding and brave until his last breath, without ever seeing his wife and son again. The country regained peace as the son turned sixteen, having journeyed to the ends of the earth in search of his father. Knowing his father had gone forever, he returned to his mountain home, refusing all invitations and promises from the capital. He thought: I still have a mother, the mountains, and a girl on the hill beyond. The road to the capital is still rough, steep, and dangerous. I do not wish to contradict my father.

Having heard much of the story, my daughter said: "Your story sounds a little strange, kind of like a fairy tale, but different."

* * *

My brother phoned me several times: "A guy offered me twenty million dong for the house. I want to sell now so I can build a third floor on my house and have a better, wider place for the family altar."

"Don't sell!"

"But the house is empty. Every day it gets worse."

"I want to fix it up—we'll come home now and then. . . ."

"Fine, then come home and really take care of it—let's see if you'll really do it."

Three years after my father died, I came home on the second or third day of Tet. It was a long, unsettling trip, but just one week living there made me miss it more, made me want to stay. Even so, my brother still wanted to sell. My tears would fall without end on the night of the train ride back to the city. What about when I come back again? Surely, dear Brother, we can't do it.

After cleaning up the place, my children and I investigated every detail of the house and garden. Watching the children get so excited about the flowers, looking at the old peach tree in the courtyard waiting for us to come back to show off its color, to draw us back, my tears were about to fall again. For the past two years my brother and niece had come before Tet to prepare the altar and the house. This year I didn't know why both were so cold and empty.

As the lights began to twinkle from the surrounding mountains, my brother arrived. Cakes and fruits were placed on the altar, prayers commenced and finished, the smell of incense for Tet wafted through the air, and brother and sister dined together. My brother unburdened his heart, maybe trying to justify his tardiness and failure to fulfill his obligation to our ancestors: "Come on, Sis, for the past two years we haven't been able to celebrate the new year in the city. This year, I told my daughter we needed to come up here sooner, but she refused to do it—we argued endlessly. The whole family's been turned upside down lately. Her brother's about to get married but doesn't have a house, and Nga spent a ton of money applying for a job that didn't work out."

I kept silent. After a moment, he continued: "And you, returning, coming back, regretting things from the past or being nostalgic, it all blocks your way and interferes too much in your life in the present—it blurs other priorities and doesn't do you any good. Be more practical! Being so bound to the past will only put your back in front of you. The future will reproach you. Does your husband sympathize with you? Every year, will you and your children take the trouble to travel such a long way, leaving your husband without his family? Won't it affect everyone's happiness?"

Listening to my brother speak, I felt confused, trapped, and disheartened. My husband's cold silence while the children and I prepared for the trip loomed in my mind. I had to suppress my discomfort to put on a good face, but Song remained impassive. We both needed each other. He felt I was putting my heart into something trivial, wasting both visible and invisible things. For my part, I felt alone. Unloved. Not a few times, my weariness made the man of the sea worry for me. All the same, his presence remained solely in my mind to make me feel less lonely.

Late into the night, we sat talking by the fire. Gradually, I wore down his enthusiasm for selling the house. From then on I didn't hear him talking about selling or not selling the house. But a few months later, he wrote me a letter to tell me the house was sold. I seethed but remained silent. On the anniversary of my parents' deaths that year, I placed sticky rice, chicken, and flowers on the ancestral altar in my own house to remember them, refusing to go to my brother's to see his third-floor altar renovations.

*   *   *

My native home. I had only the graves my brother could not move. Mountain people always burn incense for all the graves in the cemetery. The souls of my parents and grandparents must have been warmed as well. I returned to my homeland again. So much time had passed!

Accustomed to a cheery welcome in my village, this time I felt something missing, something out of tune. I could still stay in my house—it was just that it and the things in it no longer belonged to me. Nothing felt emptier or crueler than the strangeness toward the things that used to be my blood, flesh, and breath. The new owner shook his head when I offered to buy back the house. People want to settle down and prosper, not turn their peaceful lives upside down. The affairs of the ancestral home and the family were surely the most important things. Would my brother's hair gray—would time soak into him a love for his home that included both the sour and the sweet? Did he lie awake at night, tossing and turning for Thung Lam, for his homeland?

This time, I felt afraid when making my plans to visit Thung Lam. The new owner's wife told me some disturbing things about it. My disquiet led me instead into town, and I found my way to my old office at the Culture Publishing House. The site had changed a lot. But the most surprising and interesting thing to me was that the "New Boss" turned out to be "Bảo the Geographer," who had been the best student at geography in my old school days. The joy was indescribable. Stories without beginning or end came one after another. We sat to have a meal with many tasty dishes, but we merely picked up bites with our chopsticks, tasted them, and put them down to keep talking.

"You came back several years ago, right? You were the first to leave and the first to come back. That's great!"

Bảo stood by the window looking out for a moment, then pulled a file from the cabinet and handed it to me, saying: "Read it, Nguyện—maybe you'll like it."

I read Bảo's article about how humans interact with nature while he paced, waiting. When I laid it on the table, I hadn't yet had a chance to speak before Bảo demanded, "So?"

"Do you write newspaper articles now too?"

"Is it okay?"

"Will you go with me tomorrow, Bảo?"

"Where? But what about the article? I want to send it to the province newspaper."

"Go with me tomorrow and you'll know."

The next morning, we hiked up to Thung Lam. As we stood at the summit of the mountain road, the sky fell dark. In the distance, we could see where a wide strip of forest had been completely cut down.

"Now what do you think?" I asked Bảo. "You think ghosts are sucking the blood of the forest? Never a sound, very silent. First the shirt, then the skin and flesh, finally the bones and marrow. What does a Man of Culture* like you think about how people interact with nature now?"

---

* Referring to Bao's work at the Culture Publishing House.

"There's so much to do, Nguyện!"

"Can we gather enough wind to make a storm?"

We walked to the lake. A thunderstorm barreled in over our heads. The hut appeared in my imagination. My childhood self ran up to the hut and sat looking at the rain in the forest, at the surface of the lake sipping drops.

"Nguyện! Why just stand there? What's wrong?"

Bảo brought me to my senses. We were both getting soaked. I blushed, remembering when Song carried me in his arms. Bảo seemed strange placing his hand on my forehead. I felt what was about to happen and blushed. Bảo hugged me. I squirmed in his tight embrace, cringing as he said out of tune, "It's all so right!"

He hovered like a gentle breeze, easily nudged away as I regained my calm. I knew in that moment that Bảo just barely managed to suppress emotions other men would yield to, thinking they were wonderful. The image of a former lover, so keen on reading and writing that he forgot everything else around him, loomed large in my mind.

We came back late to the house. Bảo's wife did not look happy. I didn't want to stay, and Bảo awkwardly took his leave of me in the twilight at the town station.

Back in the city, I received news that the man of the sea was in serious pain. I feared it might take him away. I felt exhausted, tortured by the fact that I had never taken him to Thung Lam. Pacing to and fro with worry, my compassion expressed itself in tears. People whispered. My husband didn't believe me and turned cold, then frozen. I imagined a strange smell on his body. Was I losing him? The pain of life surged up like a monster eager to devour me.

These days, I often find myself returning to Thung Lam. Sometimes I stand at the top of the slope, looking at the high sunny peaks. The splendid green overcoat flares cheerfully in a simple dance. Then I see my mother as she transforms into thousands of green trees. My brother steps down from the hut, and I mistake him for my father. Sometimes I see Song and me swimming, changing into fish in the lake. Sometimes the man of the sea—or sometimes Bảo—rides a bicycle along the road to my ancient and lushly forested valley.

Translated by Lê Thế Quế and Charles Waugh

Sounds of the Evening Bell

Lê Hoài Lương

I DON'T WANT TO WASTE YOUR TIME WITH DESCRIPTIONS OF THE BEAUtiful scenery and the beautiful pagoda in the beautiful mountains that have long been considered a tourist goldmine. When I'm exhausted by the dizzying endless contest of modern life, I seek out the pagoda's head monk, renowned for his deep religious knowledge and unassailable virtue. He's always willing to sit with me all afternoon long—for some time now he has considered me his friend. He loves me because I can sit quietly for hours or talk with him about Buddhist books but have never asked a word about his private history. And then, one day I told him that I'd just found the remains of a martyred brother thanks to the telepathic ability of Ms. Hằng,* and asked the monk what he thought about this sort of mysticism. He did not answer directly but, after a moment of reflection, told me the story of his life. . . .

* * *

In those long ago days, there was a Saigon soldier who had become an army ranger, a wild beast, stationed along the Bến Hải River. Before becoming a soldier beast, he had been conscripted many times, but he had also deserted many times as well. To avoid being convicted as a draft dodger and sentenced to a chain gang, both shameful and dangerously easy to kill—not to mention leading to the same end—he volunteered to join the army, then volunteered for ranger training, and was immediately sent to reinforce a unit suffering heavy casualties because of the strategic value of their position. Just across the river lay North Vietnam. Day after day, they shelled the other side with artillery; when their hands itched, they shot their rifles to relieve their boredom. Occasionally, through a loudspeaker they arranged several hours or sometimes a whole day of ceasefire, with

* The narrator's reference is to Phan Thị Bích Hằng, a psychic in Vietnam famous for helping families find their loved ones' lost remains.

177

both sides complying with these impromptu "initiatives." Both sides Vietnamese. Many among them relatives. War and shooting to kill, there was nothing fun about that. Communists have ideals, but soldiers like him were all reluctant to hold guns; ideals were shit! He had a family of ten hungry mouths, including his parents, his wife, and seven children. His wife and children were given a family allowance, but just barely enough to live. Wanting to earn more, he asked permission to open a unit canteen. His commanders knew he had many children and agreed immediately. He didn't dare sell very much: soldiers live today but die tomorrow; they gamble, eat, drink, and take on reckless debts; sometimes debtors would die before settling, and he'd never get his money back. He sold intermittently and perfunctorily, and every month he'd mail home the canteen's income along with his salary.

He also raised a dog to keep at the canteen. Adopted as a puppy, the dog was accustomed to hearing bombs and bullets; while the ranger worked in the canteen, the dog usually wandered around camp. Up to a mile was its usual range, the surrounding area just sand and low-lying scrub. Nothing had the time to grow higher than about a foot there. The dog roamed to relieve his boredom; certainly it was impossible to find a mate anywhere nearby; all the local people and their animals were long gone. The barracks actually had a female dog, but the one time he visited he was nearly killed, saved only by the bitch's master's poor shooting. The panicked dog ran home and gave up its dream of finding a mate. It seemed to understand that during war it could not ask for more. So, it roamed, seeking comfort in its wanderings.

One day, the dog brought back a piece of a shinbone. A human bone! The guy recognized it immediately. Nothing strange about finding a human bone when people were dying like frogs. The dog gnawed on the bone just for the sake of chomping. Dry, as if it had been roasted, not a scrap was left on it. But he couldn't let him have it. He shooed the dog away. Surprised for a moment, the dog sat and listened. Then it took off. The guy knew the dog had given up so easily because it could find another piece of bone right away. He put the bone up and sneaked after the dog. A few hundred yards from camp, the dog disappeared into a sandy hole, burrowed further in, and then emerged with another piece of bone. The guy rushed over and shooed the dog away. It whined, this time obviously feeling angry but also afraid of its owner. Using his hands, he dug into the sand and soon found the whole skeleton, most likely dead from a tunnel collapse. A small tin of Gold Star balm and a pair of rubber sandals clearly indicated the dead guy was Viet Cong. If he'd met this guy when he was still alive, it would've meant losing his own life. He stared at the corpse. Thinking. It's a human being. A human corpse. He couldn't bear it. Sure it was dead, but to leave a human being—even an enemy—to be gnawed away bit by bit by a dog was something he could not do.

He returned to camp, found a wooden artillery shell box and a small shovel, retrieved the shin bone, and then went back to the hole. He carefully removed the whole skeleton, placed it neatly in the box, and dug a proper grave. Rest in peace my comrade-in-arms from the other side; I don't know how old you are, but this skeleton certainly came from a man; maybe you have a wife and children, but if you're still just a virgin boy then what a pity for your life; if you have a wife and a crowd of kids like me, it's still a pity for them; fuck this goddamn war!

He took the shovel and went home, feeling peaceful. Then he forgot all about it.

But not long after, he was forced to reconsider this good deed when his life was spared in puzzling ways, making him feel overwhelmingly that some guardian spirit had been watching over him. Hearing the howl of artillery shells, he rolled into a friend's foxhole, only to have the guy tell him to move to the next hole because that one was too cramped; he had just emerged above ground when shells began to whistle overhead and an invisible force hurled him five yards to the next foxhole. His friend had been obliterated. Another time, his battalion was sent to reinforce a division setting up a command post on Cù Hon peak but came under fire before reaching them. Later, he always remembered, as if etched in his mind, the evening clouds that day were tinged red as blood. Looking at his comrades' faces, he saw flickering souls and dim shadows. He rubbed his eyes and felt a chill in his spine more evil than good. And then the attack began. The enemy emerged from the earth as the battalion reached a sandy area humped with false graves. Countless enemy soldiers rose from the graves, their bayonets shining red, reflecting the evening sun. At times during the close battle, the only sounds were wrestling and struggling, bodies falling and a few cries of pain. Then would come bursts of machine-gun fire and clusters of exploding grenades. His limbs trembled as he ran around and around his comrades who were too frightened to fight and kept clumping together and disintegrating in the type of close combat where bayonets and decisive action won the day. At least three times, a three-bladed blue steel bayonet rushed toward him only to swerve away at the last moment, nearby comrades taking the thrusts. He ran, peeing his pants but still running. A shell exploded just behind him, but he kept running, gradually realizing that his calf had been torn apart. The battalion had been beaten to pieces.

Making it to a safe place, he fell like a cut banana tree. The field doctor marveled that he had run so far without first aid. Damn it! First aid? The enemy right behind, lucky just to escape, no time for that. If it's infected, go ahead and amputate by God, I'll go home on a pair of wooden crutches, I'll be a one-legged general. . . . He grimaced, babbling over and over again while the doctor treated his wound. That night, he slipped into a feverish coma.

He saw an enemy soldier kneeling beside him and massaging his calf; he could tell the soldier was the enemy by the uniform he wore; the face flickered, hazily unclear, but still young, very young. He wasn't afraid, truly not afraid at all. The enemy soldier continued to caress his wounded leg gently, and the pain let up. And very quickly, his calf began to heal. The doctor was more surprised each time he came to check on him. The doctor tried to explain his recovery, speculating that he must have some very special antibodies. The ranger remained quiet, saying nothing. He stopped cursing. Some vague and solemn understanding emerged from the dreams he saw and from the incredible escapes he had made. He shivered with the knowledge that the enemy soldier had begun to take care of him. He felt cold all through his body as he remembered everything. He resolved that he would, after getting out of the hospital and going back to his unit, bring offerings to the soldier's grave to show his gratitude.

But he did not get that chance. Nor to take his superiors' offer to allow him to take two weeks leave to visit his family. He knew he'd never get that leave; the command always made excuses to postpone leave for soldiers stationed in I Corps. Just as he arrived at the unit, the large-scale operation called Lam Sơn 719 began.* It was an unprecedentedly large joint attack that moved swiftly and noisily to the west, toward the mountains, toward a major Viet Cong base. He only learned the codename of the historic attack later; at the time, all he knew was that he had to obey his orders.

Artillery and bombers attacked ferociously to clear landing sites. Then came the troops. Paratroopers darkened the sky, landing at their predetermined coordinates. These guys were truly intimidating; their whole thing was to appear massive, not to mention their fighting; they and the marines were the only guys rangers like him respected. His battalion came in by

* Lam Sơn 719 refers to the operation conducted between February and March 1971 in which soldiers from the Army of the Republic of Viet Nam, supported by U.S. Air Force bombing and U.S. Army helicopter strikes, invaded Laotian territory to disrupt People's Army of Viet Nam supply lines and staging areas. The campaign was meant to demonstrate ARVN's capability to wage the war without American ground troops. Both sides claimed victory, but ARVN sustained heavy, debilitating losses.

helicopter, the sky densely black with planes, bombs, and explosions. For all his time in the army, this was the first time in such a huge, fierce operation; word was it was being led by the commanding general of I Corps himself.

Gunfire came from all sides. He couldn't tell whose fire was whose, the shots a complete chaos. He was just an ordinary soldier; listening to chaotic gunfire didn't tell him anything about the progress of the operation. His company came under attack before fully deploying. It seemed the enemy was somewhere very near, and that they'd waited to ambush them. The plan was to send battalions out in both directions from the landing zone to encircle the large Viet Cong base called Xê-pôn and then to tighten the noose; but instead, both battalions were intercepted and attacked before they could close the circle. Hearing the commanding officers' panicked murmuring, he could guess things weren't going well. But the Viet Cong didn't hold every battlefield. It seemed they didn't have enough strength. After ambushing a platoon that had just landed or that was trying to flank their base, they would withdraw. They'd go silent, and then they'd suddenly hit somewhere else, appearing and disappearing. Every battalion was hit this way. There were some fierce clashes, but while the victory was still inconclusive, they disappeared. The commanders' desperate efforts gradually got the battalions into formation, but by then they had taken too many casualties. Dead bodies lay everywhere. He bent down to an infantryman waving his hand desperately. The guy's lower jaw had flown off somewhere, his torn and bloody tongue still wriggling but unable to speak, his throat choked with blood. Tears streamed down his face, begging, whether for a bullet in the head or to be carried on his back he did not know. He found a towel and spent a long time trying to bind the wound, but because of the difficult angle, he could not stop the blood; he wiped the guy's tears before going away. The guy would die for sure, but he couldn't put a bullet into his head. He trembled at the thought of it. He ran. His knees gave out but still he ran. All the soldiers still alive like him were scurrying this way and that, scared, having nothing left.

When the circle was finally closed, only traces of the Viet Cong camp and their communication wires remained. Still bewildered by the failed strategy, the Saigon forces were hit from behind. The Viet Cong could attack during the day or at night, at any moment, from any position, on a grassy hill or in the forest or from down a stream. Now they hit right in the middle of their own camp, their stoves still hot, attacking the field command headquarters. The big offensive to raid the Viet Cong base had been turned into a meat grinder. The Americans and the Saigon generals faced a dilemma:

their advance was complete but the enemy controlled the battlefield, and
a retreat wouldn't keep their men alive. Fighter jets screamed overhead,
but the pilots could not identify targets to bomb without hitting their own
troops. The longer the sparring between the two armies lasted, the worse it
got because the Viet Cong really knew the mountains. Reserve troops were
sent in. Like adding salt to the sea. Each battalion fell into the Viet Cong's
mysterious and magical mountain forest. All of them were frightened. All
were shattered. From officers to grunts. From heavenly sons in red berets
to the riffraff in camouflage. Reconnaissance planes made wide circles well
out of harm's way and then disappeared. They were right to report they saw
no trace, made no contact. There were no more orders.

Variously clad soldiers from the beaten and broken battalions clustered
together to soothe their fears, but as their numbers grew, they worried they
might attract the Viet Cong's attention. They split up only to clump back
together. Then split up again. No one was in command, but the officers
were still respected. At least they had some education; surely they had better plans to escape than the know-nothing peasant guys like him. The way
he found the guys he was with was strange. Thrown by an exploding bomb
into a ravine, he woke up in the dark. Gunfire in the distance reminded
him he was alive. He pulled himself to sit up, then patted himself all over to
check for injuries. He had no idea what to do in the deadly pitch black, but
then in front of him appeared a light. A blinking blue light. Concentrated
in one place and then dispersed into many shapes as if under a magician's
spell. Fireflies. He rubbed his eyes; for sure, they were fireflies. Many times,
in the old peaceful days on the river of his mountainous home village,
on nights of the high tide he would wade into the river to catch crayfish,
frightening them with the sound of his footsteps from where they clung
to the stones, so that they would be swept by the current into the square
net he held downstream; he alone with the darkness and thousands and
thousands of fireflies would hold their own festival of lanterns above the
lush foliage on the banks. In those moments, he felt that the dark nights of
the mountains were less lonely. His wife and children would welcome the
rich, delicious crayfish. Into the distance flickered the soft green lights of
the fireflies and his poor but peaceful village. But now only fierce war and
death stood nearby. Tears overflowing, he felt a thrill looking at the fireflies. They hovered in just one place instead of flying around, illuminating
every stone of the ground below. A chill crept down his spine as a familiar
figure took shape in the blue lights; yes, before him hovered the cold but
dear human figure who had stroked his calf until there was no more pain,
his guardian spirit. Previously, he had seen him only in a dream. But at this

moment . . . he pinched himself . . . and still the wavering blue figure continued to illuminate every stone in the ravine. He shuddered, stood, and followed the light of the guardian spirit. He forced himself to stumble on, knowing for sure that the sacred enemy soldier would rescue him. He kept walking, rejoicing the chill in his spine and brain. When he finally heard soldiers nearby, whispering with fear in the night, the glowing blue shape disappeared. He dropped to his knees as if in prayer. The surprised soldiers had no idea why.

The soldiers now had an infantry lieutenant. In times of danger, people stuck together like a pack, and the soldiers' aggressiveness had to yield to the mind. The time had come for the mind to be respected again. The mind, after trying unsuccessfully to reach the operations command on the PRC 25 radio and after sending into the atmosphere an innumerable number of Morse signals, wisely concluded that they really had been abandoned, and the mind drooped like a withered leaf. But then it sprang back up; it would not die; it rose up clearheaded again: surrender! The way to live was to surrender! Everything was clear. At the end of the tunnel appeared a flickering light. The signs of life were stronger than those of death. But still fragile. The mind pointed out the need to move to the top of a grassy hill where they would be easily observed, and so would not make the "respected gentlemen" suspicious. The mind called the enemy "respected gentlemen" instead of Viet Cong as before. The pack climbed the hill, luckily not meeting any "respected gentlemen" along the way. They piled their weapons at the edge of the clearing. Then they all screamed together, resounding low and high: "Hey . . . Communists . . . ! We . . . surrender . . . !" They screamed until hoarse. Both afraid and relieved, screaming. Going into a trance screaming. Soon they could hear the rat-a-tat of AK-47 gunfire. More screaming. Five minutes later, the gunfire was closer. Shooting up into the sky because no one fell down. The soldiers who had set down their weapons were as afraid as if they'd lost their minds and souls, but no one fell down. And then the "respected gentlemen" appeared, just five of them, more than enough to receive over thirty battered people; of course, somewhere nearby more "gentlemen" would be hiding in case it was a trick. There was no need to say this out loud, the mind knew it well!

Then the whole captured pack marched the famed Ho Chi Minh Trail to the North. On the way he heard a "red beret" guy whispering that their colonel had also been captured alive. The pack continued to be exhausted by the American bombs.

On the day prisoners of war were exchanged, the captive soldiers took a look at the four-party delegation and grumbled their disapproval for the other side. Only he remained silent. When given leave to visit his family, after sharing tears and joy, he surprised them all by shaving his head and leaving for the pagoda on the mountain. Some said it was just a way not to be thrown back to the battlefields. But after '75, no, this monk did not return to secular life. . . .

* * *

"A few years after liberation, I had the chance to follow my teacher to Quảng Trị, and I tried to find that grave I'd dug to burn incense. Just vaguely remembering all the trenches and shelters, I could only offer my prayers up to the infinite sky."

The afternoon had fallen. The monk sat in silence. Somewhere in the pagodas of these five scenic mountains, the evening bell began to toll peacefully. Stunned, I could not help asking, "All these strange things . . . did they really happen, Teacher?"

He stood up to see me off and said slowly, "You know, I have spent thirty years living the life of a monk, but I still feel like an imposter."

Alone, I descended the stone steps, attuned to the rebounding sound of the evening bell.

Translated by Nguyễn Hùng and Charles Waugh

The Land

Nguyễn Danh Lam

MY FATHER CAME HOME AT MIDNIGHT. A DOG WAS BARKING OUTSIDE the village.

"Ten more days to go," he said. "We just have to. The whole village has gone already."

Mother sat on threshold.

"Really? Oh God . . ."

My mother put her face between her knees. She let her hair down in the light of the only lamp on our ancestor's altar. My father rinsed his mouth with eugenia tea* and spat into a pot on the table.

"The Đôngs have gone, the Tács have gone. More than half the Trần families are gone, almost all the Nguyễn families. All gone. Who will we stay here with?"

"It's up to you. I've been by your side for ten-something years now. But what about our ancestors' graves? How about our house? The kids . . . ?"

My mother looked up at the mosquito net, beneath which my brother and I lay curled together. Neither of us were asleep, but we lay absolutely still. Father shook his head.

"If the ancestors' graves don't have us, they'll at least have our neighbors to care for them. This house will be—" Some desperate thought overtook him—"Burn, burn it all, until nothing's left. We've lost everything!"

I didn't understand anything. I knew we would have a long journey. Very long. But when I heard the Tács would go too, I felt a sudden joy inside.

The lamp on the altar still had a spark, as tiny as the head of soybean. The wind rustled the banana leaves at the back of the house. I seemed to hear the footsteps of my father's father outside the door.

* * *

* Eugenia tea is made from the small dried berries of a species of myrtle related to clove, guava, and eucalyptus.

Father placed a hand of bananas at the head of his parents' graves, just between the two plots. He lit and placed some incense and stepped back. He didn't cry; only the muscles of his jaw hardened.

"Father and Mother, stay here. I will take the whole family down there. . . ."

A winter afternoon. A wind swept gently over the surface of the paddy. The paddy water lapped the yellow grass at both ends of my grandparents' graves. My father said: "Pray to your grandparents."

I prayed. Tears spilled from my eyes.

Thảo's voice called, "Will your family also go, Còi?"

I looked up. My friend Thảo had perched on top of the grave and held a lead rope in his hand. His buffalo's jaws chomped the grass noisily. The grass was hard as steel plate.

"Yeah, my family will go. How about yours? Going down there should be great!"

Thảo's head shook.

"We still have Grandma. She refuses to go, so we have to stay."

Arriving at our gate, I saw the Tács in the yard near the well and the persimmon tree planted by my grandfather. The well still belonged to my family, but the part of the tree close to the bamboo grove on the side by the dike was on public land. When they attempted to cut the persimmon tree down, my grandfather stripped off his shirt, even though it was the middle of winter, and held the trunk of the tree very tightly and screamed. His skin turned gray. His eyes rolled back. His mouth sputtered. They stood in a circle around him, watching until my grandfather's skin turned purple, and then they left. The persimmon tree wasn't cut, but I could not pick the fruit. Once, when my father was away, I climbed the tree. The watchman caught me, and they locked me in the commune warehouse until midnight. By the time my father came to rescue me, rats had eaten a portion of my heel. For more than half a year, I limped.

Mr. Tác said, "There are five buses to take thirteen households this time. Bring everything to the station gate. You should consider selling your heavy belongings. When we get to the station, we'll have to transfer everything from the buses to the train. Heavy things will be hard to carry."

My father said, "We have nothing to bring . . . and who's left to buy?"

Mr. Tác's daughter Mắm clung to his side. She smiled at me. She had lost three or four teeth in the front; the ones left were very yellow.

"Will you go with me, Còi?"

"Sure; Father? Can our family and Uncle Tác's share a bus?"

My father grumbled, "It's childish, I've got too much to think of already."

Mắm picked a hibiscus flower, stripped the petals, and stuck them to her forehead over the place where she had a red horizontal birthmark.

I said, "Are you a princess?"

She said, "Going to such a happy place, I'll turn into a princess."

Mr. Tác left. All that night, my father sat bowing his head down before our ancestors' altar, without moving, without prayers, without even breathing. Dew pattered on the palm leaf roof. My mother said it was frost, and tomorrow morning we'd have to get up early to catch surfacing fish.

I asked my mother, "How many days until we leave?"

Mother was silent for a moment and then said, "Five days." She turned her face toward the earth and bamboo wall. I fell asleep while still calculating in my head, four days after tomorrow, three days after the day after that. . . .

*   *   *

I was awakened by Mắm's voice. "Hey Còi, get up and catch the fish coming up. My brother, Cà, caught two basins full already!"

I got up intending to rush out of bed, but the cold immediately splashed into my face, making my eyes and nose burn. I had to squat down for a moment.

My father's voice came from the kitchen: "Last night, another two neighborhood buffalos died. Such wicked cold."

My mother's voice replied: "Hear tell down there it's not cold."

I heard everything down there was good.

Carrying the fish basket out to the veranda, I stopped to wipe out one of the marks under the palm leaf roof. Four marks left.

The dike was full of people. Mist from the paddy spiraled up. I strained my eyes but couldn't see a thing. Walking a little ways, I decided I needed to step down into the paddy. But as soon as my feet touched the water, I felt a crack. My heel had split, bleeding profusely, the blood spreading across the surface of the water. I threw the basket down to hold my heel. Mắm came over to me. She must've been following me the whole time.

"Oh God, what's the matter with your heel, Còi?"

"It split."

"Down there, it won't split."

Like others, I longed to go, but I was also fed up with the "down there" refrain, and I said to Mắm, "Down there, if you become a princess, I won't like you!" I didn't think my way of reproaching her would bother her. I was angry because of the pain.

Mắm looked stunned. She stared at me, the birthmark on her forehead turning from blood-red to dark brown. She pointed at my face.

"I don't like you!"

Drops of blood from my heel spotted the withered paddy grass when I ran after her. She sped off, but my foot hurt badly. The grass cut into the wound, the pain flooded my brain. I had to sit down.

* * *

Five buses had been parked at the village gate since three that morning. The cold could not prevent people from flocking in. Sounds of people calling, sounds of crying, sounds of chests clunking. . . . I held on tightly to my guava-wood top, made from the tree cut from the edge of the garden yesterday afternoon, and looked for Mắm. Dozens of yellow lanterns winked back and forth. The village road seemed like a market fair from another world.

At dawn, luggage and people were packed into the bus. I still didn't see Mắm anywhere. Standing in the middle of the village road I cried, "Mắm ơi!"

My mother yanked me along.

"Do you want to stay here? Get in the bus! We'll find her down there."

I gritted my teeth to keep from crying. My mother grasped my hand tightly and the guava-wood top fell into the duckweed pond, sank, and disappeared. My apology gift for Mắm would never be put into her hands.

Inside the bus, I poked my head out the window. Scenery streamed past. I felt something painful surge up inside me. The dike flew past. Myrtle bushes. Shadows of buffalos and houses, shadows of bamboo and rice plants. . . . Would I see them again? I asked, "Mother, is going like this goodbye or just see you later?" I'd started to think about this since the day my grandfather died.

My mother said, "Goodbye, meaning we'll never see this place again. . . ." Tears welled in her eyes too.

The sky brightened gradually, but the wet landscape remained blurred with the frosty morning mist. A few adults told me to close the window. I insisted on keeping it open, poking my head out to peer forward and back, hoping to see Mắm's hair also whipping out like mine. Was she on this bus? Was she still angry with me? My mother broke a sweet potato in half for me and told me to eat it. I shook my head, still watching things outside the bus fly past.

The bus traveled a long way from the village. The landscape became strange, and my feelings lightened. Little Quắt, my sister, lay sleeping soundly on my father's lap. My father didn't sleep but kept silent as if asleep. For nights on end, he had not slept. First arranging our things and then sitting before the ancestors' altar. At first, my mother reminded him to eat. Then, seeing he'd only grumble, she stopped.

* * *

As night approached, the bus entered the city. Father stood and sat, stood and sat. The whole bus fidgeted. Children clung to the bus windows, pointing. The adults grew impatient and worried. They began to grouse. A village elder, perhaps the most experienced in the bus and regarded as the head of our group, stood and shouted loudly: "Tonight we'll make a pile of all the belongings, with the young boys and men circled all around. Women and children will lie on top of the pile to sleep. Here in the north, thieves are rampant as sand fleas. If we're not vigilant, down there we'll have to eat dirt."

It was the first time I had seen the city. Nothing turned out to be very different. All the same trucks I'd seen running in the countryside. All the same figures wearing the same hooded jackets. The same dark gray sky. . . .

The children were made to stay in one place, forbidden to run about. I saw a dishevelled Mầm step down from the bus ahead of mine. I shouted, my eyes blurring: "Mầm! Mầm!"

She turned to look at me. Her eyes opened wide with fear. Her skin, once so pale, had now turned dark gray. I approached her, intending to hold her hand, then thought better of it.

"What happened to you, Mầm?"

She remained silent.

Someone cried out, "Grandfather ơi, our family has seven bags. Why do I now see only six?"

Then crying. Explanations, interrogations. Fear spread like contagion through the thirteen households, all squawking like a flock of chickens with hawks circling in the sky above.

That night, I startled awake repeatedly because of the cold, because I felt homesick, and because of the wet, yellow station platform and its wafts of urine, strong tobacco, and smelly people. I wriggled free from the blanket. Some trunks below creaked. My mother opened her eyes. She had not been asleep, maybe not all night. My mother squeezed my hand, pulling it into her lap. I couldn't tell if she was protecting me or asking me to protect her.

I looked up toward Mầm's family, only to see heaping piles of blankets. Some dim figures of men sat talking and smoking. Ten yards away, five teenage boys wandered around. Each of them had a woolen hat pulled low over his brow and his hands in his pockets. My brain reeled. I was justifiably frightened, but I didn't dare to speak. I knew my mother was more frightened than me. I was a boy of thirteen for the first time realizing he was growing up.

In the morning, I lay there for a while in a haze before rising. The station platform had become packed with people. Not just the thirteen households from my village, but hundreds of others like us had also flocked there. Just like us.

The drenched train stood there panting and puffing. Dozens of carriages connected like chicken coops hooked together. Dilapidated, destroyed. . . .

Starting off! The train whistle tore through the morning mist. The cold dashed into the carriage. I clung to the window, feeling light, wishing even to sing. There were very few seats left; people sat back to back, swaying from side to side with the rhythm of the rails. Blankets, mosquito nets, and other belongings had been stacked at the end of the carriage, each family with a different way of marking their things. The whole car was filled with people from my village.

Little Mắm neither laughed nor cried. All morning, she remained silent. I didn't know whether she was still angry with me, or if she missed our homeland as it became distant. I desperately wanted to talk with her, but I didn't know how to start.

The train stopped. I knew somehow the girls would take time to pee, unlike us boys who just stuck our things out the windows.

A strange area. Some bushes here and there. The sky remained dark gray. I pushed at the crushed grass with my feet, waiting for my mother. She came out of the bushes, her pants not yet zipped. I saw a part of her white belly and quickly turned away. Mắm walked past me. I darted out a hand to hold her tightly.

"Don't be angry with me, Mắm!"

She tried to dredge up half a smile.

I asked, "What happened yesterday?"

"I got really carsick!"

It turned out to be just that. She was not angry with me, much to my relief. I let out a sigh.

"It's cold, why did you dress so lightly?"

"My warm shirt was packed in a trunk; where it's hidden I'll never know."

"Should we look for it?"

Mắm and I shoved some trunks aside. All around, the belongings were piled up like mountains. Piles of blankets and mosquito nets all toppled over. That spot was a lot warmer than the front of the car. After finding Mắm's shirt, I said: "Let's sit back here. Not go up front and freeze."

She listened to me and sat back down. We pulled a blanket from nearby and covered ourselves up to our chins, looking at each other and laughing silently.

"We should stay here until we get down there!"

She nodded. We sat for a long time, chatting, then at some point fell asleep.

When I woke, I found Mắm leaning into me, snoring lightly. The smell of her body was difficult to bear, like the smell of pee. Her birthmark looked dark in the twilight from outside. She was so close to me. A little confusion mixed with pleasure rose lightly inside me. I wanted to stretch my arms across her but was afraid.

The adults in the car filled their minds with worry, with strain, leaving the kids to hang about as they pleased. Mắm and I settled into our nest of blankets and mosquito nets behind the trunks in the back of the car. In another world. I told her, don't let the other kids know. She agreed completely with our exciting hiding game.

I was thirteen. And Mắm was twelve. It was like we had a special secret. And inside each of us was a secret of our own. But they were the same secret, and silently known. I dared to hug Mắm. She let me. Rocked by the train, we fell asleep together. It was getting warmer. . . .

* * *

Dark green forest mixed with plots of grass extended to the horizon. In our homeland, I had never had such an immense impression as that.

From the train, we again traveled by bus. Another half day of sitting packed together, jostling back and forth until the forest opened up. I kept asking my father when we would arrive. Half-worried, half-sick, instead of answering my question, my father just kept looking out the window.

"This land will be very, very . . ."

Maybe he had grand expectations for bumper crops, once people were free to farm. I gazed out at the land. An assorted red color, spongy like chili powder, it gave me a feeling of peppery, prickly heat in my nose. The path wound its way through the twilight. Narrowing. Rising incessantly. The forest darkened as the road rose higher.

Going farther, and farther again, some men spoke as if shouting a refrain, "The farther the freer, the easier to work!" The last town I could remember passing by the window was half a day back. But on the plots of land along the road I could see the lights of scattered houses. Which meant this land had some owners already. . . .

The next time I woke, I saw not a trace of other humans. All around me were moonlit plots of tall grass, head high, bending in the wind. A cool breeze ran through the bus, nothing like the freezing-to-the-bone winds of our homeland blowing in violent, frenzied gusts. The headlights wedged into the darkness, reflecting off the glowing yellow eyes of wild animals along the road. Such a different land. My homeland was now very distant. Like a dream. Like a completely separate incarnation despite the same human existence.

Without warning, the head of the group told the driver to stop. He'd been here before, so even though the sun had not quite come up, he knew we'd arrived.

Over the next few days, we discovered the large river that ran nearby, along with many small contributing streams—plenty of water for cultivation. And that was at the height of the dry season. The trees were still green, and the grass was as high as sugarcane, but dry. We'd need to throw just one spark, and the land would open for cultivation practically by itself. Whether the burning grass would catch the forest on fire wasn't a concern. Forest fires would also come to an end. It was impossible to burn the whole earth. But even if we did, we'd still have a place to sow seeds, and sow them we would.

The grass burned like gasoline. Smoke and dust darkened the sky. Sparks and ash rocketed into the upper layer of the atmosphere. Occasionally, I would hear the echo of an explosion amid the perpetual crackling. People said they came from old bombs. Burning the grass was also a way to clear them from the surface of the earth.

The grass burned and burned. Then the forest burned too. More than half a month passed, and at night in the distance, I could still see the fire flickering along the mountain ridges. A motley layer of black ash covered the light red earth, like the skin of a man pulled from a fire. Nothing remained. Worms disappeared. Crickets ceased to sing. Nothing but rough black trunks of trees rose up in the bleeding twilight.

Each family received a temporary plot of land, enough for planting, and then later a plan would account for the whole area. Our only fear was that our efforts would not equal the task. The first strokes of the hoes began with resounding shouts of freedom.

We had not yet distributed land to each family, each household. Under a centuries-old tree, the "village command" was established. Work all day; at night, gather at the campfires to eat and drink and tell stories. For me, those were the happiest, most carefree days of my life. No studies, no restrictions. Day as well as night, besides helping their families, the kids stuck together, playing every game imaginable.

Mắm was responsible for the washing for her whole family. Each day, dancing like a mynah, she carried a dented washbasin to the nearby stream. I watched her stealthily, and when my parents weren't paying attention, I rushed after her.

A fairy-tale scene. A stream burbled from the secluded and quiet jungle. It swirled around rocks covered with green moss. The water was piercingly clear. Mắm's shadow shook between the colors of the rustling green forest. The sunshine, golden yellow like honey, scattered on the surface of the stream. It seemed to me that she really had become a princess, but not in the way I'd complained about on that winter morning so many weeks ago.

After washing awhile, Mắm's clothes would get soaked from splashing. They were almost transparent. I always kept myself concealed while watching. One day, I saw the raised circle of her breast bulging higher than the one on my breast. I lost my balance and rustled in the brush and Mắm discovered me. She chose to escape by sinking into the water.

"Go home, I'm washing. When a girl is washing by herself, you are not allowed to watch! For shame!"

Self-consciously, I climbed up the slope. When I'd nearly reached the top, I heard her call out playfully: "I'm joking, come back down. Come down . . . and wash with me!"

I came back with the step of different person. Mắm stood in the middle of the stream, her two arms covering her breasts, her hair clinging to her shoulders. Her birthmark was bright red, like the color of her lips, making an appealing spotlight on her face.

At dawn the next day, I had a strange dream. Both interesting and startling, I didn't dare share it with anyone. . . .

* * *

Then famine, like a perpetual black cloud, spread to cover even the brief moments of happiness. Our villagers had left aiming for the middle of the dry season. Seeds sown in the new land remained dormant despite the people's hopeless expectations. Scoops of water from the stream would whirl a layer of dust up from the violent red earth. The exciting red color of our arrival was gone, now it seemed to slap into our blackening faces and reddening eyes. There were still some months until the rainy season. Seeds could not be turned up from the soil to replant later. The famine tightened its grip. . . .

Hands used to farming now had to spread nets and to comb the forest in search for food. The previously clear stream now began to seethe. The forest was murky, more threat than promise. Husks of people dried up and decomposed.

Little by little, my clothes tore to shreds. Even the thickest cotton coats frayed away. Each day, I held Mắm's hand going along the stream, going up to the pool. We seized a fig tree protruding to the edge of the water. Its bunches of fruits were dark red. Our saliva ran. Our jaws strained tight. Like wild boars, we devoured them, forgetting to breathe. Ten minutes later, drops of cold sweat beaded on the fine hair on the back of our hands. We held our bellies, writhing in pain from wrenching bowels. I stuck my fingers down my throat to vomit. Mắm grasped me tightly. Her body flexed, her muscles jumping out of her skin. It was too far from the village to call for help or rescue. We held each other tightly, struggling in rhythm, slackening. . . .

When I opened my eyes, I saw only the flicker of campfire flames. The surrounding air felt stifling. My belly still hurt. I couldn't tell whether it was actual pain or hunger. But what mattered was that I'd been rescued! The first thing I thought about was Mắm, how was she? I tried to murmur: "Mắm ơi, Mắm. . . . Are you all right?"

My mother turned me over and held my hand.

"Are you awake again? You two were found at the edge of the stream. A few more moments and you would've been eaten by beasts. There's nothing wrong with Mắm. She's sleeping over there."

I burst out crying from the pain, mixed with disgrace and some relief.

* * *

In fact, the first real disaster befalling us because of that famine was not that we ate wild figs, but the death of Mắm's brother, Cà.

That morning, like any other morning, Cà took his knife into the forest to search for food. Usually, he went with Mr. Tác. But that day Mr. Tác had a fever and stayed shivering in his hut with his teeth chattering. Cà left early in the morning and did not come home at dusk. The whole village lit torches and went to look for him.

Cà's corpse was dark purple, swollen, huddled into the slope of a hill. In the middle of his face were two black bite marks. He was killed by the poisonous bite of a forest snake. We didn't know why the snake bit him in the face. The poison penetrated straight into his brain. He died, unable to drag his legs back to the village.

Mourning. Mr. and Mrs. Tác fainted again and again. Mắm was disheveled, her eyes swollen. She could not recognize it was me standing before her. She held my side, shaking.

"Brother Cà *ơi*, Brother Cà is here, why is everyone saying he's dead already?"

We dug Cà's red grave in the top of a windswept hill. He had just turned sixteen. The grave of a youth would now be the beginning of our new village cemetery.

I replaced Cà as a brother to Mắm. Mr. Tác became bleary, all day crushing up dry grass to cram like a pinch of tobacco into the bowl of his water pipe, puffing deeply by snatches, and then wheezing and coughing and holding his breath and squirming. His eyes were red, ready to destroy everything within reach, without understanding reason. Mrs. Tác was like a salted cabbage leaf, withered and mushy. Seeing I was close to Mắm, sometimes she would call me and hold my hand in a daze. Her eyes looked to the wild hills. She cried, confusing the two names Còi and Cà.

Spring curled up like a dry leaf. The earth roasted dry. Then the winds poured forth. The land and the sky intermingled with deep orange color. The whole village held on with forest vegetables, stream fish, and sometimes with squirrels and weasels. . . . No one had had much experience hunting.

Mắm was like a dried tree, without leaves, but nevertheless continued to grow. I staggered beside her. She had become a bit taller than me. . . .

* * *

One night at midnight, the whole village seemed to be thrown from their beds. Thunder rolled from the horizon. The wind howled. Beseeching hands raised into the air toward the glittering strikes of lightning. Rain! Rain! Rain!

The next morning, a thick layer of mud and water covered the surface of the earth. The land had changed to brown and black, lithe and flexible like dough. Adults and children alike squeezed out the last of their energy, followed by the strokes of hoes. A week later, green shoots began to appear.

Mrs. Tác looked at me and cried, "My child, the village is going to survive. Corn and beans have started to come up. Only Cà cannot enjoy them. . . . Oh my child, oh Cà, oh. . . . Why did you go so early?"

The land came back to life. Just picking grass, putting it in our mouths, our hunger disappeared. I held Mắm's hand as we wandered the hills. Cà's grave lay surrounded by green. We sat beside the burial mound.

"My brother must have gone back to our old village. With my ancestors."

"That's right, don't be sad. The dead can go like clouds and wind. Maybe Cà brings our ancestors to see us here sometimes."

Mắm trembled. She held me tight. I rubbed my hand across her shoulders.

"Let's go home. Spending time sitting here just makes you afraid."

Mắm's eyes looked far away. I felt dizzy. Her hair smelled like grass. A strange, unsettling feeling spread inside me.

We sat down on the far side of the hill. From the direction of the village rose a plume of smoke. Farther beyond rose immense hills and mountains. Mắm lay back on the grass. After a moment, she seized my hand.

"Lie down!"

Bewildered, I fell like a log. Mắm tilted her head to look into my eyes.

"You . . . are my husband, Còi!"

I startled.

"You naughty girl!"

Mắm giggled. Just laughed. I asked her more questions, but she just kept laughing. Annoyed, I wrestled with her to give her a pinch. Our hair filled with crushed grass. Mắm lay in my arms. . . . I squeezed her. . . . I felt a tingling down my spine. . . .

*   *   *

Mắm was not a salted fish* anymore! She sprouted more every day. Each day when we met face to face, I found she was totally different from the day before. But strangely, she started to avoid me, saying some quick thing as soon as she saw me, and then she'd jog away.

The village divided land into plots for each family to build a home. The plots for cultivation were farther away. Large households received permission to expand their share to the horizon. My house was not far from Mắm's. Mr. Tác only put up a shabby hut, just large enough for three shadows to come in and out. When I came to find her, Mắm would steal away behind the house. Seeing Mr. Tác's shadow, I'd get scared and stagger home again.

What was happening to Mắm? Maybe I'd done something wrong. I couldn't restrain myself. I'd feel indebted to her forever for that strange cry at dusk on the wild hill that day. But as the weeks went by, her attitude toward me didn't change. She remained hot and cold. It seemed like everything that had happened had been necessary. But now, I had only some dream version of my desire, and I'd struggle awake at midnight . . . partly frightened, partly delighted. Several phases of the moon passed in torment, impatience, and worry. . . .

---

* *Mắm* means "salted fish."

Then one afternoon, as I chopped wood in the middle of the yard, I heard a shout from the direction of Mắm's house. All the neighbors out at that moment rushed over. I held an axe, standing on tiptoe to look through the fence. Mắm was running around the yard. Mr. Tác held a long stick horizontally, swinging it at her belly.

Mrs. Tác reeled, shouting, "What a misery you are my child! Why does heaven keep punishing me?"

Mr. Tác's face turned red as he sputtered weakly, "I'll beat you! I'll beat you until it spurts out! Then I'll kill its father too! I'll kill him! I'll burn his house!"

My knees seemed about to collapse. Mắm fell down in the middle of the yard. Part of her belly showed, bigger, and whiter . . . and then I caught sight of Mr. Tác with a glittering knife in his hand, rushing toward me. . . .

* * *

In the old yard, there remained only a part of the gable, falling over to the side and leaning against some shaky beams. I stood motionless on the old foundation. The water in the well had gone a stagnant yellow. The persimmon tree had disappeared without a trace. . . .

"Còi? It's you, isn't it? Why are you here?"

My buddy Thảo was still leading his buffalo on a rope. I'd never thought of him other than as one whose most memorable moments were full of trifling things.

"Yeah, I came back . . . to visit my grandparents' graves."

"Why'd you come back so soon? How's everyone down there?"

Tears welled in my eyes, forcing me to look away.

"Everyone's fine—only I had to come back. . . .'"

A yellow afternoon. A deserted river. The buffalo rope dropped from Thảo's hand. He sluggishly followed me out to the village cemetery.

Somehow, I'd come back to this place. My father intervened to prevent Mr. Tác from . . . and then immediately that night . . . and in the days following . . . interminable panic. . . .

I ran like a thief. I didn't get any more news about Mắm. The trip back was infinitely long. That night, my mother emptied her pockets of every last coin. There wasn't enough for both father and son. It was just me, forced to escape. Everything had just seemed to be starting, but in an instant everything crumbled.

My grandparents' tombs had flooded to the lower edge. If I hadn't been a young buffalo boy, knowing the village cemetery like the back of my hand, I never would have found it. I prayed, bowing three times. I looked up along the river. Although my village was small, I still couldn't see it all at once. Wide as it was, did it have any place for me?

"Grandmother, you left me already. Passed last winter. It was so cold for weeks on end. And then just like that, my father could follow the whole village to go down there."

I stood motionless. I couldn't speak. If Thảo went too, whom could I rely on? I choked with emotion.

"When will your family go?"

"Maybe in a few months. After the harvest. You can stay with my family, help my parents with the farmwork."

A few more months. Maybe Mr. Tác's anger would subside. "Mắm ơi! I will come back!" I shouted along the windswept river. I knew I had to save myself. To save myself for a place far, far away, a place not my homeland, for a drop of my blood. Of course, if she could keep it. Oh, Mắm ơi . . .

Translated by Lê Thế Quế and Charles Waugh

Rain of White Plum Blossoms

Phạm Duy Nghĩa

Since the first day she came up to Kin Chu Phìn, Thuận felt she lived in a hushed and isolated world. Her bedroom shared a wall with a classroom in a small thatched house nestled beside a bamboo forest. Spring nights, Thuận could hear the rustling sounds of porcupines chewing bamboo shoots behind the house. All year round, a thick fog enveloped Rú Mountain's cold air, scarred gray walls, and thick carpet of wild trees. Now and then, the slippery grinding sound of a rockslide would echo from the mountain. Wind whistled in the bitter bamboo forest, sounding like a congregation of whispers beneath the dense canopy. Afternoons in the forest collecting firewood, Thuận would catch glimpses through the blinding fog of undulating silhouettes and indigo shirts. Dao girls bundling dry wood and cutting grass for their horses.* Just little girls, but their woven back-baskets were always filled with big branches, double the height of their bodies. At the entrance of their village, in the shimmering blue light of the sunset, the girls returned in silence. Their dirty little faces always looked so sad.

Thuận left her husband and child to come here, after graduating three years earlier, to teach Dao children how to read. Buffeted with mountain winds and clouds, her skin was no longer as soft and fair as it used to be, but she was still a fresh, energetic woman full of life. "What type of person are you," Principal Tiến had asked her on her first day, "sweating so sweet like fig juice. Looking at your hills and valleys inspires a person to have sexy thoughts not easy to put into words." Tiến was at least two years younger than Thuận, and the sort of person who liked bawdy jokes. And now, after three years living alone in Kin Chu Phìn, Thuận felt very deeply the fear and sadness of a teacher who had to work in a school far away from her family and the city. When she first began, she had to use a stick to walk

---

* The Dao (pronounced Zao in northern Vietnam)—or the Yao in southern China—are one of Vietnam's fifty-four ethnic minority peoples. They live mainly in the mountainous areas of the north and west and are often subcategorized into Red Dao and Black Dao.

through the rain and fog, slipping in slimy mud full of horse manure, just to come and try to persuade the children to come to school. Sometimes, because of flooding, the stream outside the village would be so swollen that she couldn't make it to the market to buy rice and dried fish; for a whole week, she ate nothing but the mice she was able to trap and grill. One night, a green snake slithered into her house to get out of the rain, waking her as it writhed over her chest. Waiting for it to pass through to the classroom, she rolled herself in her blankets to return to sleep, but she startled awake again when a second snake rippled to the middle of her mat. When the sun blazed in the dry season, she worried about forest fires. The year before last, one of the Dao men burning forest land for farming let the fire reach a strip of lychee trees on Rú Mountain, and the sparks flew all the way up to Kin Chu Phìn, nearly catching the thatched houses in nearby Ha Nhi village on fire. Mister Tấn Phù Siểu, a Kin Chu Phìn village leader, came back from Rú Mountain that day carrying a charred dead she-monkey with white eyes and singed black fur. He said, "For you, Teacher. Enjoy eating it if you want. Its face looks like an old woman's—I don't think I can eat it." Thuận took the chance of butchering the monkey and called Mister Siểu's daughter to share the meal with her. The pot of monkey meat smelled terrible and gave her a dreadful headache. That night, Thuận lapsed into convulsions, her whole body cold as ice. While delirious, Thuận hallucinated that the monkey came back and splashed blood all over her face. It sat on the bed crying bitterly like a real person. After hearing the story, an older, experienced teacher named Thanh told her, "Many years ago in this commune, a woman who hated her husband's family left the house in the middle of the night and disappeared on Rú Mountain. People said they saw her in the forest, coming and going as fast as an ape. I don't know for sure, but it's possible you've eaten her." Sweating with fear, Thuận gathered the bones, wrapped them in plastic, and buried them in the sloping yard in front of her house. Above the grave, sage and wild ginseng grew thick and green.

At the beginning of June, Principal Tiến brought a young man named Kiên to start a new class up in Kin Chu Phìn. Kiên had just finished his first year at the provincial teacher's training college and had been mobilized for a six-month literacy campaign in remote areas. The appearance of such a young and enthusiastic student was like a spring breeze blowing into Thuận's foggy life. She and Principal Tiến pulled down some bamboo trees to make a bed. In the small, rathole of a bedroom, the places for Thuận and her new friend were just an arm's length apart. Principal Tiến chuckled. "What a fragile boundary! I have to go back. Help her gather firewood and cook rice, and remember not to spy on her in the bath."

One day, a young education officer from town came to check in on them. Seeing Thuận and Kiên's eating and sleeping situation, he rolled his eyes. "Making a man and woman live in the same room—what are you trying to tempt them to do?" Principal Tiến stuffed tobacco into his water pipe and said calmly, "Please sympathize with us, we're in the highlands! It's asking too much to make the people here contribute labor and materials to make a second house. The best way is just to take advantage of what we already have. Besides, they're adults—if they have a-little-this-a-little-that, it's no big deal. Their lives will be a little rosier, heh heh. . . ."

Living with this young man just a short time, Thuận sensed in Kiên something unusual, something different from other boys. Tough jobs, such as getting filthy with mud, mixing manure with ashes, being swarmed by mosquitoes while passing through the jungle, helping farmers plant and harvest rice, chopping grass for horses, or packing and hauling fruit, never bothered Kiên. He remained perpetually eager, enthusiastic, and joyful, as if all those difficult jobs were just fun games to play. But when he lay down on the bed, his two eyes closed tightly. He never showed an interest in the sensual sighs or the soft sounds of clothes being removed in the night from the bed beside him. There was the time Thuận was showering in the little area fenced with bamboo behind the kitchen, and she called Kiên to bring her a towel. Sitting in the house, he seemed not to hear a thing. Several times, Thuận invited Kiên to stroll along the bulrushes beside the stream bordering the dense bamboo forest. She liked to bathe in the stream at night. In the past, she had to bathe this way by herself. Before undressing, she always told Kiên, "Just sit somewhere nearby. This place is so deserted, it makes me a little scared." But each time Kiên walked far away. He let her swim and dive in the water for hours, her senses thrilled by the water's caresses, her uninhibited body invigorated by the sensational mingling of flesh and water. Then she'd calmly step ashore, exposing her luscious young body in the glow of midnight, full of vitality. Far away, in the pitch black rocks rising above the banks of thick bulrushes, Kiên would stand as immovable as a devoted palace guard. And never once did he glance back.

After times like this, Thuận felt completely humiliated. A woman—though still wanting her husband, and despite abundant wind and moon—still likes it when an awkward and clumsy younger man takes a look at her.

One day, Kiên received a letter. Yellowed with rain, the envelope brought him a photo of a very young girl standing in a plum orchard. His eyes shone with joy. "My girlfriend here—pretty, right?" "In the same class with you?" "Yes. In the literacy campaign, my Ha went to Cán Hồ."

In the envelope were some tiny crumpled white flowers. Kiên brought the letter out in the sun and held it up, touching each word as if to trace something special. The next day, he wandered in the woods all afternoon, clutching a pile of withered leaves from some glowing red tree. He stayed up the whole night writing to her, his face contorted with deep thought. Each time he went to the commune office to ask someone to post one of his letters, he never forgot to include one of the red leaves with three lobes.

* * *

In autumn it rained relentlessly. With the perpetual rushing and pattering in the bamboo forest, it was as if Kin Chu Phìn had disappeared beneath a blinding white waterfall. Thuận's cottage creaked and groaned beneath the pouring water; it seemed it might buckle with just one more big storm and give way for the sage to grow and flower without end.

When the rain finally let up, the forests had been washed clean and left sparkling wet. Only Rú Mountain remained locked in dense sea of fog. The terraces glistened with overflowing water.

Afternoons, Kiên would follow Mr. Siểu's sons to graze the buffaloes on the grassy hillside fields. Each night, he taught them their ABCs, and in the afternoons they taught him how to plow and harrow. Returning home, his face looked merry, but his body had become like a muscular golden eel from the bottom of the pond. Thuận washed rice in a bowl and stared at Kiên's sinewy legs. She felt queasy because of a foul smell at once both familiar and strange. The smell of mud.

The smell woke an array of disturbing memories that had been sleeping deep in Thuận's mind. She recalled the days long ago when she was a girl tending buffaloes and hunting crabs and snails in her own rural homeland. At fifteen, Thuận's body blossomed like the buds of banyan trees and rice plants in the cattle fields behind her village. In her knot of buffalo herding friends was a boy named Tốn. Tốn rode a buffalo without horns, but it still managed to look intimidating with its bulging flanks and constantly munching lips. Roasted insects were Tốn's favorite food. Sometimes his love for them was so overpowering, he'd even eat them raw. Many of the kids had seen him gnawing on a freshly caught red dragonfly. More horribly, some swore they'd seen him plunge a locust thorn into a live snail shell, draw out the snail, and pop the wriggling meat into his mouth and swallow while the snail's lumpy eggs and green intestines still hung from his mouth! Maybe because of all this extra protein in his diet, he looked as rough and blocky as a slag brick. He ate like a dragon fish, but he took only the most cursory care of himself; mud might be crusted on his heels for a week at a time.

One sunny summer afternoon, Thuận was looking for her buffalo on a hill of palm trees when all at once she smelled mud and the hornless buffalo head poked through the tall grass. Whump! Without warning, Tốn's dirty, dusty body jumped from the palm leaves and landed on top of her. He laughed and shoved his hands into her pants. The buffalo devouring grass nearby seemed to turn its head and grin. The frightening image of his mouth full of sticky snails popped into Thuận's mind, and she hid her face in the grass. She resisted at first by thrashing madly, and then, unexpectedly, she stiffened. From somewhere far away came some quivering, flowing stream. It paralyzed her senses. It erased all notions of purity. All repulsion. When she was alone again, Thuận sat up and in a daze looked at the bright rays of the sun shining through the palm leaves. The adolescent girl did not understand why she had stopped resisting. The smell of mud wafted up to her nose. At end of the day, returning through the crushed grass, Thuận saw some drops of blood, the red color glittering in the setting summer sun.

That red color seemed to congeal over her memories of that age, and it was not easily scoured away. Despite the shuddering dread she felt when remembering the painful rape, sometimes Thuận surprised herself by wanting to return to wade through the grass and find the smell of that mud again.

Besides mud, Thuận was also haunted by the smell of fish.

After she'd just left her homeland for the highlands, Thuận lived with her uncle's wife in a house near the river, every day stripping sedge for her aunt to weave into hats to sell. At sunset, she often sat beneath a cottonwood tree, waiting for the boatman who brought the sedge up and down the river. She watched the guy on his boat with a curious delight. He sat shirtless in the prow, mending his nets and flexing his bulging chest, his mouth hidden by a red beard that reeked of foul tobacco. She had no idea where he'd drifted in from but had heard he also cut wood from the forest and traded fruits as he traveled the river. One night, Thuận heard flute music coming from the river. She gathered up her unfinished work and made her way down to her cottonwood tree. A hazy silvery blue mist lay on the surface of the water, gathering into little clouds of fog along the bushes. Fishermen knocking oars against the sides of their boats clunked through the mist. And the boatman sat in the prow of his boat anchored just offshore playing a sad melody. The sound of that melody gnawed at her insides and made it hard to think about anything else. Then the mist cleared, the moon rose, and it seemed that in the fresh air there was something inspirational and very warm. An atmosphere of proliferation, of rapture. The blue moonlight glistened through the grass. Bullfrogs plopped into the water. A pair of tree frogs embraced one another in a sandal-wood tree. Thuận felt the pull of desire. The smell of mud from the past reawakened inside her. She went back and forth along the riverbank. Then she called to him. She rolled up her pantlegs, waded out to the boat, and said, "You play so beautifully." But he remained focused only on his song. She picked up his bamboo fishing rod and tapped him on the head. He continued to play. She wrestled the flute from his grasp and threw it into the river. He scowled, and then grinned. A fierce struggle erupted at the front of the boat. She thrashed like a river carp beginning to lay its eggs. A steel bucket full of sardines hit the deck—*choang!*—and in the cabin dark-ness, the spilt fish glowed like silver doubloons. Wet slippery fish slithered over the backs and bellies of their now naked bodies. Fish in their armpits. Fish between their legs. In a whirlwind of passion, she bit his shoulder and tasted the salt of his blood in her mouth. They held each other on the slip-pery deck, the smell of fish all around them. He sighed, "What a pity!" She gave him a playful slap. "What's a pity? That you didn't meet me earlier?" He smacked his lips. "No. A pity for the flute. Tomorrow, I'll have to cut another reed."

A month later, they became husband and wife. He quit fishing and took a job in a pottery factory. They had a child, and Thuận went to the teacher's training school, and after graduation she got a job in Kin Chu Phìn, begin-ning a new phase of her life in a remote mountainous area. From then on, the smell of fish, of the river, of the fishing boat remained powerful in her imagination.

"Any love that passes through our lives may leave some odor," said Prin-cipal Tiến to Thuận once. "The smell can haunt us a whole lifetime, Sister. For example, my first love imbued me with the smell of buffalo dung. At the age of fourteen, I fell for a girl from my village. Night after night we met secretly at the jackfruit tree in the garden in front of her house. Right where they tied the buffalo. Some of the dung was dry, some wet—it all looked very filthy. Why didn't I take her somewhere else? Bad luck, I suppose. One time, I called for her too loudly when I didn't realize she'd already come out, and her father came out to the yard and looked around. We hid from him by climbing into the jackfruit tree. High up in the tree, she began to cry silently in pain. It turned out she had accidentally touched her head to an ant's nest made of buffalo dung wrapped around a tree branch. The ants had swarmed out and bit her. The next day, I found a dry scab of dung in her hair. Later, when I left the village, I never forgot the smell of warm dung. It was attached to my first tremor of love. So, whether sweet or wretched, we should still cherish and enjoy whatever we have, ha! My second love—much luckier—had the smell of eucalyptus leaves. . . ."

* * *

Night. Another night. To teachers in the highlands, nights feel truly long.

By day, with Kiên being friendly, Thuận's loneliness was halved. But at night, not only had the gap not been filled, it seemed to crack even further. It was like a deep and dark thirsty hole opening up. She missed her husband; she missed her child. For nearly a year she hadn't been able to rub her face in his beard, hadn't been able to care for or inhale the smell of the sunshine in the hair of her daughter, now six years old with a pair of eyes as black as two beans dropped in water.

The previous fall, she had received a letter from him. The letter set the date he would come visit her. The day before he promised to arrive, at dusk, a terrible lightning storm burst the giant ironwood on the steep mountain summit, shaking all of Kin Chu Phìn. Under dark clouds slit by chaotic lightning, the white orchids covering the hills created a ghostly atmosphere. The storm lasted until the next day, with the village completely engulfed by white rain. Thuận's heart felt on fire. After two days of waiting with tired eyes, she heard that a flood had swept away the bridge leading to the commune. Water roared, raging like a fall. People and traffic from the city all had to turn back. A foolhardy boy risked swimming across but was swept headlong into the rocks.

Thuận fought with herself and everything else for several days, angry with the sky, hating the land. In her dreams, she saw herself and her husband turn into fish swimming in the flooded stream. He was a big white fish circling around her. Her chest heaved up and down like twin throbbing red gills. . . . Time after time, in her heart, she hoped for some fulfillment of her distant love that continued to thrive and spread as fast as ginseng in the forest.

In the spring, after taking their daughter to celebrate Tet in his hometown for a month, he took two more days off from work to visit her. Remembering this visit later made her half laugh, half cry. Apparently, as he neared Kin Chu Phìn, he'd seen two horses in a field of grass along the mountain path in the red light of sunset. On the other side of the path sat two Dao men smoking tobacco. Having had a passion for horses ever since he was a boy, when he saw the magnificent horse black as midnight, he dropped his bag to the grass. God! A horse with charming eyes, as smooth as ice. Its black coat was like satin, rippling in the wind. "A beautiful princess," he told her. "A noble lady with a mane, not a horse." And the other one with dirt brown hair, a belly like a toad's, bony ribs, and pustules under its squinting eyes. He looked at it with pity, thinking, Such an ugly creature! He stroked the horse's mane, intending to show her some sympathy. Immediately, the horse reared its head and whinnied, exhaling a foul stench and trying to bite him. He stood up, wiping his hands on his pants. "God damn beast! Half a second more and you'd have two knuckles in your mouth. Ugly and bad tempered too!"

Turning to the black horse, he stroked its shoulder lovingly. Perhaps its heart was in harmony with his thoughts; it glanced at him with its fanciful hazel eyes, then started to eat grass. After checking its hooves and teeth, he stepped back and stood up straight to admire its smooth hips. But without warning the horse reared up, knocking its head straight into his groin. He sprawled onto the ground, reeling, then picked up his bag and stumbled through the grass to the dark mossy stream.

One of the Dao men fell down to the ground laughing. The old man sitting next to him rubbed his beard and shook his head.

That night at Kin Chu Phìn, he squirmed at her side like a big kid, his gestures awkward and sickly, sliding all over, drifting like a wick in oil. Pain throbbed in his groin up through his guts. She buried her face in his foul chest, clawing him and crying all night. For the past several days, she had been a tree dying of thirst waiting for life-giving rain. . . .

* * *

After several rainy nights, sage grass grows quickly.

Where trampled by hooves, sage emits a strong aroma. Horse manure meets the new sun, softens, and gradually covers with white mold.

In the forest of Rú Mountain, game hens crowed at noon, and the wilderness seemed more desolate because of it. Early in the morning until noon, the fog settled into thick curds impossible to escape, curled into spheres that clung to the trees and tumbled over the rocks.

The day before Kiên left Kin Chu Phìn, the sunny weather gave way again to rain. The farewell party for practicum students who had finished teaching their literacy courses was held in the evening at the commune primary school. The tables had been arranged into long rows. Besides the teachers and practicum students, Mr. Tẩn Phù Siểu, the vice-president of the commune and former village chief of Kin Chu Phìn, attended. The harder it rained, the more wine people drank. His face red and leering, Principal Tiến gnawed leisurely on some dogmeat bones and encouraged Kiên: "After graduation you should come back up here to teach, Kiên. It'd be a goddamn crime to go to a town or a city. Those people are always pressed and clumped together, weak as molting crabs. There's not even space to sneeze! Come up here and you can breathe clean air, eat clean vegetables, and sleep with clean girls. Drink wine 'til your lips get soft, savor wild game 'til your teeth are tired, and sometimes see naked Meo and Man girls bathe in the stream, and you'll never have to know a damn thing about technology or the war in the Gulf. Ha!"

Sitting next to Tiến was Thanh. Thanh's face was as black as grease mixed with soot. His voice sounded as gravelly as someone who'd eaten rocks.

"Kiên has lived in Kin Chu Phìn for half a year, we can't fool him. The only clean wild game left on Rú Mountain is just some monkeys, and whoever shoots them eats them. Sure, there's unspoiled girls here, but you and I are no longer bachelors. Coming up here to teach is like Trương growing a tail!"

Thuận burst out laughing. "What Trương grew a tail? You're kidding!"

Thanh said, "I don't know the guy. He came up here a decade or so ago, with some timber company, and then stayed to work as a forest ranger. One time, he went back home and caught his wife in the act with another guy, got really angry, and began to hate women. He was living in Tả Lé but then moved deep into the forest and built a hut to escape seeing other people. Back then Rú Mountain was full of bears and deer and other wild game. Swarms of monkeys saw him appear and thought he was smart. They saw him living off the forest and thought he was virtuous, so they made his acquaintance. Sometimes, they'd toss fruit down to Trương, and he'd sit beneath the tree picking up the fruit for his meal. Living with the monkeys for a long time, he began to laugh like a monkey—*khẹc khẹc khẹc*. One day, while bathing in the stream, he discovered something had sprouted above the crack of his ass. He thought it was a pimple. Each day, it became more of a nuisance, and finally he came out of the woods to have someone take a look at it. It turned out to be a four-and-a-half-inch tail. Why the hell are you laughing? If you ever go to Long Khánh, just ask people about Trương who used to work in the forest, or if you meet him, ask him to take off his pants. He went to the hospital to have the tail removed, but there's still a scar."

Remembering Thanh's story about the woman missing on Rú Mountain, Thuận chuckled.

"In your dark eyes, everyone can turn into a monkey. Monkey man, monkey woman. . . ."

"Turning into a monkey when you're really sad is a common story!" Thanh grinned. "I know what's going on. Books and movies about the highlands are all so glorified and untrue. The cameras only catch places where it's all beautiful white orchid tree flowers or crimson peach flowers. Then the pretty flute music starts up—*pặp pặp pù pù, tí tí tủ, tí tí tủ*—and the rice wine bamboo straws are bent into use and boys and girls hold hands and dance. All the girls in the films have light skin too. Sure, all their lives are spent working hard in the fields, so where does all this sweet-smelling white come from? I've lived in the highlands for years and years and never smelled anything but horse shit."

"Looking at life like that is too shallow!" said Principal Tiến in a patronizing tone. "I'm emptying a cup of wine into your mouth right now!" He crossed one hand over the other. "Life must be optimistic. There have been changes to the highlands. In years to come, schools will be built in a well-organized way, and more roads will be built to connect the villages. Fertilizers will be brought to the soil, entering into every corn root. Who knows, in ten or fifteen years, Dao people might go down the street driving in cars, right, Mr. Siểu?"

Mr. Siểu nodded in agreement.

"Principal Tiến speaks the truth. Many Mong and Dao people have TVs and motorbikes already. With the right will, anything can be done. My only fear is the time when we will have so much money we won't know what to buy."

Principal Tiến tossed the dog bones under the table and wiped his mouth. "Please, clap your hands for Mr. Siểu! In short, we can take this lesson: life must be optimistic, and you have to know how to make the most of what you've got. Like right here, good clean dogmeat and good clean wine, cheers!"

The noise of the party rose up. The cups went upside down. Thuận went along the rows of tables, bending to invite people to have a drink, smiling and talking. She drank one cup of wine, then another. Kiên was surprised. "Why are you so merry today?"

Principal Tiến whispered, "Since we're both men, I have a question for you, okay? Have you ever been allowed . . . to sniff Thuận's armpit?"

Kiên did not reply. He focused on the wine pouring into the cup in front of his face. The Nậm Pung wine* came from the bottle like a glistening thread.

"A woman with heavy feet, moaning sighs, and a hairy lip, especially one who rarely gets to smell her husband, is often very thirsty!" suggested Tiến.

Kiên looked around, smiling sheepishly.

---

* A type of rice wine made by the Red Dao people of the Vietnamese highlands.

"She looks as succulent as a strawberry hanging before your eyes—what man wouldn't like her? But . . ."

He left his sentence unfinished, looking away. The rain let up though blue lightning still flashed in the distance. Kiên imagined in the blue lightning the face of a virgin girl, innocent and holy—her holiness so soaring that no man would dare have trivial sex with her, even if it was on his mind.

When seeing Kiên and Thuận off, Principal Tiến poked Kiên's ribs, whispering, "Just look at Thuận, a stallion who craves her, says something. Don't turn your heart to iron or stone. You have to make the most of what you've got."

"For my sweetheart," Kiên responded in a cold voice, "I am completely faithful."

Leering, Tiến said, "Wait and see!"

Kin Chu Phìn was a two-hour walk from the commune primary school. Kiên went first, carrying a flashlight. Thuận reeled after him as if in a dream. The smell of decaying leaves in the forest rose up, musty and unavoidable. The sloping dirt path they walked was slippery. Disturbed by their passing, birds fluttered their wings in the dark canopy, scattering down drops of rain. Thuận slipped and fell forward, crying out. Kiên turned around just as Thuận crashed into him. In that moment, he felt an extremely smooth power overcome his body. His hands inadvertently grasped her waist and hips, his fingers sank into her soft, cool skin. Thuận's eyes rolled, her mouth exhaled a cloud of alcohol into Kiên's face. A great thirst flared, making Kiên feel weak, but he quickly dropped his hands.

"Those damn birds, they startled me!" Thuận seemed to be awake now. She gave a brittle laugh and took the flashlight, volunteering to walk ahead.

The two of them returned home at nearly eleven o'clock. In her bed, Thuận tossed and turned a long time, unable to sleep. Still heady with wine, her body on fire, Thuận felt the thirst inside her return. The warming of the wine along with the shadows cast by the lamp's dim and flickering blue flame mingled with her wild thoughts. On the next bed, Kiên also turned over again and again, unable to sleep. In just a few hours, he would leave this house and its desolate forest and return to the teachers' training college in the happy crowd of the city. Remembering their embrace in the forest, Thuận felt excited and restless. A male body as well built as bamboo lay just an arm's length away. He reeked with the smell of man—a burning, salty smell mixed with sun and wind that only an experienced woman like her would recognize. The whole past half year existing with Kiên, his smell tormented her. It kindled in her mind the smell of fish and the smell of mud.

A too silent night. Thuận could hear and feel the blood flowing inside her. She knew she was no longer at a silly, romantic age, no longer able to believe in the spiritual matters of life as Kiên did. She knew only that she was a woman. A woman with a husband who needed pleasures in real life, the way wormwood grass needs heavy rains, fruit trees need wet land in the woods, or lush bamboo needs to breathe mist. A woman is close to the earth. A woman is synonymous with nature and a life cycle both idyllic and mortal.

Thuận remembered, in days past, a widow in her hometown who resolved to be faithful to her late husband her whole life, gaining a reputation as a virtuous and sincere girl. In her thirties, a young boy hired for work in the village often came to her house to help her with the farming and gardening. Whenever she saw him without his shirt or scratching his eyebrows that were curly like sprouting corn, the woman blushed and turned to burn incense on the altar of her husband. One night, a thunderstorm forced the boy to sleep at her house. In her dark bedroom, the woman struggled all night. No one knew what she was thinking. People only knew that the next morning she woke to find her long hair had turned completely white, where before it had been completely black. The white of clouds, of frost.

Thuận felt her lungs swell, suffocate. The fire from the alcohol burned. She pulled the blanket to cover her body, and then peeked over to Kiên's bed while fumbling with her shirt buttons to reveal her fulsome breasts. Her body bucked under the blanket like a trapped young animal. Why do people have to cover themselves and hide the desires that every person has? Why do we bind ourselves with a cord called ethics and make desire something guilty and evil? In the past few years, she'd been throttling her youth to show her devotion to the education of the nation. She had no regret about that. Being devoted was the greatest pleasure of humanity. She only regretted having so few moments to be a woman in her life. And human life was truly so short.

Kiên stirred, turning his face toward her. In the dimly glimmering light, his chest swelled, and the long black hair above his forehead looked wild. Thuận's body shook. She could not resist her instincts any longer. She would strike down across his bed like an uprooted banana tree. Claw him frantically. Fill herself with sexual pleasure. Sin with four people all at one time. She no longer cared. She sat up. But she froze in the instant she glanced down into the gap between the two beds, this time as deep and dark as a sewer.

There was some invisible thing forcing her to stop. It was like the fear of a person about to bury herself alive.

Minutes later, Thuận lay down. Sweat rolled down her breasts. Her body verged on collapse. She could feel the hair on her head gradually turning white. The white color of a fierce tension, of protecting herself until the dire end. Near morning, she fell asleep. She dreamed about Tốn drowning, his body floating on the river Thao. The hornless buffalo had gone mad, its muzzle foaming, its eyes rolling back, the wind tearing crazily over the riverbank and fields. She recoiled at the red rice flower in Tốn's mouth, his young body pink like the body of the boy hugging a carp in the Hồ village paintings.*

Tốn's clean chubby body slowly disappeared. A cyclone swept in, scattering red leaves with three lobes into the air. A burning flame spun and then vanished, briefly illuminating Kiên's girlfriend Hà, whom Thuận knew only vaguely through photographs. They were in Càn Hồ, then lost themselves in the plum forest. Strangely, neither Thuận nor Hà wore clothes. They were pure, primitive, virginal. Petals fell continuously like a rain of white plum blossoms, flooding the forest to their calves with white. They walked together in the rain of white flowers, naked and unashamed, their bodies light and airy with the thoughts of ethereal souls. Hà's body radiated the sweet fragrance of a fairy. Thuận's mind felt clean and clear and free of desire. To be free of all desire in the diversity of real life is to be free of the root of all suffering. Buddhist truth is like that: simple, fresh, and pure as an eternal rain.

Translated by Lê Thế Quý and Charles Waugh

---

* Đông Hồ village has been making woodcut paintings since the eleventh century.

Ghost Cat

Phong Điệp

THE SMILES ON THE TWO CHILDREN'S LIPS DIE WHEN THE HARSH SOUND-
ing bell from their father clangs. One wheelchair rolls after the other down
the dark, narrow corridor. An old cat purrs creakily at the entrance to the
warehouse, its still green eyes wide open and glaring with reflected light.

"Do you think anything's wrong?" says the girl. "Daddy's home earlier
than usual."

"The bell makes him sound angry too."

"So you think . . ."

The two wheelchairs turn into the building's living quarters. Unexpectedly, all the lights have been turned on, sparkling on the polished floor of
the entryway. The front doors have been left wide open, and next to their
father's big shoes on the mat is a pair of small sandals.

The owner of the sandals must have been in a rush—one edge of the
doorstep mat is turned over.

"You think Daddy wants us to go in there? It's been a long time. . . ." The
bell clangs again, the sound short and sharp. The two children roll their
wheelchairs to the entrance to the living room. A woman stands nervously
in the middle of the room, apparently waiting for the children to come have
a look. Her face is cold and sad, her skin pale in the overly bright lights.

Their father sits on the couch in silence. Crushed cigarette butts fill the
ashtray on the table to overflowing.

"From now on, Ms. Bội will be your teacher."

Their father is silent for a moment to look at them sternly.

"No one is allowed to argue with Ms. Bội. Are you clear? Not allowed,
that's it. Now go to your room."

The tired woman raises her hand to greet them. A long hand with dry,
papery fingers.

"We will meet again tomorrow morning," she says.

The two wheelchairs turn back to the long and narrow corridor. The old
cat is still sitting at the entrance to the warehouse, its eyes ghostly green.

The trees in the garden rustle against one another as the wind whirls round and round.

"Anh, I feel scared."

"Dad leaves again tomorrow morning," says the boy. "More long trips. And probably a lot of gifts."

"But he never talks to us."

"Because he's so busy. He comes home to rest."

"I feel sorry for Daddy. What if he gets tired of having to take care of us?"

"You don't know what you're talking about!"

The children put themselves to bed.

With incessant peals the morning bell wakes the children at seven o'clock. They dress hurriedly and drag their bodies into the wheelchairs next to their beds. From the hall comes the sound of Ms. Bội's sandals clicking on the tiled floor. Without hesitation, the bedroom door swings open. The children hadn't given a thought to locking the door from inside.

In the light of day, Ms. Bội looks even thinner, paler. Her deeply sunken eyes settle into a cold look on the children. She has dressed in a thick fabric that she has wound around her flat, skinny body. Women her age never dress like that.

"Children, say, 'Good morning, Ms. Bội.'"

The children force themselves to mouth the words. Ms. Bội appears to have no reply for them. Instead, she goes straight to the beds. The disorderly piles of blankets and mosquito nets are neat and tidy within seconds, the two bedcovers pulled taut and smooth.

The little girl, with a deep breath, tries to break the ice. "Ms. Bội, did you sleep well last night?"

But the boy reaches over to her wheel with one hand and rolls them both slowly toward the door.

"Are you going somewhere?" asks Ms. Bội, her metallic voice somewhat cross.

"I want to go to the garden," says the boy.

"Not allowed. Please go wash your face and sit at the breakfast table. After that, we'll begin our studies."

The girl looks with worry at her older brother squirming in his wheelchair.

"What's wrong?"

Ms. Bội silently rolls each wheelchair into the hall and closes the door. Breakfast begins in an orderly fashion. Ms. Bội eats quickly, barely causing even a clink or a scrape. The children take their time, chewing and swallowing reluctantly. Ms. Bội has to wait more than ten minutes for them to finish.

"Healthy food like this helps make a body healthy," says Ms. Bội as she begins to clear the table. "Why didn't you finish?"

The girl's plate still contains a third of her portion.

"It's for Két."

"Our crazy old cat," says the boy. He wipes his mouth.

"A crazy old cat?" Ms. Bội says weakly.

"It screams all night and bites everyone it meets."

"That's not true at all," says the girl. "He's really old. He keeps losing clumps of fur. But he doesn't go out prowling around like other cats."

Ms. Bội silently lowers herself into a chair. Without a word, the children leave the table and settle into their lesson room where their books lie about in disarray. A clump of cat fur flutters from the windowsill.

Ms. Bội comes in, looking serious, and sits down facing them as if to begin the lesson.

"Feline spirits often manifest themselves at night," she says, "yowling and calling to each other in wretched voices and roving around in large, noisy packs."

The girl casts a worried look to her brother. But they keep listening without saying a word.

The end of the lesson comes when Ms. Bội has become completely haggard, her face lifeless and pale.

* * *

Két does not appear at subsequent meals. Thin clumps of his gray fur lie scattered around the house.

The children are forbidden to stay up late. At the end of their evening lessons, they are sent to bed and the lights turned off immediately, making the girl anxious.

"Do you think he's going to die?"

"Who? That stinky Két? Of course—he's so old."

"That's not what I meant," she says unhappily. "No one's fed him. It's been days. He doesn't hurt anyone."

"Ms. Bội will tell more cat ghost stories if you keep saying that." The boy takes some delight in this. "Ms. Bội always has a lot of those stories."

"I don't like them." The girl sighs and pulls the blanket over her face.

"He's going to die, for sure."

But the cat is not yet dead, because at midnight the boy wakes to the sound of its crying tiredly at the back of the warehouse. He tries to wake his sister but she won't get up, lying curled around a painful stomachache and sweating profusely.

Outside, the corridor is very dark. The yowling of the cat fades away. The boy rolls his wheelchair forward. Ms. Bội's room at the front of the warehouse is still bright with lights, as if nothing has happened. The little boy takes a deep breath and raises his voice, calling, "Ms. Bội? Ms. Bội?"

He stops in front of her door. A strong wind whips toward Ms. Bội's bed. There is no one in it.

"Ms. Bội? Ms. Bội!"

A crashing sound like a cascade of falling rocks comes from the back garden, and then everything is again completely silent. Frightened, the boy wheels around to return to his room, but even his wheels squeaking on the polished tiles of floor sound overloud and terrifying in the middle of the night. In his room, he finds his sister already sound asleep, drool spilling from the corners of her mouth. He hauls his sister's unresponsive body into her wheelchair and pushes it out ahead of him into the garden.

Fluttering in a panicked voice, their elderly next-door neighbor, Mrs. Hàng rushes out to open the door for the children. Voices can be heard arguing back in the house. Running footsteps clatter toward the gate. Water flushes. The girl is lifted into a bed. People fill the room, talking loudly. The boy's wheelchair is pushed into the corner. Mosquitoes swarm his face, but in his exhaustion he falls asleep.

In the afternoon three men and a beautiful woman arrive in an old jeep with an engine as noisy as a rice-milling machine. They've come to look for Ms. Bội, but she cannot be found.

Mrs. Hàng continues to cook for the children. In the backyard garden, all the vegetables have been trampled. The children spend their days reading all the way until dinner.

The children's father finally comes home after a long journey. His skin has darkened and his cheeks have become gaunt.

"With all that crazy business, what actually happened?"

"We don't know. But we keep hearing a cat crying at the back of the warehouse."

Their father sighs. "There have been a lot of stories about crazy cats. That they bite a person, and then the person dies because of something the cat infects them with. Ms. Bội had a child who died like that."

The children sit in silence. After a very long time, the girl says, "Daddy, we want Ms. Bội."

Their father stands up, looking exhausted.

"You kids go back to your room. Starting tomorrow, you'll be back in school."

The two children quietly roll their wheelchairs down the dark corridor.

"Anh," says the girl, "Két is not crazy."

"But that's not what we said before," says her brother.

*　*　*

The new school year begins, and the children have to get used to rising earlier than before. The alarm bells echo down the narrow corridor full of bright sunlight. Mrs. Hàng from next door is already waiting for them in the courtyard.

The children call out their goodbyes to their father.

The door of the guest room remains closed. The welcome mat is pushed away toward the corridor, one edge curled up.

Near the school, a woman in clothes made of coarse fabric wrapped closely around her flat, skinny body waits for them to pass by and then quietly slips away.

Translated by Nguyễn Hùng and Charles Waugh

Gifts of Heaven

Nguyễn Thế Hùng

THE WINDS NO LONGER BLEW SO STRONGLY AND THE WEATHER WAS still cold, but it looked like warmer, more humid air was on its way. At night, gnats flew into the houses, signaling that the lilacs would soon bloom and that the deer in their pens would shed their old coats for new smooth golden ones lined with white dots, as sleek as if glowing with oil. The stags rubbed their heads against the bamboo enclosure, preparing for the antlers that would soon grow. The does wagged their short tails to attract the stags. Mating season. Also the time for my grandfather to carefully sharpen the saw that had been hanging in the shed since last season. My father woke early each day to practice the old traditional way of catching the deer. My mother began to grind up small pieces of charcoal in a chipped washbowl to dry out the velvety new antlers we'd soon have.

I don't know when my village began raising deer or who had the idea to begin with. I only know for sure that as I was growing up, my grandfather was the best antler cutter in the whole village. My father had only just begun to learn. Starting the year I turned ten, every morning, in one corner of the yard, my father taught me the traditional way to catch deer. On big farms, people usually catch them with ropes, but my village didn't go in for that, choosing instead to keep the ways of our ancestors. Because to our understanding, raising deer wasn't just a way to earn money by selling antlers, the antlers themselves were gifts of heaven bestowed specially on our village. So the day we cut the antlers was a day of celebration. The men who cut the antlers had to be chosen with special care since a poor cut would mean those deer wouldn't be able to grow new antlers the next season, wasting a whole year's worth of care. All the rice, beans, corn, peanuts . . . everything wasted. It seemed that heaven had given this sacred duty to my family, from one generation to the next. We had been antler cutters from the beginning. Of the many people needed to harvest antlers, the most important was the starter. The starter had to be fast, strong, and very delicate to keep the antlers unbroken and both the catcher and the deer safe. Many inexperienced starters will break an antler, dropping the value of the broken horn down a third. Many have broken a deer's leg or blinded one—an unlucky omen for the whole year. So I had to run and do chin-ups to strengthen my arms until they were as hard and yet as flexible as a thick rope—only then could I practice the skills of being a starter. There were no official rules, but everyone always looked up to and admired a skillful starter. Many years passed with my father and me practicing every day. As usual, we'd finish by standing opposite each other. He'd make some crazy moves, and I'd have to match him, take some chances, very fast, and catch both of my hands exactly around his wrists and press them down. At first, my father needed only to take a wide, low stance no matter what I did. But then, day by day, he began to need all his energy to withstand my attacks. One day at the beginning of the mating season I turned seventeen, after practicing together for so long, as if learning a dance, face to face, I finally caught my father's wrists perfectly and focused all my energy to press them down. His pillarlike legs began to shake. Several seconds passed, and I inhaled deeply into my lungs and continued to press him down. His stance weakened bit by bit, and his breathing became forced. Finally, with a gasp, he gave in. As we walked home, he said to me: "You are a man now, you've proven you can take my place. Remember how very strong you are. Never drink the deer's blood." I saw in his eyes a spark of happiness from seeing his son reach manhood, but also a little sadness from feeling he was now passing into a new stage of his own life.

My father's arms hung down limply as he entered the house and stood beside my grandfather, whose eyes were nearly blind. He stood there waiting sadly. It was as difficult for him to accept being replaced as it was for him to replace my grandfather, who pushed his creaking knees to stand, went upstairs to take down the saw, and brought it to my father. My father sharpened it diligently in preparation for the new mating season.

*   *   *

The young stag in our shed was a rare breed, already as large as an adult. Every year, in the middle of the mating season, a pair of pinkish white antlers appeared on his head, with three long, proud branches. A well-tempered sort of deer, everyone in the village wanted to bring their does to my house to mate with him. Each year, he could satisfy five or six does. But the year I became a starter, my father did not allow him to mate. He wanted him full of energy and as strong as possible to make one last test for me before I became a starter officially. The day finally came, beginning early in the morning with the noisy sounds of knives on chopping blocks and chopsticks in bowls. In the shed, we had stored hundreds of kinds of fresh leaves and blossoms that had been gathered from the high mountains in preparation for our unusual party. In the house, the smells of sticky rice, fermented rice, and rice wine wafted fragrantly through the air. My father placed a platter of food and fresh blossoms with a bottle of spring water on the altar of the god of good luck. Then, chanting in the way of my ancestors, my grandfather prayed: "The old father has made way for his son, we hope Thần Lộc* agrees. My grandson's strength can help him to replace his father and become a starter. Now I have no strength, my eyes nearly blind, my hands weak. I want to give the saw to my son. Our small ceremonial gift of spring water and fresh blossoms from the high mountain comes from our hearts. We pray you come and bring us luck. Our family, thanks to your blessings, has never forgotten to teach our children to express gratitude to you. We use your gifts† to accomplish useful and fair things, to make medicine. Anyone who breaks these traditions would not be spared. I pray you can accept our rude speech, these small gifts, and our kind hearts."

The prayer ended, and six strong young men stood ready behind me, the door of the shed half-open. After a moment of working himself into a frenzy, the young stag found it impossible to escape. He froze and raised his fresh pink horns defiantly. In an instant of panic, my face flushed red, and I breathed deeply to calm my nerves. I gazed into the red eyes of the stag. I knew a dozen more eyes observed my every move from behind. I held his gaze. He seemed to feel cowed and blinked slowly. Conquered by my gaze, he came out of the shed and turned around in the corral, somewhat desperately. My helpers all stepped into the corral, their backs pressed against the bamboo fence, wary of the stressed stag's every quiver. The circle closed in. The crucial moment approached. The stag wanted to see what I was made of. He lifted his head and took a step. I retreated. He stumbled and lowered his head. That's all I needed. As fast as a tiger seizing its prey, I threw out my hands and caught both his horns. In my father's strong, low stance, I set all my weight into them. He did not give in. With a flick of his hard, strong neck, he lifted me from the ground and then flung me back down. Inhaling deeply into my eighteen-year-old chest, I kept the pressure on his head until it lowered to my legs. Instantly, I wrapped one leg around his head to cover his eyes. He bore up, chuffing, but he couldn't withstand my powerful leglock. With his sight blocked and his strength failing, his knees finally buckled. I shouted, "Come on!" Moving as one, the more experienced men

---

* Thần Lộc is the name of this god of good fortune.
† The word *lộc* can mean luck, antler, or blossom, and is used here as all three.

all pinned the stag to the ground. I sat on some dry straw on the ground with his head locked in my legs to raise his horns. My father, with a respectful look on his face like he was presiding over some ceremony, stepped toward us with the saw in his hands. He knelt down and asked, "Ready?" I nodded. He gripped an antler and lined the saw on the base. Before the first stroke, he asked again, "Ready?" and then the saw buzzed as it bit into the antler. The stag shivered, and the stiff fur of his neck bristled. I held the head firmly as my father sawed through the horn. Blood from the cut gushed into a bowl of rice wine below. A spurt of the blood flew straight into my mouth and my father shouted, "Don't drink it!" The blood tasted sharp, sweet, and delicious all at once. The stag's healthy, well-nourished body spurted blood as if being pressed by a cylinder. I reluctantly kept my mouth shut. But the stag's warm blood had spurted all over my face, and when my father bent his head to his work, I couldn't resist opening my mouth to swallow more. As he finished cutting the second horn, I drank even more of the fresh, warm blood.

But then I had to pay the price for these acts of sheer stupidity.

* * *

My village was near the border, so the Lao wind needed only to slip down the mountain to blow through our village all day and all night. But the light of civilization from the lowlands had to climb many slopes along poor roads with many potholes. If we had no special antlers, then surely no one would know my village—it was as anonymous as any of a hundred other poor villages. But then, the border crossing at Cầu Gác was opened, and the paved National Highway 8A crossed the pass. My village now found itself located in an important economic triangle. After that, many people rushed to my village, bringing the noise of city with them. Our little border town began to sparkle at night with colorful lights, beautiful dresses, pinked cheeks, reddened lips and nails, and long stockinged legs, the whole place burbling with voices from the north, south, and center. Our special deer had truly become a blessing. Men have always been confident in all things, except making love. Lacking this confidence, they seek antler velvet, cinnamon, geckoes, sea horses, snakes—all sorts of lusty things. The price for antlers increased every day, and money rushed into my village, bringing a mess along with it. The more crowded the border crossing became, the emptier the schools. I also dropped out of school my last year. I was on my way to becoming a skillful starter, and the price of antlers had skyrocketed, so what would I need to learn at school? Why make myself tired? Some friends who had dropped out worked as porters at the border and kept telling me about a long-legged girl named Thi who worked at a bar called La Da. They just talked about her, admiring her from afar because they themselves had only the starving salary of porters. Sometimes, after a long day working like horses carrying goods across the border, they'd use their remaining energy to relax and to share a cheap old hooker who came up from the low-lands to wander the forests satisfying young men's urges. Miserable! Men usually sow their seeds healthily, into another healthy body, and don't cast them to all kinds of places they can't sprout, like a tree through a bunch of fruit. Hearing my friends talk about Thi, my desire stirred but I didn't dare to go. It was my first year as a starter. My father wouldn't even let the young stag mate. I'd resisted my friends' provocations, but then I gave in to the sharp, sweet, delicious taste of the deer's blood. Not listening to my father's advice meant I would have to pay. . . .

The stag was bandaged carefully, everyone let go, and he bolted to his feet, shaking his head now lightened by the loss of his heavy horns. We climbed out of the corral. As if I'd drunk a holy medicine, my body felt strangely excited, my groin tensed, and my blood boomed through my body like blows from a hammer. Even so, I kept my cool, raising up my blood smeared face. I felt as proud as a boxing champion stepping out of the ring in front of all the envious village boys and the mating season's virginal girls. I had earned a bona fide certificate of adulthood. The ant-ler cutting done, we began the celebration. I was invited to sit at the head platter with the village elders. The platter with the freshest blossoms, the biggest shrimp, the most delicious cuts of pork, and the most fragrant rice. Like other times, I wanted to make a spring roll and enjoy the taste of the special leaves—the bitter *trâm*, the buttery *mít*, the sweet and sour *ngút*—as well as the delicious mango blossoms, the savory shrimp, the fatty pork, the spicy chilis. But this time, no, I couldn't concentrate on the food. I felt an intense, burning desire all through my body. Not permitted to drink rice wine, I drank two cups of brandy mixed with the deer's blood, thinking that the brandy would help squelch my desire. I thought wrong. When flames meet flames, the fire only burns hotter. Not able to stand it any more, I sneaked out of the party and found my friends behind the house. We'd just reached the fence when I was transfixed by the sight of a girl named Lành stepping from the kitchen, her cheeks flushed from the kitchen's flames, her pink bra holding her big, soft, virgin breasts revealed through her sweat-soaked blouse. Seeing me, she smiled coyly and raised a hand to put up her hair, inadvertently pulling up the short blouse to reveal her smooth belly and deep navel. Ghosts tempted me, devils compelled me. I pretended to stumble as if drunk and then pressed my body to hers. She gasped in panic as I hurriedly groped her body. And then I trembled as a cold electric current ran along my spine, and I felt as if a blocked sewer had been drained. My groin no longer strained, my body felt light as cotton, my eyes blurred by smoke and fog. Like paradise?! Lost in my euphoria, I was not prepared to be seized by the collar by my father and yanked to the ground. He said out loud: "Are you so drunk you fell down? Get up, I'm taking you home." Then to Lành he said, "And Lành holding up such a heavy guy, you poor girl. He's so drunk, he fell." Lành hastily rearranged her blouse and ran into kitchen. I stood up awkwardly, hunching over to hide the big wet spot in the crotch of my pants. Dragging me by my hand, my father said through clenched teeth: "You lying fool. You're like that crazy stag. You've got endless vitality, but you gulped down the deer blood anyway, and then you gulped down blood brandy too. You didn't listen to me. Our family will come to ruin all because of you." Drunk and ashamed, I thought about a crazy stag from many years ago. In his first season, he grew only tiny little antlers, and my father confined him to a pen next to one holding an old doe. When mating season came, he was so excited that he thrust his penis through the bamboo fence, and the doe took a bite out of it. After several seasons, he grew big antlers. But seeing him struggle so pitifully during mating season was hard for me to bear, so I asked my father to castrate him. He said, "Buffaloes are born to plow, horses to pull carts, and deer for us to take their antlers. If we castrate him, the antlers won't grow, and then what would we do with him?" No matter what I said, my father wouldn't castrate him. The more the crazy stag grew, the more he suffered during mating season. When he couldn't take it any more, he butted one of the shed posts until his skull fractured and he died. His death continued to haunt me. But now I understood. Sex is the strongest obsession, overruling all other obsessions and desires.

*   *   *

That afternoon, my mother prepared charcoal in a large pan. My father rolled a big barrel into the house to trap me in my room. When the charcoal burned red hot, my mother dumped it into the barrel. Then my father carefully placed the antlers in the barrel to be dried. The barrel and my father sitting there tending it kept me in my room all day. They kept me there for three days and nights. Slowly, the urgency of my hot animal desires began to dissipate. I slept better and had fewer wet dreams. The antlers continued to dry as my mother put less and less charcoal in to avoid breaking them. Seeing that I was no longer crazed with desire, my father let me out of my room. Like a stag escaped from the shed, I went looking for my friends.

My small town sparkled with colorful lights, and the long legs with short skirts were still out enticing people to come in. All the stories boys my age wanted to listen to and imagine, money could buy. But what got me was the porno movie at Café Phố Núi. Sure, I thought, why not see what that was about, just to know. All my friends and even a bunch of the younger boys had all talked about it so nonchalantly, but I'm about as dumb as a stupid deer. I couldn't let them look down on me, especially not now, after I'd been a starter to cut the antlers. And after seeing that movie, I felt even more urgently that I had to unblock the drain after my victory with the young stag. No one else in the village was as strong as me. I had to do it with Thi, and then all my friends would admire me. The next night, I snuck out of the house and went to the bar where she worked.

Trying to act like I'd been there many times, I raised my chin to ask the bouncer, "Got any new girls?"

He looked at me and grinned, and then said, "New or old, what's the difference? In and out, that's the important thing, in out, in out. . . . Got any money in your pocket?"

He thrust his hand into my T-shirt pocket and found nothing, checked the left and right pockets of my pants and found them empty as well. He paused a second, then thrust his hand all the way into my pocket and grabbed my manhood and squeezed it painfully. I felt the sting all the way into my brain. All the blood drained from my face. Before I knew what was happening, he'd dragged me out of the bar and kicked me in the ass out into the street. Faking a southern accent, he said, "You tryin' to mock me, son? You got no money but want to put on airs." I was hurt, angry, and ashamed to the point that tears filled my eyes. The gods were torturing me. I remembered the death of the crazy stag. It made a kind of sense now. The pain in my groin settled, but the images from the porno movie at Café Phố Núi surfaced in my mind again. I had to come back to La Da!

Saying it made it so. I snuck into my house quiet as a cat, opened the lid of the barrel, removed one of the warm, drying antlers, tucked it under my arm, and returned to La Da. Before the bouncer could check my pockets, I pulled the antler from my shirt. He opened his mouth, jumped back a step to seize a sword hidden behind the door and shouted to the other bouncer. I calmly stepped closer to him and said condescendingly: "Look again, don't worry, it's not a weapon. Fuck, did you wet yourself?" I waived the antler in front of his face. He snatched it, hooting with joy. I raised my chin and demanded: "Thi!"

He fumbled over himself agreeing and called inside: "Thi, give it all you've got. Room number three." I swaggered with excitement, but when

I reached room number three, I felt hesitant. I wanted to turn back. The antlers should only be used for higher purposes . . . only to make medicines to help people . . . anyone who dared to break the rule would be cursed . . . the lost antler . . . everyone would know . . . my grandfather sick again . . . I never thought things through. But then the door to room number three opened. Thi stepped out, took my hand, and pulled me in. She was more beautiful than my friends could describe. So beautiful! If only she were my girlfriend—or my wife. . . . I was still daydreaming like this when Thi took off her clothes.

As I stood there gaping, she lay back on the bed. And then . . . my gun went off, out of my control. Fortunately, with the deer blood I drank and the stamina of a young buck during mating season, I was already ready to go again. Thi gasped: "You're number one! Other men can only wish to have such virility."

"It's a blessing and a curse."

"Anytime you want, come to me."

"Hey, I'm not rich. All year, I get by on several antlers. If I spend it all on sex, I'll have to eat dirt."

"I'm free for you. Show me your house. Naturally, I like you. If I'm with you, it's not for the money."

"You'll work without pay? How will you live?"

"It's a gift of heaven. Heaven gave me beauty, a gift I enjoy that I can share with you. If I keep it for myself, heaven will punish me."

"Really? My house is at the end of the village. I'm a starter."

"Wow! I got the village hero's virginity. . . ."

It seemed my antler for one night was quite a gift, so the bouncer never came knocking at my door. Strangely, my stamina was like a subterranean stream, flowing endlessly, never empty. The sunrise came early, and I had to return home. When I stood up, my legs trembled, and I had to lean on Thi. She giggled.

"Do you surrender, or can you muster one last shot?"

"Is that a challenge? I'll knock you out!"

Without hesitation I rushed into her a final time. Afterward, I got dressed, and haggard as a fighting cock leaving the ring, I dragged my body home. A bright new sun had risen. The blossoms sparkled with the color of love.

* * *

Mating season is the time when all species copulate and reproduce. For plants it's the time to sprout, for flowers to blossom. Not many people die during mating season. Because of this, when my grandfather fell sick, no one thought he would go far away. But maybe his case was an exception. And I'm the one who helped bring a miserable end to his long life a little faster. That morning, I came back home. Not needing to ask, my father knew I'd taken the antler and what I'd done all night. No accusations, not even looking at me, not a word. He saw me as a lost child. It all might have ended right there except that a few days later I felt a stinging when taking a piss, and a few days after that I couldn't piss at all—all that came out was just a little pus. My body burned with fever.

Seeing that, reluctantly my father knelt beside my grandfather's bed and said, crying, "I've dishonored you, father, I couldn't raise my son properly."

"Stand up, my boy. I'm afraid this is also the will of heaven. Heaven has given our house many blessings for many generations. Now heaven wants to take them back."

"But if I'd taught him better . . ."

"For the first time since our village began, prostitution has appeared. The new thing makes things strange. Men crave this novelty. Every little boy likes anything new. But when it comes so fast, comes so recklessly, our villagers don't yet know how to guard themselves against it."

"Now he . . . he . . . gets . . ."

"What?"

Lying there listening to my father speak, my grandfather began to shake, but so weakly that the deerskin blanket on his belly barely moved. Trying to control his wheezing, Grandfather told my father to fetch a pen and paper and to write down the herbs he dictated. The medicine was a secret family formula. It seemed in all our generations, I was the only one who had to use it personally. And I had to use a lot of it. When my father finished writing, Grandfather said in an agonized voice, "Anyway, this year the house could use more coat hooks. . . ."

Then my mother brought in a bowl of rice porridge with ground antler for him. My grandfather reminded her of the time when her father had been bedridden like that. After my maternal grandfather's illness, my mother and father had become a couple. The story was that at eighteen, my father had already become a notable starter. All the village girls dreamed of him, except for my mother, who at sixteen was so proudly beautiful that all the village boys thought they'd die wanting her. An extremely talented boy like my father and an exceptionally proud girl like my mother would never sit down to talk with each other. The year my mother turned eighteen, the village had a horrible outbreak of dysentery. My mother's father lay seriously ill, all week no treatment could help him, his body becoming so thin it looked like a leaf on the bed. Finally taking people's advice, my mother resigned herself to knock on my paternal grandfather's door. Only with thin slivers of dried antler cooked with rice porridge and several cups of honey could my mother's father be saved. Touched by my grandfather's tender care, my mother decided to marry my father. In all my life, I'd never even once seen them quarrel with each other. Seeing my grandfather open his eyes, my mother said: "Let me give you a spoonful."

"It's all right," he said. "Save the antlers for some other medicine—no more porridge, this is enough. I won't eat any more. Gifts from heaven like this I've had more than enough of already."

Hearing my grandfather speak like this, my mother did not dare insist. My whole family understood: after this mating season, the antlers remaining on the deer in the shed could never be cut again. They would grow old, lose their velvet, scale off, thin, and next mating season drop by themselves. Then the only thing we could do with them would be to hang them on the wall as coat hooks. Our karma. Because of me, the antlers' gold had again become just some thin, dried bone. I blamed myself for kicking everything down. Never, never had anyone dared even to think to trade antlers for their own personal pleasure. Until me. I stole the food from my family's mouths, the clothes from their backs, all their honor and everything good for generations. My lust led me astray, far from the path my ancestors had always walked. And I no longer had the strength to be a starter. My father was an antler cutter now. He couldn't return to starting as before. My grandfather had given him the saw. He couldn't take it back. The pride of a family accustomed to leading the village in reaping its gifts from heaven, in thanking the heavens, would not allow my father to ask for help from another villager to catch the deer in our shed for him to cut the antlers. Even though my grandfather didn't unequivocally insist that we should give up for good, it seemed that would be the way. We had to wait for the antlers to grow old and drop. We resigned ourselves to waiting until the next season, hoping everything would be better. It seemed my grandfather had crossed a threshold. From that day on, he wouldn't eat or drink anything. He just stayed in bed, his eyes open wide, staring at the ceiling where my father had hung the saw with which he used to cut the virgin stag's antlers. In the middle of the mating season, my grandfather passed away. The elders in my village all talked. They said he was only the second villager to die in the middle of a mating season. The first didn't die of old age but collapsed during sex and died on the belly of his wife.

* * *

All my family thought: We just need to wait until next season. But in our deer sheds there would never be another mating season. The bugling of the stags and the tail-flicking of the receptive does, the plaintive sounds, the sounds of love—all were a thing of the past. I recovered my strength but couldn't reach the sheds. The herd tore around the enclosure, jumped and bucked, fierce as wild beasts. When they saw me or smelled me, the whole herd bolted like tigers. When the stags with the fresh pinkish-white antler velvets saw me, they'd butt their heads into the bamboo poles, breaking their antlers and bleeding. The pregnant deer butted one another until they miscarried. The unmated stag also behaved differently. When he saw me approach, his eyes went red as blood, his body tensed, his hind legs spread defensively, and he'd raise his long neck. If I didn't pay attention, he'd rush right at me. The corral's bamboo fence protected me from his attack, but his butting shook the whole fence.

We all saw that the herd teetered between life and death but couldn't see a way forward. After my grandfather's funeral, with the problem of the herd came many sleepless nights. My father's hair turned white. Not one black hair remained. My mother looked at him with pain. An atmosphere of mourning, of endless sorrow, pervaded our home. I also spent many sleepless nights. All these torments, everything too late. Too late already for even a master of deer raising like my father to do anything, so what could I do? I decided to go away. I would go away forever so the herd in our shed could live and reproduce, so heaven would once again bestow blessings on my family. But when they learned what I intended to do, my mother and father wouldn't let me. I was their only heir—if I left, no one could replace me. What good are heaven's gifts if life has no meaning? Heaven's gifts were for me, for my children, and grandchildren. My grandparents and my parents didn't need it anymore. They only wished to save the gifts of heaven for their grandchildren. But now . . . the price I had to pay was too high.

* * *

After several more sleepless nights, one morning my father rose early, dressed in his best clothes, and solemnly cleaned both our ancestral altar as well as Thần Lộc's. He lit incense and mumbled his prayers. He pulled the machete from the wall, sharpened it so carefully it could cut a hair, then rose and walked out into the forest. Frightened, my mother ran after him. My father smiled and said, "Don't worry, I'll be back this afternoon." True to his word, near evening he came home with a large bundle of fresh bamboo on his shoulders, all of them as big around as his ankle. That evening, he made a fire ring behind the deer sheds, and then lit a huge bonfire, placing

the freshest bamboo on top. Finally, he opened the enclosure gate and solemnly released all the latches inside the shed. All at once, the fresh bamboo
exploded. Startled and frightened, the herd bolted out of the shed, bound-
ing toward the main road. My father shouted and ran behind them with a
lit torch. The unmated stag stopped and blocked my father's path so that
the other deer could escape. His eyes sparkled a fierce red in the light of
the fire. His shaggy mane ruffled up. The village dogs barked, raising a riot
of sound. My father advanced with the torch in his hand. The stag stepped
back, then stepped back again, and when he saw the other deer had run
far away, he spun around and ran after them. After a moment's hesitation,
the herd got used to the dark and then ran like crazy. They ran and ran and
disappeared into the black night. My father followed them to the edge of
the forest before turning back. The herd returned to the place where their
ancestors had lived. They would go on forever and never come back to
humans. Yes. It seemed these deer were a special breed that would never
be tamed, even though many generations of them had lived with humans.
They could never bear the life humans forced them to live. Fastidious
about what they ate, they could force humans to serve them like kings and
queens, and in return they gave the gift of their antler velvets. If the humans
didn't coddle them, they would get angry, be fierce, not eat or drink until
they died. They had always craved their freedom and the vast land of the
wild, the forest. Because of this, they only needed to escape and the deer
could rejoin the green jungle—their magnanimous, sacred forest.

Coming back home with the dying torch, my father no longer looked
like an illustrious former starter. Dropping the spent torch in a corner of
the yard, he stretched his back, pushed back his white hair, and entered
the house. My mother stared at him with concern. After a while, he called
me to him and said: "You are an adult now and you saw all that happened.
Before this, our village has lived on the gifts from heaven. But the gifts of
heaven have limits, taking too much will exhaust them, and now they've
truly run out. You're still young, look for a way forward. Go anywhere, but
I suggest you not go west—not to the border. . . ." That's all he said—the
people of my mountains don't talk much. And I wasn't waiting for him to
say that, but when he did, I made up my mind to go.

Yes, tomorrow I will go away. I will search for a job based on my abilities, and for sure I will not depend on the gifts of heaven forever. I will go.
Going is also how I will find a way to come back.

Translated by Di Li and Charles Waugh

Forever on the Road

Phan Triều Hải

1.

Rain pours down as my car passes the quarry. It's four-thirty in the afternoon, and the quarry workers have begun to bicycle home.

The wind lashes curtains of dust and rain onto the hunched workers. To get from the quarry to the big road will take thirty minutes at least, and the thick gray dust lying everywhere—on the road, on the leaves, on the zinc fencing between the low roadside shacks—has been transformed into a quaggy mess that occasionally sucks the car and bikes down into the puddles. As the car spins its wheels past a hole, I see one of the workers pedaling behind us get drenched in mud up to his lips. With one hand he keeps the bicycle straight against the wind, and with the other he wipes his face. I get goose bumps when I see him look at us so calmly, like he'd seen some inanimate thing without heart or soul passing by.

I admonish the driver to drive more slowly. I don't know his name but I also don't intend to ask, because I know after only a short distance along the road, I'll forget it. This is just one of many sad, boring journeys, the kind that has already become old hat, arriving anywhere, doing anything, turning around whenever. Every part of a journey like this has already been predetermined for a number of decades or more. When I am forty or fifty, or however old I am when I die, I'll still have this job. From now until then, the details of one day, one week, one month, or one year are so clear and so simple that any unusual thing, if it exists, is just a fleeting connection, and because of that there's no difference between drivers or vehicles, between a day that's rainy or a day that's hot, this place or that.

At the beginning of this journey, an acquaintance hired a strong young driver for me, but his tires were so old and worn, they looked like a thin stretch of intestines, their sides about to pop. With his hand tightly gripping the steering wheel he had argued, "I've run from the south to the north a million times and never had a problem, and definitely not on flat Western roads like these. You're worrying over nothing." I didn't buy his argument, because essentially I'm a traveling tire salesman—he obviously didn't see my two rubber-blackened hands. In the old days, the unusual trouble of changing vehicles just before leaving meant bad luck. But it's different for me because of the work I do. In the past, my mother had special rules, handed down from her mother, about going for a ride. The number one rule was never to have conversations with the driver for fear of distracting him. But my father held the exact opposite opinion: one must speak with drivers, otherwise they'll fall asleep. Sure, the hands will still grasp the wheel, and the face will still point straight ahead, but the guy will have fallen sound asleep. My mother said my father went on like that, but then he always defended his own bad habits, like never finding anything he needed even when it was right in front of his face and kicking up a fuss anyway: "Where are my socks? Find my socks for me, I just had them here." My mother would then quickly pick up the socks or whatever it was, pass them to him, and then launch into some sharp, irrefutable scolding: "It's like the old man's always asleep!"

But I had no other choice in this case because if I'm late even one day, my whole schedule will be thrown off, totally messing up my life, which for a long time has been completely dependent on plans made in advance. And so I had to find another car, the car I'm in right now, and a different driver, the person whose back I see before me. I can't tell his age. His face is young and at the same time both gentle and firm, but his hair has already turned silver. I figure the important thing is the contrast between his straight nose and fearless eyes.

This whole morning he spoke very little, remaining virtually silent. I discovered in his seatback a small, already curled dictionary and a collection of short stories that I tried to read to put myself to sleep during that first long section of the road. But after passing the quarry, I can no longer read or sleep because the driver has begun to talk.

2.

Rain splatters the windshield. The two overwrought wipers slide back and forth like two tennis players battling in Roland Garros stadium, their feet sliding right, then speeding back to the left. In France it's tennis season, June, the stadium clay beginning to raise red dust, but on the road we're traveling there is only rain, pouring down on a place already the most oozingly wet. The car passes the last group of workers. I take a final look at them, at their profoundly bent backs beneath the curtain of rain. Workers everywhere have the same backs, like farmers everywhere have the same feet. It seems that to be able to wear new clothes, or even nice clothes, none of them can escape looking so exhausted.

"With rain like this, smoking becomes a very interesting matter," says the driver.

"Feel free to smoke, if you want."

"Thanks."

He lights a cigarette with one hand and with the other puts the window down a little to let out the smoke. Rain spatters in, dotting the side of the seat and headrest.

"You travel a lot?"

"Always on the road," I say, "like you."

"I'm always on *this* road, each day spent like the next."

He stubs out his cigarette and gives it a flick. The butt sticks desperately to the glass, then blows back behind.

"So, smoking in the rain any different?" I ask.

"I don't know what I was thinking," he says, a little embarrassed. "I tried to do something unusual to see if it made things more interesting, but it made no difference."

He raises his gaze to look back in the rearview mirror, and I see a wide, flat forehead. Somehow, I got a driver who dresses in beautiful clothes. From looking at a pair of hands can one know whether they know how to drive? From a pair of dark-circled eyes, that someone has stayed up late? From their knowledge of places, about roads? It's a tough one—drivers are like brainy civil servants, they have no outward sign like the backs of workers or the feet of farmers.

I say, "When I come to a strange place I probably also think like you: I'll shower, change clothes, and go down the street and buy any old thing so that when I have the chance to see it again I'll remember that whole time, date, and place. But usually I can only get so far. Shower over, I turn on the TV, my eyes get heavy, and I sleep, promising myself I just need a little nap before I get up completely alert to do whatever I had planned. Satisfied with my promise, I lie down and sleep all the way through to the white light of morning and then begin the new day with this desperate feeling that time is like sand in my fist. The more I try to grasp it, the more easily it slips away."

The driver is silent. The road stretches out straight in front of us. Houses on both sides slip out of view into the leaves, lamps twinkle like fireflies, and darkness descends gently over the gardens.

3.

The sky is now completely black.

On the right side of the road is a wide, straight canal with an extremely peaceful current. In the dry season, farmers relaxing at night pile straw and sit with their backs to the road chatting, a bottle of rice wine tucked into the grass. Each time a vehicle passes, the wind blows their hair and clothes, the lights glistening like off the back of a fish. But now the sky is still raining, a rain that could fall with no warning and stop just as suddenly, and the car continues endlessly, going forever like this into any kind of weather.

The driver says, "If you keep looking forward on this road, you'll get depressed by the monotony. You'll ask yourself, must I drive all my life? Sit behind the steering wheel and stare at the road running past for all eternity like this? These gauges are of no use to you at all, because from the first day of your life you figured out how to do this job already. With a highway you finally understand that the long road is your time on earth, and going along that road is a countdown of that time, and at that point you'll hope the road is endless. But at the end of every afternoon there's always a place to stop and rest. There, a day can end its reckoning."

Five years ago, I traveled this road, and that long canal stretching as far as the eye can see is the thing I remember best about that crazy, dark, eight-hour trip. At that time, I was twenty-six. For the first part of the trip back to the city, I sat in the front of the bus with Vũ, the guy who had invited our gang of friends to visit his family home with him. Vũ had just turned twenty, and still had the naiveté of a student. He looked unhappy because the whole trip many people had moaned about not being able to go to the bathroom and about having nothing to eat or drink; the rest stop water had had a lot of alum in it, the restroom was just a wall of coconut trees, and the only thing to eat was some nasty boiled seafood. Through the open window, Vũ spotted a school of fish swimming in the canal alongside us, the water rippling over them, but the school of fish just kept going, their tails waving back and forth. The wind blew our hair and our clothes flew out behind. At that time, I'd only just started to work and was still an apprentice. I was weak-chested and skinny-armed, despite lifting weights every morning, and when I sat near the open door, the wind blew me all over the place. I saw quite clearly that I only needed the wind to be a little bit stronger and I would be blown away like a leaf.

A leaf blown to the middle of the ocean has no way to find its path back. Terrible. Terrible because when the leaf dies it knows how many regrets it has, and because when I was still very young, every morning I always had some song forever in my head, and everything seemed melodious and cheery. For me then, every day was a new day, at the same time both joyful and strange. I remember asking Vũ what he would do after school. "I'll come back home, here," he'd said immediately. Going along, I said, "It really is beautiful here. The sky is clear. The shrimp are plentiful." And Vũ said, "I'll come back because my grandmother is here. I love Grandma. In Saigon there are so many nights I don't miss my mother or father; I miss only my grandmother's smiling kiss, and I want to cry."

Anyone can talk this way, but not everyone can compete with time, and in my mind Vũ is still always like this, bright and bewildered by life.

Giving me a smile, the driver says, "Really what you've got here is an unlucky guy, what with my bulging round wrists, bloated fingers, and my big fat sagging belly. You know, one night a while back, I turned into a different person, maybe even a completely different kind of person. I tell everybody who travels this stretch of road they've got to listen to this story."

4.

The road narrows like a city street. The cars and trucks plod uphill, the bridges allowing only one vehicle through at a time. Alongside the canal, a string of multicolored lights stretches between two old wooden houses. The car creeps along the guardrail. A light rain falls on the disheveled thatch roofs. Inside, beneath white lights, young red-lipped and round-cheeked farm girls wearing green mascara and thin dresses sit on wooden platform beds, clustered together playing cards and chatting and drinking from worn plastic bottles.

"At that time," says the driver, "my dream was to be able to send my daughter up to Saigon to study. I was already working day and night, scrimping and saving through the year. When she went to school and I saw the way she stepped through the gate so elegantly and without pretension, instead of feeling happy because I had fulfilled the expectations of a father and accomplished my lifelong ambition, I felt only the insipid set of my lips, my exhaustion. Strange, isn't it? I had this clearly absurd feeling—I'd spent twenty years of my life taking care of my daughter, presumably just like my father spent the same number of years nurturing me into adulthood. Then, after that, what? My daughter would continue on this road, would spend some number of months at school, and then still end up with the expectation to become a mother. It's not every day we get the chance for a new life, so it's completely natural to deliberate on or to have recommendations or some expectations for the lives of others, so it's easy to go around worrying about someone else's life. We keep muddling along like this—one generation goes, another one comes, like blooming flowers will always wilt, like rippling circles give birth to rippling circles, on and on forever. I went home but in my heart there was only blankness; I didn't know I was close to needing to do something else. At that time I saw the life ahead of me as both long and without reason. Being in this world or not was all the same, no more, no less. That day the heavens also rained like this, and that feeling of vacuousness led me into a café like one of these."

He meant the little brown huts we'd just passed. On that side now is only the pitch-black canal continuing adjacent to the road, running on and on forever.

"In those cafés, all stories are strange. Young girls sit calmly drinking and chatting with guests' hands in their skirts checking to see if they're of age, playing naughty games leading to you know what. Behind them, mattresses and bedding are strewn on patches of wet floor, very rank, not even a curtain drawn when a crew of carpenters comes to put on a new roof. Everyone minds his own business. But what surprised me the most was the really big shit-hole in the restroom. A big hole to let guests drop themselves into a boat waiting below on the canal in case they need to escape. And when falling like that, ninety-nine percent of the guests must have the exact feeling that they are a big lump of shit, no better or worse."

"An extraordinary feeling."

"Really extraordinary," says the driver. "I went into one of those cafés and didn't know what to do next. But those girls are really ingenious, so I did things like I just said with a clever, vulgar girl. Unfortunately—or fortunately?—that day I was forced to break through the rotten plank covering the hole to find a way to escape. Sitting in the getaway boat, I was still in shock, not knowing who I was. When I fell through, I saw clearly I was a big turd, weighing 130 pounds, but otherwise exactly the same in color and substance. The story is absurd but the truth is like that too. I sat in that boat thinking over and over again, not able to understand who I was. I kept thinking like that until I returned home. But after a long sleep, the insipid feeling disappeared and I began to feel happy again. Because nothing can compare to the moment when we rediscover ourselves like that."

5.

The canal disappeared at some point. In the darkness I can no longer see the water glistening anymore. Just the mountains, rolling slowly out before us into blackness.

The road winds between the sea and a narrow strip of barren flooded fields below the foothills. For fifteen minutes the car speeds along without us seeing another person, without seeing even a house. All around us is indistinct black night, the only light reflecting back from the top of the guardrails, road signs, and billboards. And in the crowd of signs glancing by there is a name I don't understand because I know the road has far to go until it reaches the next town: the Hotel Rose. Printed in huge letters. In the middle of these withered hills, it's a damned preposterous name. Beneath the lettering, an arrow flashes, pointing toward an utterly dark mountain.

I can't see anything, but I think if there really are roses over there, they must certainly be in the most beautiful of gardens.

6.

When I shut the car door and step into the hotel courtyard it's just 10 P.M. The hotel entrance is closed, the metal security gate rolled down smooth as glass and locked tight. The hotel receptionist, a scrawny youth with the proud thirsting eyes of a working student, busies himself spreading out a sleeping mat along with an old gray pillow and a thin blanket. He stands up, resting his arms on the counter and looking serious in his thin T-shirt.

"Are you going for a walk?" asks the driver. "There's nothing here."

"The ocean's here."

"Nobody goes to the ocean at this hour," he says.

There's also a lot of wind, I'm sure of that. I can even feel it blowing on my hands inside my pockets. While he fumbles with his keys, I speak, realizing I've already spoken a lot today, but still want to say more.

"Have you ever flown in an airplane?" I ask. "Never? If you get the chance, just wait 'til you get to see a city from up high. You'll see each house, no matter how big or small, all become as tiny as a box of matches, and the boxes of matches will all look jumbled and crowded and piled up. Some people spend their whole lives digging a grave just to find a box of matches like that, happily running to and fro over the same ground. But me, I need to go down to the ocean. Have you ever gone down to the sea at this time? If not, how would you know what it's like?"

He looks at me like I'm a psychopath. And then, smiling benevolently, he replies, "Feel free to go by yourself—you look tense, but that's okay. It's really safe here, in fact, there's no place safer. I'll stay by the door and wait for you to get back."

7.

Crossing the bay, a pontoon bridge bobs on the soft waves like silk flowing from the dark black mountains. The wind blows inside my shirt onto my chest when I bend down to slip beneath the barred gate. Inside the bridge's dark tollbooth a cigarette glows. The security guard is not yet asleep. Each time the cigarette glows brightly, I can see white words on a greenish-black background. I stop in the middle of the bridge and lean on the thick rope guardrails.

Now I can see clearly that some of the pontoons are actually boats floating up and down. In the front of one boat, two young women sit leaning against one another, their curved backs very beautiful, their long hair waving on their shoulders, flying back and forth. A thin scarf. A heel touching down to the water when the boat undulates with the waves. I watch them silently and realize it seems like I've never had the chance to really look at anyone. Because I don't have the time or the peace of mind, or maybe because I have scruples. In the city, people can read each others' eyes and know what the other thinks and wants, and because of this I rarely have the time to look for long, to look straight. But in this out-of-the-way place, things are different; certainly between them and me there must be some distance in the way of perceiving life, and here silent dialogues like this are not likely to be completely understood. This is a tiny village that goes to sleep before even ten at night, the time the action in the city I live in is just beginning, the biggest city in this country, a city exactly fiftieth in all the big cities in the world.

And I'm right here in the night watching them, as uninhibited as if looking at a painting in a museum or at souvenir shells for sale along the beach. Far out on the sea are many white lanterns, and I try to imagine my position at this moment, one dilapidated small dot in an out-of-the-way corner of the map, the place name of the district longer than all the streets themselves.

8.

I smell the faint scent of roses as both women climb back to the bridge and stroll away, and in that little moment, a breeze passes through my spine. Without warning, right in front of me, two chalky white faces appear. Rough red blotches mark these young men's cheeks where they've pawed one another. Their faces divide into patches of light and dark, the hollows like black holes, the lumps pale and white. They look at me with glassy, vacant eyes; no one speaks a word, and both of them stand up from their bench quietly, like lions turning over lazily when they sense prey approaching during a nap.

I let drop the big rope stretching along the bridge and step away, unhurriedly resuming my walk. I take a long deep breath as if I'm taking the whole sky into my chest, and because there is nothing around me except empty space, I listen to the sound of feet echoing on the pontoon bridge. When I come to the toll booth at the other end, I realize if I turn the wrong way, I might keep going until the end of my life; in front of my face I have nothing at all, no house or station, just the mountains and the long road back to the city. I intend to return to the car, but those two guys from the bridge are lurking silently in that direction. Maybe they live over there, but even so, I just want to keep going a little bit farther.

I pass several small pagodas, lifeless and cold without their incense smoke. Then I pass a bulldozer standing tilted at the side of the road.

No one keeps watch over the bulldozer. In the dark it's just a worthless heap of scrap iron.

9.

I climb to the road girdling the dry land and the sprawling mountain rubble. Behind me still are those footsteps, sounding monotonously alike. I listen to the sandals scraping on the surface of the road, their noise muffled but confident. They echo up regularly, without a bit of hesitation. Misgiving sprouts in my chest, and I try to find a way to adapt to it, just as I've already adapted to so many things in my life. I'm not sure if these things matter or not, or if they are so taken for granted I wouldn't even notice them except in a strange place, in fresh cool air like this, where I realize every crack in the shell of my confidence is as natural and ancient as the shell itself.

I try to think of other stories, the gentle, airy ones that usually are the delight of a peaceful stroll.

I remember my dog at home, a terror with people but terrified by any stuffed animal made with smooth hair. I remember the long-dead rat in the cabinet after a weekend had passed, but with all the brave heroes in the house, not a one who dared to volunteer to take it out.

Then I think about the driver at that moment, sleeping back in the car. He'd had a lot to say about this and that, but after all of it, he could still sleep. He knew how to keep his strength for another trip. No matter how many times opinions or tastes might change in one day, everyone always begrudgingly returns to this. He was asleep. Truly ordinary, but also completely reassuring.

10.

I don't know how long I've been going. As I walk along the sea, the sky darkens. And signs for the hotel successively appear in reverse order. I know for sure I've already gone far, gone in the direction of my home city. A city that seems stranger each time I come home because I know at some point if I keep traveling the road like this, I'll never be able to return. Each time I feel like lying down to sleep, footsteps come echoing up from behind, unhurried, regular, taut.

I go slowly and the footsteps go slowly, I go fast and they also go fast.

I spin around or try to go even faster, but instantly the footsteps from behind echo up just as fast, like an alarm signaling any attempt to run away. At home, if I want to have a bit of news from thousands of miles away, I only need to turn on a machine, click on the network, and everything is at my fingertips. But now just ten steps behind me are some simple and rustic people whose intentions I cannot begin to fathom. A huge gap in understanding, a silent mystery. And a strange overwhelming fear rises swiftly as I realize everything I've ever come to understand has become useless beneath this curtain of darkness along this deserted road; realize that the things that used to bring me self-confidence truly only helped to disguise the fragility of the composure of a person used to living in peace.

My thoughts have become a weary jumble, but my legs keep going. Plodding on.

Translated by Charles Waugh

Author Notes

Di Li was born in 1978 in Hanoi. Since graduating from the English department at the University of Foreign Languages, she has taught English at the School for Tourism. She has published ten collections of short stories and a novel, *Trại hoa đỏ*, which was awarded the Police Publishing House's second prize in 2008.

Đinh Ngọc Hùng was born in1975 in Hải Dương. A graduate of the Faculty of Literary Writing and Criticism at the University of Culture, Hanoi, he now lives and writes in Ho Chi Minh City. In addition to publishing many short stories in newspapers and magazines, his collection *Nắng Gió Miền Đông* was published by Kim Dong Press in 2006.

Đỗ Bích Thúy was born in 1974 in Hà Giang. After graduating from the Academy of Journalism and Communication in 1997, she worked as a journalist for the *Army Literature and Arts* magazine, of which she is now associate editor-in-chief. She enjoys writing short stories and has received several Vietnam Writers' Union prizes for her fiction, including the *Army Literature and Arts* first-place prize in 2000 for the story appearing in this volume, "Sage on the Mountain." She has published five collections of short stories, a poetry collection, and a collection of essays.

Đỗ Tiến Thụy was born in 1970 in Chương Mỹ District, Hà Tây Province. He is a 2006 graduate of the Faculty of Literary Writing and Criticism at the University of Culture, Hanoi, and is an editor for *Army Literature and Arts*. He has published three short-story collections, with Youth Press, Young People Press, and the People's Army Press. The story appearing in this volume, "Wounds of the City," won second place in the *Army Literature and Arts* 2006 contest.

Dường Bình Nguyễn was born in 1979 in Thái Nguyên. A 2001 graduate of the Institute of Security, he now lives and writes in Ho Chi Minh City, where he works as a reporter for the People's Police newspaper. His story collections, *Hoa ẩn hương* and *Giày đỏ*, were published by the Vietnam Writers' Union Press in 2005 and 2007, and his short stories have appeared in many magazines and newspapers.

Hồ Thị Ngọc Hoài was born in 1972 in Nghẹ An and graduated from the University of Pedagogy in Hue. She has published several novels and short stories and is an editor for *The Purple Ink & Red Shawl* journal. Hoài is also a high school teacher in Nghe An. Her story in this collection, "Thung Lam," earned first prize in the *Literature and Arts* 2005 short story contest.

Kiều Bích Hậu was born in 1972 in Hưng Yên. After graduating from Hanoi Foreign Languages University, she found work reporting for several newspapers in Hanoi. She published a short story collection, *Lovers' Lane*, with the Vietnam Writers' Union Press in 2007 and a novel, *Xuyến chi xanh*, in 2010. Her story in this volume, "Waiting for the Ferry," won second place in the *Literature and Arts* short story contest in 2007.

Lê Hoài Lương was born 1971 in Bình Định, where he continues to live and work as a freelance writer. He has published two short story collections: *Each Month Has a Full Moon* with the Vietnam Writers' Union Press in 2000 and *An Uncultivated Time* with Thuan Hoa Press in 2005.

Nguyễn Anh Vũ was born in Hanoi in 1979, graduated from the University of the Arts, and now lives and works in Hanoi. He has published many poems and short stories in *Van Nghe* magazine and in *Army Literature and Arts*. His story in this collection, "Sleeping in the Lotus Flowers" won first place in the *Army Literature and Arts* 2009 short story contest.

Nguyễn Danh Lam, born in 1972 in Bắc Ninh, now lives and writes in Ho Chi Minh City. His novel *Giữa dòng chảy lạc* was awarded the Vietnam Writers' Union's novel prize in 2010.

Nguyễn Đình Tú was born in 1974 in Hai Phong and graduated from the University of Law in Hanoi. He is an editor for *Army Literature and Arts* and has published three short story collections and five novels since 2001.

Nguyễn Ngọc Tú was born in 1976 in Cà Mau, where she continues to live. She has published ten short story collections since 2001, many of which have been published by the Vietnam Writers' Union Press, and her stories have appeared in many newspapers and journals from around the country.

Nguyễn Thế Hùng was born in 1972 in Hà Tính. After graduating from the Faculty of Literature and Criticism at the University of Culture, Hanoi in 2006, he began editing for *Army Literature and Arts* in Hanoi. His story

"Gifts of Heaven" won third place in that magazine's short story contest in 2006.

NGUYỄN VAN TOÀN was born in 1973 in Quảng Ngãi and graduated from the Nguyễn Du School of Creative Writing in 2006. He now lives in Binh Dinh, where he reports for the magazine *Life and Law*. His story collection, *Sowing Grain*, was published by the Vietnam Writers' Union Press in 2007, and his stories have appeared in many newspapers and journals around the country.

NGUYỄN VĨNH NGUYỄN. Born in 1979 in Ninh Thuận, Nguyễn is a graduate of Dalat University and now works as a reporter for *Saigon Marketing*. His short story collection, *Ở Lưng Chừng Nhìn Xuống Đám Đông*, was published by the Vietnam Writers' Union Press in 2011.

NIÊ THANH MAI was born in 1980 and graduated from the Dalat University of Pedagogy. She teaches at the N'Trang Long boarding school, which is an elementary school for children from Vietnam's many ethnic minority groups. She has published three collections of short stories, and her story in this volume, "In the White Rain," was a winner of the *Army Literature and Arts* 2005 short story contest.

PHẠM DUY NGHĨA. Born in 1973 in Yên Bái, Nghĩa holds a PhD in literature from Vietnam National University. He lives and writes in Hanoi and is an editor for *Army Literature and Arts*. His story in this volume, "Rain of White Plum Flowers," won first prize in *Van Nghe* magazine's short story contest in 2004.

PHAN TRIỀU HẢI was born in1969 in Quy Nhơn. A 1993 graduate from Ho Chi Minh University, he continues to live and write in Ho Chi Minh City. His story "There Was a Man Lying on the Roof" appears in *Love After War: Contemporary Fiction from Viet Nam*, edited by Wayne Karlin and Ho Anh Thai. Hải was a 1998 participant in the International Writing Program at the University of Iowa. He has published five collections of short stories and was awarded best young writer from *Avant Garde* newspaper in 2000.

PHONG DIỆP was born in 1976 in Nam Định. After graduating from the Hanoi University of Law, she began writing fiction and is now an editor for *Army Literature and Arts*. She has published five short story collections with Youth, Young People, and the Vietnam Writers' Union Presses, and most recently, the novel *Blogger* in 2009.

Editor and Translator Notes

Di Li is also one of this volume's authors. She teaches English at the School for Tourism and has published a volume of her own stories in English, *The Black Diamond* (Hanoi: The Gioi, 2012).

Lê Thế Quế is former department head and professor emeritus from the Faculty of International Studies at the University of Social Sciences and Humanities, Vietnam National University. A former diplomat, lover of languages, and multilingual punster, he continues to delight his students by teaching undergraduate courses in American Studies and graduate courses in International Relations at VNU.

Lê Thế Quý is a translator, interpreter, and lecturer who has taught at the College of Languages and International Studies, Vietnam National University, Southern Leyte University in the Philippines, the People's Police Academy in Hanoi, and Hòa Bình University. His first literary translation into Vietnamese is the novel *All that Remains* by Patricia Cornwell.

Nguyễn Hùng was born and raised in Hanoi. He received his MA in International Studies at the University of Oregon and a PhD in Bioengineering from the University of Osaka in Japan. He now lives in Sydney, Australia.

Nguyễn Lien was a writer, translator, scholar, and teacher who championed world literature in translation for nearly fifty years. He passed away in 2014 after a long struggle with Parkinson's disease. He translated many international works of literature into Vietnamese, including *The Glass Menagerie*, *The Prince of Tides*, and the textbook *A Contemporary Approach to American Culture*. With Charles Waugh, he is the coeditor and cotranslator of *Family of Fallen Leaves: Stories of Agent Orange from Vietnamese Writers* (University of Georgia Press, 2010).

Peter Ross is a writer, teacher, and translator who has lived in Southeast Asia for more than twenty years. He translates Vietnamese and Thai into English and currently teaches English in Hue, Vietnam.

Thúy Tranviet received her PhD in Asian Studies at Cornell University, where she is a Vietnamese Language senior lecturer. Her research focuses on International Service Learning. Her publications include a translation of "The Industry of Marrying Europeans" by Vũ Trọng Phụng, and she has filmed a short documentary, *"Streets and Sidewalks: The (Re)Public Space of Vietnam."*

VĂN GIÁ is the dean of the Faculty of Literary Writing and Criticism at the University of Culture, Hanoi. A professional journalist as well as a beloved teacher, he is a prolific writer of literary reviews and nonfiction essays.

VŨ THỊ TUYẾT MÀI teaches English in the public school system in Hanoi.

CHARLES WAUGH lives in the mountains of Logan, Utah, where he teaches at Utah State University. With Nguyễn Lien, he is coeditor and cotranslator of *Family of Fallen Leaves: Stories of Agent Orange from Vietnamese Writers* (University of Georgia Press, 2010). His essays, stories, and translations have appeared in journals and magazines such as *Words without Borders, The Literary Review, Two Lines, Flyway, Sycamore Review, Foreign Policy, ISLE,* and *saltfront.*